*Her Heart Sang with*
## *Tender Dreams*

# Her Heart Sang with Tender Dreams

## Julia Robertson

This is a work of fiction. All characters, organizations and events portrayed in this novel are products of the author's imagination or are used fictitiously.

Tender Dreams  Copyright 2021 by Julia Robertson

All rights reserved Printed in the United States

**ISBN:** 9798500031488
**Imprint:** Independently published

## Acknowledgments

My thanks to those who have helped me along the way. My cousins Terri, Katheryn and Paula. To my sister-in-law, Jan, and friends, Cindy, Tina, Vikki, Lila and my brother Dennis. To Ron R. Paradis whose editing skills found my many mistakes and put up with my endless questions and changes. To my husband, Roy, for your beautiful cover photo and guiding my manuscript into print.

*Her Heart Sang with*
*Tender Dreams*

*Tender Dreams*

## Prologue

Late afternoon sunlight filtered through the neatly gathered lace curtains and sprinkled pinpoints of light across the dark room. The results were stunning and romantic but lost on those nearby. She lay motionless on a sea of soft pillows and blankets, drifting helplessly from sleep to drowsy wakefulness. His whispered words seeped into her weary mind.

"I'm here," he said as he knelt next to the bed.

When her eyes fluttered open, she struggled to focus on him. His eyes had always spoken to her without words. How long had it been since she lost the ability to see all the specks of color in the deep blue of his eyes. Though her world had turned gray and all concept of time eluded her, every cherished memory was hers for eternity. His warm hand gently slid in under hers. She yearned to reach out for him, to once again cuddle close to him. It took supreme effort to turn her muddled thoughts into spoken words.

"Love, love you with," she whispered, pausing to draw in a shallow breath, "with all my heart."

"I love you too. Sleep now," he replied.

Summoning a little more strength, she lifted her eyelids and again saw only the faintest image of him. "Let her take care of it," she whispered. "Please," she said, at peace with what was coming.

"But," he began.

"My spirit is," she whispered. "My spirit will already be set free. Please."

"Okay, I promise," he said.

"Hold me," she whispered.

"No, you can't," he objected, for they both knew even the slightest movement caused her pain.

"Hold me," she begged, vaguely aware of the desperation in her own voice.

"Honey," he said, waiting for her to fall asleep.

"It's, it's time," she said, her voice faltering. She felt his weight press down on the mattress. Felt his arm slide beneath her body before he drew her close. She sighed as she melted into his familiar warmth. In that instant her spirit filled with joy and rose toward the beckoning light.

"I love you. I'll always love you," he wept.

Beyond the bedroom window the sky became a watercolor in pinks and yellows. A mourning dove cooed twice before it fluttered its wings and soared away from the corner of the house. The sun dropped behind the mountains, pulled all the colors from the sky and left the valley shrouded in soft gray twilight.

## Chapter 1

"This is all wrong. We shouldn't be here. Not like this."

Numb with grief, Brian Cooper sat on the edge of the chair with his elbows on his knees. A few feet away, Alicia wore a pale green dress, gold hoop earrings and a white beaded necklace. They were all things she would not have chosen for herself. For a moment she appeared to be sinking deeper into the quilted ivory satin. Brian rubbed his hands over his face. He kept his promise to have her parents handle the arrangements, but even though it eased the financial burden it simply was not worth it.

Gruffly he cursed, stood up and stepped closer to his wife. He wanted to run his fingers through her hair but curled his fingers into his palms instead. Alicia typically wore her dark blonde hair loose and flowing over her shoulders, but now it was short and sparse. He turned his wedding band while he stared at the rings on her finger. She wanted him to take them, but now was not the time. Not now. Not yet. He wanted to touch her but resisted and tugged the sleeves of his coat down to his wrists. She would not feel like the warm and soft Alicia he loved so dearly. As the walls closed in on him, he turned and walked out of the room.

Eyes raw, Brian sat in the rental car parked outside the funeral home. He looked up at the old Victorian house and wondered how everything in his life had fallen to pieces. All the dreams they once shared were shattered, lost and buried forever. Being back here in Massachusetts was worse than he imagined. Every step of the ritual magnified the pain in his heart. He held onto the steering wheel, laid his forehead down against his hands and wept.

When Brian sat back, images of Alicia danced before his eyes. He saw her arranging a bouquet of sunny yellow daffodils on the dining room table. Watched her eyes sparkle with delight as she opened a Christmas gift. Saw her spin around on the kitchen floor to show off her pretty new dress. The skirt lifted, flared out and dropped down below her knees as she reached out for him. When her image yellowed and suddenly disintegrated, Brian squeezed his eyes closed. He forced his thoughts back to the here and now.

Alicia loved this time of the year, but this spring of 1990 held no promises. The sky should not be blue, and the birds should not be singing on this terrible day. Hands shaking, he wiped away his tears, turned the key and started the car.

Two hours later, Brian stood up from the pew when the organist began playing a mournful hymn. He refused to watch the procession coming up the wide aisle. Her body was imprisoned inside the coffin. His sweet Alicia. His kind and loving Alicia.

"Daddy," whispered Erin as she tugged on his coat pocket.

Brian turned away from his dark thoughts and leaned down close to her. He hoped she did not need to use the restroom again.

"What's that box for?" she asked. "I want Mommy." She knew something was wrong, but at age four and a half she simply did not understand.

"Momma," cried three-year-old Jack.

Brian picked up Jack before he saw Erin's tears. He struggled to keep from crying himself as he lifted Erin up from the pew. "We need to be quiet," he whispered.

With the children clinging to him, Brian glanced back at Marlene and Justin. Marlene was Alicia's closest childhood friend. When Brian went to the funeral home earlier in the day, Marlene watched over Erin and Jack. She had not been able to cope with seeing her best friend laid out in a coffin. Having witnessed it firsthand, he knew the image was going to haunt him forever. Brian watched Marlene lean into Justin. The brave face she had put on to weather the ceremony had crumbled. Brian's eyes shifted to Justin and wordlessly thanked him for being there for Marlene. He turned in time to see the pallbearers take their final steps.

With barely a sound, the coffin was placed in clear view of the congregation. Brian immediately closed his eyes. The acidic flavors of the coffee and toast he had forced himself to eat earlier burned his throat. He breathed in and swallowed hard before opening his eyes again.

Brian was shocked to find the lid had been lifted on the coffin, exposing Alicia's still form. Though the sight turned his stomach, he subdued his outrage. Contessa had set this up, but Brian refused to give her any sense of satisfaction. He wished he and the kids were not here. Wished they did not have a reason to be here.

"Daddy, its Mommy," said Erin. "Can she come sit with us?"

"Momma," sobbed Jack. His face was overheated and wet with tears.

As the children's cries grew louder, Brian knew it was too much for all of them. He turned toward Marlene and Justin and whispered, "I'm sorry."

"We understand," Justin replied as he reached out and squeezed Brian's arm.

Brian nodded, then stepped out into the aisle. For an instant he saw Alicia's parents standing in the opposite row of pews. Contessa glared his way, no doubt damning him for leaving. Brian felt the pain as though she were jabbing a knife into his heart. Alicia's father stood rigid with his eyes locked straight ahead. Brian wondered what the man felt after seeing his only daughter's body. Garrison lacked the backbone to stand up to his wife's cruelty. Before he turned away, Brian heard Contessa spit out, "Filthy Bastard."

Brian did not so much as blink in acknowledgement of her words. She was a bitter woman with a heart of stone. Neither of Alicia's parents would ever know the depth of their loss.

Even while he felt the disapproval of some who watched him, Brian kept his head up as he moved toward the back of the church. Many of those in attendance were here to mourn the loss of Alicia, but others came simply to satisfy their morbid curiosity. When the organ music suddenly stopped, his footsteps sounded like hammer blows on the hardwood floor. Brian felt every eye bearing down on him as he neared the last row of pews.

Murmuring voices floated across the sea of people.

"How can he say he loved her?" whispered one voice.

"What kind of man leaves like that?" said another.

"Those poor children. They've lost their mother and they're so young," murmured someone who cared.

"They made a beautiful family," cried another.

The whispering voices were cut off when the door clicked closed behind Brian. He stood at the top of the steps with his eyes closed. The only sounds came from passing cars and a group of boys playing basketball at the nearby playground. Erin and Jack did not move nor say anything. Jack rested against his shoulder and Erin held onto the collar of his coat.

"Let's go," Brian said as he started down the steps. "You two hungry?"

"Can Mommy come with us?" Erin asked.

"No, honey. Mommy's gone to live with God in Heaven." Brian kept walking away from the church.

"Yeah, but," Erin said as she twisted around and looked back at the closed doors.

"Let's talk about it later, Erin. It is making Jack sad. We need to make him happy," Brian told his daughter.

Erin reached over and touched her brother's face. "I'm gonna tickle you," she said.

Jack reacted immediately. He loved being tickled. "No," he chuckled.

"I'm gonna get you," she teased. When she saw him smile and lift his head, she grinned.

"You're a good girl," Brian said. "Let's get you two buckled in. We'll go get some food and then go to the park."

"Swing," Jack announced as he bounced up and down.

Getting the kids into their car seats and fastening the seat belts was routine, but nothing else about today was routine. Brian pulled off his dark gray coat, tugged off the burgundy tie and dropped them on the passenger side seat. He stood and rested his hands on the car's sun warmed roof and looked up at St. Luke's Church. The historic wooden structure was painted white with wide concrete steps spread out in front of the ornately carved wooden doors. A single bell was suspended inside a square frame topped with a tall narrow spire. Two maple trees stood on either side of the building, their long bare branches reaching out and up toward the blue sky. Before long, the branches would be filled with green leaves, like they had been when he and Alicia were married here nearly seven years ago.

It had been a long, drawn out affair orchestrated by Contessa Rivers. They endured the extravagant wedding ceremony, which her parents insisted upon and paid for. Alicia never understood the need for such lavish affairs. She preferred simple and pretty things. Given the choice, they would have had a quiet ceremony with their closest friends and relatives. Contessa had her way back then, just as she was having her way today. He would never know what inspired Alicia's decision to be buried so far from their home.

Shortly after he and Alicia were married, Brian accepted a job offer on the West Coast. Living here had not been an option due to her mother's need to control Alicia's every breath. Filled with joy and anticipation for their future, the newlyweds had eagerly packed their few belongings and headed to Oregon.

After stopping for a quick meal, Brian took the kids to the park to burn off their excess energy. Erin and Jack ran for the swings first. Brian stepped back and forth between them, pushing the swings and finding pleasure in their laughter. After a time, he picked up Jack and sat down on the swing seat with the little boy on his lap. Erin rushed over and joined in the silent hug.

While the kids played chase, Brian watched a flock of birds fly helter skelter across the expanse of blue sky. His life seemed to be just like that, with everything going on, but in no logical order. He and Alicia often talked of how life was going to be when they grew old. She worried most about becoming forgetful and he loved to tease her about her hair turning white.

"You'll be the most beautiful little old lady with your soft white hair pinned up in a tidy bun," he'd teased. He remembered hugging her close when her eyes glistened with tears. Neither of them ever imagined their lives taking such a drastic turn.

Brian tucked away the sadness and turned toward the soccer game at the far end of the immense park. The teams appeared to be 5th and 6th graders by the way they moved. No longer clumsy, but not quite graceful seemed a suitable description. Uniforms of vivid purple and gold mixed with glowing green and black flashed back and forth across the grass. Enthusiastic cheers erupted from the spectators lined up on either side of the game.

Out beyond the playground, a young man tossed a bright red Frisbee with a quick snap of his wrist. His black and white Border Collie shot across the grass and leapt up just in time to snatch it out of the air. The dog's paws barely touched the ground before it raced back for another throw.

Brian sensed Alicia sitting next to him. Though he knew she was not there, knew she could not possibly be there, he turned and looked anyway. "Damn," he muttered. A quick glance at his watch told him he had to pull the kids away from the playground. Though he avoided thinking about the scheduled appointment at the funeral home, Brian had no other choice than to keep it. He stood up and called out, "Let's go guys." When they came running toward him, Brian knelt down and caught both of them in a hug. He held them close, missing Alicia so much it hurt.

Twenty minutes later, Brian stepped into the funeral home with Jack and Erin. The smothering feeling hit him without warning.

"Stinks in here," Erin said, holding her hand over her mouth and nose.

"We'll be here for just a few minutes," Brian whispered. He picked up Jack and held Erin's hand.

"Mr. Cooper, please come in," said Lawrence Ashcroft.

Brian tugged on Erin's hand when she hesitated. "It's been a long day," Brian said.

"Yes, of course," agreed Lawrence, handing over a small velvet bag. "Please be sure they are the correct rings. Please," he urged.

Brian had a difficult time opening the tiny bag. It took his breath away when he poured Alicia's rings out onto his palm. A minute passed before he was able to gather his thoughts and speak again. "I'm sorry, yes these are her, her rings." Feeling clumsy, Brian slid the rings back into the bag and held it in his fisted hand. "Is everything finished here? Is there anything else I need to do?"

"No, everything has been taken care of," Lawrence replied. "I'll pray you find peace in your memories."

"Yes, of course. Thank you," Brian said. He secured the small bag deep in his pocket and took hold of his daughter's hand. A cloud of grief shrouded their every step as they left the funeral home.

Brian slipped the car into park in front of the Brookside Motor Lodge, a single-story structure built in among a grove of towering hemlock trees. The tranquil setting and natural earth tones welcomed weary travelers. The rooms carried the same theme, painted in shades of beige and forest green with soft brown carpeting and dusty rose bedspreads.

Once they were inside, Brian turned the deadbolt lock and leaned his head against the door. He had no regrets about leaving the church and avoiding the burial ceremony. Their ordeal here was nearly over. By this time tomorrow they would be back home, but he was not ready to face going on without Alicia. Once again Brian set aside his grief in order to take care of the kids.

"Okay, time for a bath," he said. "Shoes first."

Brian lifted Jack up on the bed and pulled off his shoes and socks. He turned when Erin tapped his arm. "What's wrong?"

"I got knots," Erin said with dismay.

"Aw, baby, come here." Brian sat Erin next to her brother and loosened the stubborn knots in her shoelaces. "Socks too," he reminded her.

Erin tugged off one sock. "Can we have bubbles?" she asked, wiggling her bare toes.

"When we get home," he replied.

While the bathtub filled with water Brian wondered if the pain in his heart was ever going to go away. A few minutes later he sat back on his heels and watched the kids in the tub. They both had light blonde hair. Alicia had wondered if their hair was going to darken as they grew older. It was another of the mysteries revealed only by the passage of time.

Erin's hair curled around her face and was just long enough to braid or put up in a ponytail. Jack's was cut short like a little gentleman. Erin's eyes were the same soft brown as Alicia's and Jack's were blue like his own.

Brian lifted Erin out first and wrapped a towel around her. "Go careful now. Don't trip on the towel."

Brian followed after Erin with Jack bundled up in a towel.

Everything in their lives evoked memories of Alicia. Even the red pajamas with blue and yellow balloons he pulled out of the duffel bag were reminders of Alicia and happier times. Alicia always brightened when he finished bathing the kids and brought them in to her. He liked to hold them and announce, "Look what I found. Two little babes."

"Not babies, Daddy. We're big kids," Erin corrected.

"Babies," laughed Jack.

The memories felt so real while he held Jack on his lap and combed his hair. "You're a good boy," he said and kissed his warm cheek. With that Jack wiggled down to the floor.

"It's your turn, Erin," said Brian. He gingerly ran the comb through her tangled hair. He'd forgotten the conditioner and she knew it. "I'm sorry, honey," he apologized.

"It's okay," replied Erin.

Brian fiddled with the comb for a moment, running his thumb up and down its wide teeth. He reluctantly pulled himself up out of the chair and checked the lock. "Hey, you two be good while I shower, okay?"

Erin looked up and said, "I'll take care of Jack." She turned her attention back to the coloring book on the floor.

Brian let the hot water ease some of his tension while he unwillingly revisited the past few days. Alicia was the most loving and giving person he had ever known, but her parents were another story entirely. Her mother blamed Brian for the events of the past two years. All of it was his fault, she said over and over again, even with the children near enough to hear her. She wanted everyone to think he had condemned his wife to death. Suddenly he remembered where he was and finished his shower. He toweled off and came out to find his children right where he had left them.

Once he had their clothes set out for morning, Brian packed the duffel bags and backpack. He carefully tucked the tiny velvet bag containing Alicia's rings into the pocket of the jeans he was going to wear for the flight home. He needed to keep them close.

*Tender Dreams*

## Chapter 2

Quilting came as naturally as breathing to Grace Marshall. Stretched out on the quilting frame before her, the beautiful pastel-colored pieces of fabric formed pinwheel designs on a background of ivory. She guided the silver needle through the multiple layers of fabric and batting as though the needle were an extension of her fingers. Though the intricate work was tedious and took countless hours to complete, Grace loved each and every minute of it. The work kept her busy, brought her joy and helped to pay the bills.

Grace set the scissors aside before scooting the old wooden chair a little further to the left. Her stomach growled, but she ignored it while she kept thinking of the completed quilt wrapped in tissue paper and tucked into a gift box. The toughest part of her projects came when she handed the quilts over to the clients. Whether the attachment she felt for each quilt was silly or insane did not matter, it always happened. She wanted her quilts to be cherished and then perhaps passed along to the next generation. Her thoughts strayed to an antique quilt stored in a trunk upstairs. Though it had come down through three generations to her, she knew it had no chance to be passed on again.

Grace dropped the needle onto the quilt and covered her face with both hands. A wave of self-pity and hopelessness washed over her. She abruptly sat up, wiped away the tears and dried her hands on her jeans. She had to focus on her work and remember she had a deadline to meet and bills to pay. Between her day job and the quilting projects she needed every penny she earned to meet her expenses. She always felt like she was barely treading water. Grace was grateful for her life, but wished she had the power to change the past. Wished she could keep from thinking about her unattainable dreams. Her mother's words came back to her at that moment.

"Life is a gift. Get up every morning and be grateful for it. Life changes. Be patient," Marianna had advised.

Grace felt her mother's lingering presence in the room. With her eyes closed, she saw herself helping to stack up cut pieces of fabric. Remembered creating towers with spools of thread. Envisioned her mother's steady hand cutting a perfectly straight line across a width of batting or backing material. Her mother's love for the craft had created the same passion in Grace.

With another adjustment of the chair, she moved the lamp and began working again. The breeze picked up outside and sent the wind chimes dancing. Their deep tones rang out like church bells.

Grace smiled when she heard a robin chirping in the back yard. She imagined him hopping through the grass in search of the perfect worm for supper. Her stomach growled again, reminding her she still had not had anything to eat. Just a few more stitches and she would take a break. Grace examined her work with a critical eye. It looked good. No, it looked perfect. She trailed her fingertips over the stitches, then pulled them away.

"It's past time to eat," she whispered. When she switched off the floor lamp the entire house went dark. Grace knew every inch of her childhood home and moved with ease toward the narrow hallway. With her fingertips running along the wall, she silently padded toward the kitchen. A quick glance at the clock on the stove told her it was already 9 o'clock. No wonder her stomach had protested. Quick and easy seemed most important at this hour. With a bowl of cereal and a glass of juice, Grace walked to her bedroom.

"Breakfast in bed, for supper," she said out loud. She knew what her mother would say to that.

"No meat and potatoes?" Marianna would have scolded. "Shame, shame."

Once the final quilting began Grace typically neglected everything else. She flipped on the television to check out the 24-hour news channel. After a few minutes of depressing stories, she turned off the set and finished her supper in silence. It was that silence that followed Grace through the next steps. Familiar steps. Routine steps.

After loosening her braided hair, she methodically brushed it out. Her chestnut brown hair reached down to her waist.

Grace slipped into her well-worn flannel nightgown and crawled in under the comforter. She always liked how the dark of night wrapped around her and cloaked her with peace. It was not long before she cleared her mind and fell asleep.

Without warning Grace found herself running in the dark. She could not see anything behind her, but she knew something, or someone, was chasing after her.

Abruptly, Grace sat up overheated and breathing hard. She tossed the comforter aside, frantic to get cooled off. A minute passed before the silvery threads of moonlight let her see she was safe. Grace pushed her hair back from her face, dropped her feet to the floor and slowly made her way to the bathroom. The darkness hid her reflection in the mirror. She rinsed her face with cool water, then reached for the towel. Her heart was still thumping like crazy.

"Calm down," she told herself as she walked back into the bedroom. "Just a dream, nothing more."

Grace picked the comforter up from the floor and flung it out over her bed. Once it settled into place, the moonlight created images of white ribbons scattered across the dark fabric. The simple beauty made her feel better, but the dream kept replaying in her mind. The frantic running and overwhelming sense of doom frightened her. She ran her fingers through her hair and stood there in the moonlight.

Though her dreams rarely came true, Grace knew they held merit. Shortly after her 21st birthday, Grace's parents made plans to go on a boat trip off the coast of California. Although it was a trip they had taken many times before, she wanted them to stay home. A nightmarish dream of a terrible explosion had taken the breath out of her. Even after she explained her reason for asking them to cancel the trip, they assured her they were going to be fine.

When she received the horrific news two days later her heart sank. Grace fell into a bottomless well of despair. Rational thought escaped her. Devastated by the tragedy Grace lost all sense of time, mentally punishing herself for failing to save their lives.

Even now she denied herself the chance for anything resembling happiness. The years had not diminished her feelings of inadequacy. She lived life day to day, keeping a safe distance between her solitary life and the contentment her parents had once shared. Grace was alone in the world, the only branch still clinging to the withering family tree. She drew the comforter up and willed herself back to sleep.

*Julia Robertson*

## Chapter 3

Brian found a quiet corner near the gate at the airport where the windows afforded the kids a clear view of the activity on the ground below. When the baggage handlers started loading luggage into the plane's cargo compartment, he told Erin and Jack to watch for their car seats and sat down in a nearby chair.

He had had a restless night, waking several times to the unsettling sight of Alicia in that damned coffin. He checked his jeans pocket to be sure the small bag containing her rings was still there. Brian kept Lawrence Ashcroft's words in mind, though he doubted he would ever find peace in his memories. While he watched his children, he revisited a special day two years into their marriage.

After a hectic day at work, Brian arrived at home long after dark. He noticed the only light in the house came from the kitchen. "I'm home," he called out. Brian unlaced his work boots, pushed them off and set them aside. After leaving his jacket on a peg near the front door, he walked into the kitchen. When he lifted the lid on one of the pots on the stove and breathed in the aroma, he sighed.

Alicia suddenly popped out of the dining room. "Hi, my favorite husband. How was your day?"

Brian had to laugh. Her expression told him she was up to something. "Hey cutie, what's going on?" He walked up to her and skimmed his fingers over her cheek. From the corner of his eye, he saw the candles flickering in the dining room. "Do we have company coming?"

Alicia bit her lip to conceal the news a little longer. "Company coming? We sure do," she said as she raised her hands to his face.

"Should I go get cleaned up? Who is it?" he asked, resting his hands on her slender waist.

"There's no reason to change, my love. You look perfect to me." She ran her thumbs over his dirt-streaked face. "I love the way you look after a hard day at work. You look, well, so macho."

"Macho," he whispered and leaned in close to her. "Want me to show you macho?" He pulled her close and kissed her.

"Such a man," giggled Alicia. She ran her hands up his strong back. "My man. The father of our baby."

"Are you kidding?" he exclaimed. "For real?" He picked her up and spun around the room. "We're having a baby!" he shouted.

Alicia's laughter stopped as she pushed back from him, frantic to get away. "Let me go!" she cried out.

She ran from the room while Brian stood stunned. Had he done something wrong? He followed after her, ready to apologize immediately. He found her sitting on the floor in the bathroom. "Alicia? Are you okay?" he asked, kneeling down next to her.

"Isn't it wonderful?" she said with tears running from her eyes.

Brian wet a washcloth and handed it to her. "Wait, let me help you," he said when she started to get up. "Is it normal to puke like that?"

"Perfectly normal," she laughed. "I thought I was sick, but never imagined being pregnant. It's a harmless condition that will pass in, oh, about seven more months."

Brian listened, counted, and then said, "June?"

"Yes," she said with surprise. "How'd you do that so fast? I fumbled with the months trying to figure it out and you, it just pops right out."

"Sorry, it's just that," he began, but stopped when she pressed her fingers to his lips.

"I started dinner, but now," she moaned with her hand on her stomach.

"What can you eat that'll help?" he asked.

"Hot tea, I think. Maybe some crackers."

Brian scooped her up and carried her back to the kitchen. "What's in there?" he asked as they passed by the stove.

"My best ever red sauce. You just have to cook the pasta. Can you do that?" Alicia giggled at the expression on his face. "Like I said, sweetie, such a man."

"We'll begin boarding with rows," Began the airline agent at the counter.

Startled out of the past by the crackling voice coming over the speakers, Brian bolted upright on the chair. He did his best to calm his ravaged heart as he gathered up the kids and joined the line waiting to board the plane.

Half an hour into the flight Jack was sound asleep leaning against Brian. He knew it wouldn't be long before Erin joined him. Once both kids were asleep, Brian relaxed and closed his eyes.

From the window of the airplane on their final approach, something caught Erin's eye. "Looks like a red ladybug," she said.

Brian leaned over and saw the small car. "It sure does," he agreed.

"I like pink best," said Erin. She looked at her tennis shoes and bounced them up and down. "Make your shoes do this," she told Jack.

Brian watched his children. Raising them without Alicia brought tears to his eyes, but this was the wrong place to let his feelings of inadequacy get the better of him. He reminded himself to take things one step at a time.

When the plane came to a stop at the terminal, Brian waited their turn to stand up. He felt anxious to get away from the chaos and into the fresh air outside.

"Stay close and hold my hand, Erin. Don't let go," he said as they began to move toward the front of the plane. The line kept slowing and stopping while people blocked the aisle, reaching overhead for their belongings. Brian thought of the nearly empty refrigerator at home. They needed to get milk and juice on the way home. And a loaf of bread.

Once they spilled out into the terminal with the other passengers, Brian sighed. If Clay Hancock was here to pick them up, they would be home in no time. Minutes later he spotted his friend in the crowd.

"Hey, Brian," Clay called out. "How's it going, old man."

"Old man," Brian said. Clay was four years older than Brian, but it never mattered between friends.

"Let me take that big boy of yours. Come here, Jackson. And how about you, Lady Erin. Wanna come up?" He squatted down and lifted her up.

"Thanks," Brian said. "Let's head for the baggage claim. We're ready to go home."

When Erin rested her head on his shoulder, Clay said, "You're a sweetie, Lady Erin." He turned to Jack. "You went on the big plane."

"Way up high," said Jack with his hand up in the air.

"Way up high," agreed Erin. "I need to go to the bathroom."

"Give me your backpack," Clay told Brian. "I'll watch for your bags."

"Hey, the car seats too," Brian said.

"Got it," said Clay.

"Do you have time to stop at the grocery?" Brian asked once they were in the car. "If you don't mind staying with the kids it'll make it easier for me."

"I can do that," replied Clay, slowing to a stop at the first traffic light outside the airport.

"The ladybug. Over there," Erin announced from the back seat.

Brian glanced over and saw the little red car parked where they had seen it from the airplane. "It's bigger down here," he said.

"Ladybug?" Clay asked. He looked away from the light and saw the car and the woman inside. "She's pretty."

"She's the Ladybug Lady," Erin sang out with delight.

Brian absently watched the car until his attention was drawn toward the passenger side window. A swirling mist swept around him and took his breath away. Before he had time to comprehend what was happening, Brian heard her.

*"Please don't live the rest of your life alone," she whispered.*

Brian's mouth went dry as cotton. He turned to see if Clay had heard what he had just heard, but he obviously had not. Tension he had never known before crawled up Brian's back and bore into his head. He stared out the passenger side window with his heart pounding like a jackhammer. Alicia had spoken those same words to him several times over the past few months, but she was no longer here with him. He had no desire to look for someone else. There was no one else. He would never consider replacing the only woman to capture his heart. "No," he said as he nervously rubbed his hands against his thighs.

"What's up?" Clay asked.

"Nothing," Brian replied. "Just tired."

"I bet. How did yesterday go?" Clay asked cautiously.

"It went," Brian said, silently finishing with 'right to hell'. "It's done. But," he said.

"It's all right, Brian. It's all right. We have things covered for the next month. You figure things out and we'll make it work. We're right there with you, whatever it takes." Clay tapped the steering wheel, creating a much-needed distraction. "How's the engine sound to you?"

"Like a dream," Brian replied. "Seriously, it sounds great."

"Now that it's running, I can get to the body work," Clay said, beaming with pride.

"It's not the best-looking car on the road," remarked Brian.

"It does need a little touch-up paint," Clay laughed.

When they pulled into the driveway after stopping at the grocery store, Brian stared at the house, suddenly feeling sick to his stomach. He had to get out of the car. Had to get on with his life.

"Brian," Clay said as he gently squeezed his friend's shoulder. "You okay?"

"I just, it just," Brian stammered. Without another word he shoved the door open and stood up with the bag of groceries. His legs felt numb as he stepped into the house. "Keep moving," he told himself.

By the time he reached the kitchen Brian heard the kids coming in behind him. He felt ashamed for having left Clay alone with them.

"We're home!" Erin shouted as she ran in through the front door. "Come on, Jack. Let's go play in our room." Their tennis shoes thudded down the short hallway and their squeals of delight flowed through the house.

"Cool," laughed Clay. He set the car seats on the floor and went back outside.

"Thanks for coming for us, Clay," Brian said, following behind him.

Clay handed him the smaller duffel bag. "No problem. Your backpack's in the back seat."

"Okay, thanks," Brian said and pulled the door open.

"I'll bring this one in," Clay said as he closed the trunk lid. The whole car shuddered and squeaked. "It's musical ain't it," he laughed.

"Rattletrap," Brian remarked with a grin. "I'd better get the kids to the bathroom again. We made the entire trip without a wet pair of pants," he said, walking back inside the house.

"It's probably easier to pull your own tooth out than teach a kid to use a toilet," Clay groaned, following Brian. He put the duffel bag down on the floor just inside the front door and called out, "Hey Brian, I'm heading out. Need anything while I'm still here?"

At the bathroom doorway, Brian turned back toward his friend. "No, we're fine. Thanks Clay. Call me tomorrow. I want to keep up on the work progress."

"You got it, boss man. Bye kids!" Clay shouted before heading for his car.

Once the kids were back in their bedroom playing, Brian stood in the hallway for a moment. He was bone tired, but it was far too early to put the kids to bed and expect them to sleep through the night. He imagined them up at 3 o'clock in the morning, ready for a day of play.

After shaking off his weariness, he headed back to get the duffel bags. He might as well dump everything into the hamper and get the laundry going. He set the first bag on the bed and started to pull the zipper open. His hands froze when his eyes focused on the bed.

"Our bed," he whispered. She would never sleep there with him again. He would never make love with her again. The cold reality of it made him feel sick. Brian knew he should have been prepared for her death, but it hurt even more now that they were home again. Home without her.

Alicia had always been energetic and happy. She took everything in stride. It did not matter whether it was too little money in the bank to pay the bills or a flat tire on the car, she faced it with a smile and determination to make things work out. When Erin came along her high spirits soared even higher. It was wonderful to see her with Erin. The way she looked at their baby with love. The way she stroked her soft hair and held the tiny hands in hers spoke of tenderness and devotion.

By the time Erin mastered crawling and standing next to any immobile object, Alicia learned she was pregnant again. She fairly danced around the house with delight. Why she did not dread the upcoming labor was beyond Brian's comprehension. He did not want her to have to endure it all over again. She told him not to worry because she was young, and she was strong. Her eyes sparkled when she held up her arms to show him her muscles.

"My little powerhouse," he loved telling her. Alicia had been very strong back then. Brian knew it was counterproductive to dwell on the past and the things he could not change, but he had no idea how to deal with it.

"Get busy, keep busy," he told himself.

While he purposefully worked at a slow pace unloading the duffel bags, Brian remembered washing diapers when the kids were babies. With his thoughts focused once again on the past, the dirty diapers were here when Alicia was here. He recollected her expression as she dumped a pail full of raunchy smelling diapers into the washer. Nothing smelled quite so bad.

"Daddy, I can't find Jack! Hurry!" Erin called out.

"Okay, I'm coming," Brian said as he followed her into the bedroom. He stopped just inside the door but did not see the boy anywhere. He quickly looked behind the door, then knelt down and checked beneath the beds.

He sat back on his heels and asked, "Where is he?"

Erin giggled and hid her eyes behind her hands. Her giggles grew louder as she dropped down on the floor.

"Come on, silly girl, where's your brother? Where's he hiding?" Brian crawled over and rolled her onto her back. "The tickle bug is going to get you," he said with his hand walking toward her like a big spider.

"No, no," Erin squealed. "Over there, over there," she said through her giggles.

Brian blew bubbles of air on her bare tummy, then scooped her up and draped her over his shoulder. He scanned the room and caught sight of Jack.

"Just look at you, little man. How'd you get in there?"

Jack peeked out from a pile of stuffed animals in the toy box. He looked like a doll on a toy shop shelf. Kneeling on the floor, Brian patted Erin's bottom and then reached out and tapped Jack's nose. He let Erin slide down onto his lap and lifted Jack out of the pile of animals. "I need a bunch of hugs. Who's going to help me out?"

*Suspended between the past and hereafter, she watched them, no longer able to reach out and touch them. Her death left a huge hole in their lives. It showed in Brian's eyes. His pain radiated throughout the room like hot sparks of electricity. She vowed to stay close and help him find peace.*

Brian instinctively sheltered the kids when he felt an eerie presence in the room. "Hey, I'm sorry," he said as soon as he realized he had frightened them. When he looked up at the doorway, the strange feeling was gone. There was no one there. Had not been anyone there.

"Are you two getting hungry?" Brian asked, hoping to distract them.

"Yeah," they both sang out.

"Okay, you guys play while I get supper ready." Brian grabbed two stuffed animals and handed one to Erin and the other to Jack.

"We gotta be good, Daddy's sad," Erin whispered to her brother. She patted Jack's cheek.

Brian dragged the full hamper down the hallway and into the kitchen. He put the first load into the washer and added a scoop of laundry detergent. He listened to the water filling the tub and thought about supper.

*Tender Dreams*

## Chapter 4

 Grace spent her late afternoon lunch hour watching the planes land at the airport. They looked like mysterious silver birds floating down from the blue sky. The idle time away from work and the day-to-day routine gave her a chance to daydream. She wondered about all of the people on board the planes, where they had come from or where they were going. She had never been inside an airplane, let alone 30,000 feet above the ground. The mere idea made her stomach feel jumpy. Though she had no fear of flying, she had no idea what it might be like. Grace's father had been a pilot during World War II. He never offered her stories of any kind, but she learned too late that he was a hero.
 After her parents died, she found the medals and a few items from his time in the service. Grace cherished those things even though she did not fully understand their meaning. She had taken time to sort through their belongings, saving what she knew were family heirlooms and discarding things that were just things. Despite the overwhelming mortgage payments, Grace chose to keep the house and all the memories within its walls. She could not bear to part with her home. It had been a difficult journey for her to travel all alone.
 Grace caught sight of the next plane coming in as she scooped up another bite of pasta salad. One day, she promised herself, she would take a flight to somewhere else. Grace's eyes drifted toward the traffic coming from the airport parking lot. She followed the path of what she considered a project car, apparently held together with just enough duct tape. Primer gray blotches covered up whatever color it might have been and one of the headlights was missing. As it drew nearer, she saw two men in the front seats. Her imagination filled in the details she had no chance of actually seeing from where she was parked.
 The driver had scraggly hair, a set of dark eyes and a heavy mustache. She decided he was a tall, thin man with a tattoo on his upper arm. No doubt it was some girl's name. He probably had a gold

tooth that showed when he smiled. She chuckled at her imagined description.

When her eyes landed on the second man, the one in the passenger seat, she sighed. This time she let her creative energy lean in the opposite direction.

Talk about drop-dead gorgeous. His hair was neatly trimmed and the color of silky chocolate ice cream. Grace momentarily wondered where she had come up with the color comparison. She decided his eyes had to be a stunning shade of dark blue. Imagining him standing before her, she saw his strong athletic body with toned muscles and sun-bronzed skin. Grace wanted to call out, "A phone number, a name, anything," but remained silent and confused.

The car sped away and he was gone. Had she seen children in the back seat? Who did they belong to? The scraggly haired man or the gorgeous guy? Or had she simply imagined them too? It didn't matter since she would never see any of them again. She bit her lip and pushed away her crazy thoughts.

Grace returned to work, unable to stop thinking about the handsome guy in the car. She had never had a lasting relationship and felt foolish for allowing herself to daydream about a total stranger. If there had been kids in the car, they might be his. If the kids were his, then he was probably married. If he was married, he was off limits. Besides, Grace admitted to herself, she did not deserve to have anyone. She knew in her heart she was destined to spend the remainder of her life alone. The emptiness made her stomach burn.

Back at work Grace crammed her purse into the bottom drawer of her desk and growled at her stupid thoughts. When her phone rang, she stared at it. She did not want to be here. She knew Roger Phelps was watching her from his nearby desk. He was a friend, but also her immediate supervisor. Her unhappy and unsettled self wanted to run away and hide. Her responsible side silently reminded her of the mounting bills, forcing her to sit up straight and focus on her job.

"Answer it," Roger snapped under his breath.

Grace could not resist glaring at him before picking up the phone. "Valley Post, this is Grace." Her calm tone masked her personal frustration. "Sure, I can help you with that. Give me a sec," she said as she tapped keys on her computer keyboard. "All right now, which section?" She paused and listened to the caller. "Yes, we have one specifically for garage sales. I suggest you list the days, then your address. Listing your phone number will have you answering questions all day long. Okay," she said. On the other end of the line, she heard the woman laughing. "You're busy, aren't you?"

"I've got three kids. They think when I'm on the phone it's a signal for them to act up. Same goes when I try to go to the bathroom alone. Geez, quiet down, Mandy," she said. "Okay, I think I'm here."

Grace typed "Friday, Saturday," then paused. "Okay, do you have big items you'd like to list? You know, things that will draw in the garage salers."

"Oh yeah, a baby crib, cause we're not having more kids. Geez, I have changed enough diapers. And a really old trunk, you know, with fancy brass trim all over it," she said.

Grace finished typing and read the ad back to the woman. "How does that sound?"

"Great, I like it. I'd go myself except it's my sale."

Grace pulled the phone from her ear as the woman hooted with delight. "Good one," said Grace, using her best customer relations voice. "It will run in Friday and Saturday's papers. Thank you, Mrs. Wheeler. Have a nice day."

"You too," responded Mrs. Wheeler.

Grace heard her calling for Mandy again. The kid sounded like a terror. She reread the ad on the computer screen one more time, then pressed the key to send it to print. "I've written more garage sale ads than ever this month. It must be spring cleaning time."

"Sounds like," agreed Roger. He leaned back on his chair and folded his arms over his chest. "Maggie wants me to clean out our garage. I cannot stand doing it. I make a pile of boxes to get rid of, then Maggie comes out and says we need to keep this, and we need to keep that. I cannot get rid of any of the treasures she stashes out there all year long. We don't need any of it, but there they sit, boxes to the ceiling."

"What's a guy to do?" Grace said, hiding her smile behind her hand. Roger's desk always looked like it had been hit by a tornado. There were several trophies and four or five stacks of sports magazines. Countless pens and pencils were scattered from one side to the other. He used a football tee as a holder for photos and she knew he had a football somewhere nearby. A bright yellow coffee mug with a grass green "O" on it could always be found half submerged amid the clutter. She wondered if Maggie had ever seen Roger's desk. She knew Maggie loved to save things, but so did Roger.

Out of habit Grace kept her eyes averted from the large clock on the far wall. When her work was caught up, she dared to take a peek. She was relieved to see it was almost quitting time. She began cleaning off her desk, anticipating the evening ahead. She had several more nights of work to do on the current quilt. Her quilting gave her more joy and satisfaction than any of her work here.

## Chapter 5

The kids fell asleep in record time that first night. Brian gently stroked Jack's hair with his fingers. The little boy's chubby hands were fisted under his chin. Brian kissed the top of his head, then turned to Erin. While Jack slept all cuddled into himself, Erin had one arm flung up over her head, laying on her back. Her blonde hair fanned out across her pink pillowcase. She usually had a list of questions for him at bedtime, but the room was silent tonight. Silent but for his thundering heart. Brian sat down with his back against the wall between the two beds wishing Alicia were here with him. They were supposed to raise their kids and grow old together.

Alicia's life had been all about nurturing their children, keeping their home and loving him with all her heart. She had endless patience and handled each and every task with delight. Brian cherished precious images of her nursing Jack while Erin "read" her favorite story books. Life had settled into a comfortable routine for all of them. Every day had been filled with love and laughter, perfect in every way possible. Things began changing around the time Jack turned 18 months old.

Alicia seemed to be tired all the time, even when she slept through the night. She napped whenever the kids were sleeping. Her eyes became shadowed with fatigue and she always seemed to have a cold. When Brian noticed she had bruises that were not healing, the alarm bells started going off. Their world began unraveling shortly after Alicia's first appointment.

Once the final lab test results came in, they sat together and listened as the doctor explained the diagnosis to them. Most of the terminology went right over his head, but Brian caught one single word before he mentally escaped from the room. The word leukemia virtually ripped out his heart. When he finally came around again, he struggled to understand what he was hearing. The cancer cells had already invaded her body. The doctor said they would attack the cancer but offered no promises. He offered no false hope for her future. Brian knew she had been handed a death sentence. The chemo began immediately. The doctor said it was not like a weapon fired at a specific target. Instead, it was more like an atomic bomb set off in hopes of killing those enemy cells, endangering every other cell in her body. Worse than a game of chance in Brian's eyes.

Although Alicia had insisted on going for the chemotherapy on her own, it was not long before she could not drive herself into town. The cost of her treatments, lab tests and doctor visits overwhelmed their savings in a heartbeat. They sold their home in Chelsea Creek and moved into a compact rental house in Jameson where they were closer to the medical facilities Alicia's poor health demanded. Alicia often reminded him the most important thing was that they were all together. Even while dealing with the relentless and unforgiving illness, her positive attitude never wavered.

The tragic memories forced Brian to his feet. He walked out of the small bedroom and down the hall to the kitchen where he gripped the edge of the counter. He had cursed everyone and everything for destroying Alicia's precious life. He felt angry with everyone from God to the doctors to her mother and father.

Once the worst of his rage began to subside Brian stepped back and ran his fingers through his hair. He was too tired to be angry. Besides, the anger would not change anything.

He double-checked the kitchen, switched off the lights and headed to his bedroom. After he brushed his teeth, Brian scanned the things on the bathroom counter. He thought of Alicia's bright eyes when she showed him the stoneware toothbrush holder and soap pumper she found at a local pottery show. He reached out and touched her various containers of makeup and lotions. Her things, he thought with sadness.

Brian tugged the velvet bag out of his pocket and ran his thumb over the fabric. Unsteady on his feet, he crossed the room and opened the ring box Alicia kept on top of their shared chest of drawers. The memory of the night he had asked her to marry him came back with vivid clarity. It had been the right question for the right woman at the right time in his life.

Brian slid her ring over the tip of his pinky finger. It was a simple, yet beautiful engagement ring. He wanted to buy her the biggest and most expensive ring in the jewelry store, but Alicia had put her foot down.

"It's not the size of the diamond or the cost, Brian, it's our love that counts. Besides, we cannot afford anything expensive right now. If you need to give me an expensive ring, do it for our 25th anniversary. We will be older, wiser and perhaps richer by then. Please, I like that set," Alicia said as she pointed out the simple white gold band with the tiny square-cut diamond.

Her words rang out inside his head. They would never celebrate their 25th anniversary together. Hands shaking, Brian settled the ring into the little box. He held her wedding band between his thumb and index finger, a much smaller version of the band he wore. A few silent seconds passed before he put the wedding band in next to her engagement ring. Tears ran down his cheeks.

Contessa Rivers had insisted her daughter be buried with her wedding band on, but Brian knew Alicia wanted him to keep the rings forever.

"Please," Alicia had whispered late one night. "Please take them off before they put my body in the ground. I want to know that you will keep them."

Brian took off his own ring and rolled it between his thumb and finger. He did not know whether to keep wearing it or put it away. Was he still married? Did a widower wear his ring? Though his mother was gone, Brian had no idea if his father still wore his wedding band.

Brian's fingers grew cold when he began to slip his ring in next to Alicia's rings. He abruptly slid it back on his finger. He would keep wearing it because he was still married to her. He still loved and needed her. He snapped the lid closed and put the box back in its place. He rubbed his hands over his face and took in a deep breath.

Brian crawled in under the comforter, but sleep eluded him. With his eyes open in the dark room, he could not stop thinking. Alicia had been his whole world. With her at his side he could do anything. Now he had been forced to turn the page to a new chapter in his life.

Brian's mind pulled a vivid image from the past into focus as though it were in real time. It was summer break at college, and he had volunteered to help paint houses for several area families in need. He set the ladder up on the front porch of the old house, steadied it as he stepped up and reached down for the paint can. Brian lost track of what he was doing when the most beautiful woman in the world stepped into a beam of sunlight on the porch. She wore faded jeans, a sleeveless brown T-shirt and red tennis shoes. Her honey-gold blonde hair was pulled up into a long ponytail and tied with a red ribbon. How long he stared at her he would never know. It might have been for just ten seconds, but Brian wished it had been forever.

"Cooper, take this thing," Andy grumbled, thumping Brian's knee with the paint brush.

"What?" asked Brian. He looked down and saw Andy's angry expression. "Sorry, I just," he began as he took the brush and looked across the porch again. She was gone. The paint can nearly fell from the ladder when he turned abruptly.

"Hey, watch out," warned Andy. "She'll be right back, don't worry."

"Who is she?" Brian asked.

"Alicia," Andy replied. "She's going to paint the trim right behind you. Get busy."

Brian dipped the brush into the paint and looked up when Alicia came back out onto the porch. All concentration was gone when she walked over to the ladder and looked up at him.

"Hi," she said.

The paint brush slipped out of his hand the moment his eyes met hers. Brian caught it before it hit her. He frowned, feeling like a fool. When she laughed, a charge of electricity shot through him and he knew he was going to marry her.

It was the beginning of their life together. Even if he had known the consequences, he still would have asked her to marry him. Brian rolled onto his side and tucked the pillow under his head. If Alicia were here, she would be cuddled up against him with her back to his chest. He would wrap his arm around her beautiful body and breathe in the scent of her hair. He would lay there and think of how lucky he was to be married to the woman he loved with all his heart, but Brian was all alone in his bed. He laid his hand on the bare sheet beside him and whispered, "I love you."

Shortly after 10 o'clock that night, Brian rolled off his bed and sleepily made his way toward the sound of Erin's crying. It was not the first time and he knew it would not be the last.

"It's okay, honey. Go back to sleep," he said softly. He gently massaged her back.

"Mommy," cried Erin.

"I know, shh," he said. He wondered how long Erin was going to feel like this. For months? Maybe for years? He knew he would miss Alicia forever. When Erin relaxed, he stayed close until he felt certain she was sound asleep. Brian stumbled back across the hall and fell onto his bed.

*Julia Robertson*

*Tender Dreams*

Chapter 6

With crickets chirping outside the window, Grace set a bowl of chicken rice soup on the kitchen table. Though her fingers itched to get back to her quilting, she had to eat first. She chose a newspaper from the growing stack on the table. Grace wrote classified ads, birth announcements, obituaries and police reports, but hoped to write human interest stories in the near future. She spooned up some soup and scanned the birth announcements. Each one was structured in the same manner, but of course the names were different. She read the new baby names out loud, skipping over the rest of the information.

"Cassandra Josephine. Cassie Jo," she mused. "Jaidyn Nicole, Conner Weston, Brooklynn Summer, Matthew James, Royce Daniel, Alyssa Diane." She went back to the top of the list and read through the weight of each baby. Conner James topped out at 9 pounds, 10 ounces, while Cassandra Josephine weighed just 5 pounds, 4 ounces. "Cassie Jo," she said again.

Grace almost let herself imagine what name she would choose if she had a baby of her own. Before she came up with anything, she pushed aside the idea. She dared not think about the things she could not have.

She spooned up more soup as she slowly passed along the narrow columns of words in the obituary section. Grace whispered the words aloud, "Willa Mae Caruthers, age 99, died on Tuesday night."

She read through the names of her children, grandchildren and great grandchildren. Grace wondered about everything the woman had experienced in her long life. She took another spoonful of soup and went on to the next one.

"Barton Miles Standford, age 85, passed on to Heaven with his beloved wife at his side."

Grace remembered putting the article together while she talked with his widow. They had been married for 60 years. Mrs. Standford had

33

wanted a nice tribute to her husband. He had served in World War II and was a true American hero.

"Not a braggart," Mrs. Standford had told her.

Grace wrote the majority of the obituaries, but the next one wasn't familiar to her. Marilyn must have written it. She pushed aside the empty bowl and began reading out loud.

"Alicia," she whispered. "You were so young. What happened to you?" She bit her lip and looked away. Before her hands managed to fold the newspaper up and hide it from view, Grace looked again. "Survived by her husband and two children," she read aloud. The young woman's parents were listed as well, but no other family members.

Grace slowly shook her head, thinking of how her own obituary would read. "Grace Marshall, died alone, survived by nobody." She began tapping the floor with her foot. Grace dragged herself through life day after day, doing what needed doing. Her only goals were to keep up with the bills, preserve her fragile spirit and maintain an outward sense of happiness. She did not have time, nor did she deserve to enjoy life like others around her. Wishing for and dreaming of did not make things any different.

"Stop it! Nothing is going to change. Block it out. Let it go," she scolded herself.

Aggravated with having allowed her negativity to get the better of her, she clumsily folded the newspaper, picked up the empty bowl and carried it to the sink. She stared into the inky darkness beyond the window, feeling more alone than ever.

Once the kitchen was put in order, Grace went back to her sewing. She adjusted the floor lamp, illuminating the area of the quilt she was working on. She threaded the needle, expertly knotted the end and began stitching again. Her mind wandered back to the young woman's name in the obituary. Alicia was a pretty name. She wondered if anyone called her Ali. Then she wondered if she pronounced her name Ah-lee-shah or Ah-lee-see-ya. Her own name was impossible to mispronounce. Just plain Grace.

With the pattern completed, Grace clipped the loose ends of the thread and set the scissors aside. She examined her work, satisfied to find the stitches neat and perfectly uniform. She thought of the quilts she had won ribbons for in the County Fairs. It had been many years since she entered a quilt in any sort of competition. One day she ought to do it again, but for now the quilts she created served to pay some of the bills her full-time paycheck did not cover.

As soon as this quilt was finished, she would start the next one. She had been given several boxes of fabric scraps left over from projects a woman had completed over the past four decades. The woman's daughter had hired her to create a quilt as a gift for her mother's birthday. No doubt she would wonder what had been made from each piece of fabric. When the needle began to blur before her eyes, Grace set the scissors into a small box, slid the needle into one of her pincushions and stood up from the chair. She switched off the lamp and dragged herself to her bedroom.

*Julia Robertson*

*Tender Dreams*

## Chapter 7

"He's sleeping," Erin told Jack. She pushed the comforter out of the way. "Let's climb up." Erin boosted Jack onto the bed and scrambled up next to him. "Under here," she said. "Get really close, Jack."

Brian heard their voices from somewhere beyond the sleepy clouds around him. He clung to sleep for a moment longer as the kids climbed into bed with him. Maybe if he pretended he did not hear them, they would go back to sleep.

Jack scooted in closer and laid his hand on Daddy's cheek. "Ouch," he whispered when he felt the coarse stubble.

"Shh," Erin said as she reached over Jack and felt Daddy's cheek for herself. "Needs to shave," she whispered. "Not you, not me," she said when Jack laughed and wiggled closer to Daddy. "Be quiet," she reminded Jack.

Brian felt hopeful when the children stopped whispering and held still. He knew they were watching him. Every time they did it, he felt their beady eyes penetrating his mind. He held his breath and wished they would conk out even though he knew there was no hope.

"Gotta pee," Jack said.

Brian pushed the comforter back and stood up. "Come on, Jack," he said, his voice gruff from sleep. He scooped up his little boy and walked to the bathroom. Brian rubbed his hand over his face and wondered what time it was. Hadn't he just calmed Erin after her bad dream? It could not be morning yet. It just could not be.

"All done," said Jack, swinging his feet back and forth from the toilet seat.

Brian looked down at Jack's bright eyes and big smile. The boy was wide awake and ready to go.

"Can we have Cheerios?" Erin asked.

"I don't know. Let me get dressed."

"Okay, but we want Cheerios."

Brian had no idea what kind of cereal they had left in the cupboard. "Sure," he agreed.

With the dryer running and the washer filling, Brian sat at the table eating Cheerios with Erin and Jack. He needed to take inventory of the freezer and kitchen cupboards and make a grocery list.

Brian was no stranger to cooking anymore. Shortly after Alicia started chemo, he took over most of the household chores. They hired a part-time housekeeper, but he still needed to learn. Alicia talked him through each step, often laughing at his fumbling attempts to prepare an edible meal. Her patient tutoring helped him learn how to wash their clothes, make up their beds, clean the house and put together a shopping list. She taught him everything about taking care of the children, even how to French braid Erin's hair.

Traveling alone with the kids had been a challenge, but there had been no other choice. If Alicia had not insisted on having her parents handle her funeral arrangements, Brian knew he would have managed that as well. He might never know what motivated her decision, but he had honored her wishes. After all she had been through, he could not tell her no.

Brian let go of his thoughts when Jack started smacking his cereal bowl with the spoon. "Okay, enough of that," he told the boy. He wiped milk off Jack's face and set him down on the floor. Erin had already disappeared. Jack ran off toward their bedroom.

While Brian rinsed their breakfast dishes and loaded them into the dishwasher, the dryer buzzed. Resisting the desire to pour another cup of coffee, he emptied the dryer into the laundry basket. He mechanically followed through the next steps, loading the dryer and pushing the last of the dirty clothes into the washer. Focusing on the simple tasks kept him from giving in to the impulse to sit down and cry.

On the way to his bedroom with the full laundry basket, he stopped to look in on the kids. Erin was trying to pull a shirt on over Jack's head. Jack was sitting still, but Erin was not having any luck with the shirt. "Hey, Missy, take his pajamas off first." Brian turned and stepped into his bedroom. He stood at the foot of the bed folding laundry and listening to the kids. He threw several more socks onto a growing pile.

"Hold still, Jack. Your head is too big," Erin giggled.

Brian walked to the doorway and watched her for a minute. "Erin, you can't pull the sleeve over his head. Need help?"

"Okay, but Jack is silly," Erin said, pointing at his face.

"Let me see," Brian told her. He stopped when he saw Jack's eyes scrunched up tight and his lips sticking out. "What happened to your face, boy? Open your eyes." Brian took the shirt from Erin and turned it right side out. "The pajamas come off first."

Jack giggled when Erin poked his tummy. "Want monkey shirt," he said.

"You got it, Jack. Hands up," he said and smiled when Jack's chubby little hands reached up toward the ceiling. "Here we go, now we're making progress." He pulled the pajama top off over Jack's head.

Erin listened and watched. "What's that?" she asked seriously.

"What's what?" asked Brian as he slid the T-shirt down over Jack's head.

"You said it," groaned Erin. "Um, prah, prah, I don't know. You said it, Daddy."

Brian stopped and thought about what he had said. "Okay, I think I know. Progress?"

"Yeah, what's that?" she asked.

Erin always asked things like that. He wondered how she kept all the information inside her small head. "I said we were making progress. It means we are getting something accomplished. You know, it was working, instead of the way you were doing it."

"Progress," she repeated with obvious concentration. "I didn't have progress?" she asked, using the word with caution.

"You usually do, but not this time. It was all tangled up." He smoothed his hand over Jack's soft hair.

"Twangle dup," said Jack.

Erin rolled on the floor with laughter. "Silly Jack," giggled Erin.

Loving her reaction, Jack said, "Twangle dup, twangle dup."

Brian watched them for a moment longer before he left to finish folding the laundry. It felt good to see them having fun. Once the basket was empty, Brian sorted the socks and tucked them into matching pairs. He stared at the pillows at the head of the bed, aching to step back in time and recapture what once was.

"I want you to come back." Before he drowned in sadness, Brian quickly gathered up the clothes and carried them into the kids' bedroom. He stepped over Jack and his coloring book and knelt down in front of their small chest of drawers.

Erin stopped playing and asked, "When can Mommy come home?"

Brian felt the walls closing in on him. He turned and pulled her onto his lap. "Erin, honey, I know it's hard to understand, but Mommy can't come home. She's in Heaven now."

"But I want her here," Erin wept. She clung to him with tears spilling down her cheeks. "I need her."

"I'm sorry, but we can't always have what we want. We have to live without Mommy, but she's right here," he told her. "Here, in you," he said as he touched her over her heart. "A part of Mommy will always be with you." Brian knew it was more than Erin could possibly comprehend.

"Is she in you too? And Jack?" she asked.

"Yes. A little part of her will always be with each of us." Brian stroked her hair and struggled with his own brittle emotions.

## Chapter 8

Running late Grace hit every red light on the way to work. She had stayed up too late last night and had no one to blame but herself. Though she had made good progress on the quilt, the lack of sleep left her mind feeling fuzzy. An invisible thread had tugged her back to the young woman's obituary only minutes before she headed out the front door this morning. The mental barrier she usually kept between her private life and the obits had crumbled this time. In addition to her uneasy feelings, she had unwillingly brought back the image of her own obituary. It suddenly occurred to her it would have been better all the way around if she had been the one to die rather than Alicia. Certainly would be better for the husband and their children.

Angry with herself, Grace parked her car and ran across the parking lot to the newspaper office. She felt foolish coming to work late. It rarely happened and everyone in the office noticed her tardiness.

"Hey Grace, forget to set your alarm clock?" Josh called out. He swiveled on his chair and watched her make her way to her desk. He glanced over at Marilyn. "It's nice it isn't me this time."

Marilyn laughed at Josh. "Yeah, I'm always stunned when I come in and you're already here," she said with a big grin, shoving his chair with the toe of her boot. "Get back to work before the boss sees you goofing off again."

"Again? What's with that?" Josh snapped with mock anger in his voice.

"I have tons of work for you today," Roxanne said as she dropped a stack of paperwork in the box on Grace's desk. She walked away without another word, but slowed down long enough to pop Josh on top of his head.

"Huh?" Josh cried out. "Man, what is this, pick on Josh day?" He rubbed his head and sighed as he turned back to his work.

The humorous exchange barely registered as Grace clumsily pushed her purse into the bottom drawer and turned to her computer. When she sensed Roger watching her, she kept her eyes averted from him. She did not want to be rude, but she felt the tension growing stronger. Though she confided in Roger and Maggie from time to time, she needed to keep her thoughts to herself for now. If he began prying, she would pop. She clicked on her computer and impatiently waited for it to boot up. The whirring fan barely muffled the sound of her shoe tapping the floor. Without thinking she picked up a pen and tapped it to the same beat. She absently looked up and saw Roger watching her. "What," she snarled.

"Nothing," he replied, wincing at her angry tone.

Grace dropped the pen and stopped her foot. If it were possible, she would crawl inside her desk and hide. She regretted snapping at Roger and typed a message to him. Her fingers flew over the keys. "I'm trying to work out some personal issues. I'm not angry with you." Without looking up she waited and unwittingly began tapping her foot again. When she saw her fingers reaching for the pen she groaned. Her computer beeped, drawing her attention back to the screen.

"Rough night?" he wrote.

She looked up and nodded. He nodded back and she knew they were all right. She reached for the notes in her basket and began organizing an obituary for the next issue of the newspaper. Was there ever a day without another obituary?

"Harriett Winnifred Parsons, age 92." Grace's fingers froze on the keys when her thoughts slipped back to the obituary she had found at home. She closed her eyes and wondered how the family was coping with their loss. Were the children old enough to comprehend the death of their mother? At times like this she wondered if life was worth living. She knew all too well how loss and grief tore at one's spirit. Grace wiped away the unwanted tears and noticed Roger watching her again. She shrugged and turned her attention back to her work, dreading the long day ahead of her.

## Chapter 9

Brian held the pencil between his fingers, staring at a blank sheet of paper. He used to sketch house plans when he had things to think about, but nothing came to mind now. Alicia had been right when she told him to take some time off after she was gone.

"Life is all about changes, honey," Alicia whispered when she first felt herself slipping away. "We have to be ready for whatever comes along."

He closed his eyes and almost felt her hand on his chest. He had held her on that day. Held her close for a long time. She was so frail. He asked God to take away her pain and give her life back to her. He asked God to let him take her place. His prayers had all gone unanswered. While he knew things could not be changed, he could not let go of the anger and resentment either.

Brian put the pencil down and held his hands up before him. Would they ever stop shaking? He needed Alicia here to help him put things into perspective. As many times as she assured him he would be okay, that he had the inner strength to do what needed doing, he found it impossible to believe.

"Please come back," he whispered. Brian rubbed his hands over his face and sighed. He stood up from the stool, unsteady on his feet. Alicia had been right. If he had gone back to work right away, he probably would have caused an accident.

Brian sat back down on the stool. He had been set adrift in a raging storm without his guiding light. If Alicia were here, he thought, then angrily stood up again. "Damn," he muttered.

Brian pushed away his anger and walked into the kitchen. He looked out the window without seeing the yard or the trees. He had to think about the days and weeks ahead. He also had to keep in mind he had friends to lean on.

When Alicia began having trouble keeping up with the kids and the housework, she looked for outside help. She knew at first sight

Kathleen was the right woman to take over the responsibilities as housekeeper and caregiver. Kathleen Hodges had become a part of their family during the final months of Alicia's life. She loved Erin and Jack as though they were her own grandchildren. Brian trusted her to take good care of them when he returned to work. Going back to work did not bother him at all. In fact, he needed the physical work and constant demands of the job. It was coming home and knowing Alicia was not going to be here that frightened him. The kitchen counter should have cracked under the pressure of his hands.

"Give me strength," he prayed through his clenched teeth. His children and his job depended on him. Letting them down was the same as letting Alicia down. She had been the focal point of his life. Everything was connected to her: His love, his family, his business.

Brian and Clay started their own construction business while Alicia was still in good health. Although Brian was the boss, they shared in every aspect of the work. In the end Brian had the final say, but he trusted Clay implicitly. During Brian's absence from work, issues arose from time to time that required a fresh perspective. Today Clay came to Brian with a problem he had not been able to resolve on his own.

"We've hit a brick wall here," Clay said as he tapped the outside wall on the blueprint. "We either order new lumber for this or we take out this section, which will set us back at least a week." He stood up and slowly stretched his back. "Looks like I, uh," he began before he looked behind him. "Looks like I messed up," he said.

Brian saw the glint of mischief in Clay's expression. "That was close," he said, understanding without words that Clay was relieved he had not blurted out something Erin might pick up on. Brian went back to studying the blueprints.

"Hey, where are your kids?" asked Clay.

"Nap time. They're zonked out on my bed. Okay, I think I've got it here. If you," Brian said as he shifted on the stool. "Right here," he indicated and went on to explain his solution. "What do you think?" He looked up when Clay did not answer him right away.

"Maybe I need to get me some glasses." He rubbed his eyes and leaned in closer, straining to see what Brian was talking about. "How the hell did I miss that?"

"It's no big deal. You're carrying a heavy load here. I'm sorry for dumping everything on you. Things are, I mean you shouldn't, we shouldn't, nothing's like," Brian stammered as the room suddenly grew too hot. He stepped away from Clay and lurched toward the kitchen counter.

"No, I can do this. Must be the cobwebs," Clay said, tapping his head.

"Want something to drink?" Brian asked, fighting to hide his emotional upset.

Clay rolled up the blueprints and slid them into the cardboard tube. "Yeah, sure."

"Got big plans for tomorrow?" Brian asked as he poured iced tea into two glasses. Tea splashed out onto the counter, but he did not bother to wipe it up.

Clay took the glass and sat down at the table. "Naw, just planning to sleep in and be lazy. How about you guys?"

"I don't know," Brian replied, staring down at the scuffed linoleum floor. "Maybe we'll go to the park. Maybe we won't. I don't know. The grass, the yard, I have to," he mumbled as his hand tightened around the glass. He clumsily put it down before he dropped it.

Brian felt confident while they worked through the troubles at the construction site. He had been totally focused on the work. Though his patience was strained at times while taking care of the kids, he was handling it. Handling it, but for how long without Alicia. Brian suddenly felt the darkness rising, taking hold of the edges of his sanity and stripping all the colors from his world. Before he was able to regain his composure, he knew he was losing the battle.

"Brian, you okay?" Clay asked, bearing witness to the sudden change. "You don't look so good."

"I'm fine," Brian said, pushing the words out past the lump in his throat. Overwhelmed, Brian turned away from Clay and stumbled toward the back door.

Without a sound, Clay crossed the room, pushed the screen door open and shoved Brian outside. He grabbed him, slammed him up against the house and got right in his face. "I'm not gonna sit on my ass and watch this eat you alive," growled Clay. "You can't let yourself fall apart. Those kids in there, they need you."

Brian tried to get loose but gave up when Clay knocked his head back against the wall. Stunned, he shut his eyes. Ashamed of his weakness, Brian could not stop the tears now scorching his skin. "I miss her, miss her all the time. Every second of every day. I can't, it won't, I'll never," he stammered incoherently.

"Damn it, Brian, it's gotta hurt like hell. You lost the woman you love. Giving up ain't gonna fix it," Clay replied gruffly.

"Yeah, you're right, I know. Sorry, it just," Brian began.

"Shut up," Clay barked. He shoved Brian back and stepped away. "You've got nothing to be sorry about. You need time, more time." Clay walked to the edge of the patio and rubbed his hands over his face.

Brian leaned forward with his hands on his knees, trying to catch his breath. Overheated with the unexpected exchange, he pulled up the lower edge of his T-shirt and wiped his face. He stepped away from the wall as Clay turned around and walked back to the door.

"Stupid jerk, you look like shit," Clay remarked.

Brian looked away before following Clay inside. He watched Clay put the empty glass on the counter before he moved a few steps further into the kitchen.

"Look, I've gotta get back to work. I'll come by tomorrow morning around 10 o'clock and pick up the kids. I'll take them to the park and let you have time to do stuff around here without worrying about them," Clay said without giving Brian a chance to object. He gripped the cardboard tube and tapped it against his leg.

Brian wiped at his eyes again. "You don't need to," he said, but realized Clay had his mind set. "Thanks."

"You're tougher than you think, Boss. I'm out of here."

"Yeah, okay," Brian replied, but Clay was already gone.

*Tender Dreams*

## Chapter 10

Grace concentrated on threading the needle, determined to finish the quilt today. The simple task grew frustrating as the small slit seemingly shrunk, denying the thread easy passage. When the needle fell from her fingers, Grace pushed the chair back, leaned down and scanned the hardwood floor under the quilting frame. She slid off the chair and reached out to grab the elusive needle, misjudged where she was, bumped her head on the heavy frame and dropped the needle again. Grace sat down on the floor before she reached out and finally picked up the needle.

Her eyes burned with overwhelming frustration. She wished her parents were still alive. Wished she had forced them to stay home. Had she joined them she would not be living with the guilt. Death offered the only real escape from her misery. Grace momentarily felt ashamed of herself, but she could not stop her negative thoughts. The loss of her parents had sapped the happiness from her life. After a few more minutes of self-pity, Grace opened her eyes and angrily wiped away her tears. "Let it go," she scolded herself as she sat down on the chair and stared at the quilt.

A treasured story from the past replayed in her mind. Grace was once again a young teenager listening to her mother's words and watching her expressive eyes. Marianna gave her stories the same attention to details as she put into her sewing projects.

"I remember that day like it was yesterday," Marianna began. "Daddy and I had been married for 18 years. By that time, I was almost 41 years old and knew we were destined to live our lives alone. Dreams of having children had all but faded away. Menopause came early and my doctor ordered a few tests, but I never gave those tests a second thought.

It was late August 1958, and the summer heat made our house feel like we were locked inside an oven. The fans moved the air but did nothing to cool it down. I was sliding a platter of sandwiches into the refrigerator when the phone rang. I held the phone to my ear and turned to be sure the refrigerator door was closed tight when I heard the news. I stopped breathing and lost my grip on the phone.

Dumbfounded, I watched the receiver swing back and forth against the wall before I came to my senses and picked it up again. I quickly apologized to the nurse on the line and asked her to repeat the message. Trembling, I set the receiver back in place and held my hands over my mouth. After a minute passed, disbelief shadowed my joy as I lifted the phone and clumsily dialed the doctor's office number. The nurse repeated the message and I squealed with delight.

I rushed out to the back yard where Daddy was mowing the grass. I must have looked like a mad woman running toward him. He stepped away from the mower and stood ready to catch me.

The words spilled out of my mouth so fast they were incomprehensible. I repeated my words and his face drained of all color. I asked him if he was okay, but he said nothing as he walked toward the shade on the patio with his arms holding me tight. I could not help but giggle when he sat down on the chair, took hold of my hands and asked, 'Tell me again, Annie.'

I could see he was fighting to remain calm. I told him once more, 'We're pregnant. We are pregnant.'

Grace sighed once the remembered tale reached the final lines. Their marriage had been a true love story from start to finish. Grace found it impossible to imagine having a family of her own. Some things were simply unattainable. Grace wiped her eyes and struggled to focus on her work.

## Chapter 11

"Use my car," Brian said. "The kids' seats are already buckled in. It will be easier."

"Okay," agreed Clay. "So, where are they?"

"Are you sure about this? I mean," Brian began.

"Shut up, jerk," grumbled Clay. "I wouldn't say it if I didn't mean it. We'll have a blast. I'm thinking the taco place for lunch. They like tacos, right?"

"Yeah, they do, but you don't have to do that," Brian said.

"Whatever," muttered Clay.

Jack came running down the hallway with his tennis shoes thumping the hardwood floor. "Going to park!" he shouted.

"Hi Jackson, how are you?" Clay said as he squatted down and picked up the boy.

"Swing, swing!" Jack shouted with delight.

"Where is your big sister?" Clay asked.

"Lost shoe," Jack said with a sad face.

Brian found Erin laying on the floor looking under her bed. "Do you need help?"

"Daddy, do monsters eat shoes?" she asked.

"Naw, here it is," Brian said after finding it under Jack's bed. "Too bad we have two feet. One shoe is always easier to find."

"Daddy, one shoe? One foot? Hop, hop," she said as he carried her down the hallway.

"Lady Erin, there you are," Clay said. "Got your shoes?"

"The monster didn't eat it," she replied, waving her shoes in the air.

Brian put Erin's shoes on and laced them up for her. "You be a good girl and help watch Jack today."

"I will," said Erin.

"Here's a tote bag to go with the kids. A change of clothes, just in case. Be sure to get Jack to the bathroom every hour or so. He'll tell you," Brian explained, trying to cover all the bases.

"Don't worry," Clay reassured his friend. He shouldered the tote bag and took Erin from Brian. "Hey, take my keys, Brian. If you need to go somewhere, take my car."

Brian held onto the keys and reluctantly stepped back from his children. "Wait," he said quickly. "Give me a kiss."

"I'd rather not," groaned Clay.

"Not you," Brian said and kissed both of his children. He followed Clay outside to help buckle the kids into their seats.

As the car moved out onto the road, Brian realized he had not been away from the kids since Marlene had taken care of them while he was at the funeral home. The overwhelming emptiness hit him hard as he stumbled back inside the house. He leaned back against the door and wept. What if something happened and the kids never came home again. What if he had to spend the rest of his life missing Alicia and their children too? He leaned forward and braced his hands on his knees, fighting back nausea. "Get a grip," he told himself.

Brian dragged two empty boxes in from the garage. At the end of the hallway, he dropped them on the floor at the bedroom door. He stood there staring into the room, unsure how to begin. Alicia would have urged him to do the job and put it behind him.

"I hate this!" Brian cried out. Eyes burning, he grabbed the smaller box and turned back to the bathroom.

Brian had contacted a shelter that provided a safe haven for abused women and their children. Donating Alicia's things felt right. Hands shaking, he filled the box with makeup, lotions, soaps and shower gels. The top of the vanity looked too empty without her things there.

When Brian picked up Alicia's toothbrush, he wondered if Erin would notice it was missing. He refused to look as he tossed it into a paper sack, along with her used shaver and a nearly empty can of shaving cream. Brian reached into the space beneath the sink and pulled out a small box of pads.

"Damn," he groaned. How the hell was he going to explain menstrual cycles to Erin? If that was not bad enough, he realized he would have to talk to her about intimate relationships one day. He hit the wall with his fist, then crammed the box of pads into the box for the shelter.

Brian found himself standing in the doorway to his bedroom a few minutes later. "Just do it," he ordered himself, taking the bigger box over to the chest of drawers. His hands shook as he put several pairs of jeans into the bottom of the box. He lay in soft camisoles and T-shirts, tank tops and shorts. Sentimental memories brought on more tears when he came across her cloth hankies and two handmade lace doilies. He held them to his face and breathed in her lingering scent. Lightheaded, he tucked them into the back of the top drawer, along with her jewelry box. Brian eyed the ring box, picked it up to put into the drawer, then put it back down again. It had to stay within sight for now. Maybe forever.

    Brian dragged the cardboard box over to the closet. Moving from one hanger to the next he folded her blouses and dresses. Alicia's wedding gown hung on a padded hanger inside a long garment bag. He unzipped it far enough to look at it, ran his fingers over the soft lace and frowned. Unsettled, he pulled the zipper closed. Along with her wedding dress, he kept Alicia's favorite dress and a long nightgown he thought Erin might like to wear one day.

    The row of empty hangers stunned him. Leave them there or put them into the box, he debated. Leave them or give them away? Breathing too hard, he stared up at the ceiling, then grabbed the hangers and pushed them down into the box. It felt as though he were throwing Alicia away.

    "Damn," Brian whispered as he looked up at the closet shelf. He took down a fisherman's style hat and held it up before him. A row of embroidered bugs marched around the yellow fabric. He turned it and smiled at the crazy little beetles, a green inchworm and a bright red ladybug. She had worked with such determination on the fun project. Her delightful laughter echoed through his mind. He ran his thumb over the tiny stitches on the ladybug. When a strange prickly sensation stung his skin, he quickly returned the hat to the shelf.

    His hands stilled as he reached up for a shoebox. He never had any reason before now to look through what Alicia kept in her side of their closet. Something about the box made him feel uneasy. He held it in his hands for a few seconds knowing there were shoes in it. What else would be in a shoebox after all? Upon lifting the lid Brian felt the room tip sideways.

    Alicia had always kept note cards and several packages of stationery in her nightstand. She often sat up against the headboard and wrote letters once the kids were asleep at night. Now he sat down on the side of the bed and stared at the stack of paper in the shoebox. How long had she been writing these letters? The one on top had been written only weeks before she died. Brian squeezed his eyes closed. After a minute he picked up the letter and held it in his trembling hand.

> *My dear Brian,*
> *How it hurts to think of leaving you all alone. I love you with all my heart. You are my lover and my best friend. You've given me such joy and happiness. Soon I will be gone, but know I am ready for that time to come. Share your life with someone again, Brian. Please do this for me, my love.*
> *Missing you already,*
> *Alicia*

Brian fell back on the bed holding the letter close to his heart. He covered his eyes with his arm and wept. "Alicia," he cried out. He could never love anyone but Alicia. His heart belonged to her forever.

Brian put the letter back in the box and resisted picking up another one. He had to take his time reading through them, for it might shred his heart to read them all at once. Envelopes marked for Erin and Jack were standing up next to the stack of letters. Another envelope was addressed to her parents with a note taped to it.

*"Please mail this a month after I am gone."*

Puzzled, Brian returned the sealed envelope to the box and looked up at the shelf. Alicia could not have been the one who put the box up there. At least not in the past few months. Kathleen must have helped Alicia and kept the secret between them. Their friendship had been wonderful for both of them.

"Thank you," whispered Brian.

He returned the box to the shelf and wiped his damp hands against his jeans. Determined to finish the job, Brian loaded all but one pair of her shoes into the box. He placed the white high heeled sandals on the shelf next to the yellow hat. He fingered the narrow straps that crisscrossed the toes, remembering how they looked on Alicia's feet.

"Find peace in your memories," Brian whispered. Was Lawrence Ashcroft crazy for saying that? Peace was never going to replace the pain in his heart. He shoved the cardboard box away with his foot and yanked the closet door closed.

Brian still felt on edge when he dropped the paper sack on the kitchen floor and opened the cupboard door. He grabbed all of Alicia's prescription bottles and threw them into the sack. None of the pills had helped Alicia get better. In fact, like the chemo, it had all been a terrible waste. Maybe they should not have tried any of it. Maybe she would still be here if they had left her alone.

Anger spiked as Brian slammed the cupboard door. He grabbed the sack and rumpled the top down as though it were full of deadly snakes. He wanted to put the blame on someone. Wanted to pound out his anger on something. Wanted Alicia to come home.

Brian stashed the boxes in the garage, jammed the paper sack into the garbage can and worked off his anger mowing the grass. When he emptied the catcher for the last time he was overheated and breathing hard. The smell of the fresh cut grass triggered more memories as he carried the last of the clippings out to the front yard. It was something Alicia always loved on warm afternoons just like this one. Back when they lived in their house in Chelsea Creek, they did the yard work together and then sat on the patio afterwards. Those had been wonderful days.

Brian pushed his boots off at the garage door and walked into the house. He pulled his damp T-shirt off and tossed it on top of the washer. While he stood by the kitchen window with his second glass of water, he spotted a small red car driving by on the road. "The Ladybug Lady," he said, remembering how excited Erin had been when she spotted a red car from the airplane. He frowned as he revisited the day they had come home. The day they came home without Alicia. He shoved aside his dark mood. He drained the glass, thinking of his kids and wondering how Clay was fairing.

*Julia Robertson*

## Chapter 12

Utterly wiped out, Clay flopped back on the grass at the park. The kids played on the complicated wooden playground structure for a short time before they hit the swings. Then they headed for the wide wooden slide, the merry-go-round and charged over to the teeter-totter without slowing down. Clay had to take a break before he collapsed.

Erin and Jack sat side-by-side watching Clay. "Let's climb on top," she whispered. Without a word, Jack jumped up and Erin scrambled after him.

The attack caught Clay by surprise. As the air whooshed out of him, he grabbed both kids. "Hey, what," he gasped, but his words were drowned out with their laughter. "You two are nothing but trouble." He easily overpowered them, pushed them down on the grass and tickled them.

"No," Jack laughed.

"    No, no," Erin squealed with delight.

"How about we go for tacos," Clay suggested once they calmed down.

Both kids shouted, "Yeah!"

Clay lifted Jack onto the bench at the taco stand. He was glad to be sitting outside with the kids. Anything that fell from the concrete table was food for the birds. "You guys want hot sauce?" Clay watched as Jack nodded and Erin shook her head. "Okay, the lady says no thank you and the big boy wants it hot."

"I like the park," Erin said.

"Me too," agreed Jack.

"I liked the slide best," said Clay. "Next time we'll bring your old man with us."

Erin frowned in concentration. "Who?" she asked.

Clay knew he had blown it again. "I mean your dad," he laughed.

"Old man," she thought out loud. "Daddy's not old."

"You're right, I'm sorry." Clay was relieved when the tray of drinks and tacos were delivered to their table. He set each of them up with a kid sized taco and flattened the paper out in front of them.

Erin dropped strands of cheese into her mouth. "Yummy," she giggled.

Clay knew it had to be tough for Brian to see so much of Alicia in Erin's eyes. The little girl was a living reminder of everything he had lost. Although Jack had Brian's blue eyes, he saw Alicia in him too. He sure was a happy little guy. Even when part of his taco shell cracked apart, he kept smiling. Brian had his work cut out for him for the next sixteen years or so.

"The Ladybug!" Erin exclaimed. "Look, it's the Ladybug!"

Clay expected to see a little bug on the table, but Erin was pointing out at a car on the street. "You are silly, Erin."

"The Ladybug Lady. She's pretty," said Erin as she ate the remnants of her first taco.

"Who?" Clay asked.

"The lady in the Ladybug car," she said.

"Hot sauce," said Jack.

"Say please," Erin reminded him.

"Please," said Jack.

"Good boy. Thank you, Erin." Clay watched Jack's eyes light up when he dribbled a tiny amount of hot sauce on what was left of his taco. "I need to fix you some hot wings, Jackson. You'll like them."

"Hot wings?" asked Erin.

"Yeah," Clay mumbled with his mouth full. "Buffalo wings."

Puzzled, Erin chewed the crunchy taco shell. "Buffaloes don't have wings," she stated seriously.

"What?" Clay asked. He had lost track of what she was talking about.

Again, she said, "Buffaloes don't have wings."

"I suppose," Clay agreed. "It's just a name, Erin. You know, Buffalo wings. They're chicken wings with hot sauce on them."

"Why do they call them Buffalo wings?"

"Well, I don't know the answer to that. Want another taco?" he asked, hoping she would forget the question. "I'm going to order more. How about you, Jack?"

Shortly after 1 o'clock, Clay pulled into Brian's driveway with the kids sleeping in the back seat. Brian came outside and peered into the car. "Looks like your trip was a success," he said.

"Bored them to sleep," laughed Clay.

They carried the kids into the house and put them down on their beds. Pausing at the doorway, Clay watched Brian pull Jack's shoes off. He momentarily felt like an alien being. He shook off the awkward sensation and headed toward the kitchen.

"How's it going?" asked Clay. He stood at the counter, aware of the weariness showing on Brian's face.

"I mowed the grass and, well, sorted through," Brian said, unable to finish his thoughts.

"You're doing a good job, Brian," Clay said. "Those kids of yours are happy. That says a lot."

Brian shrugged, ran his fingers through his hair and sighed. "Today wasn't easy." He rolled his shoulders and looked out toward the road.

*Julia Robertson*

*Tender Dreams*

## Chapter 13

Grace placed the finished quilt into the elegant gift box, tucked the ivory tissue paper over it and settled the lid on top. With Mrs. Glover's approval she would bid the new quilt farewell and be on her way home by noon. As she pulled out onto the road Grace noticed the gas gauge needle hovering on empty. Ten minutes later she sat in the car at the gas station while the tank filled and the attendant washed the windshield. She tapped her foot, checked her watch, glanced back to see if the pump had stopped yet and began drumming her fingers on the steering wheel.

Back on the road Grace stopped at the red light, feeling frustrated with her ill timing. If she paid more attention to things like the gas level in her car, she would have fewer delays in her life. She saw a man with two small children at the taco stand, then realized he was the scruffy guy in the ratty car at the airport. Not as scruffy as she had imagined, dressed in a blue T-shirt and faded blue jeans. So there had been children in the car, and he was their dad. There it was plain as day. A girl with blonde hair in a bouncy ponytail sat next to a smiling little boy. When the girl pointed her way Grace glanced around, then looked back again. She realized then that the child was actually pointing at her. Was she that funny looking? Shouldn't the father correct the child's bad manners? She took off when the light turned green, thinking about what had just happened.

Grace drove up the steep driveway to the Glover's home on Hillcrest Road. Southern plantation came to mind as it had the first time she had seen the two-story structure. She loved the wrought iron lamp suspended between two tall, white columns. The front door opened before Grace lifted the box from the back seat.

"Miss Marshall, I was worried you may have forgotten about our appointment," said Theona Glover. "Will you require assistance?"

"No, I'm fine. Thank you," Grace replied as she stepped up onto the porch. "I forgot to fill the gas tank yesterday, so I'm running a little late."

"Do not give it another thought, my dear. Please come in," Theona said as she stepped inside ahead of Grace. "Let's go into the parlor. The light is best in there this time of the day. I can't wait to see it. You may set the box down right here," Theona said, pushing aside a stack of magazines. "Let's spread it out over the sofa."

"Perfect," Grace replied as she lifted off the lid. "Here we go," she said, feeling her heart flutter at the sight of her work. Quiet anticipation tangled with her jittery nerves whenever she presented a finished quilt to a client.

"Allow me to help," said Theona. "Oh my, I am speechless, Miss Marshall."

Grace smiled at the formal use of her name as she watched the woman inspect her work. She felt like she was back in grade school presenting her penmanship paper to the teacher.

"You are a true artist," said Theona. "I will never be able to thank you enough. It is absolutely marvelous! Let me get Patricia. She needs to see this right away. Please sit down, I'll be right back."

Grace watched the excited woman scurry out of the room. Rather than sit down, she walked over to a beautiful cherry wood bookshelf holding a vast collection of books. Most of them were leather bound, but on one of the lower shelves she saw stacks of paperback books, including many titles by Louis L'Amour and Tom Clancy. Turning toward the approaching voices, she wondered if the paperbacks were the books that were actually read, while the others were there simply for show.

"Look at this, Patricia," sang out Theona. "Can you believe what you are seeing? Isn't it astounding?"

With her fingers laced together, Grace watched the older woman lean in close and gently run her fingertips over the tiny stitches.

"Absolute perfection, Mrs. Glover. Oh yes, she is an artist, no doubt about it," Patricia said, looking up from the quilt with a bright smile. "Did it take you long to learn?"

Grace realized the woman was employed here. "No, it comes naturally to me," replied Grace. "I learned by watching my mother quilt. I love it."

"It shows, my dear. You have a talent that is no less than God-given," she whispered.

"I agree with you, Patricia," said Theona. "I'll be giving your name to my closest friends, Miss Marshall. Now let me get your check."

Patricia looked behind her, then stepped closer to Grace. "Miss Marshall, she doesn't praise many things in this world. I've worked for her for thirty-three years and I know. You have touched a rare spot in her. God bless you," she said. "I must get back to my work. Thank you for sharing your gift with me."

Grace did not have a chance to respond before the woman left the room. She carefully folded the quilt and placed it back inside the box. She tucked the tissue paper around it, then slid the lid in place.

"Here you are, Miss Marshall. Now, I've added a bit extra on it, but don't you argue with me. I am extremely pleased. I cannot wait until Charlotte sees it," said Theona.

"Thank you," Grace said as she took the sealed envelope.

"You're welcome. You have made me very happy," Theona said as they walked to the door.

Grace drove back into town and glanced over as she passed by the taco stand. She found herself wishing they were still sitting there. The little girl's smile came to mind again as she turned into the grocery store parking lot. She made sure she had her list and decided to take a little peek at the check from Mrs. Glover. She opened the envelope and pulled out the check. She was breathless when she saw Mrs. Glover had paid her half again as much as she originally asked for. Grace eased her head back against the headrest and closed her eyes. "And she's telling her friends," sighed Grace. Perhaps she would splurge on something special for dinner. Or tuck the extra money away toward the skylight. Most likely, she would pay another bill. Feeling let down, Grace put the envelope back in her purse and zipped it closed.

*Julia Robertson*

## Chapter 14

Though Brian knew falling apart was not a logical option, the temptation to let go and hide from reality remained close at hand. He understood why so many people used alcohol or drugs to dull the tragedies in their lives. He reminded himself every day that it was the coward's way out; that destroying himself would ruin what little his children had left in their lives. Even with Clay's not so subtle message replaying in his mind, Brian constantly feared he was going to end up falling into a dark void.

The day had gotten off to a rough start after another restless night, but Brian managed to get lunch prepared early so they could get out to the job site before naptime. While the kids played in the back yard, Brian rushed out to the garage. It was time to drop the boxes off at the shelter. When second thoughts about giving away Alicia's things crept into his head Brian quickly sealed the boxes with tape. He angrily tossed the roll of tape aside, grabbed an empty box and hurried back inside. At the open doorway to the hallway closet Brian filled the box with Alicia's sweaters, jackets and boots. His hands felt numb as he loaded the trunk and slammed it closed.

Leaving the boxes at the shelter was heartbreaking. Not for the first time Brian felt like he was throwing a part of Alicia away. At the same time, he knew it was something Alicia had wanted him to do. Brian held onto those final thoughts, taking comfort in them as they drove away.

"Daddy makes houses, Jack. See," Erin explained as she tapped on the side window.

As Brian pulled up in front of the work site, he turned and looked back at his children. "This is a dangerous place for kids. Do not pick up anything at all! Understand?"

Jack nodded with his eyes locked on the house.

"We'll be good," Erin said. "Is Clay here?"

"Yes, he's here somewhere. Watch for him." Brian released the kids from their car seats and held onto their hands as they walked toward the first house.

"Will there be kids here, Daddy?" Erin asked.

"Maybe after the house is finished, honey. I don't know." He thought of the long stairway that would eventually be carpeted. He pictured Jack and Erin playing there with a lineup of little cars and trucks.

"Will they have a swing?" she asked next. "And a puppy?"

"They might," replied Brian. "Nobody lives here yet. Hang on," he said.

Brian wore his work boots, but there was too much debris on the ground for their small shoes. He made a mental note to have the crew do a serious cleanup today. He squatted down and picked up Jack.

At the same time, Erin shouted, "Clay! Hi!"

Clay raised a hand in greeting. He wore heavy construction boots and a leather tool belt. The red bandana around his head made him look like he had just come off a movie set.

"Give me one of those brats," he told Brian. "Lady Erin, you smell sweet," he laughed as he picked her up.

Erin grimaced and held her nose. "Stinky Clay," she said.

"That's not stink. That is a working man smell," he said and kissed her cheek.

"Scratchy," she squealed when his beard-roughened face touched hers.

Jack bounced with excitement. "Way up high," he said, pointing up at the second floor of the house.

"Not today. Let's check out the downstairs," Brian said.

"We just set the tubs in the second house," said Clay.

"Good, right on schedule," Brian said.

"You bet," replied Clay. "Had a potential buyer come by earlier today. We might have this one sold before we get much further."

"Do they have a puppy?" Erin asked. She fiddled with the red bandana where it was knotted at the back of his head. "A puppy is fun," she said seriously.

"Puppies chew up shoes and fingers," Clay said in reply.

"Looks great," Brian commented as they stepped inside. "I like the way this floor plan is working out."

"Yeah, me too. The lookers agreed with that. The kitchen is exactly what they were looking for," Clay remarked.

Brian loved everything from the initial sketches and blueprints to the finish work. He had created four different floor plans for this group of houses. Brian looked through the downstairs level with a critical eye. "Hey, the dormer windows look great from the road."

"You missed putting them in, but they slid into place like a dream," remarked Clay. He squeezed his eyes closed and rubbed them with his hand. "Must be the dust," he said as he shifted Erin on his arm.

"I plan on being back here by the time this one is ready to finish," Brian said. The second house was at least two weeks behind this one. Brian loved building things since he was a little kid. He wondered if Jack was going to follow in his footsteps. Of course, he could not discount the idea of Erin joining his business as well.

"By the time you're back we'll have the countertops in," Clay said.

"Good, perfect," Brian said as he walked down the temporary ramp and out into the sunshine. Before long they would pour a concrete porch and a narrow sidewalk leading to the driveway. The house already had a welcoming look to it. He imagined two shade trees in the front yard. "You have anyone scheduled for cleanup?" Brian asked.

"Sure do," replied Clay. "Mike and Danny have it this afternoon. I know it looks bad, but we've been busy here."

"It shows. I appreciate the time you've given me, Clay. I couldn't have held the business together without you," Brian said.

"We're a team, Brian. These precious babies are well worth the extra work," Clay said and patted Erin's cheek.

"We're not babies," Erin corrected. "We're big."

"Excuse me, Lady Erin, you are right. Please forgive me," he said with a frown.

"No sad face," Erin pleaded as she tried to push up the corners of his mouth.

Brian watched his daughter with his best friend. He enjoyed seeing his tough, no nonsense friend melt like butter in her hands. Jack slumped down against his shoulder. "I better get these two home. Jack's losing it here."

"Okay, I need to get back to work. Give me a kiss, Lady Erin." Clay buckled her into her car seat. "See you later."

After settling the kids down for a nap Brian walked out to the mailbox, mentally reviewing the progress at the work site. He pulled the envelopes out of the box and frowned at the credit card applications with Alicia's name on them. Seeing her name in print broke his heart. He angrily ripped them to pieces and threw them away. He slapped the bills on top of his checkbook.

Alicia had purchased a life insurance policy shortly after they were married. At the time it seemed extreme to him, but she thought differently. Now he was supposed to watch the mail for the check, which made him feel sick. He planned on putting it into a certificate of deposit as Alicia had suggested. If the kids decided to go to college, the money would be there for them.

Brian had to focus on what the kids needed. Right now, that meant preparing dinner. Nutrition, a word he had recently added to his vocabulary, guided his choices for their meals. If anyone had asked Brian to prepare a healthy meal ten years ago, he would have laughed at the crazy request. A decent meal at that time consisted of a burger and fries. A milkshake and an order of onion rings made it even better. Everything had changed since then. He had to make healthy choices for the kids and himself.

Brian switched the oven on and pulled a deep roasting dish out of the cupboard. After checking the recipe card, he gathered the ingredients he needed. Over the past year, Alicia had put together easy to follow recipes for him. She included notes on which vegetables went best with different meats, how to mix salads and even how to bake desserts. Though he still fumbled with some things, Brian had become a fairly decent cook. His successes had all been made possible through her love, understanding and endless patience. How he missed her.

Naptime over, wide awake and ready to go, Erin and Jack wanted to play with Play-Doh. Despite the mess it always created, Brian gave in when he saw their eager expressions. He reached up and took the familiar round tubs out of the cupboard above the refrigerator. He wondered how long it would be before one of them figured out how to get into that cupboard. For now, it was a safe place to keep things out of reach. When Erin came running with a plastic bucket in her hands Brian warned her to slow down.

"This is gonna be fun," she said. She stopped next to the small wooden table and shook the bucket. "Can't get the top off," Erin complained.

Already sitting on a chair, Jack slapped his hands on the table. Brian walked over with the tubs and squatted down between Erin and Jack.

"Settle down, mister! Let me help you," he told Erin. "One of these days your hands will be big enough to pry the lid off."

"How?" she asked with her hands held up in front of her.

Brian grinned at her bewildered expression and could not help but laugh. "You are a prize, Erin. Just wait, you'll see when you get older. Now, choose a color." He sat down on the floor and joined the kids.

When the kitchen timer buzzed a short time later, Jack exclaimed, "Cookies!"

"Chicken," corrected Brian as he stood up. "Don't smash my Play-Doh." He quickly grabbed the hot mitts, checked the thermometer and reset the timer.

"Worms," said Jack.

"I made my hand," Erin said.

Brian looked over their projects. "Great worms, Jack. Do they have eyes?"

Jack turned serious. He picked up one of the plastic tools and made two pokey holes at the end of each worm. "Eyes," he said and clapped his hands.

Later that night Brian read to the kids while they sat on his bed. Tonight's story was about Clifford the Red Dog, a seriously huge dog whose imposing bulk nearly filled each page of the storybook. Erin studied the pictures and concentrated on the words while Jack simply listened.

"Can we have a puppy like him?" asked Erin.

"Where would we keep him, Erin? He's bigger than our house," Brian replied.

She studied the pictures. "We have to get a bigger house first," she decided.

"The story is pretend. He's not a real dog," Brian cautiously explained.

"Okay," she said.

Brian moved Jack up against his chest. His little boy was fast asleep, but Brian turned the page to continue reading for Erin.

"Daddy," said Erin.

"Hmm?" Brian said, feeling sleepy.

"How long does Mommy have to stay in Heaven?" Erin asked.

Reading time was over. Brian set the book aside, shifted Jack once more and pulled Erin closer. "She has to stay there forever, honey. It is a beautiful place." His words were as much for her as for himself.

"Can I ask God to let her come home? I need her."

"You can ask God to let Mommy watch over us, but she cannot come home." He waited and hoped it was enough to console her for now.

"Daddy," she said.

"What is it?"

"I miss Mommy," she mumbled.

"I do too," he whispered.

Brian slowly became aware of his awkward position and pried his eyes open. He had apparently nodded off after talking with Erin. Moving slowly, he eased Jack down onto the pillow, lifted Erin in his arms and stood up. The room swayed for a moment before he found his way to the other bedroom. Once Erin was tucked into her bed, he went back for Jack.

Alicia had been given too little time with their children. She said they were gifts from God, and though he agreed, he also felt angry her life had been taken away. At times like this his fear and resentment grew stronger even though there was no one to blame. He desperately needed her patience and love.

Brian stared out through the bedroom window. Was she sparkling like one of the stars in the sky? Was she watching over them? A shooting star streaked across the ebony sky. He kept his eyes on it and whispered, "Please help me. Give me strength." Brian leaned his forehead against the cool glass and wept.

## Chapter 15

Once she put the groceries away, Grace stepped into her work room ready to start the new quilt project. The quilting frame stood folded up against the far wall. Remnants from the last project were boxed up or discarded. Her worktable was set up and loaded with new supplies, waiting for her skilled hands. A familiar buzz tickled through her fingers as she walked up to the table and pressed her palms down on its marred surface.

"It's all put together in my mind, Mom. I wish you were here to work with me," she whispered as her mood grew unsettled. Hopelessness converged with loneliness and her eyes burned. She squeezed them closed and bit her lower lip. "My life will never settle on the right path."

Disgusted with herself, Grace stepped back, pulled the chair up to the table and sat down hard. "Every time. Damn, I hate this."

Before she sank any further into despair Grace flipped open her notebook and picked up the stubby pencil. Each item she needed had been checked off the first page. The templates were stacked in a shallow box and the fabrics were arranged in order, matching the list on the second page.

Once she picked up the first piece of fabric, Grace easily slipped into a well-practiced rhythm. With each new cut, her imagination revved up and worries about the future slid to the back of her mind. Grace pictured the woman for whom the quilt was being made, sitting on an overstuffed sofa surrounded by her family. With the quilt spread open across her lap she would tell stories of the things she had made. Grace concentrated as she positioned the template on the fabric. She created her own stories while she worked.

Dark blue-gray plaid sparked an image of a man splitting wood with a long-handled ax. Sunny yellow gingham had Grace seeing curtains framing a bright window in the farmhouse kitchen. Warm sunshine shone through the glass and spread across a kitchen table adorned with a runner of yellow, brown, and blue calico. Centered on the runner was a mud-colored stoneware bowl filled with glossy red apples.

Grace stacked the cut pieces of calico, set them aside and picked up the next scrap. This time Grace found herself imagining the same man dressed in blue chambray. A row of dark blue buttons ran down the front placket of his shirt. Beside the man stood a small girl with her auburn hair tied up with a length of narrow yellow ribbon. She wore a pale blue and white striped pinafore over her moss-green calico dress. The dress skimmed her ankles. Her bare feet were one atop the other, attempting to hide her dirt-streaked skin.

Grace stretched her hands up over her head, then looked over the spools of thread in her basket. Rather than stitch the quilt in white, Grace had chosen soft blue and pale green thread to use as a highlight for some of the design stitches. Her client had requested daisies and ivy leaves to accent the corners. Grace saw the finished stitches even while the thread remained in the basket. She had a long way to go before stitching the designs. When she took a break from cutting, Grace glanced over at the thick roll of batting, the bolts of white cotton backing material and soft muslin used to piece the squares together. Quilting was a giant jigsaw puzzle that created a useful and treasured gift. Grace found herself comparing her work to that of a pastry chef, a musician, a writer or a carpenter as she reached out for the next template. They all used the same basic plan to gather the essential ingredients and design their own unique creations. The gratification she gained must surely be mirrored in each of them no matter the end result.

Grace hummed as she set the next piece of fabric on the stack. She counted the cut pieces, then counted them one more time. Satisfied, she set the template aside and switched the radio on, tuned to an oldies station.

While The New Christy Minstrels sang about gum drop trees and lemonade springs, Grace sat back and looked up at her imaginary skylight. It would be the perfect place to watch thunderstorms as they rolled through the valley. Maybe one day, she sighed. Then again, she dared not allow such frivolous thinking. Grace knew in her heart it was not the material things that mattered most in life. From her earliest days she had wanted what her parents had with each other. That is, someone to share her life with.

"Stop it," Grace scolded when she realized what she had been thinking. "It won't happen, it can't happen. I don't deserve it." She angrily shoved away her dark feelings and focused on her work.

Grace double-checked the notes pinned to each stack of cut fabric pieces. They matched the list in her notebook, numbered in order to line up with her sketch of the quilt.

Grace put down the pencil, pulled the elastic band from her braid and ran her tired fingers through her hair. As she stretched her hands over her head and looked up, Grace let herself imagine she was seeing a million twinkling stars. When she walked over to the window and looked up into the night sky, she spotted a shooting star. The sight caught Grace by surprise. She found herself making a silent wish to be loved and to love someone with all her heart. It was a foolish thing to do, she thought as she turned toward the hallway. She should have wished for the bad dreams to stop haunting her sleep at night. Grace switched off the lights as she soundlessly padded down the hallway to her bedroom.

*Julia Robertson*

*Tender Dreams*

## Chapter 16

Clay loved his work, but he did not have the artistic drive to design houses or create the blueprints like Brian did. He preferred following the prepared plans and putting all the pieces together. Because of those differences he and Brian worked together with ease. They had a mental telepathy thing going on between them on the job.

After Brian drove away with his kids, Clay walked around to the back of the house. He joined part of the crew working on the exterior siding.

"Check the level for me," Bill called out.

"Okay," replied Clay. "Looking good."

"Say what?" Danny said. The young worker leaned down next to Clay. "Doesn't look like it to me."

"And who made you the boss?" barked Clay.

"Check it again," Bill called out.

Irritated, Clay rubbed his eyes and did as Bill suggested. Sure enough, the kid was right. "Damn," he sputtered. "Now it looks good," he said as he looked over his shoulder.

"Sorry," Danny apologized.

"No big deal," Clay said. It was not the first time he had trouble with something like this. He had put off going in for an eye exam for too long. Getting glasses at his age was not all that unusual, but it bugged the hell out of him.

By mid-afternoon Clay welcomed the end of the workday. Coming in at 6 o'clock on a Saturday put a dent in the weekend, but they all knew putting in the extra hours was going to pay off. Barring any major delays, they would be ready to start the next two houses right on schedule. It looked like taking some time off late this summer might work out. Clay planned on spending most of the time doing the body work on his car. Everything he needed was gathered up and stored in his garage. Along the way to getting the car running Clay had taken a lot of ribbing. Everyone told him he could have saved time by buying something more intact. To those kinds of remarks he only shrugged. Clay loved to take something that was nearly condemned and bring it back to life. One day in the not-too-distant future, he would drive his shining car around and receive words of admiration and praise for a job well done.

With the rest of the crew already gone, Clay and Bill each grabbed a handle and carried the large ice chest to Clay's truck. They lifted it up onto the tailgate, then shoved it onto the truck bed.

"Thanks, Bill. You guys did a great job today. Appreciate it," Clay said. He watched Bill walk away as he wiped his face with his dirty bandana and shoved it into his back pocket. Clay made one more walk around to double-check the windows and doors before going back to his truck.

As he stepped up into the cab Clay grabbed hold of the steering wheel with sudden desperation. "What the hell," he groaned, leaning back on the seat. The dizziness faded after a few minutes, but it left him feeling sick to his stomach.

As soon as he walked into his house Clay switched on the washer, dumped in some detergent and pulled off his dirty shirt. He kicked his boots out of the way, then emptied his pockets onto the dryer. Grimacing, Clay peeled off his socks and threw them into the sudsy water. He sorted through the dirty laundry on the floor, left the jeans behind and stuffed everything else into the washer.

Erin's words tumbled through his brain again. "Stinky Clay," she had said. Clay smiled just thinking about how cute she was. No doubt Brian would be carrying a baseball bat with him when the boys started showing up at his door. With that thought still tripping through the cloudiness in his head, Clay stepped into the hot shower. Ten minutes later he was stretched out across his bed, sound asleep.

Clay found himself in total darkness when he opened his eyes again. The darkness was so unexpected he felt a momentary sense of panic. A quick pass of his hand in front of his face convinced him his vision was fine, that it was nighttime and nothing more. He eventually convinced himself he needed to lock the front door and get something to eat. Heaving a great sigh, Clay rolled to the edge of the bed. He shuffled out to the living room in the dark, turned the deadbolt lock and closed the drapes.

Seconds later he stood in front of the open refrigerator and decided he was not hungry. He let the door close and stood there in full darkness for another minute. Back in the bedroom Clay yawned sleepily, dropped down on his bed and pulled up the blankets.

## Chapter 17

Brian parted the lace curtains on the bedroom window and peered outside. Countless sparrows darted in and out of the mulberry tree growing near the corner of the house. Alicia had painted each of the four bird houses suspended from the bare branches. While they still lived in Chelsea Creek, she spent several days coordinating the bright primary and pastel paints, so each house had its own unique personality. Brian had been fascinated while watching Alicia's obvious delight in the work and Erin's wide eyes as the colors appeared to flow from the tip of the brush. The memories lingered on. Sighing, he let the curtains drop back into place. Brian straightened the blankets on his bed and threw the comforter on top.

He had been counting the days since coming home as if he would feel more at peace when he reached some mystical number. It was not working. Nearing the end of April, with 30 days behind him, he realized he had to mail the envelope to Alicia's parents. He took it out of the shoebox and removed the taped-on note. The return address read, "Mrs. Brian P. Cooper". Alicia's parents never used her married name. No Mrs. anything. He was curious about what Alicia had written. Could not help but wonder if they would even bother to open it.

Before heading out to start breakfast, Brian walked out to the mailbox, put the envelope inside and lifted the red flag. He closed the small door and then opened it again to be sure the envelope was still there for the mail carrier to pick up.

*\*\*\**

The envelope arrived at its destination point on the East Coast five days later. From where she stood at the kitchen window, Anna Cole, the long-time housekeeper, watched the mail carrier slide a bundle of mail into the roadside mailbox. Since it was one of the first houses on the route, the mail arrived early every morning.

She dried her hands and walked out to the road. Anna typically made quick work of bringing in the mail, but today she stood paralyzed at the sight of the envelope that slid out onto the open door. Her hands trembled as she clumsily stacked the magazines and other envelopes, leaving the hand addressed one until last. She gently picked it up and stared at the return address. Time slowed while her mind replayed images from the past.

The little blonde-haired girl dressed in rumpled pajamas appeared before her. Anna would never forget the toothless smile, the wary expression or the fragile spirit hiding behind those beautiful soft brown eyes. She was the same girl who made Anna's otherwise dismal life shine with vivid colors. If not for Alicia, Anna did not know how she would have lived for so long.

Anna brushed at her eyes and looked up at the house. She had to get back inside before someone realized she was not in the kitchen. She could not afford to lose her job. Anna drew in a long breath and closed the mailbox door. Every step to the front door took supreme effort.

Anna placed the mail on the foyer table. The sound of footsteps on the stairway reminded her she had work to do. She did not need to look to know it was Mr. Rivers approaching the foyer. What kind of reaction was the letter going to evoke? It was none of her business, of course, but she could not help but wonder as the quiet footsteps grew closer. With a heavy heart, Anna rushed off toward the kitchen and the duties awaiting her.

## Chapter 18

The word meticulous most appropriately described Garrison River's daily routine. He entered the dining room for breakfast at precisely the same time every morning. Already showered and shaved, he wore neatly pressed tobacco-brown cashmere lounging pajamas. The shirt's long sleeves reached just shy of his wrists and his long pants barely touched his imported handmade leather slippers. He sat down at the head of the table covered with a perfectly pressed ivory linen tablecloth and spooned sugar into the steaming cup of coffee. He stirred it around and around in a pattern he had repeated for many years. After setting the spoon on the saucer, he lifted the cup and sipped.

Exactly five minutes later, Anna walked in with his breakfast platter. Three eggs over-easy, two slices of buttered rye toast and four strips of bacon as per his request. When she set the platter before him, he glanced up and said, "Thank you, Anna."

Garrison watched Anna walk out of the room, then quickly brought his attention back to his meal. He nodded as he spread the linen napkin across his lap. After finishing the first egg and one-half slice of toast, he ate a single strip of bacon. He wiped his fingers on the napkin, then dabbed it against his lips. To Garrison's dismay his wife appeared in the doorway. He had come to relish this time alone contemplating the day ahead. He resented the disruption and gave his full attention to finishing his meal without acknowledging her presence.

"Garrison," hissed Contessa.

"Contessa," he reluctantly replied. Garrison looked up only when she repeated his name. It was not what he wanted to hear as he bit into the second-half slice of toast.

"This is wrong," Contessa snapped as she slapped an envelope down next to Garrison's right hand.

"Damn it," Garrison sighed as he set the half-eaten slice of toast down. On any other morning he was gone from the house long before Contessa emerged from her bedroom. Sharing meals rarely occurred since he intentionally worked late hours. Garrison considered walking out of the room but remained sitting when she started talking again.

"Look at this!" Contessa demanded. "What sort of game do you suppose he's playing? How can he think we'd believe it's actually from her?" Contessa fumed as she tapped her polished red fingernail on the envelope.

"Open it, Tessa," he said, using her nickname in hopes of settling her down.

"You do it!" Contessa demanded harshly. She slammed the antique ivory-handled letter opener down on top of the envelope.

"He wants money from us. That filthy bastard," she said as she had when he left the church before the funeral service began. "She's dead!"

"I'm well aware of that," groaned Garrison. The tension in his shoulders increased as he ran the opener along the envelope's flap. With great care Garrison removed the single sheet of folded stationery. He set the envelope to his left and eased back from his breakfast platter. Garrison pursed his lips upon recognizing his only daughter's handwriting.

"What does that mean?" demanded Contessa.

"Alicia wrote this, not him," Garrison replied, purposefully avoiding Alicia's husband's name. "Please give me a minute to read."

Contessa looked away, ready to scream if he did not say something soon. She dragged her fingers through her newly cut and dyed raven-black hair. Frustrated, she cinched the belt of her midnight blue silk robe tighter and stomped toward the hallway. After another minute passed without a word, she could stand it no longer. "Read it out loud, damn it," demanded Contessa.

"As you wish," Garrison replied.

> *Dear Mother and Father,*
>
> *By the time you read this I will be gone. I may have a few months left, but the doctors cannot be certain of that. Little by little my body is withering away. Before it is too late, I must thank you for creating me. Knowing neither of you wanted me was a burden I carried until Brian came into my life. He showed me I am a good and precious person in every way possible. Love is a healing gift. His love lifted my spirits and opened my heart to dreams. I want you to know I am happy. Even as I am nearing*

*death, I am very, very happy. I wish you had told me you loved me. I needed it while I was growing up. I will tell you now that I loved you both as a child. As I move into the life after this life, I will remember you as the cold-hearted people you have always been. I can almost see Mother scowling. I can hear Father sighing because I have disrupted his daily routine. You will never understand what might have been.*
*I will sign this simply,*
*Alicia*

    Garrison gripped the edges of the letter while his heart skipped every other beat and Alicia's lovely script blurred before his eyes. He had never given any consideration to anything beyond his day-to-day routine. Unable to stand up for his rights as a father, Garrison had long ago separated himself from Alicia's life. His life was a matter of making money and running his business. He kept his eyes averted from his wife while the brittle ties that bound them together snapped apart.

    Contessa scowled at her daughter's words and at the expression on Garrison's face. Her hands bunched into fists as she breathed through her clenched teeth. When she caught sight of her breakfast being brought in, Contessa shouted, "Go away!"

    Garrison watched Anna disappear from sight. When Contessa reached out for the letter, he quickly pushed away from the table, folded the stationery and tucked it back into the envelope. After securing it deep inside his pocket, Garrison walked away, leaving Contessa alone in the dining room. Her angry cursing accompanied by a low guttural sound might have had anyone who did not know her running for cover. Garrison kept his steps steady as he mounted the long stairway to the second floor of their shared home. He had no desire to bear witness to what was coming next.

    On the verge of a total meltdown, Contessa stared at Garrison's abandoned breakfast and slammed her fist on the table. The impact made the spoon jump from the saucer under the coffee cup. She picked up the cup and threw it at the wall. She grinned when the fine porcelain cup shattered, giving herself the perfect excuse to buy new dinnerware. The pattern she had now was beautiful, but there were so many new designs available for purchase and she wanted to have them all.

Contessa pulled back the heavy chair and sat down as she mentally organized a busy shopping day. There was nothing more therapeutic than slapping a credit card down on a department store counter. The meltdown that had threatened her only seconds ago floated away like dust on the wind. She narrowed her eyes when Anna appeared in the dining room doorway.

Anna quietly asked, "Mrs. Rivers, may I serve your breakfast?"

"Yes, damn it!" Contessa shouted. Was the woman a lunatic? Of course she wanted her breakfast.

Contessa glared as Anna brought the tray of food to the table. Watched the woman begin gathering the remains of Garrison's breakfast. Grinned when Anna caught sight of the broken cup and the coffee smeared on the wallpaper.

"Clean that up later," scolded Contessa. "Leave me alone right now!" Contessa kept an eye on the woman until she was out of sight, then snapped her attention back to the meal before her. With the gleaming silver spoon in hand, she stirred the hot coffee so abruptly it sloshed over onto the expensive linen tablecloth. She watched the stain grow wider as the fine fabric greedily absorbed the dark liquid. While she added new linens to her shopping list, Contessa wondered what she had ever done to deserve such hatred from her daughter. It was that damned jackass Alicia had married. The bastard had forced two children on Alicia before she had even grown up. What kind of freedom could a woman have with two children screaming and clawing at her every day of the week? As far as Contessa was concerned they were not married. She knew God agreed with her. "God's on my side. On my side," she muttered as she slapped the spoon back and forth in the cup.

*Tender Dreams*

Chapter 19

    Garrison opened the double doors to his walk-in closet upstairs. The brightly illuminated and perfectly organized space kept everything at his fingertips. Each personally tailored suit had a lineup of pressed shirts and coordinating silk ties hanging next to it. Lacquered wooden shelves displayed his Italian-leather shoes. Absolutely everything in its place. Once he removed his pajamas and placed them on the appropriate hanger, Garrison dressed with precision, fastening each button with his fingers still shaking. Haunted eyes stared back at him from the full-length mirror while he heard his voice reading his daughter's written words. He pulled on steel-gray pants and tucked in the tail of the white shirt. He brushed his hand down the length of his brick-red silk tie and fastened the diamond studded tie-tack in place. After putting on a pair of black leather shoes, Garrison pulled on his jacket and slid his wallet and Alicia's letter into the inside pocket. He ran a comb through his thinning hair and studied his grim expression in the mirror.
    Before leaving the room, Garrison took a garment bag out of the back of the closet and placed a second suit, several shirts and ties and a pair of shoes inside. He placed his bathroom essentials and several changes of undergarments and socks into the bag and looked around his bedroom. He closed the zipper, lifted the garment bag and walked down the hallway to his den. He gathered up a few personal papers and several folders from his desk, slid them inside his briefcase and snapped it shut. Out in the hallway, he turned and locked the bedroom door, returned to the den and locked that door as well.
    Garrison moved down the stairway to the front door, stepped outside and closed it behind him. Inside his leather upholstered Mercedes, he turned the key, started the engine and drove away from the house. A short time later he pulled out into the left lane of the steady stream of traffic heading into the busy city. When horns began honking behind him, he realized he was losing control. He moved into the right lane, struggling to concentrate on his driving. Several more drivers blasted

their horns at him before Garrison finally moved off the road and came to a stop in the emergency lane. Beads of perspiration ran down his face. Overwhelmed with emotion, Garrison Rivers rested his forehead against the steering wheel and wept out loud.

A tapping noise startled Garrison. He momentarily wondered where he was. Garrison focused on the police officer standing at the side window.

"Roll down the window, sir," the officer said loudly.

Garrison complied. "I am sorry," he apologized.

"May I see your license, sir," requested the officer.

"Yes, of course," Garrison replied. He reached inside his jacket and took out his slim leather wallet. "Here it is," Garrison said, holding it out.

"Please take it out of the wallet, sir," the officer said, watching the man's hands as he did so. After taking the license, he quickly scanned the information and looked up. "Tell me your address, sir."

Garrison recited his home address correctly. "I am fine, officer," Garrison said, struggling to keep his emotions intact.

"Yes, sir. Why did you stop here?"

Garrison slid his license back into the slot in his wallet. "My daughter died a short time ago. I am not coping well with it."

"Perhaps you ought to go home until you feel better," suggested the officer.

"I am going to see my lawyer. Thank you for your concern."

"Be careful, Mr. Rivers," he warned.

"Thank you," said Garrison. He did not intend to go home and face Contessa again.

Garrison's thoughts strayed back in time. When Contessa learned she was pregnant, a new level of violence emerged right before his eyes. Up until then she had displayed her anger with verbal outbursts and a degree of physical tantrums, but he drew into himself when she began destroying anything within reach. After Contessa had two rooms stripped down to the studs, the chaos became unbearable. She screamed at all of the hired workers, then tore down the wallpaper when she decided it wasn't what she wanted and threw any tools she came across against the newly painted walls. During her violent outbursts she turned on anyone who crossed her path, so Garrison made it a point to be away from home as often as possible. Immediately following Alicia's birth, Contessa swore there would be no more children.

Garrison's life was riddled with bad choices and poor decisions. Owing to strict religious instructions during his younger years, Garrison felt committed to his marriage vows. The man was to be the provider and Garrison had never swayed from his role. While Contessa set the house rules, he completely missed how controlled his life had been. His past mistakes had become crystal clear today.

Alicia was gone. He had not slept with his wife in years. Their communication remained minimal. He had clearly become a pawn in Contessa's kingdom. The wall between them had been there for decades but had grown many times higher since Alicia's death. Contessa's behavior at the funeral service had pushed him closer toward the breaking point. Alicia's letter toppled him over the brink. No bigger fool had there ever been than the fool who sat behind the wheel of his car at this moment.

Garrison pulled back out onto the road. The plan formulated in his mind as he brought the car up to speed.

Though he did not have an appointment with Nathan Farrell, Garrison felt certain the lawyer would make time for him. Besides their families being longtime friends, Nathan and his father had handled the family's legal affairs for many years. He stepped up to the receptionist's desk and requested a few minutes of Nathan's time. The message had barely been relayed to Nathan when the man stepped out into the wide corridor.

"Hello, Garrison," Nathan said, offering his hand in greeting. "What's on your mind?"

"Nathan, thank you for seeing me. I need your help," Garrison said as he sat down and curled his fingers around the hand-carved arms of the high-backed Windsor chair. "I have some changes I need to make right away."

Nathan deftly gathered up the papers on his desk and slipped them into a folder. As was his nature, he directed his total focus to the task at hand. Back straight, fingers interlaced before him, he sat ready to take action. "You name it, I'll handle it," Nathan replied, facing Garrison across the wide expanse of the polished desktop.

"I will start with the beneficiaries named in my Will and on my life insurance policies," Garrison said. "I want you to list my daughter's husband as the main beneficiary and then their two children as equal second beneficiaries on each document. Please have a new power-of-attorney ready for changes as well. Know that I will also be doing the same on most of my bank accounts as well as my investment accounts and deeds in the coming days."

Obviously caught off guard by the positive tone in Garrison's voice, Nathan set out a yellow legal pad and began writing. "This is big, Garrison. Is everything all right?" he asked cautiously.

Garrison felt himself rising up higher on the chair as though every word lifted another invisible weight from his shoulders. "Yes, Nathan, everything is fine. Now," he said, pressing his palms flat against his knees, "how long will this take to be ready for my signature?"

"Give me a day or two, Garrison. Meanwhile, understand things are not changed until you sign the new documents," Nathan warned.

"I understand. Work it up as soon as possible and give me a call at the office. Leave a message if I am not there," Garrison added.

"Hold on, Garrison. Before you leave, we need to go over the spelling of the names. They must be correct," Nathan explained.

"Yes, that makes perfect sense, go ahead," Garrison agreed.

Nathan paused when he recognized Garrison's sudden unease. He raised his eyebrows and waited patiently.

"Hell, Nathan, I don't know. How can I be sure?" Garrison asked.

"You must contact Brian, Garrison. Give him a call and tell him what you are up to. Do it today, then get back to me," Nathan urged.

"I will," Garrison agreed as his enthusiasm slowly deflated. "Thank you, Nathan. I appreciate what you are doing for me."

"You'll get my bill," Nathan said with a smile. "May I be so bold as to ask what happened? You look different."

"I have learned a hard lesson, Nathan. I should have learned it decades ago. It is not too late to change, is it?" Garrison asked, standing to face his lawyer and friend.

"No, you have made a wise decision," Nathan replied without hesitation. "Alicia would have been proud of you."

"Do you think so?" Garrison asked tentatively.

"Absolutely, absolutely," Nathan replied as he rounded the desk and stepped closer.

"Fine," nodded Garrison as the two men shook hands one more time. "Get to work and stop jabbering, Nathan. I pay you good money for what you do." With that said, Garrison turned and walked out of the office.

Left in the wake of Garrison's hasty departure, Nathan interlaced his fingers behind his head and whispered, "It's about time."

## Chapter 20

Garrison dialed the house phone number, then set a clean sheet of paper on his desk. The phone rang twice before it was picked up.

"Hello, this is the Rivers' residence, Anna speaking."

"Is she there?" he asked.

"Excuse me, who," Anna began. "I'm sorry, Mr. Rivers, your wife left for the Bayside Club 20 minutes ago. Would you like me to call for her?"

"Please listen, Anna," Garrison said.

"Yes sir," replied Anna.

"What we are going to discuss needs to remain between the two of us, Anna. Do you understand?" Garrison waited for her reply, then said, "Good, good. I need the full names of Alicia's husband, their children and their birth dates. Can you do that for me?"

"Let me go to my room and get my address book. I'll be right back," Anna said. "Are you ready, sir?" she asked a few minutes later.

"Go ahead," Garrison replied. He listened, printing the names as Anna spelled Brian Patrick Cooper. "The girl is next, is that correct?" he asked cautiously.

"Yes sir, Erin Madison," she said, spelling it as well.

"Now the boy. Is he John or?" Garrison began.

"No, he's Jackson Graham," Anna interrupted.

"How did they come up with that?" Garrison asked, printing the boy's name.

"Jackson, well, Alicia always liked the name. She told Brian she wanted to marry someone named Jack, but she fell in love with him instead. I believe Graham is Brian's mother's maiden name," Anna said. "I'm sorry, sir."

"Why are you apologizing?" Garrison asked.

"I should not have carried on about Alicia," she sighed.

"You have always loved her," Garrison said, hearing the strain in his own voice.

"She's very special to me. I miss her," Anna said softly.

A moment of silence passed between them before Garrison cleared his throat and spoke again. "Anna, I will not be coming home tonight. I will talk to you tomorrow or the next day. Meanwhile please do not say anything about our conversation to my wife."

"Yes sir," replied Anna.

Following the phone call Garrison sat in the quiet office and looked at the names of his son-in-law and grandchildren. For the first time in his life, he admitted he had deserted his only daughter. He was an idiot. Garrison knew he had just taken the first steps toward correcting his past mistakes. Without delay he tapped the intercom button.

"Yes sir," answered Elaine.

"Please reserve a room for me at the Bennington," Garrison told his assistant.

"Sir?" Elaine replied. "Excuse me, sir. How many nights shall I reserve?"

"Two weeks for now, thank you," he replied. Garrison sat back on his chair and stared up at the ceiling. While he contemplated the documents Nathan was preparing for him, an image from his past crept back with alarming clarity.

"Before you marry, be sure to have papers drawn up to protect what is yours. You cannot know if she is going to eat you alive," warned his father.

Garrison had followed his father's advice even though he felt it paranoid at the time. Now he realized it was going to save him.

Garrison took the call the following afternoon. "Yes, Nathan?"

"I have the paperwork ready for you to sign," said Nathan.

"Let me see," Garrison replied as he checked his appointment calendar. "I can come in tomorrow morning first thing."

"See you then," said Nathan.

The call reminded Garrison he needed to contact Brian and explain everything to him. He picked up the phone and dialed the house. "Anna, do you have Brian's phone number?" For a moment he heard nothing from the other end of the line and thought perhaps the call had not connected. "Anna?" he said cautiously.

"Garrison! What the hell are you doing!" screamed Contessa.

Without another word Garrison disconnected the call. He realized it was too early to call the West Coast anyway. Brian was probably still working. He tapped the intercom button.

"Elaine, will you please locate a phone number for me?"

Contessa's anger echoed through Garrison's head. While he admitted he was the biggest fool for putting up with her all these years, he could not lay all the blame on Contessa. He promised himself that he would never return to the house again. As soon as he purchased a new house, he would contact Anna and offer her employment.

Garrison winced when he considered what might be happening at the house. Should he call back and try to calm Contessa, or would it only prove to make the situation worse? He frowned at the picture that came to life in his mind. Contessa was most likely firing her rage point blank at Anna. Garrison could not know how correct his assumption was at that moment.

***

Anna thought Contessa Rivers was angry enough to burst into flames. Their personal affairs were none of her business, but she feared she might lose her job over the matter. She had not said a word about her conversation with Mr. Rivers. It was too late now, but Anna wished she had answered the phone herself. Contessa still held the phone against her ear. With every click of the wall clock the rage grew stronger in her dark eyes. "Monkey-in-the-middle," Anna thought to herself.

"Say something!" Contessa screamed into the phone.

Anna guessed Mr. Rivers was no longer on the other end of the line. Her theory was proved correct when Contessa threw the phone at her. It fell to the floor and bounced back against the cupboard door thanks to the thick cord that tethered it to the wall above the counter. Anna stood perfectly still with her fingers laced together.

"I know you are in on whatever he's doing! You pack your bags and get out of here by morning!" ordered Contessa.

"Yes ma'am," Anna replied. She did not move an inch. She waited until Contessa charged out of the room, heels clacking on the tiled kitchen floor. Contessa grabbed her purse, flung the door open wide and ran out to her car. A moment later Anna saw the car pull out onto the road.

Relieved, Anna closed the door, came back into the kitchen and picked up the phone. She suddenly realized where Contessa might be going. She quickly dialed the number and spoke to Elaine. Anna kept her eyes on the road while she waited for his voice to come on the line.

"Mr. Rivers, I have the number you requested, but Anna needs to speak with you right away," said Elaine. "Good, thank you," Garrison replied. "Anna?" Garrison said once the call was connected.

"Mr. Rivers, I'm pretty sure she's on her way to your office," warned Anna.

Garrison did not waste any time deciding how to react. "We will work this out," he assured his housekeeper. "I believe you ought to leave the house. Do you have somewhere to stay for the time being?"

"Yes, I think so," Anna replied. "I haven't prepared dinner yet," sighed Anna.

"Forget about dinner, Anna," Garrison interjected as an unfamiliar sense of power straightened his spine. "Gather up your things and get out of there before my wife returns. I will be getting my own place soon, Anna. I will need a housekeeper right away. There will be no lapse in pay. In fact, a pay raise is in order immediately. Leave a number on my office answering machine when you decide where to go for tonight," Garrison instructed.

"Umm, okay, but," Anna argued.

"Do as I asked, please," Garrison urged.

"Yes sir," replied Anna.

After speaking with Anna, Garrison buzzed Elaine again. "We are leaving early today," he ordered, surprised with his own abrupt tone.

"Sir?" Elaine replied.

"You will be paid for your regular hours," Garrison explained. He rarely strayed from routine and understood Elaine's hesitation. "I feel we need to be gone before my wife arrives. She is unhappy with me at the moment."

"Yes, of course, sir. I will be out of here before you know it. Thank you," she added.

Garrison slid the paperwork he had been reviewing into his briefcase, grabbed his jacket and headed for the door. Elaine came around the corner and handed him a slip of paper.

"Brian's number, sir," she chirped, and rushed out into the hallway.

Garrison nodded his thanks, but Elaine was already out of sight. He secured the paper in his pocket and stepped toward the hallway. Even if Contessa drove like mad, it would take her at least 20 minutes to arrive. He switched off the lights, set the security code and locked the door. At the downstairs desk he left his hotel number with strict instructions not to give it to Contessa. The security guard nodded and smiled. Garrison wondered if he had been the only one who had not seen through the smoke screen all these years. Before walking outside, he requested the use of the phone at the desk.

"Nathan, can you see me immediately? Good, I am on my way," he replied.

By the time Garrison stepped into Nathan's office, Nathan had a pen in his hand and the papers set out on the desk.

"Take your time, Garrison," Nathan said, instructions he offered any client when presenting legal documents.

"I have always trusted you, Nathan," replied Garrison. He took the pen and began signing the papers, barely glancing at the content of each document. "There is something else I need you to do for me. I believe you have the prenuptial agreement we signed before our wedding, do you not?" He watched Nathan nod slowly. "I want you to file the paperwork for my divorce. Push it through as quickly as possible. I want every coin accounted for. Other than my personal wardrobe, she can have the house and its contents as well as the account I set up for her, but nothing else. I may not be the brightest star, but I have finally come to my senses. How long will the process take?"

Garrison felt like he was floating on air after leaving Nathan's office, but his high spirit crumbled as he neared his car. Why had he not listen when his parents and his brother warned him about Contessa? He steadied himself against the car when images of her greedy fingers pulling cash from his wallet flashed before his eyes. She always bought anything and everything she wanted. Until reading Alicia's letter, Garrison had not realized how much control Contessa held over him. He had ruined his own life, but far worse than that he had destroyed Alicia's childhood.

He opened the car door and sat down thinking about how easily Anna talked about his daughter. She truly loved Alicia. She knew about the grandchildren and the young man Alicia had married. Was it too late for him to get to know them? Would putting them in his Will look like a bribe? Would Brian reject the idea? Could he blame him if he did? Would Anna have any helpful suggestions?

After closing himself in the two-room suite at the Bennington, Garrison shed his jacket and pushed off his shoes. He automatically reached out for a heavy wooden hanger, then stopped and turned away from the closet. Instead, he draped the expensive suit jacket over the back of an oak armchair. He stepped back and stared at it, then glanced over at the shoes on the floor in front of the antique dresser. He was never so careless at the house. It simply was not tolerated. Garrison ordered room service before calling to check his office answering machine. He recognized her voice even before she stated her name.

"Hello, Mr. Rivers, sir," she said. A full minute of silence passed before she spoke again. "This is Anna, Anna Cole. I'm going to my friend's house for the night. Her name is Paige and her number, umm, let me see," she said, drifting off before returning to recite the phone number before hanging up.

Garrison listened to the message twice more before he put the phone down. Her simple words evoked a strange feeling inside him.

After finishing his late supper, Garrison sat alone in the semi darkness. With his mind settled he reached for the phone and dialed the number from the slip of paper. While the call connected over 3000 miles away, Garrison wondered if he would recognize the sound of his voice.

## Chapter 21

Anna calmly drove toward the home of her childhood friend, Paige Kelsey. When she called earlier and explained her situation, Paige jumped at the opportunity to help.

"Of course, get over here this minute. If you don't stop talking, you'll never get here. Shut up and move," Paige said with delight.

It did not take Anna long to pack her belongings into three boxes and her two battered suitcases. In a matter of minutes, she had emptied the small space she had occupied for the past two decades. She found herself surprised with how easy it had been to leave. As Anna approached her friend's home, she sighed with relief. While the house she worked in was lavish and eye-catching, Paige's little home had more appeal. The cozy cottage-style structure looked like every other house on the narrow street. Each had a small porch, a single driveway and a little lawn out front. Tulips bloomed profusely in planters on several of the porches.

Anna had always secretly envied Paige's life. She had spunk and enthusiasm that Anna had never experienced for herself. Paige was waiting outside, bouncing up and down on her toes. With her usual enthusiasm Paige jumped down from the porch, raced up and hugged Anna.

"Welcome!" Paige exclaimed. "You have done a very brave thing. I'm proud of you."

"Oh Paige, are you sure about…" Anna said before Paige slapped her hand over Anna's mouth and kissed her cheek.

"Tell me what we're bringing inside. My boy has been away for nearly a year, and I'm thrilled to have someone fill the emptiness. Now, how long are you staying?" Paige asked enthusiastically.

Anna did not argue when Paige insisted she join her in the kitchen. She sat down and rested her joined hands on the red gingham tablecloth. Anna knew Paige made the table covering as well as the matching curtains framing the nearby window. Like Anna, Paige had grown up cutting corners to make ends meet. Witnessing wealth did not make either of them jealous. In fact, they often admitted they preferred to earn their way in the world. Paige and her late husband had done their best to raise their son with the same values. Anna knew Paige had dealt with their son's defiance for the past few years.

Right now, Paige was wielding a long serrated knife, still bouncing on her toes. Anna thought her friend's excess energy ought to be harnessed and might be enough to power an entire city. Anna suddenly recalled Contessa's rage from earlier today. Her eyes closed and her interlaced fingers tightened while she tried to erase the stark images. She looked up at the sound of Paige's happy chatter.

"This will be like a vacation for us, Anna," Paige said as she ran the knife through the spice cake at the counter. "We can talk over old times and keep talking until we drop."

"I'm too old for that," Anna sighed, grimacing when Paige set the plate down in front of her. The piece of cake was larger than the plate itself. "I can't eat all of this. Goodness sake, I haven't even had dinner yet," Anna mumbled.

"Let's go shopping tomorrow. I'll pick out a place for lunch and treat you to a day of fun. We'll have a blast," Paige said.

"I don't know. I never go shopping like that," confessed Anna.

"Then it's about time you do. We can try on clothes like teenagers. And we'll do it while they are in school," she cackled with delight.

"Paige, you still haven't grown up. You're using words like a kid and thinking of silly things to do," sighed Anna.

"You get one chance at life and you have to make the best of the time," scolded Paige.

"I don't know," Anna said, slowly sinking the fork into the cake. "Did you bake this from scratch?" she asked.

"Who, me?" Paige squealed. "No way!"

"Where did you get that?" Anna asked, all too aware of her sheltered life.

"Kids have such fun expressions and I listen. We aren't too old to learn," replied Paige. "Eat your cake, then we can talk in the bedroom while we look at old photographs and stuff."

## Chapter 22

Brian choked back laughter when he glanced over at Jack. The kid had food smeared all over his face. How he managed to get anything into his stomach was a mystery. Erin used her fork and spoon with perfect manners, lending hope to the idea her little brother might one day follow her lead.

The phone rang as they were finishing dinner. Brian narrowed his eyes at Jack as he reached back for the wall phone. "Mashed potatoes in your hair isn't cool, Jack. Maybe we ought to shave your hair off and make life easier," he said as he pressed the phone to his ear.

"Hello," he said into the phone. Jack's face lit up with a huge smile.

"Don't shave off his hair, Daddy," pleaded Erin.

"Okay, I won't," Brian replied. "Sorry about that, this is Brian," he said into the phone.

"Brian, Garrison Rivers here."

"Well, yes," Brian said, stunned to hear the caller's voice.

"If you have the time, I need to talk with you," Garrison said.

"Let me get my kids down from the table. Hold on for a few minutes," Brian replied.

Garrison had never made any direct contact with them over the years of their marriage. Part of Brian considered hanging up the phone and letting the action speak for itself. On the other hand, he had been raised to respect his elders even when he felt they did not deserve it.

Determined to keep his emotions in check, Brian set the phone down on the counter and grabbed the dish towel off the edge of the sink. "Come here, monster boy. Let's get you cleaned up." He held the dish towel under warm water, wrung it out and worked on Jack until he was safe to set free. "Erin, please take him to your room and get out his cars and trucks. I need to be on the phone for a little while, okay?"

Erin slid down from her chair and walked over to Jack. "Please don't shave his hair off."

Brian kissed her and tugged lightly on her ponytail. "I promise I won't. It's yucky when he does that, don't you agree?"

"It's because he's little," Erin replied.

"You're right," Brian agreed. "Now go and play for a bit." Brian leaned against the counter and calmed his nerves before reluctantly reaching for the phone.

Garrison must have heard his exchange with the kids. Brian knew the man had never experienced a similar interaction with Alicia. He drew in a deep breath, let it out slowly and pressed the phone to his ear. The words came out before Brian realized he was speaking. "Excuse me, sir. We were finishing up dinner," he said. Under normal circumstances it would have been a perfectly acceptable thing to say, but he was speaking to Alicia's father, a man who did not know anything about children or family. Arrogant, cold hearted and strictly business described Garrison Rivers. Brian remained quiet, waiting for the man to say something. He had after all, initiated the call.

"I apologize for the interruption," Garrison said after an awkward moment of silence passed between them.

"What's on your mind?" Brian asked.

"I read Alicia's letter. It made me realize what a fool I have been," Garrison said.

"Yes sir," Brian said in return.

"Alicia and I were strangers living in the same house. I deeply regret that," Garrison explained. "Her letter opened my eyes to the reality of what I did to her. I accept full responsibility and understand if you would rather not hear me out."

Brian felt the phone growing hot in his hand. He shifted it to his other ear and rubbed his palm on his jeans. The call had to be the most awkward conversation he had ever experienced.

"I filed for divorce a few hours ago," Garrison said softly.

"Sir? Are you all right?" Brian asked, thinking the man must have lost his marbles.

"I believe so. You need to be aware I have changed my Will and named you and your children as my main beneficiaries."

Brian held his breath and stared at the aftermath of dinner with Erin and Jack. Spilled milk, blobs of mashed potatoes and a few stray green beans littered the space between the plates. "What did you say?" he asked.

"You heard me, Brian. You and your children, Alicia's children, are now my main beneficiaries. My family has always had money. When I married Contessa, she took charge of our financial output. She also controlled me and the life of our daughter. Until now I never realized how foolish it was of me to allow her to do so. Things have changed drastically now that I have seen the wrong of it all," Garrison continued. "I would like to meet you and my grandchildren sometime in the near future. I know this is a lot to take in all at once, but please give it serious consideration. I will honor your wishes without question, but I hope you will give me a chance," Garrison concluded.

"I'm not, I'm not sure what to say," Brian stammered. The sudden need to move forced him away from the counter until the phone cord halted his progress. He turned back and stared out through the kitchen window. "This is a shock," he said, though he had not meant to say it out loud.

"You can say that again," Garrison agreed. "It is a new beginning for me."

"Yes, I suppose so," Brian commented, trying to absorb everything he had just heard.

"I am sorry for the discomfort I created for you and Alicia over the years. It is not easy for me to admit to so many mistakes, but I hope you can accept my apology," Garrison said. "Let me give you a phone number where you can reach me. Leave a message if I am not in. I will no longer be at the house."

"Okay, but," said Brian.

Garrison continued, "I will do whatever I can to make amends for the past. There will be a substantial inheritance coming to you and your children in the future. Consider what I have told you and call me when you are ready to go over the details. I need to fix things between us. Let me know what you think, but do not feel rushed."

"Yeah, okay, I will," Brian replied. He jotted down the phone number and stared at the paper with disbelief. Was this really happening or was he dreaming? When he heard the children laughing down the hallway, Brian said, "Look, I need to go check on my kids. I'll think about what you have said."

"Thank you, Brian. Have a good night," Garrison said.

Brian stared at the phone for a moment before hanging it up. Hands shaking, he wiped the tears from his eyes and whispered, "Alicia."

"Daddy, Jack's stuck!" shouted Erin.

Brian put aside his confused feelings for now. "I'm coming," he replied as he stuffed the paper into his pocket and hurried down the hallway.

Brian was surprised to discover Jack really was trapped under his bed. "What are you doing under there?" he asked, kneeling down next to his son's legs. Brian raised the bed up and pulled Jack out.

"Fire truck, fire truck," Jack announced, rolling over onto his back and holding up the little red truck.

Erin dropped down on her knees next to Jack. "He found it!" she exclaimed, patting Jack's tummy.

"I love you two," Brian said, gathering his children in his arms. "You're the best kids ever. I love you." Brian thought about how Alicia's parents never hugged her. She should have been bitter and resentful, but she refused to let the past dictate her future.

Once Erin and Jack were down for the night, Brian returned to the kitchen. Spending time with them had taken priority over cleaning up. He turned on the water and set the plates in the sink as the strange conversation with Garrison Rivers replayed in his head. He rinsed off the dishes and loaded the dishwasher. Garrison and Contessa had never been grandparents to Erin and Jack.

Since his own mother died before he met Alicia, the only other grandparent was his father. Patrick Cooper lived alone in a retirement home. He had long ago lost interest in life, content to watch the world from the window in his small room. The way Brian saw it his father had expected to die first. Elise Cooper had lovingly cared for her husband, who was twenty years older. She often talked of her plans to travel the world after Patrick was gone, something Patrick had encouraged her to do from the beginning of their marriage. Brian had been an unplanned surprise that brightened her every day. Elise was a devoted wife and loving mother whose life was cut short when she suffered a massive heart attack. If not for Erin and Jack, Brian might have followed in his father's footsteps.

Without Alicia, Brian was virtually alone raising their children. He so missed having her near when life became overwhelming. Brian sponged off the table, knowing his situation had no chance of changing.

Garrison had sounded sincere, but it was impossible to know the truth of it all. Why had it taken Alicia's death to open the man's eyes? He could only imagine how Alicia might have reacted if Garrison had called her and relayed the same information. Anger surged through

Brian at that moment. He glanced over at the phone and considered calling the number he had taken down. Shaking his head, Brian rinsed out the sponge and grabbed the dish towel to dry his hands. He realized too late it was the same one he had used on Jack. "Aw hell," he groaned.

*Julia Robertson*

Chapter 23

    Garrison felt hopeful following the conversation with his son-in-law. He sat in the quiet hotel suite contemplating what he needed to do next. He drummed his fingers on the arms of the chair and realized he had not made any decisions other than for his business over the past three decades. Had it really been that many years? Contessa had directed his every step, from his clothing and food to where he could or could not go on an everyday basis. She designated who came to their house parties, when and where they went out for dinners and what kind of stage shows they attended. It occurred to him she had refurnished their house at least twice a year without any objections from him. Her wardrobe experienced constant updates, as did her hair and her makeup and her nails. If he so much as lifted an eyebrow at her, she lit into him like a screaming tornado. Now that he acknowledged those events, he knew he had been too weak to stand up to her fury. What a fool he had been, he thought, pounding the arms of the chair with his fists.
    Garrison shook off the anger and focused instead on the future. Locating a new place to live seemed of the utmost importance. Was it better to have a new house built, like the one he had just given up to Contessa, or should he buy an existing house that might require renovation? How did one go about finding the answers? Perhaps he ought to ask Elaine to research the topic for him. She was a very resourceful employee. Garrison's thoughts turned to Anna. He had offered her a job and a place to live, but had he ever actually talked with her? He knew she was a good cook and an excellent housekeeper, but who was Anna Cole? "Anna," he whispered into the quiet.

*Julia Robertson*

## Chapter 24

Contessa smashed the gas pedal down and roared out of the driveway. Since Garrison refused to talk to her on the phone, she would just get right in his face. She would straighten him out one way or another. The man had no idea what was coming. Contessa was wrapped around the steering wheel like a coiled spring. She jerked her car into the fast lane and stomped on the gas pedal.

Coming to a screeching halt at the office building, Contessa did not see Garrison's car in his reserved parking space. He probably parked it somewhere else to conceal the fact he was still here. She pulled her car into his spot and stormed into the lobby without a glance at the security guard. Her temper reached the boiling point while she stabbed the elevator button, momentarily giving thought to running for the stairs. As soon as the elevator reached the proper floor she squeezed through the barely opened doors and raced down the wide carpeted hallway.

Contessa screamed when the doorknob did not turn in her hand. She grabbed the knob with both hands and tried furiously to twist it open. She kicked the door and pounded it with her fists without a single response from inside. She pressed her face against the narrow pane of glass next to the door and saw nothing but darkness. Garrison had obviously taken off for his hiding place. Contessa screamed again and wondered how far away her voice carried.

She did not deserve to be treated like this. Forgiving him was out of the question. She fumed as she charged back toward the elevators. The moment the elevator doors opened she remembered her purse, shrieked and raced back to pick it up.

Contessa ran to her car a few minutes later, flung the door open and dropped down on the driver's seat. She slammed the door with revenge on her mind. "The battle has just begun," she hissed.

Contessa knew good things came to those who fired first. There was no time to waste. Buying something expensive or getting something strong to drink might help calm her nerves. Contessa mulled it over for two seconds, then made her decision as she slapped on a thick layer of lipstick. Given the time of day she set aside shopping for a new diamond bracelet, which she most certainly deserved, and headed out of the parking lot for the Bayside Club.

Half an hour later Contessa slid onto an empty bar stool and drummed her manicured Raging Red acrylic fingernails on the shining surface of the bar until the bartender delivered her drink. He knew exactly what she wanted, so she did not need to waste her time spelling it out for him. While she waited, fingernails drumming, she checked out the people behind her in the reflection in the mirrored wall in front of her. She grabbed the glass from the bartender and waved him away. Eyes closed Contessa swallowed a good portion of the Cosmopolitan, heavy on the vodka, and waited for it to smooth the outer edges of her rage. She began sorting through the past two days in search of exactly what had destroyed her control over her husband. After a few minutes she banged the empty glass on the bar and impatiently waited for the bartender to bring her a second round.

The sun set long before Contessa returned to the house. Powered up after her stop at the Club, she walked inside and clumsily searched for the light switch. Contessa had never come home to total darkness before. Anna was most certainly not getting a severance package. She was out of here cold-turkey.

Contessa made her way to the kitchen and found it deserted as well. There was not so much as a single pot on the stove and no dishes on the counters. Every surface gleamed under the bright overhead lights.

"Anna, where are you?" she shouted. Contessa expected the woman to appear instantly. "Anna! Anna!" she screamed at the top of her lungs. With her fists clenched tight, Contessa marched toward the servant's quarters at the back of the house. It was unfamiliar territory for her. When she entered the narrow hallway and felt the closeness squeeze the air from her lungs, Contessa gasped and teetered on her high heels. She stumbled to the first doorway and looked inside. Both bedrooms were unoccupied and there was not even a toothbrush in the bathroom.

Contessa spun around and raced back to the kitchen. Surely the woman had prepared dinner before running off. Contessa opened the oven and found it empty. She rushed down the hall to the dining room expecting to find her meal already on the table. The bare linen tablecloth, free of wrinkles and stains, was the only thing on the long table.  Everything looked exactly as she demanded, with barely an inch of space between table and chairs.

What the hell was she supposed to do about dinner?  Rising rage slammed headlong into drunken frustration as Contessa threw her high heels into the glass doors of the antique china cabinet.

*Julia Robertson*

## Chapter 25

Brian watched his children drawing together while he reflected upon Alicia's decision to bring Kathleen Hodges into their lives. Alicia's words were imprinted on his mind. He recalled his grim feelings as he leaned against the door jamb.

"We need help," Alicia had said. "I'm not going to get better. We both know that."

While Alicia accepted the inevitable, Brian tried to pretend it was not happening. When she welcomed Kathleen into their lives, he felt the outer layer of their dreams begin to peel away. He sat on the side of their bed and cried like a baby. Alicia had wrapped her arms around him and comforted him.

"You're going to love her like I do. Give her a chance, honey," Alicia patiently encouraged.

As Alicia's illness progressed Brian began to understand how important Kathleen's role was in their lives. Her sunny attitude became a vital part of Erin and Jack's days. Tentative greetings at the front door as Brian left for work evolved into brief conversations. Brian began to share stories about Erin and Jack, as well as how the night had gone for Alicia. Kathleen welcomed the chance to talk about her own past and her need to be needed. Their shared grief eventually drew them closer together.

Brian learned Kathleen Hodges had been married for 37 years when she lost her husband. Though her friends encouraged her to start dating, Kathleen had no interest in getting married again. After meeting Alicia through a mutual friend, her life changed dramatically. Kathleen and Alicia grew as close as mother and daughter, something neither had known before. Brian knew the bond they shared was genuine. Kathleen promised she would be there for him for as long as he needed her.

Brian was grateful for everything Kathleen did for him. The kids loved her dearly. The daily routines she established made life easier for all of them. Even though she was well into her 60's, Kathleen never seemed to run out of energy.

When the time came to return to work, Brian found it difficult to leave the kids behind. He settled back into the normal work schedule with relative ease. It was the coming home part that hurt the most. His heart cracked a little more every time he came into the house and faced the fact that Alicia was not there, and never would be there. Kathleen knew exactly what he was feeling. It showed in her eyes, so he did his best to hide his dark moods from her. He focused on work during the day, trained his thoughts on the kids in the evening and saved his sorrow for his brief alone time at night.

Despite his best efforts to make his life work, Brian missed Alicia all the time. He ran his hand over his eyes in an effort to settle his emotions. He refocused his attention on the kids once again. Erin was anxious to start kindergarten in the fall. He hoped to make the transition as smooth as possible for both kids since they were used to having each other around all the time. Right now they were laying side-by-side on the floor with a large piece of white paper spread out in front of them.

"I'm gonna be five," Erin announced with her fingers spread wide. "One, two, three, four, five!"

"Five," Jack said, holding his hand up like Erin.

Erin reached over and tucked his thumb and littlest finger down against his palm. "One, two, three. Jack is three." Erin clapped her hands, hopped up and did a little dance.

Jack looked at his fingers and said, "Wanna be five." He let his tucked down fingers pop back up again.

Erin knelt down next to her brother. She traced her hand and carefully drew a smiling face on each fingertip.

"Make my faces," said Jack.

Erin positioned Jack's fingers, then ran her pencil around them. She drew little faces on his three fingertips. "Three for Jack. Five for me."

Laughing, Jack rolled over onto his back. Brian knelt between the kids. He laid his hand on Jack's tummy and looked over their drawings.

"I'm gonna be five," said Erin.

"It won't be long. Are you happy?" he asked.

"Yes!" she replied as she stepped up on his knees and wrapped her arms around his neck.

Erin suddenly looked sad, but she did not say anything. Brian knew she was thinking about Alicia and wanted her here for her birthday. He felt the excitement drain from his daughter. He kissed her hair and hugged her tight. "It's okay to be sad, Erin. I understand."

"Hug me too," Jack said as he jumped up and scooted up close to Erin.

"Can we have balloons at my birthday?" Erin asked.

"What color?" Brian asked.

"Red," Jack said.

"Pink," replied Erin. "Can Clay come?"

"You'll have to ask him. He'll be over later," Brian replied.

*Julia Robertson*

## Chapter 26

Several weeks had passed since Clay had gone in for his eye exam. The doctor told him to use the prescription eye drops for two weeks and then come back for a second examination. Once things calmed down, he would be fitted with prescription glasses. Clay refused to admit he had a problem and figured it would all go away if he ignored it long enough. At that time he tossed the prescription for the drops into the glove box and intentionally forgotten about it.

When May rolled around and things had not improved, he reluctantly had the prescription filled at the pharmacy. Clay wrapped his long fingers around the bag containing the expensive little bottle of eye drops and walked out to his truck. He put the rumpled bag down on the seat next to him and stared out through the windshield.

A steady stream of people came in and out of the busy store. A woman with two little boys sitting in a shopping cart barreled across the blacktop parking lot. Their delightful laughter ricocheted around the parked cars. Clay spotted two teens walking hand in hand. The boy carried a small paper sack and the girl kept pulling her bright red purse strap up on her narrow shoulder. Clay figured he knew what they had in mind once they found a little privacy. Remembering his own teen years made him grin until he thought of Erin ten years from now. For a moment he considered going out to lecture them on what real love was supposed to be like, but since he had not yet experienced it on a personal level, he had no right to interfere. The way he saw it, if what they had in the little bag prevented a possible pregnancy, there was no harm done. Kids needed to have parents who talked to them about everything in life, not that talking had ever deterred him from doing the wrong things. It was best his mother did not know about all the stupid choices he had made. He leaned back against the headrest and closed his eyes for a few minutes. Feeling like an idiot Clay opened the crumpled pharmacy bag and peered inside.

Clay drove to the pizza place and ordered two pizzas to share with Brian and his kids. While he waited for his order, he sat on a long narrow bench and watched the people coming and going like he had done at the pharmacy. He unwittingly sized up each group passing in front of him.

A tall thin woman with frizzy bleached blonde hair made him think of a dandelion flower gone to seed. A stocky man with a buzz cut followed right on her heels. "Who's the boss?" Clay mused.

A couple came in with a brood of five children. The kids ranged in age from a toddler younger than Jack to a girl in her teens. The couple could have been Brian and Alicia if they had had more time together. They were well behaved children with attentive parents. They stayed together like it was the most natural way to behave.

Then along came a single woman with a bratty kid of maybe six years of age. The brat was up on the bench, climbing on the counter and smashing his face into the glass doors all at the same time. Clay would have sworn there were six of him. The woman needed to consult with the family he had just observed. When his name was called, Clay was relieved to pick up his order and be on his way.

"Pizza man!" Clay shouted as he opened Brian's front door. Before he took two steps Erin and Jack wrapped themselves around his legs.

"Clay, hi!" shouted Erin.

"Hi!" echoed Jack.

"Do I know you two grubby monsters?" Clay asked, loving what he saw in their bright smiling faces. "Wait, I think I have the wrong house."

"Don't leave, we're hungry. Help me, he's big," Erin called out as she pulled on his free hand. Jack grabbed his hand too and tugged with all his might.

Brian walked up to Clay and took the pizza boxes away. "All mine," he said as he turned and headed back to the kitchen.

Clay watched the pizzas disappear, then looked down at the kids. He squatted down and grabbed both of them. "Do you want me to toss these outside?" he called out.

"Be my guest. I'm eating pizza," Brian replied.

"Pizza!" shouted Jack, wriggling to get free.

"We're hungry," Erin whined.

"Maybe we can spare a bite or two," Clay said as he deposited Jack and Erin on their chairs at the kitchen table.

Brian put their plates down in front of them. The kids quieted down right away.

"One of those for me too, Boss," Clay said when Brian reached for a slice of the pizza. Clay opened a cupboard and took down a glass before he asked, "Drinks?"

"Yes, I forgot. Milk for the kids," Brian replied.

"Coming right up," Clay said as he poured milk into two plastic cups. He knew the drill. A half cup was better than a full one if it was spilled.

"I'm going to have my birthday," Erin said.

"No kidding," Clay said as he sat down.

"I get to be five, like this," she announced, proudly holding up her hand.

"That's cool," said Clay.

"Will you come to my party?" Erin asked with a piece of an olive on the tip of her finger.

"Yes, I'll be there. Do you remember being five, Brian?" Clay asked.

"I remember a chocolate cake with blue candles, but that's about it," Brian replied.

"We went to the beach when I turned five," Clay said, slowly turning the glass of water on the table while he revisited a long-forgotten time. "My grandmother came with us. The tide was way out, and we walked out to a cave on the backside of one of those big rocks near Sixes River. We went inside where it was dark and kind of spooky and listened to the waves. The sounds echoed off the cave walls."

"You're lucky," Brian remarked.

"Yeah, I know," Clay agreed. He knew Alicia's parents never had much to do with her life. And he knew Brian had just his dad left from his family. He watched Erin, then glanced over at Jack as the little boy licked pizza sauce off his fingers.

"Ready for another slice?" Brian asked Erin.

"Lots of olives, please," she said.

"Me too," said Jack as he lifted up his plate.

"Wait till he gets bigger, you'll be needing to buy a truckload of groceries," Clay remarked, running his hand over Jack's silky hair. He wondered what it would be like to have a son of his own. Or a daughter like Erin who was as pretty as Alicia. Having a daughter might be the end of him because he would never be able to tell her no. He figured it would be best to have either a girl who would require a good deal of his income for dresses and pretty shoes, or a son to restore cars and build houses with him. Everything he had just thought of made Clay realize he was seeing stereotypical children. If his daughter wanted to be a race car driver, or his son a world class chef, so be it. He lightly tugged on Erin's ponytail. When he looked up, he saw Brian watching him.

"You'll be a great dad some day," Brian said. "Are you still seeing Monique?"

"No," Clay groaned. "Buying her new clothes and makeup every time we were out together grew old pretty quick. I guess maybe I have my sights set too high. I'm looking for a woman who wants me, not my wallet."

"Give yourself time," Brian said.

"I guess," Clay replied.

"More pizza?" Brian asked as he pushed back from the table.

"Sure," Clay replied, wondering if Brian really thought he would make a good dad. At the rate things were going he might never find the right woman to share his life with. Clay had dated all through high school and recalled most of the girls he'd gone out with. Mary Beth, Sandra, Gina, Rebecca, Danielle, Norma, Whitney, Shawna, he mused. Cathy, Heather, Laura, Darla, Maxine, Linette, Andrea, Elaine and Samantha. Having a serious relationship had never crossed his mind. Clay figured he had all the time in the world before he had to make a commitment, but here he was in his middle 30's and he was still alone. He seemed to draw the ditzy girls instead of the ones who yearned for a family and a home. It would be great to come home to a wife and dinner on the table. Hell, he didn't care if she cooked or not because simply sharing his life was most important.

When Brian nudged him, Clay took the plate and watched him get the kids down from their chairs. He watched Brian wipe Jack's messy hands and face. Even though Brian sometimes appeared to be falling apart, he tended to Erin and Jack with no more effort than it took to pull on socks. Clay grinned when Brian tossed the washrag into the sink. He momentarily wondered how people learned to parent their children. Questioned his own ability to master such a delicate task.

"Where were you?" asked Brian.

"Nowhere," Clay replied, feeling ill at ease for getting caught daydreaming. He grabbed the first thing that came to mind in order to regain his composure. "I dated a girl named Laura for a short time. I kind of thought she might be the one, but then I met her folks. Her dad was a stubby guy with big bushy muttonchops and a beer belly. He said Laura was going to look just like her mother when she grew up. That didn't bother me until the woman walked into the room. She looked like a Saturday night wrestler. I almost screamed and ran out of the house."

Brian laughed so hard he nearly choked on the pizza. "She wasn't that bad," he argued.

"She had this steel gray hair cropped close to her head, thick black framed glasses and scarlet red lipstick. I remember looking at Laura and wondering what I was doing there. Really freaked me out," Clay sighed as he lifted the pizza up from the plate.

"You're making that up," laughed Brian.

"Yeah, maybe I am," Clay admitted, tapping his fingers on his head. "Time does a number on the mind." After a quiet moment Clay said, "Alicia was a great lady."

"Yeah, she sure was," whispered Brian.

*Julia Robertson*

*Tender Dreams*

## Chapter 27

Grace devoted most of her free time away from work to her quilting. Dusting, cleaning and outdoor chores remained at the bottom of her to-do list. It was easier to tell herself it was too hot or too cold to bother with such tasks, even while the weather was perfect. Despite her best efforts to avoid the undesirable tasks, she found herself in the bathroom trying to unclog the bathtub drain. It would have been good to have paid attention to her father's handyman work around the house, but it was too late for that now.

As she uncapped the bottle of drain cleaner, Grace worried about the condition of the pipes beneath the tub. She read the directions, sighed and began emptying the contents into the drain. It glugged slowly, making her wonder how it was going to reach the blockage if it did not go down in the first place. When it stopped glugging and pooled around the drain, she felt dismayed. She set the jug on the side of the tub and left the room. Handyman she was not.

Grace walked into the kitchen and washed her hands with plans to check the drain a little later on. While she dried her hands, she looked out into the back yard. The kitchen faucet dripped constantly. How she wished her father were here to help. Or someone, she thought. She moved the faucet so it made less noise dripping on the middle part of the sink, put the towel over the hanger near the stove and went back to work on the quilt. At least she could accomplish something with her sewing. The cost to repair all the broken things around the house left Grace feeling smothered. She forced her worries to the back of her mind.

Grace finished pressing out the seams on the last sewn sections of fabric and switched off the iron. The next step was sewing the sections to the square pieces of white cotton. She typically pinned together a half dozen pieces at a time and then stitched them in place. Her current quilt project had twenty-four squares. She stacked the pinned sections in sets of six. In order to sew them perfectly flat, Grace used an adjustable wooden frame standing on her worktable. Two 4-inch clamps held it in place. The frame was high enough to keep one hand on the underside of the fabric while she stitched the pieces together. Once all four stacks of six were completed, she would begin pinning the first of the six sections together.

While Grace worked, she listened to an oldies station on the radio. Her parents loved to have music playing and she remembered dancing around the house with her friends when she was a kid. Being an only child made the nights very lonely. Grace was never actually alone since her mother was always there. Those days were gone, and Grace was truly alone.

While The Beach Boys sang about warm summer days, Grace felt time carving new hollows in her heart. She forced her hands to keep working, sliding the pins into place, securing the fabric pieces together.

"Stop thinking about the things you can't change," she scolded herself. "Dreams are a waste of time."

Grace glanced toward the hallway knowing she had to go check on the bathtub drain. Procrastination never fixed anything. She let out a big sigh and headed for the dreaded bathroom. The drain cleaner had seeped out of sight down the drain, so she lifted the bottle and poured out another helping. Once the bottle was down to the halfway point, as the directions instructed, she replaced the cap and set the jug on the floor. Now there was nothing left to do but wait… and hope.

## Chapter 28

On an unseasonably warm June afternoon, Brian stood at a pay phone with his back to the noisy traffic on the road. "I'm out running errands. Have you thought of anything else we need for Erin's party?" he asked.

"No, I'm all set," replied Kathleen. "You have your list, don't you?"

"Yes, thanks. Are you sure about dessert? I can go by the bakery and pick up something."

"Brian, no, I'm all set. Go, before you run out of time."

"Yes ma'am," he said. "You're the best."

Fifteen minutes later Brian lifted a small bicycle into the back seat of his truck and covered it with a tarp. Shortly before Alicia died, she asked him to find a bicycle for Erin's birthday. "She'll be the perfect age to learn how to ride," she said with tears in her eyes.

Brian tapped the bicycle with his fist while her words replayed in his mind. "Shake it off," Brian sighed as he slammed the truck door and backed out of the parking space. By the time he reached the party shop Brian had regained his composure.

"Are you finding everything you need?" chirped the salesgirl.

"Um, maybe," Brian said as he scanned the overwhelming display of merchandise. He held three packages of balloons and reached for a packet of multicolored streamers.

"Who is the party for?" she asked, instantly recognizing his confusion.

"My daughter. She'll be five," Brian replied.

The salesgirl quickly surveyed the items he already had, then turned and picked up a package of colorful party plates decorated with dancing ponies. "Kids her age love these. We have cups, napkins and tablecloths to match. Everything is right here. Let me know if you need more help." She patted his arm before heading down the aisle to the next customer.

Later that night Brian took the shoebox down from the closet shelf. He sat on the bed, leaned back against the headboard and shut his eyes. Each and every one of Alicia's letters broke his heart. He replayed the last one in his mind.

> Dear Brian,
> I want you to read Erin's birthday letter before she celebrates her big day. I don't want to upset her. I only want her to know how much I love her. Please keep reminding them how much I love both of them. Read the letter beforehand and then decide if she is ready for it. Perhaps you will need to put it away until she's older. Make her birthday a happy one. I know this is not easy for you.
> I will always love you,
> Alicia

Brian lifted out the envelope for Erin and ran his fingers over the neatly printed lettering. In the quiet room with the soft light from the lamp on the nightstand, he unfolded the pale pink stationery. His body suddenly felt as cold as ice.

Brian put the letter down on the bed and walked to the window, pressed his hand to the cool glass and looked up at the night sky. Not for the first time he wanted to make a pact with God. Let him talk with Alicia in exchange for him remaining alone for the rest of his life. Or allow him to talk with Alicia if he offered his life to His service once the children were grown. Brian knew his requests were impossible and felt like an idiot. He stared up at the night sky and prayed he would make the right decisions for the future. Feeling more alone than ever, Brian walked back to the bed and picked up the letter. The words swam before his eyes.

> Dear Erin,
> Happy Birthday to my beautiful baby girl. Today is your day to celebrate being 5! I hope your day is filled with balloons and cupcakes, candles and happiness. You have a big year ahead of you. You will learn to jump rope and ride a bicycle. And you will go to school. I'll be with you in your heart as you walk into your new classroom.

You will make new friends and learn many new things.
Always be happy, my sweet little girl. Keep smiling and
find something happy to think about every day.
I love you with all my heart.
Love, Mommy

    Brian studied Alicia's words. It must have been excruciating for her to write it. He folded the single page and tucked it back into the envelope. Erin needed to hear Alicia's words of love for her. He knew he had to share it with her even before he slid the box back on the shelf.

    When he turned back toward the bed his carefully restrained control crumbled. Alicia should be here right now. Here with him. Here for Erin's birthday. Here for him to hold. His breathing grew ragged as he grabbed a pillow and threw it across the room. Heart racing, he fell to his knees.

*Julia Robertson*

*Tender Dreams*

## Chapter 29

Grace worked steadily on the quilt sections. Until her right hand went numb, she hadn't been aware of the frantic pace she had set for herself. She put the last of the squares on the stack before she realized it was dark outside. She scanned her work room, put to mind what she had to do the next day, and then dragged herself off the chair. Her back and shoulders ached. She rubbed her hand as she walked toward the bathroom. A long hot shower soothed her aching body and eased the tension in her shoulders.

Grace absently brushed out her hair as she walked toward her bed. Despite the warm daytime temperatures, the nights cooled down quickly. Grace was so exhausted she did not remember pulling up the comforter. She drifted into the peaceful quiet of deep sleep.

Under the milky white moon, the nightmare returned. Panic gripped her heart when her father's voice urged her on.

"Run faster, Gracie. Keep running, don't stop."

Her breath came in quick harsh bursts. "No, no," cried Grace. She was not, was not going to make it. Grace awoke overheated and crying for help. She shoved the comforter away, pulled her knees up and wrapped her arms around them. Her body shook with terror as she pressed her forehead against her arms and wept.

The same full moon splashed bits of hazy white light across the room as Erin silently came up beside Brian's bed.

"Daddy," she whispered, wiggling underneath the comforter and patting his cheek. "Daddy, hold me."

Brian inched his way out of sleep and pried his eyelids open. "Erin," he mumbled. He turned his hand over and felt her fingers wrap around his thumb. "Hey, what's wrong?" he asked as he rolled over and pulled her close.

"Bad dream," Erin said.

"Okay, go back to sleep. I'm right here." Brian stared into the dark. Erin seemed to have bad dreams almost every night and he had no idea how to prevent them. Alicia's death had left an indelible impression on their daughter. Was she going to carry the loss throughout her life? How was he going to help her learn from the tragedy and grow to accept it when he could not do it himself? The dark shadow of depression kept pace with his every step. What was going to happen to Erin and Jack if it swallowed him up? He ran his hand over her mussed hair and prayed for peace for all of them.

Across town, staring out into the moonlit trees, Clay lay awake unable to clear his mind. He kept imagining all the things that might be wrong with his eyes. While he tried to convince himself he only needed prescription glasses the unease kept growing.

He clumsily rolled off the bed when he realized he had forgotten the eye drops again. Not using them was not going to help. When he reached out in the dark to pick up the little bottle, he knocked it on the floor. He regretfully flipped up the light switch. "What the," he groaned with his hand over his eyes.

After a minute his eyes adjusted to the bright light. Clay found the bottle in the far corner next to the tub. Hands unsteady from fatigue, he breathed in and out until his mind calmed. He positioned the dropper above his right eye and squeezed out a single drop. Before he lost his nerve, he repeated the procedure with his left eye. He capped the bottle, flipped off the light and made his way back to his bed.

Clay knew he had to give the medication time to work. He cursed himself for waiting so long to fill the prescription. Wished he could clear his mind and fall asleep.

His mind kept flashing back to the past. He was inside the cave with his grandmother. She pointed out all the sea creatures lurking inside the tiny holes in the walls of the cave. He thought of his sister and wondered when he had last talked to her. Janine was two years older and altogether different from him. She was married, had three kids and juggled home, kids and a job with apparent ease. He admired her tenacity. Maybe he ought to go visit her when he and Brian took a week off. Soon, he thought, soon he would catch up on family stuff. The final images of Alicia came back with a rush. He could not understand how Brian functioned after losing her. He probably would have taken his gun and blown his brains out if he had been in Brian's place. Just end it all and be done with it. "Chickenshit," Clay mumbled before he finally fell asleep.

## Chapter 30

When Brian finished tacking balloons and streamers to the underside of the patio cover, he went inside and found Kathleen putting a black lacquered tray filled with cupcakes on the kitchen table. She had made pink cupcakes with pink frosting, pink sprinkles and pink candles. Erin was pink-crazy, and Kathleen clearly loved it.

"The decorations are wonderful," Kathleen said when she turned away from the table.

"Thanks, those cupcakes look super," Brian said, inching closer to the table. "Maybe I ought to test one for you." Brian laughed when Kathleen shook her finger and stepped in front of him. Far from being a threat at five foot nothing, Brian held up both hands in mock surrender.

"Behave," ordered Kathleen.

"Yes, ma'am," laughed Brian.

"What's on the menu?" asked Kathleen.

"Erin chose corn dogs, dill pickles and fruit salad," Brian replied.

Thumping footsteps told them the kids were on the way to the kitchen. Brian laughed when Kathleen tried to hide the cupcakes by standing in front of them. Erin and Jack were closing in when a knock at the front door caught everyone's attention. Brian plucked Jack up from the floor and said, "Erin, you may answer the door."

"Okay," Erin shouted on the run.

Once Brian and Kathleen saw Clay at the door, they went back to work on the party preparations. Kathleen immediately hid the cupcakes in an upper cupboard. With Jack on his shoulders, Brian picked up the napkins and plates and headed outside. He heard Erin's delightful laughter through the open window.

"Hey, there's the birthday girl!" Clay exclaimed.

"I'm five!" Erin sang out as she danced circles around Clay. "I'm five!"

Clay squatted down and set two brightly wrapped packages on the floor. "Let me see five, Lady Erin," he said as he caught her in a hug. "I believe you're much bigger than when you were four."

"This is my best day," Erin said leaning back from their hug.

"Happy birthday. Where's the party?" Clay asked.

"We're having a picnic in the back yard," Erin replied.

"Okay, let's go," Clay said as he scooped up Erin and the gifts and walked out through the kitchen.

"Look!" squealed Erin.

"Awesome," laughed Clay. The underside of the patio cover was a sea of bright pink balloons. "What's with the red one?" Clay asked.

"Jack likes red." Erin twisted around and asked, "Do you like pink?"

"Sure, as long as you're the one wearing it," Clay replied.

"Look, look," Erin giggled, reaching up and touching several streamers.

Curling ribbons in blue, purple, yellow, green and red danced in the light breeze, adding a festive flare to the small gathering. The food was on the table with party plates and napkins.

"We get corn dogs," Erin said. "My most favorite."

"Yum," said Clay. "Where do I put the birthday girl?"

"Right here. How are you doing?" Brian asked, noting the fatigue on his friend's face. He watched Clay put Erin down on her chair and stack his gifts on the card table behind her. The timer ringing at the open kitchen window drew Brian's attention away from Clay. "I'll be right back. The main course is ready," Brian said as he headed inside.

Following Kathleen's cupcakes and Erin's delightful response to her gifts, the birthday party grew quiet. Brian watched Erin lick the last of the pink icing from her fingers. With Jack perched up on Clay's shoulders, Brian decided it was time for another surprise. He lifted Erin out of her chair, then led her across the patio.

"We have one more present for you. Wait right here," Brian told his daughter.

Without another word, he ran around the corner of the house. When he returned with the pink bicycle, the look on Erin's face was priceless. She did not squeal as he had expected, but stood wide-eyed with her hands covering her mouth.

"This is my best birthday," she said as she wrapped her arms around his neck and squeezed with all her might. "Thank you," she whispered and kissed his cheek.

"You're welcome, baby. Do you like the color?" asked Brian.

"It's so pretty. But," Erin said with a frown.

"Erin, five is the perfect age to learn. Mommy and I love you," he whispered and kissed her.

"Mommy," sobbed Erin. "I want her to be here. I need to hug her too."

"I know. Hug me for her," Brian said. Erin turned and wrapped her warm arms around his neck.

Brian watched Clay lift Jack down from his shoulders. He was pretty sure Jack had seen Erin's reaction as well as her tears.

When Clay held Jack's hand up and kissed his palm, Brian smiled. He knew Jack's hand was sticky with icing, but it did not seem to bother Clay. Jack's deep laughter filled the quiet. All the while Kathleen snapped photographs, capturing Erin's birthday for later enjoyment. Brian felt blessed to have good friends who were willing to help him cope with his loss. Friends to help him sort through his troubled feelings. Friends who seemed to understand him better than he understood himself. With their help Brian felt Erin and Jack were getting plenty of attention.

Brian heard Kathleen's camera snapping another shot with Erin's hands on his face. Alicia's love was still alive and thriving.

Later that night Brian read Alicia's letter to Erin. When he finished, she touched the paper in his hand.

"Daddy," she whispered. "Can we keep it? Keep it always?"

"Yes, we love you," said Brian.

"I love you and Mommy," murmured Erin.

Brian knew he had made the right decision. Today had been a good day. A small sense of peace stole into his heart, but he knew better than to think it was going to last. Alicia should have been here to celebrate with them. He silently wept while he held Erin and watched Jack color with his red crayon.

*Julia Robertson*

## Chapter 31

Clay stayed at Brian's house long enough to help clean up after the party mess. On his way home he thought of Erin's reaction to the gifts he had found for her. She squealed with delight upon opening the box containing the pretty pink sandals. She instantly pulled off her shoes to try them on. The pink T-shirt embroidered with a small crown and the words: "Lady Erin" pleased her as well. Best of all were the thank you hugs he received afterward.

With the memories of the afternoon drifting away, Clay remembered heading out of town after high school, ready to take on the world. "Who needs rules?" he always told himself. "Who needs limitations?" he scolded his dear mother. He drove too fast, partied too hard and knew he was lucky to have survived for so long. Was Jack going to do the same stupid things as a teenager? He prayed not. Life was too precious for such crap, but he knew he had only recently gained that perspective. Being close to Brian while he was losing Alicia taught him what was most important in life.

As he rolled to a stop at the signal, Clay looked out the open passenger side window. A young boy in an old VW Bug glanced his way and gave him a thumb's up.

"Great car!" the kid shouted.

Clay had to laugh. Most people thought his car looked like a slapped together piece of shit, but the kid knew better. It took a keen eye to see the potential in his car.

As he accelerated and the Bug disappeared around the corner, Clay experienced a momentary bout of dizziness. The creepy sensation passed and left him feeling slightly out of touch with himself. Clay attributed it to the fading light. That was it, he thought, rubbing his eyes. He had heard about people with problems seeing at dusk when the light was fading and not yet overtaken by dark. There was no other way to explain it. Once he felt back in control Clay brushed the incident out of his mind and focused on the sound of the engine.

*Julia Robertson*

## Chapter 32

Brian checked the time before dialing the phone number from the wrinkled scrap of paper. He had about five minutes of quiet time left before the kids usually woke up. He should have made the call weeks ago, but it did not matter now. Between being preoccupied with work, the kids and his constant feelings of inadequacy, it was all he could do to get through the long list of everyday tasks. The coffee pot gurgled behind him while he listened to the phone ringing in his ear. His unease had him turning to hang up when the call was answered. A moment later he was put on hold.

"Good morning, Brian," Garrison said.

"Hello, sir," Brian began awkwardly. "I apologize for taking so long to get back to you."

"No need for that," Garrison said. "I presume you have made a decision, have you not?"

Brian tightened his hold on the phone, already feeling on edge. He forced his fingers to relax before replying, "I'm willing to give it a shot."

"When will you be coming to meet with me?" Garrison asked.

"I can't afford to take any time off right now," Brian replied.

"I see," Garrison said.

Brian rubbed his forehead, hoping he had not made a mistake by making the call. Maybe he should have tossed the number in the trash. Brian did not relish confrontations. After a minute of silence passed, Brian said, "Sir?"

"I will make arrangements to fly out in the near future. Of course, I will check to be sure the time and date are convenient for you," Garrison explained.

"That's fine, sir," replied Brian.

"I will make reservations to stay in a hotel while I am there. I am looking forward to meeting with you and your children," Garrison added.

"Yes sir. Look, I need to get my day going," Brian said. He was grateful when the conversation came to an end.

Brian poured hot coffee into a mug. Before it cooled enough to drink, he knew his quiet time was over. He set the mug down at the back of the counter and watched Jack plodding toward him. His little bare feet slapped against the hardwood floor.

"Hey, big boy," Brian said as he leaned down to pick him up. "You need to wake up before you get out of bed."

Brian kissed Jack's sleepy warm face and thought of Alicia. Every day brought changes to his life. Jack was growing so fast and Brian felt ill at ease about the future. "We need you, Alicia," he thought silently. Brian ran his fingers through Jack's silky hair. "Let's go potty and I'll fix your breakfast."

Brian was pouring milk into Jack's cereal bowl when Kathleen opened the front door. She wore her usual bright smile and carried a paper sack along with her bulky tote bag. "Look who's here!" he called out.

"Did you bring the puzzles?" Erin asked, skidding to a stop in front of Kathleen.

"Breakfast first, Erin. We have all day for projects. Scoot," laughed Kathleen. "Good morning, Brian. I see everyone is up early."

"Some things never change," he said. "Puzzles?"

"I told them I had some old jigsaw puzzles somewhere at home and I actually found them," she laughed. "Stirred up more dust than I care to admit having in my house. I think I sneezed a dozen times."

"Cleared the cobwebs," he remarked.

"And then some," agreed Kathleen. "If you're coming home for lunch, I can make up a meatloaf sandwich for you."

"Count on it," Brian replied. He hugged Erin and kissed the top of Jack's head. The boy was totally absorbed with capturing the floating bits of cereal in the bowl. "You kids be good. See you later."

Leaving the children in Kathleen's care freed Brian to concentrate on his job. Try as he might, he could not let go of the unease he felt when he opened the door at home each night. He found himself holding his breath waiting for Alicia to call out to him.

Brian sighed as he stepped up into his truck and pulled out onto the road. Work on the houses progressed at a steady clip. The only delays came when scheduled inspections ran late. Joking about their late arrivals eased the tense moments. The only serious distractions of late had been Clay and his health problems.

## Chapter 33

Decision made, Clay turned back toward the house where the crew was busy setting windows in place. The eye drops were not doing any good at all. Going back to the doctor for today's appointment was a waste of time and money. Staying here at the work site was far more productive. They needed every hand they had to complete the work scheduled for the last two weeks of July. Clay mentally ran down the list of tasks he could handle on his own. Curling his fingers into his palms as his boots crunched the gravel underfoot, he did not notice Brian bearing down on him.

"You're out of here, Hancock," Brian demanded.

Clay was caught off guard when Brian yanked his tool belt out of his hand. "What the hell," he snarled. The next thing he knew Brian was shoving him toward his truck. It took a few steps to catch his balance again.

"I expect you back here within the hour. Move your ass," Brian ordered.

"Brian, come on," argued Clay. "I'm fine. Let me do my work." Clay knocked Brian's hands away and started back toward the house.

"Danny, give me a hand over here!" shouted Brian.

Clay looked over his shoulder and saw the younger man coming toward him. "Brian, knock it off. Let it go, damn it," groaned Clay. He did not feel up to an argument.

"Grab him. Let's go," Brian said, dropping the tool belt on the ground.

"You got it, Boss," Danny said as he easily restrained Clay. "Where do you want him?"

"In his truck," Brian said as he lifted Clay's booted feet off the ground.

"Not funny, Brian!" yelled Clay. He felt stupid for what they were doing to him, but he lacked the strength to fight them off. His only response came verbally. Worthless words he knew would not discourage Brian, but he let them fly anyway. "Put me down, you bastards!"

"You're in no position to be name calling. I'm the boss and you're going so shut the hell up," Brian said as they approached Clay's truck. "Do I need to send Danny with you, or will you be able to get there on your own?"

Clay felt Danny's firm grip even after Brian dropped his boots to the ground. "This is horseshit, and you know it," groaned Clay.

"Good enough. Thanks Danny," Brian said. "You need to see the doctor today. Please go," Brian said softly.

"Yeah, yeah, I'm going. Shit, I feel like a ten-year-old," Clay grumbled. He brushed off his pants before pulling the truck door open. Once he regained his composure Clay looked back at Brian. "Thanks, Boss," he said as he stepped up into the cab. Though he knew Brian was rattled by their exchange, Clay was confident no permanent damage had been done to their friendship. He watched Brian walk away, saw him pick up the discarded tool belt and grinned.

Clay spent over two hours at the doctor's office. Besides looking deep inside his head through his eyeballs, the doctor sent him to the lab on the ground floor. Looked like they took enough of his blood to fill a five-gallon bucket.

"I want to see you back here next Thursday," said Dr. Baxter.

"So, what's going on, Doc?" asked Clay. Everything including the man's face appeared distorted through his dilated eyes.

"I honestly don't know. It takes time," the doctor replied.

"Yeah, well, all right." Clay felt uneasy. He felt certain the man knew more than he was letting on.

"Thursday, Clay," Dr. Baxter repeated.

Clay walked past the appointment desk and out into the hallway before he stopped. "Idiot," he growled as he turned around. The woman at the counter smiled as she set up his appointment for the following week. Though he could not quite bring her face into focus, he saw enough to know she was attractive. He took note of her sea-green eyes and glossy black hair. He considered asking her out and started formulating the request when her wedding rings glistened in the bright overhead lights. The disappointment he felt only added to his glum mood.

Clay headed back to the work site wondering if the appointment had been worth the trouble. Was he supposed to keep using the eye drops?

"What time on Thursday?" asked Brian.

"Maybe 5 o'clock," Clay said as he pulled the appointment card out of his shirt pocket and handed it to Brian. He had not been able to make out the small print on the card.

"Okay, 6 o'clock, that's no problem," Brian said, tapping the card on the countertop. "We ought to be finished up by then. You look worn out."

"Yeah, they took most of my blood back there. Don't know what they do with so much of it, but maybe that's what's making me feel kind of wacky," Clay said as he waggled his hand in front of him.

"Hang on, I'll be right back," said Brian.

Clay lost all sense of time when he tumbled head-first into a freakish light show. Hot white sparks flashed all around him. His hands grew too warm. His mind reeled. His knees shook.

"Hey," Brian said.

Clay felt like the hands of the devil were pulling him into hell. He wanted to cry out, but he could barely breathe. Strong hands pushed him back and shoved him down.

"Clay," Brian said firmly. "This is orange juice, drink it, it will help."

*Julia Robertson*

## Chapter 34

Grace rarely left work early, but once she caught up with everything she jumped on the opportunity to go home. She stepped out of the newspaper office into the warm afternoon sunshine and closed her eyes. It was a beautiful summer day in mid-July. Half an hour later Grace loaded two bags of groceries onto the back seat of her car and headed for home. After putting the groceries away, she changed into denim shorts and a ragged green sweatshirt with the sleeves torn off. Bucket in hand, she headed outside to wash her car.

Since reading the obit for the young woman, Grace had not been able to shake it off. "I'd be too afraid to do anything," she decided, talking to herself while she scrubbed the dirty car. "Maybe I'd make a list of the things I most wanted to do. Disney World? Ireland, for sure. Maybe New Zealand."

Grace stopped scrubbing and looked up at the sky. "What if Alicia was too sick to make a list? What if she lost everything without enough time to plan?"

Grace tried to imagine being in Alicia's place. The image that came to mind was a narrow bed in a dark room. Her own pathetic obituary came to mind once again. The key words were lonely, lost and unwanted. Grace knew she did not deserve anything better. She fisted her hands and forced her bitter tears to stop.

An hour later Grace was still thinking about Alicia and her family. Grace guessed her children were very young, unless she married a man who already had a family. How were they coping with the loss of their mother? Or the loss of their stepmother, she thought. She silently scolded herself for speculating about someone she did not know and dragged her mind back to the here and now.

The afternoon was slipping away. In the kitchen Grace rolled four chicken legs in sesame seeds and paprika, then set them into a foil lined dish. She cut several little red potatoes in quarters and rolled them in olive oil. After dusting the potatoes with garlic salt and chili powder, she slid both dishes into the hot oven. She set the timer and walked out into the back yard.

Grace's parents had always kept the yard immaculate, but it had grown out of control over the past few years. It looked more like a back-to-nature study than a garden. Frowning, Grace walked around trying to build up her enthusiasm for what needed doing. Resting her hand on the trunk of an old maple tree, she closed her eyes and almost felt her father standing next to her.

"The flowers grow on their own, Gracie. We're here to help them out," he explained.

"But Dad, if they grow on their own why do we need to take care of them?" complained Grace, a teenager with other things on her mind.

"The flowers, like the trees and the grass, are gifts from God. We are the caretakers of it all. It's up to us to give them fertilizer and make space for them to grow by pulling the weeds and trimming the dead flowers. Trust me, I know this is true," her father explained patiently.

"If you say so. Where do we start?" young Grace sighed.

"Where do I start?" Grace said, alone in the yard. Alone in her life. The tears came, unwanted and unstoppable. "If only," she whispered, sinking once again into the black sea of regret.

Grace gathered her wits and once again glanced around the yard. The obvious starting point was to rake up the dead leaves and find what was hidden beneath them. A little here and there, she decided as she walked toward the shed. She slid the door open, recalling her father's pride when he had built the wooden structure. He told her it was her bedroom back when she was a kid.

"Just big enough for a pipsqueak like you," he had teased.

The six-by-six-foot room had a low ceiling, a metal floor and hooks mounted along the walls. She reached out for the closest rake, determined to put some of the work behind her before her dinner was ready.

## Chapter 35

Anna absently flipped through a magazine while she sat alone in Paige's living room. Quiet moments like this were rare. Paige preferred having the television or radio on all the time. She sighed when the telephone rang and wished Paige was home from the grocery store. She hesitated before finally answering it.

"Hello," she said meekly.

"Anna? This is Garrison. How are you?"

"I'm fine, sir," she replied. It seemed strange to have telephone conversations with him. Since receiving Alicia's letter and filing for divorce from Contessa, Anna knew Garrison spent a lot of time contemplating his past mistakes. Anna had been working part-time keeping his new house clean and preparing some of his meals over the past few months, but still lived here with Paige. Though it was only a minor slice of independence, it was helping her in her search for peace in her life.

Anna might never tell anyone how damaged her spirit was after being under Contessa's reign for so many years. The truth of it was she should have left shortly after she started working for Contessa. Anna was weak, a trait she knew was visible from the outside. Anna sighed, still holding the telephone to her ear.

"Good," Garrison replied. "Anna, please accompany me to dinner tonight. I know this is short notice, but please accept my invitation."

"Me?" Anna asked with stunned surprise.

"Please come with me, Anna," Garrison urged.

"Tonight? Me? But," she began to argue.

"No buts, Anna. I will see you at 6 o'clock," he said, discontinuing the call without another word.

Anna held the telephone in her hand in a mild state of shock. "Dinner?" she mumbled.

When Paige came in with a bag of groceries a short time later, she found Anna staring at the wall. "What is it? Is there something wrong with the paint?" she asked with alarm. Paige rushed across the room, put the grocery bag on the floor and reached out for Anna's hand. "Anna, what's wrong with you?"

"I think I have a date," whispered Anna.

"Oh my goodness, Anna, that's great!" exclaimed Paige. "When? Where? Who?"

"What time is it?" Anna asked when she realized she might already be late.

"Half past five. What time are you leaving?" Paige asked, bursting into laughter when Anna jumped up from the chair and ran toward the bathroom. "Someone has the jitters," she whispered.

Anna felt like crying when the doorbell rang a short time later. She dropped down on the bed, wishing to be as small as a mouse so she could hide under it. Anna never dated. In fact, Anna could count the times she had actually gone out with someone on the fingers of one hand. She had no idea what to do. "I can't do this. Tell him I'm sick. Tell him I left town. Tell him anything," she begged her best friend. When Paige left the bedroom, Anna found herself holding her breath. She did not expect to hear the words that came next.

"She'll be right out, Garrison. Come in and sit down," Paige said. "I'll be right back."

Anna held her hands over her face, too stunned to cry. "You didn't," she groaned.

"Life is too short to hide in here," scolded Paige, grabbing Anna's hands and pulling her to her feet. "You look fine. He wants to spend time with you. I say give him a chance. Trust me, Anna, trust me."

When she finally settled down enough to think, Anna found herself being driven away from Paige's house. With Garrison, she realized with alarm. Anna became aware of her hands clenching together on her lap and forced them to relax. A million butterflies fluttered in her stomach.

"Anna, where do you prefer to dine?" Garrison slowed for a traffic light and looked over at her. "Anna?"

"Nowhere fancy, sir. I'm not dressed for fancy," confessed Anna. "Do you mind?"

"I want to take you where you like to go," he replied.

"Well, there's a nice little cafe near here. It's quiet and the food is good. Paige is friends with the owners. Is that okay with you?"

"Certainly," agreed Garrison.

Anna did not dare ask if Garrison had ever been seated in a booth or eaten at a table without a tablecloth. When she thought about it, she had never eaten in an elegant restaurant. She never considered herself worthy of candlelight dinners or expensive wines. She glanced over at Garrison, then quickly looked away when she found him watching her. She had never felt so utterly out of her league.

Garrison pulled into the parking lot and eased the car to a stop. "Anna," he said as he extracted the keys and held them tight in his hand. "I am just as nervous as you," he finally admitted.

Anna was not sure what to say. Overwhelmed, she once again looked away. "I'm sorry," she said, the words coming out on their own.

"There is nothing to be sorry for," Garrison said. "We are stepping into territory neither of us is familiar with. At least that is how it feels for me. I must admit I have feelings for you, but I need time to process the changes I am going through. Anna, please be patient with me."

Anna felt the corners of her mouth turn up. She couldn't say it, but she had feelings for him too. She touched his hand, then patted it lightly. "Let's go inside and get something to eat," she suggested.

*Julia Robertson*

## Chapter 36

Clay did his best to forget it was Thursday. Maybe he ought to cancel the damned doctor's appointment and keep working. He dreaded being cooped up in an airless office while the doctor flipped through a stack of lab papers. These days the doctor could call in the prescription and save both of them a lot of bother. They always printed the instructions for dosage and all that crap on the little labels.

Agitated, Clay began checking the work in the master bathroom to be sure everything was up to snuff for the tilers. He crossed to the oversized jetted tub and scanned the garden window. The translucent glass let sunlight in during the day, but guaranteed privacy for anyone using the room. Though interior decorating was not his thing, Clay envisioned the window filled with lush green plants and an array of stained-glass candle holders. Black and white ceramic tiles were ready to be set in place on the floor, as well as at either end of the tub to create a water-friendly backsplash.

Clay reached out to touch the burnished faucet at the same time his vision went white. Knocked off balance he crumpled to his knees. For the first time in his life Clay felt real fear. The sickening reality he might actually be losing his sight hit him like a brick. Everything in his life would take a direct hit. His job, his independence and his privacy. Confusion mixed violently with terror until his insides twisted into knots.

Alone in the house, alone with the fear, Clay held tight to the side of the tub.

For all he knew he had been there for hours when someone grasped his shoulder. "What the hell," he blurted out.

"Hey, I thought you heard me," said Brian. "What's going on?"

Clay wanted to tell Brian to go away and leave him to his misery. The white fog was clearing, but was it enough to hide what he had just experienced?

"I don't know, my stomach, it's killing me," Clay replied after a moment of deliberation. Not the whole truth, but it was all he was willing to reveal.

"Would something hot help? Coffee, hot chocolate, something, anything?" Brian asked.

Clay shook his head. "Nothing," he muttered.

"When do you see the doctor?" Brian asked.

"Late," replied Clay.

"I'll call and get you in sooner," Brian said.

Without a word, Clay raised his middle finger at Brian. The message was conveyed loud and clear.

"Okay, I give, but," Brian said.

"Go away," muttered Clay.

"Whatever," Brian sighed.

Clay shifted sideways and sat down on the floor. He rubbed his hands over his face in a futile attempt to dispel his fears. If the worst came to be, how much time did he have left to see?

Clay did not realize Brian was gone until he heard heavy boot steps outside the bathroom door. He glanced up when Brian stepped into the room and sat down on the floor next to him. Neither of them said anything for a few minutes.

"Sorry, man," Clay apologized.

"Forget it," replied Brian. "Any idea what's wrong?"

"No," Clay whispered. His vision seemed normal now, but the shock was enough to make him wonder when it was going to happen again.

"I can go to the doctor with you," said Brian. "I owe you big time for all you've done for me."

Clay rested his head back against the wall and closed his eyes. Then he asked, "Did Alicia dream after she got sick?"

"What?" Brian blurted out. "Why are you asking about that?"

"Did she?" Clay asked, turning his head and studying the alarmed expression on his friend's face.

"I'm not sure, maybe," Brian replied. "Um, maybe she didn't. I mean once she knew. Damn, once we knew she wasn't going to," he said without finishing his thoughts.

"Okay," said Clay. "I used to think life was just a one-way ride. You know, birth, life, death, nothing more, nothing less. I'm rethinking it all now."

"How's that?" Brian asked.

Clay knew Brian was upset with the topic of their conversation. He stared up at the unpainted ceiling before going on. "I think it goes beyond this life. You know, like a hereafter or an eternal resting place or something, I don't know. Did Alicia believe in God and Heaven?"

"Yes, she did," whispered Brian. "Why are you asking me this stuff?"

"I miss her," Clay said, looking over at Brian once again.

"Yeah," agreed Brian.

Clay knew it would never be easy for Brian. "Is it hard seeing her in Erin's eyes?" Clay asked.

"Not exactly," Brian replied. "Erin does have a lot of Alicia's ways. It's like Alicia left a part of herself in Erin, you know."

"I think you're right about that," Clay said, then went on. "I bet you will see more of her in Jack when he's older. He's more like you, but when he gets sad, I see Alicia."

"Yeah," agreed Brian. "It's strange. They're like miniature people with all the complex feelings growing inside them."

"It's great, isn't it," sighed Clay.

Both men looked up when Danny appeared in the doorway. Clay suspected it was Brian's doings.

"Here you go, Boss," Danny said as he handed down two Styrofoam cups. "They're hot."

"What the hell is this?" Clay asked, narrowing his eyes at the two cups.

"Shut up," growled Brian. "Hot chocolate, hot apple cider. Choose one, have both."

"I'll take the hot chocolate. You keep that one. Real men don't drink crap like that," Clay stated clearly. He took the cup and watched Brian sip the apple cider. "Wimp," he muttered, raising the cup to hide his smile.

"Jerk," Brian laughed.

Later that day, Clay met with Brian before leaving for his appointment. So far the earlier events with his vision had not reoccurred. For all he knew he was blowing the whole thing out of proportion.

"See you early tomorrow, right?" Clay said.

"Yeah, let's get the trim finished in the kitchen first thing. I'll be ready when you come by," Brian added.

"You got it, Boss," Clay said before turning toward his truck. He had not taken a single step before turning back to Brian. Their eyes locked as Clay reached out to shake his friend's hand. He almost said what he was feeling but being a man, he held it back. Had he said, "I love you," out loud he might have caused them both some level of embarrassment. The moment passed and the sound of the crew working nearby reminded him to get moving. "See you tomorrow," Clay said before he turned away.

He stepped up into his truck and watched the other men for a few minutes. It felt good to know Bill could take charge without question. The crew worked together with ease, but it was he and Brian who were the best of friends. In fact, Brian was the brother Clay never had.

Before he drove out onto the road, Clay watched Brian walk over to the men and rest his hand on Bill's shoulder. Brian exuded calm and assurance in everything he did. He put everyone at ease in any given situation. Clay always felt like Brian's equal. If they had grown up together, they would have built the most fantastic tree houses.

Clay headed for his place to get a shower and change into clean clothes. He ignored the sickening feelings creeping back into his head, focused on the road and the incoming clouds out on the horizon. Had the local weather guys predicted rain?

## Chapter 37

Billowing black storm clouds rose up over the mountains late Thursday afternoon. Fierce winds pulled at the edges of the clouds, stretched them out across the valley, blocked the sun and turned day into night. Blinding white lightning streaked through the darkened sky an instant before booming thunder rolled from one side of the valley to the other. The sudden downpour overwhelmed storm drains and turned every street into a raging river. Wielding her merciless power, Mother Nature drew their lives together with immediate and irrevocable results.

Bob Maxx began the steep downgrade into town with a load of pipe behind his tractor trailer, brooding over his upcoming vacation. His wife's plans to go on a cruise continued to fuel his anxiety. He hated the prospect of floating out on the middle of the ocean, but Nina deserved something special for having put up with him being on the road all these years. When he called her at their usual time tonight, she would tell him what they were bringing, what she still needed to buy, and what he needed to do before they left. Nina's notes and lists were posted all over the house. She stuck them on the refrigerator, the bathroom mirror, the headboard on the bed and even on the dashboard in the car. The storm and the heavy rain increased Bob's misery. He grimaced as he settled his boot on the brake pedal to slow the truck.

The image of a cruise ship bobbing on the ocean flashed before his eyes. A crack suddenly opened wide in the side of the ship and water began gushing in. The ship tipped with one end up in the air and began sinking like a rock.

Terror ripped through his mind when he saw himself grasping the ship's gleaming steel railing with both hands, holding on for dear life. Smothering panic sucked all the air from his lungs and Bob lapsed into unconsciousness. His head dropped down lower and lower until it thudded against the cold steering wheel. He had no idea how much time had passed when he jerked upright and focused on the road again. He stood on the brake pedal, but it was too late. He would never be able to stop the truck in time. Frantic, he sounded the horn and prayed for a miracle as he approached the traffic lights.

    Bob Maxx felt the truck's big tires sliding on the rain slicked road. He had to keep the truck going straight in order to keep the load behind him. If the trailer swung around or the load shifted and dumped the outcome could be catastrophic. It all happened in the blink of an eye.

## Chapter 38

While he waited for the traffic light to change, Clay ran his hands over his face. The raging storm matched his dark mood and closed him off from the rest of the world. He replayed the half hour visit with the doctor, wondering if he had missed something vital. When he asked the doctor about his chances, the man had looked away from him.

"Come on, Doc," Clay insisted. "Just spill it out."

"I can only guess at this point," the doctor began. "Your vision has already diminished. The loss of sight might be temporary. Maybe two months, or perhaps two years. You may be able to read large print, see light and color, or you might lose it altogether. You will see the difference before we see any changes. It might also be permanent. Please, I want you to," Dr. Baxter said, then stopped.

Raising his hands in objection, Clay shook his head. "Yeah, okay, I got it. Thanks." Clay stood up and walked to the door. He reached out, grasped the doorknob and turned back. "It can't be stopped?" He watched the doctor's grim expression as he shook his head.

"I want you to see a specialist up north, but it has to be done right away, without delay," Dr. Baxter explained. "I'll arrange it for you."

Clay pulled the door open and looked back again. "I'll think on it," he said and walked away.

Once Clay was outside, he lifted his eyes to the storm darkened sky. The rain ran over his face and down his neck. It soaked through his T-shirt, but he did not care. "I put it all in Your hands," he whispered before turning toward the parking lot. He slid inside his car and drew in a calming breath before heading home.

As the heavy downpour continued, Clay slowed to a stop and wondered if he would ever sleep again. The reality of losing his sight suddenly overwhelmed him. His earlier fears were coming true. How was he going to function on a day-to-day basis?

"What about work? What about my house, and my car? Hell, my very own pity party," he groaned, disgusted with his lousy attitude. "Remember how Alicia handled losing her life. Think of what Brian has to deal with every day. Don't give up," he told himself. "Whatever comes, I'll accept it. It's in Your hands."

He figured God was probably hanging around somewhere in the storm clouds. Clay stepped on the accelerator when the light turned green. In the space of a heartbeat his vision failed, leaving him enveloped in total darkness.

## Chapter 39

Grace drove toward home after an exhausting day at work. Between the remnants of a summer cold and numerous haunting dreams, she felt slightly out of touch with reality. She stopped at the red light wishing she had left work earlier. Lightning flashed in the premature darkness and momentarily lit up the intersection ahead of her. While the rain pounded the roof of her car, Grace listened for the next clap of thunder. She imagined watching the storm through the skylight she did not have. Imagined laying back on the floor while the clouds darkened.

Grace let her wishful thoughts go and looked all around her. Something felt wrong. She struggled to focus on what it was, but everything felt out of order tonight. The wind buffeted her car while the windshield wipers worked in vain to clear off the rain. The traffic lights swung crazily, creating distorted reflections in the water on the surface of the road.

Grace let her imagination dispel some of her unease. She envisioned a country road where a man on horseback rode with his black cape flying in the wind. He kept his head ducked low, unable to see while protecting his face from the bitter cold rain. Overshadowing the image, Grace felt her unease growing stronger. The air suddenly became colder and she shivered in her light cotton blouse.

Last night's dream returned in bits and pieces, a chaotic jumble of sounds, blood and shattered glass. Grace leaned forward, trying to discover what was wrong. Her fear increased with every mad swish of the windshield wipers.

She heard a horn blaring but could not tell which direction it was coming from. Grace lowered her window, ignored the rain pouring in and listened intently. Once again she heard the horn. It seemed to be getting closer.

When the light changed to green, she trusted her instincts and stayed put. At first she did not see any other cars nearby, but then she spotted the battered car she had seen at the airport. Even through the pouring rain she knew it was the same car and it was moving into the intersection. Grace gasped and held her hand up in warning.

"No!" Grace screamed. "The truck! Stop!" she cried helplessly as the car drove further into the wide intersection.

The tragedy unfolded right before her eyes. It played out like a scene from a horror movie. Lightning cast the intersection in spectacular white light while the thunderclap drowned out the sound of the tractor trailer hitting the car. In a flash the car spun away from the truck and shot across the water on the road. It hit the curb, flipped up and smashed into the light pole on the corner. When it landed with two tires in the gutter, the gas tank ruptured. One final flash of lightning cut through the dark sky, followed by a deafening explosion of thunder. The rain kept falling as the storm moved out of the valley.

Grace gasped with disbelief. Had the accident really happened? She blinked, but the wrecked car was still there.

Grace pushed her door open and ran faster than she had ever run before. The chance the children might also be in the car wrenched at her heart. Bits of the dream came to life as she reached out for the driver's door. The smell of gasoline grew stronger and she knew she had to hurry. Using both hands, she fought to pry the door open.

"You need to get out," Grace cried as she searched for the seat belt release button. As she dragged the belt out of the way Grace quickly scanned the back seat and felt some sense of relief in finding it empty. She didn't take time to consider the size of the injured man compared to her own much smaller body.

Charged with adrenalin, Grace slid in behind the man, reached under his arms and pulled him out of the car. They landed hard on the rough asphalt where water and gasoline streamed around them. Without delay, Grace dragged the man away from the car. When Grace felt they were a safe distance from danger, she eased him down and leaned over to shield him from the rain. Cradling him against her own body, she tried to see his face.

"Help is coming. Can you hear me?" Grace cried, gently wiping the blood away from his eyes. "Hang on. Please don't let go," she wept. Her tears mingled with the rain running down her face.

With an incredible whoosh, the car caught fire behind them. Flames shot into the air and swept over the pavement, radiating intense heat across the intersection.

Grace felt the ground quake beneath her, but she did not let it distract her attention from the injured man. "You're not alone, I'm right here," she said when he moved slightly. She strained to hear him over the noise from the fire and the rain.

"Tell, tell Brian Cooper. My will, my will," he whispered hoarsely.

"I hear you," assured Grace. She did not need to see him clearly to recognize the pain he was suffering. His body shivered against her.

"My Will, my sock drawer," he said. "Please, please tell Brian."

Fearing there was little time left, Grace tightened her hold on him. "What's your name?" she asked desperately. The words were barely out of her mouth when images of his children suddenly flashed before her. His beautiful children. "Hang on, they need you, please," she cried out. Grace watched his eyes flutter open again. "Your name," she begged.

"Clay," he gasped before drawing in a ragged breath.

Grace could not do anything to stop what was happening to him. As the seconds ticked by, she saw the changes as though from a distance. He relaxed in her arms as a golden light illuminated his face. Grace listened intently when his fingers closed over hers.

"Don't cry, I'm okay," he said softly.

Grace held her breath while the images became permanently imbedded in her mind. His eyes closed and the golden light lifted, hovering scant inches above him. She felt the air crackling around them as the falling rain became a shimmering crystal encrusted curtain isolating them from the rest of the world. Seconds later the golden light rose and vanished from sight. Grace knew his spirit was no longer within his body. "The children, please help them understand," she prayed.

*Julia Robertson*

## Chapter 40

Grace jumped when someone touched her shoulder and knelt down in front of her. She blinked several times to clear the blurred image of the EMT.

"He's gone," wept Grace. "It's too late, he's gone."

The rain continued falling from the dark sky while Grace watched them take the man's body away on a stretcher. She stood frozen in place unable to think past the tragedy. She barely noticed the activity around her. None of it mattered compared to what she had just experienced.

"Come with me," said the EMT." He gently guided Grace toward the ambulance.

Grace objected at first, but then complied. "I'm not hurt," she sobbed.

"Let's be sure," he said.

"I'm not hurt," she repeated, but Grace knew better. Though not physically hurt, she was injured in a very permanent way. Her entire body trembled as she was helped up into the ambulance. Grace squeezed her eyes closed against the bright lights.

"This will only take a few minutes," the EMT said as he unfolded a blanket and draped it around her.

"I was driving home. The truck," Grace cried.

"Yes, I know. Look this way," he said, checking her eyes. "Let's take a look at your hands."

Grace stared at the blood stains darkening her fingers. More blood smeared over the back of her hands. "I need to go," she said urgently.

"Are you sure you feel up to being on your own?" asked the EMT.

Grace rose to her feet with her reply slurring together. "Yeah, wanna go home." When she became aware of the policeman standing beside her, she sat down again.

"The red Honda is yours, isn't it?" the police officer asked. Hang on and we will help get you home. It's warmer where you are."

Grace waited without protest. She watched the firemen working on the wrecked car and tugged the blanket tighter around her. Though she had kept Clay from burning in the car, it had not been enough to save his life. She had watched him die and watched his spirit free itself from his body. Did death bring peace to everyone prior to their last breath? She decided that knowledge was only for those lucky enough to escape from life.

On a day-to-day basis Grace tried to appear confident, but inside she found every reason to feel worthless. She would forever hold herself to blame for losing her parents. The scars ran bone deep. Tonight's tragedy only served to intensify her dark feelings. She yearned to experience the peace she witnessed come over Clay when he let go. Death and peace, she silently considered, were they one in the same?

Grace walked away from the ambulance with the policeman. "I'm fine, really," she insisted.

"I'm sure you are, but please let us help you," the policeman said while guiding her to the patrol car. "My partner will drive your car to your home."

Grace stared out the passenger side window biting back tears. A short time later she unlocked the front door and stepped inside her house. "Thank you," Grace told the officer standing below the porch. When he nodded and turned away, she closed the door and turned the deadbolt lock. Off balance and feeling lost, Grace walked down the hallway to the bathroom. She turned on the shower, peeled off her wet clothing and stepped in under the hot spray. For all she knew she stood there for an hour.

Grace knew what it felt like to lose someone she loved, but what happened today was entirely different. When her parents died, it had been a distant and unreal event. She had not witnessed their pain or the sheer shock of it. One day they were alive and the next day they were gone. She would always carry the guilt and deep sorrow because she loved them so much.

Tonight's tragedy was all too real. She had held him in her arms, listened to his last words and felt him take his final breath. She would forever wonder if his life might have been spared if someone else had been in her place. She had not done enough, simply had not done enough.

Grace stepped out of the shower and numbly toweled herself dry. Barefoot, she crossed to her bedroom and pulled on warm sweatpants and a baggy T-shirt. She pushed her feet into well-worn slippers and returned to the bathroom. Instead of dumping her wet clothes into the bathtub, she took them out to the washer. She set her soggy shoes on top of the dryer and began dropping her clothes into the washer as it filled. That was when she noticed the blood on her blouse. Her lips trembled as she blindly pushed the blouse into the sudsy water. When Grace closed the lid, she caught her fingertips. The sharp pain brought on tears. She slid down onto the floor and cried into her hands.

Head aching, Grace pushed to her feet and unsteadily walked to her bedroom. It was already past midnight, too late to try to contact his friend. Even if she did make the call, the words would not come out right. Besides, the police probably had someone checking on next of kin by now. Grace fumbled with the switch on the bedside lamp, crawled in under the comforter and tried to fall asleep. Erasing tonight's terrible images from her mind might never happen.

*Julia Robertson*

## Chapter 41

When Clay did not show up on Friday morning, Brian called him. It was not like him to be late. He checked the time while waiting for Clay to pick up. Frustrated, he put the phone down and ran his fingers through his hair. Once the finish work was completed, they planned to put some steaks on the grill and discuss the next month's work schedule.

"You're still here?" Kathleen asked as she came into the kitchen.

"Clay's running late. If he shows up, ask him to meet me at the building site," Brian said, knowing Kathleen recognized his edginess.

"Don't worry, I bet he forgot to set his alarm clock. I'll let him know where you are," replied Kathleen.

"You're probably right," Brian agreed.

Despite Kathleen's calm assurance, Brian still worried about Clay as he backed out onto the road. Now he wished he had called Clay last night to inquire about his appointment. He decided to check on Clay before heading out to the building site. Doing the work on his own was not a problem, but he preferred working with his best friend.

Clay owned a two-bedroom house in the older part of town. Brian pulled up into the narrow driveway and saw Clay's truck parked back by the small garage. His car was gone. He knew it was not in the garage since Clay kept all of his equipment in there.

Puzzled, Brian stepped down from his truck, rubbed the back of his neck and studied the house. The drapes were open and the morning newspaper was still on the porch. He picked up the paper and knocked on the front door. After a few quiet seconds passed he thumped the door with his fist. Feelings of unease pushed him to pull his keys out of his pocket. His hands felt uncommonly cold as he shoved the key into the lock and opened the door.

Brian stepped into the quiet living room. It was typical Clay. Discarded shoes and work boots littered the floor next to the door. A small mountain of apparently clean laundry awaited folding on the battered couch. When he walked down the hallway, he found the bedroom empty. Two pillows had been tossed at the headboard and the dark blue comforter was more or less straight on the bed. Confused, Brian walked to the kitchen. A few dirty dishes were stacked in the sink, but the counters were otherwise bare.

As he locked the door behind him, Brian figured Clay must have gone in for more tests. It seemed like the most logical explanation. He decided to go on to the building site and get to work. If the need arose, Brian could call on any one of the members of the crew working on the next house.

At the intersection near the park, Brian noticed a crew working on the streetlight pole. He looked back as he drove away and saw that someone had hit the pole. Dismissing his feelings of unease, he turned his attention back to the road and the day ahead. Another mile down the road he passed by Northrup's Garage where he saw a car on a flatbed trailer behind the tow truck.

"No," he said under his breath. The car was smashed and burned. The overwhelming agony of losing Alicia came rushing back. He held onto the steering wheel as though his life depended on it.

When a horn sounded behind him, Brian jerked back to the present. He waved the car around him, pulled ahead and turned into the garage parking lot. Coming to an abrupt stop, Brian threw the door open and jumped down. It was his best friend's car. He stared at the wreckage, willing Clay to be inside the shop doing paperwork. With that thought in mind, he turned and started toward the garage. When the door swung open and Jim Northrup stepped outside, Brian stopped cold.

"What's up with Clay?" Brian asked, but read the answer in Jim's eyes before he had a chance to speak. "No," Brian gasped, stepping back from the older man. "No," he repeated and turned to run for his truck. Before he took two steps Jim grabbed his arm and stopped him in his tracks. Brian jerked free and backed away, breathing hard and feeling sick to his stomach.

"Please don't, I've got to go," Brian said desperately.

"Brian, we need to talk. Come on," Jim said, cautiously reaching around Brian's shoulders. He gently guided him into his private office, closed the door and pushed Brian down on a chair.

Jim pulled up another chair and sat knee-to-knee with Brian. "Damn, I figured you already knew. It happened last night during the storm. A trucker lost control of his rig coming into town. Clay didn't see him coming."

Brian closed his eyes and tried to block out the words. Even the loud clanging in his head did not keep him from hearing what came next.

"It happened just like that. The rain, the storm, the trucker," Jim said, snapping his fingers. "Brian, Clay didn't make it. I'm sorry." Jim gripped Brian's hand tight in an effort to keep him on the chair.

"No," Brian cried softly. "I don't believe you." Brian opened his eyes and looked right at Jim. "You're wrong. He's okay, he's not, he's not," he stammered.

"Brian, it's true. You saw his car. Clay did not make it. I'm sorry," said Jim.

"Damn it, we're doing the finish work today. He's working with me today. We have a lot to do," he cried. "It's almost finished, and we already have a buyer. He can't be," Brian cried harder. "Not again. I can't," he sobbed, refusing to accept any of it.

The two men sat in silence while Brian worked through the initial shock. After a few minutes, Jim stepped out of the office and returned with a cup of cold water. He pressed it into Brian's hands. Neither felt compelled to speak. There were no words to take away the pain.

When Brian finally left the garage, he could not help but see the car again. He did not want to believe his friend was dead. Brian stared at the ruined car for a moment longer, then walked to his truck. He had to let the other men on their crew know what happened. He also needed to call Clay's mother. Brian dragged himself up into the cab of his truck. After one more glance at the car, he drove away.

Brian sought refuge in the empty house at the work site. The need to do something with his hands had driven him here. For now his feelings were too raw to handle making the call to Clay's mother.

Brian began cutting the trim for the kitchen cabinets. The finality of death created an agonizing sense of emptiness for those left behind. He could not talk to Alicia and now he didn't even have Clay to lean on. They were both gone. They were both dead. What was he going to say to Elizabeth Hancock and how the hell was he going to explain this to Erin?

Brian knelt down on the floor and cried. He desperately wanted to escape this nightmare and return to the time when Jack was a newborn and Alicia's health was good. How easy it would be to let the darkness have its way and lead him into the abyss. Clay's blunt statement repeated itself as he wiped his face with the palms of his hands.

"Giving up ain't gonna fix it."

After a time, Brian rose to his feet. Rather than punch his fists through the wall, Brian found solace in his work. He began tacking the trim in place around the upper edges of the oak cabinets. He dropped the hammer back into his tool belt as he stepped down from the ladder.

If Clay were here, they would work as a team, one cutting and the other tacking the pieces into place. They would talk about old times and argue about where to get lunch. Clay would update him on the progress with his car. He would explain each step with great detail. Whether it was his carpentry work, the engine work or the time he spent with Erin and Jack, Clay had endless patience.

Brian's thoughts circled back to today. He wondered why Clay had not seen the truck. Had he been looking for something in the car or maybe he had been distracted by something he was thinking about. Perhaps the appointment with his doctor? Work was going great, so he knew that was not the trouble. Was it the storm? Was there a problem with his car?

While he continued to search for answers, Brian missed the nail and hit his thumb with the hammer. He shook his hand, trying to ease the hurt. He sat on the lower step of the ladder, held his thumb tight and waited for the pain to pass. It made him wonder if Clay had suffered. He thought of how Alicia endured the awful pain during her final year. Brian was thankful for each and every day he had with her, but wished she had been able to let go sooner and be freed from the pain. Before the weight of his grief crushed him, he had to go home to talk with his kids and make the call to Elizabeth Hancock.

## Chapter 42

Grace felt today had only two things going for it. It was Friday, a casual wear day at the office, and she did not have to work tomorrow. It took every bit of energy she possessed to pull on jeans, a dark teal blouse and tennis shoes. The events of the night before weighed her down like an anchor. She wanted to crawl back into bed and hide from reality.

Before Grace reached the entrance to the parking lot at the newspaper office, she saw him. It was the other man who had been in the battered car at the airport. He was driving a dark blue pickup with big tires. She was not looking at the truck, she was looking at the man. At least she was until the driver behind her blasted his horn. She glanced up at the rearview mirror, then looked back at the truck, but it was already gone. She turned abruptly on the seat and did not see it anywhere. The horn sounded again, and she felt like screaming.

Grace's frustration grew as she pulled into the parking lot. She momentarily thought about chasing after the man in the truck. Was he Clay's friend? A family member? A co-worker? If it was him, did he know what happened last night? Was he going to play a role in caring for Clay's children? Was it any of her business? She sat still while the questions bounced around in her head like a bullet ricocheting inside a tin can. Feeling lightheaded, Grace dragged herself out of her car.

"How's it going?" Josh asked as he pushed the door open on his way out to the parking lot.

Grace shrugged in reply. Making small talk was not going to happen today and she could not afford to take the day off. Even with the extra money from the finished quilt she was running short again this month. Property taxes were coming due, and she needed new tires on her car. If it wasn't one thing, it was another. Or two other things, she frowned.

"That bad?" asked Roger.

"It's worse," Grace sighed.

"Isn't your cold any better?" He walked over and sat on the edge of her desk.

Grace had forgotten all about her cold. "It's not that, Roger. I'm sure you know about the accident near the park."

"Sure, the trucker is distraught over that guy's death," he replied.

"I was there when the truck hit the car," wept Grace. Her loosely held control quickly slipped through her fingers. "Roger, he died in my arms." She covered her face with her hands.

"Grace, are you okay?" Roger asked, clearly dismayed for asking something so stupid. "I'm sorry, what can I do for you?"

"Tell me it didn't happen," she cried, clumsily wiping at her eyes. "I thought I could handle it, but it's not working."

Roger grabbed a box of tissues from a nearby desk. "Want something to drink?" he asked quietly.

With a cup of hot tea in front of her, Grace tried to focus on her work. An hour passed before she had a chance to take a break and make the phone call. She checked the phone directory, jotted the number down on a slip of paper and walked back to use the phone in the break room. She lifted the phone, set it down, tapped her fingers on the wall, and then picked it up again. She punched in the numbers, listened to the phone ring and considered hanging up. She nearly disconnected the call when a woman answered.

"Hello," said Grace. "May I speak with Brian, please?"

"I'm sorry, he's not home right now. May I take a message?" said the friendly voice.

"Um, no, I'll call back later, thanks," replied Grace. Leaving a message might have been easier, but it would have been wrong.

Back at her desk Grace began sorting through her work. Her phone rang a few minutes later. She recognized Tina Wheeler's voice right away. "Hello, how was your garage sale?"

"That's what I've called about. I meant to call before now because it was a huge success thanks to you. Most of the people who came said it was the ad that brought them to my house," she said with delight.

"I'm glad it worked out for you." Grace appreciated the positive feedback.

"I've already told my friends to ask for you when they run their ads," Tina said. "Thank you again. Mandy, put that down!" she shouted. "I've gotta go."

The phone clicked and Grace heard the dial tone buzzing in her ear. The clock kept ticking even when a precious life was lost.

*Julia Robertson*

## Chapter 43

Brian puzzled over what to say to Elizabeth Hancock as he drove toward home. How was he supposed to console a mother who had just lost her son? He had heard too many well-meant, but ill stated sympathetic words after Alicia died. He sighed heavily as the light turned green and the traffic moved on. At that moment he caught sight of the red car on the opposite side of the road. A car horn blared, and the woman turned away just before he heard the softly spoken words.

*"Please don't live the rest of your life alone,"* whispered Alicia's voice.

Her voice sounded so real, but how could that be? It was the second time he had heard the same words. Emotionally dazed, Brian dragged the back of his hand across his mouth. He was well past the red car by the time he glanced back. Stopping to look again seemed crazy. Going back to look for the woman in the car was even worse. He shook off his stupid thoughts and gave his full attention to what needed doing.

Brian stopped at the house just long enough to talk with Kathleen and call Clay's mother. He had been careful to avoid telling the kids what happened. They were still playing out in the back yard when he made his escape. Guilt followed him as he left Kathleen to deal with putting the kids down for a nap.

On the way downtown, Brian thought about his conversation with Elizabeth Hancock. Along with their tears, they shared a few happy memories of Clay. He had not mentioned anything about the wrecked and burned car. To his dismay, she asked him to go to the city morgue and identify her son for her. Elizabeth rarely drove her car any further than her neighborhood market, and facing the four-hour drive frightened her. Brian agreed even though the mere idea of seeing his friend in that place made him sick. He sat outside in the hospital parking lot trying to dredge up the courage to handle the task.

When the cover was pulled back, Brian winced. "No, Clay. What happened," he mumbled under his breath. "It's him. His name is Clayton James Hancock," he said as clearly as his voice allowed.

He saw only Clay's upper body with the sheet pulled back. The ugliness of the accident was apparent, but then Brian realized Clay had not been burned. Brian reached out to touch his hand and thought of Alicia in the coffin. The unnatural color of Clay's skin made his stomach roil. After a moment of deliberation, Brian covered his friend's hand with his own. How he wished life did not have times like this. The cold skin felt horrible against his own cool hand, but he kept it there for a moment longer. "Rest, my friend, I'll see you again."

Shrouded with grief, Brian walked out of the morgue. He stopped at the side of his truck and leaned his head against the door. Once again he had to pick up the pieces of his life. He had to put things in order and find his way. He had to do it for the kids. Brian pushed the heels of his hands against his swollen eyes.

## Chapter 44

By the time Grace had a chance to call Brian Cooper again, her tension was almost unbearable. To her relief she found the break room was empty. Her hands trembled as she lifted the phone from the wall and pressed it to her ear.

"May I please speak to Brian?" Grace asked. She considered hanging up when her stomach began hurting.

"Of course, give me a minute to find him," replied the same kind voice.

Grace heard her call out for him. She found comfort in knowing the man's wife was with him. She wiped her damp hand on her jeans and took in a steadying breath. Grace jumped when the male voice spoke into her ear.

"This is Brian," he said.

"Um, hello. You don't know me, but this concerns Clay," Grace began, unsure of how to proceed.

"What about Clay?" Brian snapped.

"I, um, I need," stammered Grace. In her mind she knew she had to go on, but he sounded angry. Frightened, she swallowed hard and bit back the tears.

"What do you want?" Brian said impatiently.

"No, no, please," she broke in, turning to face the wall, wishing the call was behind her. There was no way to know if this was a personal attack or a result of losing his friend. At least he could not see her distress. If he disconnected the call would she have the nerve to call back?

"Please give me a chance. This isn't easy for me," she explained, trying to calm her voice. "I was there," she began softly.

"You were where?" he snapped again. "Get to the point."

"I was holding him when he died. At the accident, in the rain, I pulled him out of his car," she explained in a rush. She desperately needed to finish the conversation.

"Are you serious?" asked Brian.

"Yes, please listen. He talked to me before he died. He told me to tell you his Will is in his sock drawer. I know it sounds strange, but that's what he said."

Grace imagined him processing what she had just said and perhaps thinking she was some kind of nut. It did not matter what he thought as long as she passed on the dying man's words.

"That sounds like Clay. He was," Brian whispered.

Grace waited while the silence stretched out between them. Another minute passed before she said softly, "Hello?"

"Yeah, sorry, I'm here," Brian said.

Grace heard the strained emotion in his voice. It matched her own, though she hadn't known Clay. She gathered her wits and went on. "Before he, before he let go, he said, 'don't cry, I'm okay.'" Grace pulled tissues out of her pocket and dried her face.

"He's okay," sighed Brian. "We were close. It means a lot to know he was not alone. Thank you."

"You're welcome. I'm sorry, but I need to get back to work. I hope you're okay." Grace waited and heard his heavy breathing.

"Yeah, sure. Thank you," he said.

"You're welcome. Goodbye," Grace concluded. She carefully set the phone down and hoped the sound of the dial tone didn't make him feel worse. The room grew stifling warm around her, but it still took several minutes before she turned from the wall.

Grace stepped out of the break room and walked toward her desk. Roger had questions hovering in the air, but she held up her hand to stop him. She settled down on the chair, picked up the top folder and flipped it open. For a short time Grace was able to complete her assigned tasks, but when her concentration crumbled and the air became too thick to breathe, she knew she needed to escape. Grace straightened her desk before she turned to Roger. "I'm going to take a few minutes and go for a walk," she said.

"Take the rest of the day off," Roger suggested.

"No, I need to keep busy. It all keeps replaying in my head," she said, lifting her jacket from the back of her chair. Grace stopped at the restroom and pulled the elastic band from her braid. She kept her back to the mirror while she ran her fingers through her hair.

As soon as she stepped out into the unseasonably cool afternoon, Grace zipped her jacket and pulled up the collar. When the light changed at the corner, she crossed to the other side of the street. Clay's words echoed inside her head as she stepped up on the curb. She should have felt some sense of relief for having passed along his message, but it only added to her agony.

Grace did her best to stop thinking about the awful images from the night before as she walked along the sidewalk. Her eyes focused on the pale gray concrete underfoot, lined with seams and littered with random pebbles. She was barely aware of the whirring tires on the asphalt only a few feet away. Disconnected portions of conversations from those passing by in either direction swirled around Grace. She let it all create shadows, blurring her conscious thoughts until her recent promotion came to mind.

A month ago she had been presented with the chance to create two weekly columns. The first was a column on sewing and quilting for the Saturday paper. If there were no upcoming events to announce, she would touch on local sewing classes, where to buy supplies and answer reader's questions. The second column dealt with light issues within the community. Her first topic involved the local grade school's summer program. She also had an appointment set up with the animal shelter to bring more attention to the inexpensive programs available to have cats and dogs spayed or neutered. Having her words in print and read by strangers made her nervous and excited at the same time.

Grace tucked her hands into her jacket pockets when the sorrow descended upon her like a black storm cloud. Her momentary detour from the previous night's tragedy evaporated. Grace's desire to know the peace she had seen on Clay's face grew stronger with every footstep. She ached to be freed from her life of loneliness and worry.

A near collision with a skateboarder gave her a moment of panic, but the boy's apology was sincere. His glistening braces seemingly ignited his smile. Grace could not help but smile in return.

*Julia Robertson*

## Chapter 45

Following the unexpected phone call, Brian listened to the dial tone and wished he could take back the past year. If he could only fix things and make them right again. He dropped the phone down and covered his face with his hands. He had to deal with the pain in order to get through the coming days. Erin and Jack depended on him. They depended on him alone, without Alicia, and now without Clay.

"Brian, you need to eat something," Kathleen said from the doorway.

"Yeah, okay," he replied. He looked up at the clock, then headed to the kitchen.

Brian dutifully ate the sandwich Kathleen had made for him. He intentionally rushed through the meal and left before the children came back inside. The silent hug he had shared with Kathleen told him she understood his feelings. He needed time. Just a short while ago Brian told Erin and Jack that Clay was gone.

"But we need Clay," cried Erin.

Jack listened, confused about what was being said. Erin was crushed. She loved Clay. And while he clearly loved Jack, Clay adored Erin. "Lady Erin," he always said. Brian cried with Erin in his arms. There had been no words to soften the blow.

Brian drove away from the house feeling cold and empty. He found it difficult to concentrate as he passed through town on his way to the work site. Going back to work and keeping his hands busy seemed to be his best option. When he stopped for a red light, Brian watched the people passing by on the sidewalk. How could they be happy while he felt so miserable?

Two women walking side-by-side and carrying shopping bags were engaged in an animated conversation. Alicia loved to shop, but she rarely bought anything. She told him she had everything she needed by having him. He felt the same way about her.

Brian saw a middle-aged man with a briefcase in one hand and a cane in the other. He wondered if he needed the cane or if he thought using it made him look distinguished. A woman wearing a dark blue denim jacket crossed the street in front of him. Her hands were out of sight, buried in her jacket pockets. With her eyes downcast she looked as miserable and lost as he felt. She seemed unaware of the other people around her as she stepped up on the curb. He nearly called out when a boy on a skateboard came rolling toward her. Brian raised his hand as if she could see him behind her. He felt relieved when she jumped aside before the boy collided with her. The kid apparently apologized before she gave him a smile and walked away.

Brian accelerated, but wanted to go after the woman because she looked so sad. The absurdity of it hit him as he drove away. Throwing someone else a lifeline while he was drowning in grief and depression seemed a surefire path to disaster.

Upon returning to the job site, Brian doubted he'd be able to focus on his work without constantly looking over his shoulder for Clay. As he stepped down from the cab, he wondered again why Clay hadn't seen the truck.

After tucking Jack into bed later that night, Brian carried Erin out to the kitchen. She was exhausted, but weepy after the events of the day. He held her close while he checked over the paperwork at the table. He and Clay had planned to work on the scheduling together. Sharing the workload had been routine until now. Brian gently brushed Erin's hair back from her face. For a moment he saw a treasured image of Alicia cradling their newborn baby girl. Life seemed so simple and perfect back then.

"I promise we'll be okay," he whispered. He had no business making such a promise. "Life is too damned unpredictable," he mumbled to himself.

Brian sat in the quiet, once again questioning his life and his ability to handle it all. His emotions teetered on the edge, threatening to destroy what little strength he had left. He felt as though he were sinking in quicksand, helpless to do anything to save himself. It was then that he noticed Erin's eyes flutter open.

"Will Clay get to hug Mommy in Heaven?" she asked.

Caught by surprise, Brian took a moment to answer her. "Maybe, I think so," he said.

"Good," Erin whispered before she fell asleep.

Brian marveled how she had seen beyond her own feelings of loss. A few minutes later, Brian knelt down next to his children and thanked God for his life. Erin's words helped him look at losing Clay from a new perspective. It didn't make the pain go away, but it gave him hope he might one day be able to accept the loss.

*Julia Robertson*

*Tender Dreams*

## Chapter 46

Grace caught glimpses of the house through the old oak trees as she wound her way up the long driveway. The two-story log house was situated on 20 acres of land 12 miles out of town. Once she cleared the trees it appeared larger than life. The deep porch ran the width of the structure, fronted by wide wooden steps and sturdy wrought iron railings. A dazzling display of zinnias created a four-foot wall of color from one end of the porch to the other. Shimmering white, shocking pink, blood red and pale apricot blossoms reached up toward the hot August sun and drew Grace closer. She pictured a quilt with all the colors swirling on a background the same shade of green as the zinnia leaves. She quickly catalogued the images. Grace shifted the tote bag on her shoulder and mounted the steps.

"You must be Miss Marshall," said a woman from the open screen door. "Please come in," she chirped.

"Yes, I'm Grace," she replied as she entered the house. The screen door squeaked as it closed behind her. The sound surprised Grace, but it didn't seem to bother the woman. It must not be her responsibility, but Grace knew nothing about maids and servants, housekeepers or butlers.

"Will you have a glass of sun tea?" the woman asked.

"Yes, thank you," Grace replied. She scanned the wide hallway as she followed her through the house to a lavishly appointed kitchen.

The black granite counters, wide hickory flooring and white trimmed oak cabinets looked like something out of a magazine. Two wide refrigerators standing side by side, a stovetop with six burners and double ovens stacked one above the other were all faced with hammered stainless steel. A gleaming faucet with long ivory porcelain handles curved over the double sink.

"Would you like lemon or sugar?" asked the woman as she filled a tall glass with amber colored tea.

"Plain is fine, thank you," Grace replied as she pulled her eyes back into her head. She suddenly felt embarrassed.

"It's beautiful, isn't it," said the woman as she walked toward the open French doors. "Come along, please."

Still bedazzled by the kitchen, Grace stepped out onto the back patio and came up short.

"Miss Marshall, are you feeling all right?" asked the woman.

"Uh huh," Grace replied, unable to form any sensible words.

Wrought iron chairs were arranged around six glass topped tables shaded by forest green umbrellas. Water in a white tiled swimming pool sparkled in the afternoon sunshine. Hot pink and candy red geraniums spilled out over the sides of numerous terra cotta pots.

Grace decided everything was beautiful without going overboard. She bit her lower lip and turned to the woman. "I've never seen anything so spectacular," she explained, hoping it did not sound stupid.

The woman smiled, then walked with her across the patio to where two other people were seated. "Please sit here," she said as she set the glass down on a thick napkin and pulled out a chair. "Miss Marshall, this is my daughter, Sheree," she said, gesturing toward a younger woman. "And my husband, Alexander Mills."

"I'm pleased to meet you both," said Grace.

"Oh dear," laughed the woman. "I forgot to introduce myself. I'm always doing that. If I'm thinking about something, I forget everything else. I'm Carlena. Theona told me all about you."

Until the introductions were made Grace had not been aware of the connection. The younger woman's golden-blonde hair skimmed her bare shoulders. She wore a cream and baby pink striped silk tank top and three-inch-long royal blue beaded earrings. The beautiful earrings swayed with each movement she made.

Alexander Mills reflected his wealth with polished sophistication. Grace noticed his warm smile and intriguing gray eyes right away. He looked right at home in the sage-green polo shirt, but Grace easily pictured him wearing a black tux and silk tie.

In stark contrast, Carlena wore loose fitting black cotton shorts and a white button-up blouse. Her feet were bare, which seemed to suit her personality. Grace was inwardly pleased no one knew she had seen Carlena as hired help.

"Your name is vaguely familiar to me, Miss Marshall. Do we know each other?" asked Sheree.

"Please call me Grace. It's been a long time since high school, but perhaps from back then?" suggested Grace.

"Maybe," Sheree replied. "Let me think."

Alexander stood up and shook hands with Grace. "Theona tells us you are a marvelous seamstress," he said, easing back down on his chair. "My youngest sister will be married next summer. A handmade quilt sounds like the perfect gift."

"I have a few samples and my photo album for you to look through," Grace began. "I can design anything you like. The more intricate the design, the longer it takes to complete." Grace zipped open her oversized tote bag and set the first stack of quilted squares in front of Carlena.

"Oh my," whispered Carlena. She ran her fingertips over the intricate stitches without thinking, then quickly pulled her hands away. "Are we allowed to touch them?"

"Yes, please," replied Grace. "I believe a quilt ought to bring more than simple visual pleasure." Grace took out the second stack of squares and set them on the table in front of her.

"May I?" asked Alexander.

"I'm sorry, yes," Grace replied as she quickly passed the sample squares to him.

"Not in high school," Sheree said, absently tapping her polished fingernail on the glass tabletop.

While Alexander studied the first quilted square, he reached out and stilled his daughter's hand. When the tapping stopped, Alexander lightly patted her hand. Witness to the silent exchange, Grace quickly turned her attention to Carlena Mills.

"One of the choices you will make is the thickness of the batting in the quilt. The down filling is wonderful for cold winter nights, but requires specialized cleaning. The medium weight is nice for a guest room bed or to use as an extra blanket. The lighter weight is perfect for an afternoon nap or to use for decorative purposes."

"Brianna loves to pile on the blankets when it's cold," said Carlena.

Grace noticed Alexander nod in agreement. "Then she'll use it as a comforter rather than for show?"

"Yes, she loves pretty things, but she likes to use them," Carlena replied. She set the square aside and smiled at the whimsical pattern on the next one. "Look, Sheree, this is perfect for a baby's bed, isn't it," she sighed.

"Mother, don't start," groaned Sheree.

"Yes, well," Carlena said as she traced a neat row of yellow ducks stitched into the fabric. "The stitching is perfect," she remarked.

"Thank you," Grace replied. "I love to quilt."

"It shows," said Alexander. "It's a rare gift."

Grace shrugged, feeling oddly uncomfortable with the compliment. "So I've been told," she finally replied.

"Trade with me, Alex," said Carlena.

"Cute," he remarked at the whimsical square. "I like this one too. She'd most certainly get a big tickle out of it."

Grace felt the electricity spark between the two of them. It triggered images of her parents and the love they once shared. When she noticed Sheree observing her, she dropped her eyes to the album in front of her. Grace almost missed seeing Alexander reach out and tap his daughter's shoulder.

"I'm sure Aunt Brianna would prefer something better suited for her age," Sheree remarked.

"You might be right, dear," said Carlena. "You do have to admit it's darling."

"I suppose," sighed Sheree. "Aunt Brianna has old furniture in her bedroom. Presuming they keep her furniture, why not go with the decor of that room?"

"I have several photos in my album," Grace said, passing it over to Alexander. "See if anything matches her decor."

Carlena stood up without a word and stepped closer to Grace. "Trade seats with me, please. I'll look with Alex."

"Sure," agreed Grace. She sat down on the warm cushion and reached for her glass. Grace felt Sheree watching her again, so kept her eyes on Carlena and Alexander.

Alexander stopped Carlena's hand before she turned to the next page. "That's it," he said.

"Oh my, you're right, Alex. It is perfect," Carlena sang out.

Grace saw what they were looking at and flipped through the sample squares. "Here," she said as she laid the square out before them. "This is the same pattern, but I used all shades of blue."

"It is beautiful," said Alexander. "Brianna loves flowers. Can you use all flowered fabric?"

"Of course. I suggest small print, rather than anything bold. Is blue the color you have in mind?" Grace asked. Though she kept her eyes on the couple, Grace could not help but notice Sheree's growing interest. The young woman sat up to look at the photograph, then reached out for the sample square. Sheree ran her fingertips over the designs. Watching the close inspection of her work made Grace squirm on the cushion. Doubt crept in, dashing the chances of landing the order. She quickly assessed how long it would take her to gather up her things and run for her car.

"May I make a suggestion?" Sheree said softly.

"Yes," said Alexander. "What do you have in mind?"

"Aunt Brianna isn't that much older than me. She has that old four poster bed and all. Staying with blue, which I'm certain she would love," she said, pausing for a moment. "What if you made it in the darker shades of blue and bordered it with black. A black that has, I don't know, texture?"

Grace pictured it right away. With her eyes closed, she said, "Cobalt sky at midnight."

"That's exactly what I have in mind," Sheree agreed.

"I like the idea," said Carlena while she studied the photo again.

Grace looked at Sheree. "You said black that is textured. I can do the stitching in the darkest blue on the black fabric. Here," she added as she selected another square. "I can work designs like this, maybe in stars and moons."

Upon closer examination of the stitching, Sheree remarked, "You mean you made the black look textured rather than already being that way?"

"Yes, like this stitching," Grace said, touching the heart designs on the sample in front of Sheree.

"You did that?" asked Sheree. "It looks tedious."

"I suppose it is, but I love it," Grace said.

"You must have the patience of an angel," remarked Carlena.

"Make us a sample, then we'll go from there," said Alexander. "Cost is of no consequence. Brianna deserves the best you can provide." He sat back in the chair, obviously content with the decision.

"I need to make some notes," Grace said as she pulled out her small notebook and uncapped her pen.

"You are efficient, like Theona promised," said Carlena. "Sheree dear, would you mind bringing the pitcher of sun tea down from the house?"

"Not at all," Sheree replied as she pushed her chair back from the table. "I'll be right back." At the same time Sheree stepped inside the house, she paused and looked back.

Grace glanced up in time to see Sheree looking back at her. She felt like a troll compared to Sheree. Sheree was tall and tanned, elegant and beautiful, everything Grace was not. The dark tide threatened to wash over Grace. She unwittingly slipped into the past.

Grace sat alone and watched raindrops splatter against her bedroom window. She worried about her future all the time. Feelings of loneliness swirled around her in the dark room. The long-ago childhood moments hadn't faded, even with the passage of time.

When Sheree returned to the table, Grace kept her eyes locked on the notes before her as though they were vitally important. A strange sensation rippled through her while the glasses were refilled with sun tea.

"Do you work for the Valley Post?" Sheree asked.

"Yes," Grace replied.

"You're a hero," Sheree said.

"No," whispered Grace. Her face felt like it was on fire.

"Hero?" Alexander asked.

"You read about the accident last month, didn't you? The man who died worked construction, remember Dad?" Sheree asked.

"Yes, now I do," replied Alexander. "Are you the young woman who helped that night?"

Feeling like a fish out of water, Grace wanted to slide beneath the table. "Yes," she whispered, pretending to be engrossed with her notebook.

"You risked your life to pull that poor man out of his car," Sheree said. "Talk about courageous."

"What happened?" Carlena asked as the conversation went on.

"Mom, if you read the newspaper you'd know. A trucker in one of those big rigs, you know," Sheree said as she sat forward on the chair. "He apparently suffered a blackout and lost control of his truck. He hit a car by the park in town during that big thunderstorm."

"Oh dear," sighed Carlena. "What did you do?"

"I just," Grace mumbled.

"No 'just' about it. She pulled the man out of his car only seconds before it caught fire. Wasn't it frightening?" Sheree asked with genuine interest.

Grace set the pen down on the table, then immediately picked it up again. She desperately needed something to do with her hands. She capped and uncapped the pen. "It wasn't much. Wasn't enough," she whispered.

"Good grief, Grace. I heard you talked to him in the final moments of his life. That's huge to me." Sheree waited, then gently nudged Grace's shoulder.

Grace felt Clay in her arms again. "It was awful. He died and I couldn't do anything to save him." Unable to stop herself, Grace cried, "I couldn't save him."

Sheree hopped up and wrapped her arms around Grace. "He didn't die alone. I'm honored to know you."

*Julia Robertson*

## Chapter 47

Grace replayed the meeting with Carlena and Alexander Mills as she pulled out onto the road. Sheree's suggestion inspired the images of the finished quilt in her mind. Her fingers tingled as she concentrated on the next turn in the road. Grace thought about how she felt when she first met Sheree. The woman's dark eyes, stern expression and fire engine red nail polish made her feel queasy. Her unease increased when Carlena asked her to trade places with her. Grace relaxed when Sheree became interested in planning the quilt, but was caught off guard when she brought up the accident.

Grace set aside the meeting and turned her attention to the trees along the narrow road. The massive oak trees had to be over a hundred years old. Their distinctly shaped gray-green leaves clung to the widespread branches. Though she could not see them from the road, she knew the ground was littered with rusty brown acorns. The miles ticked by while Grace enjoyed the scenery. When Grace felt a strange vibration under the car, she slowed down and eased off onto the side of the road.

"What was that?" she asked herself. She shifted the car into park, shut off the engine and pulled down on the oddly shaped button under the steering column. The emergency flashers clicked on and off, on and off. She had no idea what was wrong and wished she had taken auto shop in high school. Chances were it wouldn't have helped anyway. She knew where the engine was, could add oil, if needed and knew how to put gas in the tank. She also knew how to check the tire pressure and put air in them. "The tires," she groaned as she checked behind her and pushed the door open. It took only seconds to discover the problem.

"Well, look at that," she sighed with her hands propped on her hips. "That's a first. Do I know how to change one of those?" Grace ran her hands up into her hair and stared at the flat tire. Eyes locked on the miserable thing, she willed it to re-inflate. To her dismay it did not work. Changing a tire involved a jack and a spare tire. Whether she had either item she didn't know.

Grace stared down into the trunk. She had a jack, but no spare tire. She hated to admit she had no idea how to use the jack in the first place.

Grace closed the trunk and frowned. What was she supposed to do now? It was at least four more miles into town. Why could the tire not have held out for a few more miles? She had only two options. Either stay here and wait or start walking. Wait for what?

Grace noticed it was already 4 o'clock. She might sit here without seeing any cars for a long time. Waiting for a Sheriff's car to come by was even more unlikely. She linked her fingers on top of her head. Frustrated, she let them drop down and slap her legs.

Grace felt like the only person on the planet as she walked along the road. She had not seen any cars going in either direction since she left the Mills' house. Negative thoughts overwhelmed her common sense and convinced her she was too tired, too hot and too thirsty. She had considered joining one of those car clubs, but even if she had there was no way to call them from way out here. Phone booths were not sitting on the side of the road so far out of town. If she had Mary Poppins power, she would simply pull a telephone out of her tote bag and call for help. The mere idea made her shake her head and laugh out loud. Maybe she ought to walk back to her car and set the flat tire on fire. Someone was sure to spot the smoke and call for help. Maybe she ought to have a flare gun in her trunk. Better yet, she ought to have a spare tire in her trunk.

Grace's scattered thoughts reflected her fatigue. She was going to have to buy at least one new tire and pay for a tow truck. She had only herself to blame. Swinging her hands up in the air, Grace shouted to the sky, "Call me stupid!"

*Tender Dreams*

## Chapter 48

Brian walked across the uneven ground contemplating the possibilities. The proposed building site was a quarter mile from the road and did not have power or water out to it yet. He had been asked to work up design ideas and cost estimates for a house for the client. Potential client, he reminded himself. He already knew the general size of the home they wanted as well as the number of bedrooms and bathrooms. In addition, he had a partial list of the other features they had in mind. A large family room open to the kitchen to make easy socializing. A smaller private living room separate from the family room area. An indoor laundry room and a walk-in pantry. Sunken and jetted tubs in two of the three bathrooms. A walk-in shower large enough for two in the third bathroom.

He had plenty of time, but Brian knew he had a better chance to land the job if he put it together sooner rather than later. After checking on the kids, Brian squatted down, drew the pencil and sketch pad out of his pocket and concentrated on the preliminary sketches. Working quickly, he sketched the property, noted the existing trees and made several rough drawings of the first two houses that came to mind. After a few more minutes and a few more pages, he had the details locked in his mind.

Brian stood up and pushed the pencil and sketch pad back into his pocket. For a moment he let himself imagine living out here. Erin and Jack would have fun exploring every day. He could build a wooden swing-set with a long slide, and a big tree house. The light breeze singing through the trees gave his heart permission to dream. When Brian found himself seeing Alicia sitting on their back deck with a mug of hot tea in her hands, his happy thoughts cracked apart.

"I need you here with me," he wept silently. "I miss you all the time."

The tantalizingly perfumed mist swirled around him, drawing him in and luring him toward escape. The temptation alone created an illusion of happiness. Brian wanted it, even if only for a few minutes. He sucked in a deep breath and mentally turned away from his insane thoughts.

"Daddy, come here!" shouted Erin.

"Coming," Brian replied as he wiped his eyes dry and forced the dark thoughts away. "Keep it together," he ordered himself as he walked toward the kids.

"What did you see?" asked Erin. She crouched down next to her brother on the ground. "Come on," she urged him, but Jack only shook his head.

"What did you find?" Brian asked as he leaned over with his hands on his knees.

"Jack is tricking us," Erin grumbled.

Brian knelt down and rested his hand on Jack's back. "What is it?"

"Don't know," whispered Jack.

"Jack, was it big like your shoe?" asked Brian. Jack shook his head, but kept his eyes glued to the ground. "Little like a toy car?" Brian asked next.

Jack nodded with enthusiasm. "Long tail," he said.

"Did it have little black eyes?" Brian asked even though he already knew the answer.

"Yeah," Jack said almost reverently.

"It was a lizard, Jack. He's going to stay hidden as long as we're here. We're really big compared to him, so he's being careful."

"Will it bite?" asked Erin.

"No, but it can run fast." Brian watched Jack and wished he knew exactly what the kid was thinking. He easily pictured the little wheels whirring like mad inside his head. "We need to go home. Are you two getting hungry?"

Erin jumped up and ran with Jack close on her heels. Brian watched the two of them as they ran toward the truck. Their laughter filled the air. He glanced over, wanting Alicia to be there to take hold of his hand. Sharing his life with her had been so right. The void remained as cold as ice in his heart. He pushed his empty hands into his pockets and followed after his children.

Brian drove in and out of the bright spots of sunshine on the narrow, rutted drive leading out to the road. Erin and Jack sat contentedly in their car seats, high enough to see out the back windows. He glanced back at them every now and then. Running around in the warm sunshine had drained some of their energy. They had driven almost ten miles before the silence was broken.

"The Ladybug, look, the Ladybug!" Erin shouted, wriggling in her car seat to get a better look.

"Stay put, I'll be right back." Brian stepped down from the truck and walked around the empty car. The back right tire was flat. He didn't see anyone walking along the road, but it twisted and turned all the way into town.

"Where did she go?" Erin asked.

"The car has a flat tire," he said as he pulled back onto the road. "Someone probably stopped and gave her a ride."

"Flat tire," Jack said with a frown.

"Got a hole in it. Flat tire, sad tire," Erin chanted, patting her hands on her car seat.

"Flat tire," Jack sang out.

Brian listened to their silliness and glanced at his watch. Maybe they ought to hit the Drive In instead of scrounging up leftovers at home. Stopping there meant no mess to clean up afterward and ample time to work on the preliminary floor plans.

With his eyes on the road, Brian revisited the earlier images of Alicia sitting on the deck of the home they would never share. Every detail, from the countless green leaves fluttering in the trees to the shimmering gold highlights in her hair, came to life in his mind. He desperately wanted to feel her sun warmed skin. The weight of losing her settled on him like a boulder. Before it crushed him to death, Brian mentally shoved it away. He had to focus on today, let the past go and accept life with all of its imperfections. Try as he might, the shadow of doubt never left his side.

*Julia Robertson*

## Chapter 49

The road continued to twist and turn through the trees until it finally cut a straight path toward town with open farmland on either side of the blacktop. They were about three miles from town when Brian spotted the lone figure walking along the right side of the road. After checking for cars behind him, Brian slowed the truck and rolled to a stop next to the woman. To his surprise she kept walking without looking up.

From the back seat, Erin bounced up and down in her car seat and shouted, "It's the Ladybug Lady."

Brian did not try to quiet her down. If Alicia had been in this situation, he felt certain she would have warmed to the idea of children in a car stopping to help her. He inched ahead, kept pace beside her and called out, "Hello, can we give you a ride to town?" He waited, but she did not respond. "Look, if you have a spare, I can help change it."

"Spare," muttered Grace. She glanced to her right and realized she had no place to run if she was in danger. There were no other cars coming from either direction. She was completely alone out here with a stranger in a big pickup truck. If Sheree saw her now, she would surely see her as a coward. Feeling all the fool, Grace looked up but kept her eyes averted from the driver. She licked her lips and searched for a reply. Anything she said was going to have him thinking she was nuts. Before any sensible words formed, she noticed the child in the back window. Pretty as a picture came to mind at the sight of her gorgeous brown eyes. Grace took in a sharp breath when she realized the child had been at the taco stand with Clay. Doing her best to tamp down her jittery nerves, Grace turned her attention to the driver. "I don't have a spare, but if you'll send the tow truck out, I'll go back to my car and wait."

"It's a long way back to your car. Let me give you a ride to town instead. Someone from the garage can help you find a tire," he replied.

It was then that Grace actually focused on the man's face. Her mouth went dry when she made the connection. He was the man with Clay at the airport. He looked exactly like the image she had created in her mind. He had the same intense blue eyes and the same silky brown hair. Grace bit her lower lip and looked down at the asphalt under her shoes.

"Look," said the man. "We're going into town anyway. It's too hot to stay out here in the sun for much longer," he told her.

"I don't know," Grace replied stupidly. The child was batting at the window with her hand now. Grace guessed she was bouncing up and down in a car seat. She looked back down the road and considered how far she had walked. Grace looked at the girl again and wondered if the little boy was in the truck as well. Was this man taking care of them for their mother? Filling in the void left behind by the death of their father? How was that any of her business, Grace scolded herself.

"Don't worry, they won't bite," the driver said.

The humor of his statement was enough to make her smile, but trust had always been an issue for Grace. For the second time today, she was caught in an awkward situation. She hated the tears that threatened to spill from her eyes. She angrily swept the back of her hand across her face. She would not blame the man if he drove off and left her standing here all alone. Exhaustion had Grace giving into his offer before she had a chance to change her mind. She nodded and stepped closer to the truck. The weight of the heavy door had her stepping back and catching her balance as she examined the step up.

"There's a grab bar up to your right," the driver instructed, pointing to a large handle near the windshield.

Grace set her foot on the running board, grabbed the handle and hoisted herself up. Her temporary satisfaction after successfully landing on the seat was negated when the door swung away from her hand. She awkwardly grabbed the same handle, set her foot on the running board and reached out for the door. She nearly toppled out of the truck at the same time she was pulled back inside by the back of her jeans. Slightly stunned, Grace managed to get the door closed and clumsily brushed her hair back from her face.

"Thank you," she said breathlessly. "I'm not used to such a high vehicle."

"It does take some getting used to," said the man. "Your shoulder strap is up to the right behind you."

Grace reached back and froze at the sight of the girl's bright smile. Her heart ached for the child's recent loss.

"That's Erin behind you, and Jack's over on this side," the man said. He pressed down on the accelerator and brought the truck up to speed.

"Hi Erin," said Grace. She turned and saw the boy on the back seat. She had seen him for only a split second at the taco stand, but she had no doubt it was the same boy. He had bright blue eyes and a beautiful smile on his dirt-streaked face. "Did you say Jack?" she asked.

"Yes, we've been out at a prospective building site. They're both a bit grubby," said the man.

"Thank you for giving me a ride," Grace said as she rested back against the warm seat.

"No problem," he replied.

She waited a beat and found herself saying, "I'm Grace." She had not meant to say her name, but her mind seemed to be working on its own.

"Hi Grace. I'm Brian," he replied.

"Brian?" she said, wishing she could take back her baffled reaction.

"Yes," he said. "Are you okay?"

"Yes, of course, it's just, I can't," she said, knowing she was babbling.

"Jack found a lizard," Erin said from the back seat.

"You did? That's cool," Grace said, turning on the seat far enough to see the little girl's eager expression. "Did he look at you?" she asked.

"Got buggy eyes," Jack said, pulling his own eyes open wider with his chubby fingers.

"I bet you looked big to him," Grace said as she turned back around on the seat. It felt good to sit down after walking so far. She sighed and looked out the passenger side window. She brushed a wisp of hair from her eyes as the air blew through the open window and cooled her overheated skin. "I appreciate your help," Grace said with her eyes closed.

"You're welcome," said Brian. He glanced over and saw she had dirt smeared across her left cheek. When he found himself wanting to reach out and wipe it away, he riveted his eyes on the road. He felt agitated with his reaction to her. He did not want anyone to take Alicia's place. Even though she had encouraged him, Brian refused to let it happen. His heart belonged to Alicia. It belonged to her forever even if he could no longer hold her, kiss her or share his dreams with her.

Brian eased his foot off the gas pedal when he noticed he was driving well over the posted speed limit. If a patrol car had been behind him with its lights on it would not have surprised him. Without thinking, Brian glanced to his right and found Grace watching him.

Embarrassed to be caught staring at him, Grace snapped her eyes down to her lap. She could not believe he looked exactly like her imagined picture of him and he was sitting right there, close enough to touch. Her toes curled in her shoes when she considered scooting over next to him. She had no idea where such crazy feelings were coming from. What was she supposed to say now? Ask him who he was and why he had Clay's children with him? It was unthinkable. Flustered, Grace turned her attention to the view out the passenger side window.

"You're the Ladybug Lady," Erin said from the back seat.

Grace looked at the man with an odd sense of curiosity. "Pardon me?" she said.

"The Ladybug Lady," Erin said meekly.

"Erin saw your car from an airplane when we flew into town last spring. Erin thought it looked like a ladybug, so she decided to call you the Ladybug Lady," Brian explained.

Giving her attention to the child, Grace said, "I bet my car looked small from up in the air. I love my little red car." Grace could not erase the sight of the battered car at the airport that day. The same car Clay had been driving on the night he died. It was not easy keeping her emotions in check. She frantically searched for something else to say.

"Got flat tire," Jack said.

Grace saw his sad expression. Sad enough to make someone think he saw the car as a real being rather than a mix of metal and rubber. She was not sure what to say and was glad when Brian spoke up.

"We'll get it fixed, Jack, don't worry," Brian explained. "He's thinking all the time."

"That's wonderful," Grace replied. She relaxed and turned to the side window once again. "The Ladybug Lady," she mused silently.

All four of them remained silent for a time. The only sounds came from the tires humming along the road and the wind blowing in through the open windows. Brian looked to his left, checked the side view mirror, and then automatically glanced up at the rear-view mirror. Though he did his best to resist, he found himself sneaking a peek at Grace. He appreciated her interest in the kids, her reaction to the story about the lizard and having seen her car. A moment later he found himself wondering what she was thinking. Brian drew his mind back to the road, inwardly scolding himself for letting his mind wander into places it did not belong.

"We're going to the Drive In," Brian said, nearly biting his tongue when he heard his own words. He steadied himself and added, "Please join us, my treat."

"I can't do that," Grace objected. "I have already caused you too much trouble. Drop me off at Northrup's garage, please," she said and tightened her hold on the shoulder strap.

Brian was not surprised with her negative reply. "Look, it's getting late and the kids are hungry. You must be exhausted," he said, glancing over once again to watch for her reaction.

Grace bit her lower lip. "Okay," she agreed.

"Good," replied Brian. "The garage is open late, so it won't be a problem getting you fixed up with a tire."

Grace felt herself shrinking on the seat. His invitation sounded sincere, but now that she was committed, she felt her nerves fray even further. He was Brian, Clay's friend. Should she tell him who she was? During their phone conversation she had not mentioned her name. Part of her subconscious yelled, "Tell him, tell him!" Another part calmly said, "Let it go." Mentioning Clay with his children in the back seat felt wrong. Grace bit her lip and let the words slide down her throat. She sighed inwardly when the Drive In came into view.

Brian noticed her unease and hoped he had not upset her with his invitation. He dared not admit he had not intended to say anything. The words had come out as though his mind had been commanded by an invisible force.

Brian pushed his crazy thoughts aside and asked, "Are you guys hungry?" The excited shouts from the back seat made him smile. "It doesn't take much to get them going," he told Grace as he brought the truck to a stop.

"I guess not," Grace replied. She watched Brian step out of the truck, open the rear door and begin to unbuckle the little boy's car seat. When Erin put up a fuss, she offered to help her. Grace felt her heart melt when Brian looked up at her with his penetrating blue eyes. Her legs felt rubbery as she slid down to the ground and opened the heavy rear door. With Erin's help, Grace managed to unfasten the restraints. The little girl popped up from the seat as though powered by a spring. By the time Grace climbed back up on the front seat, both children were eagerly looking out through the windshield. They looked as if they were actually reading the black lettering on the broad white signboard.

Brian had glanced back while Grace was helping Erin, but he quickly pulled his attention away before she started climbing up across from him. He did not want to look at her, but the strangest feelings kept coming over him. He rolled his shoulders in an effort to dispel some of the tension building up in his neck. Once Grace was sitting on the front seat again, he engaged the kids in a ritual they had followed many times in the past.

"Okay guys, here's what they have. Burritos, corn dogs, burgers, cheeseburgers, fish & chips, fried shrimp, grilled whale blubber, fried frog legs."

"Daddy," giggled Erin. "Whale blubber?" she said with her hands over her eyes.

Jack shouted, "Frog legs, frog legs!"

"Oops, I made a mistake," laughed Brian. "No whale blubber today and they're out of frog legs. Sorry about that."

"Daddy?" Grace blurted out.

Brian sent her a puzzled look, then turned his attention back to the kids. "You two want to split a cheeseburger with the works? Fries or onion rings?" he asked.

"A cheeseburger," replied Erin.

"Frog legs," chuckled Jack.

"Right," laughed Brian. "Do you know what you'd like to order, Grace?"

Grace fumbled through the choices even though she feared she wouldn't be able to eat a single bite. "A cheeseburger is fine for me too," she finally told him.

Brian gave their order to the young girl at the window. Once that was taken care of, he told the kids to get their pocket games out. They sat between their car seats and focused on the games.

Brian turned to Grace and asked, "Have we met before? There's something familiar about you, but other than your car I can't place it."

Grace raised both hands and then let them drop back on her lap. "No, not exactly, I mean, sort of, but not really," she said, ashamed of the way her words tangled one with the other.

"That just about covers every angle. Are you sure about that?" asked Brian.

Grace recovered enough to look back at the children, but she could not find a single word to say in response. She reluctantly met his eyes before gazing at the children again. She couldn't get over how comfortable they were with this man after so recently losing their father. Even with the passage of time since her parents died, Grace still felt weighed down with guilt and sadness. Losing their father while they were young might be a blessing in disguise for both Erin and Jack. Grace brushed at the oncoming tears with the back of her hand.

"They're mine," Brian said.

Startled, Grace looked up. She met his eyes, but at the same time noticed he was trying to conceal his wedding band. Behind them they heard Jack erupt in laughter. The children were sweetly innocent, she thought and said, "They're happy."

"Yes, they are. Grace," Brian began.

"Don't," she said harshly. He was married and he had children. It wasn't like they were on a date, but the way he watched her gave her pause. The fact he was trying to hide it from her clenched it. She desperately needed to escape this unsettling situation.

"I'm leaving," Grace said as she reached out and took hold of the door handle.

"No," Brian demanded as he grabbed her arm. Her eyes flashed with anger. "Please, let me explain," Brian said, softening his voice.

Just then Erin popped up from the back seat. "It's stuck, Daddy," she said, holding out the game.

Brian fiddled with it until the button came loose. "There you go, baby, it's all fixed now," he said, watching her perplexed expression as he handed the game back to her. "The button got stuck again, that's all."

"What's whale blubber?" Erin asked.

"I was teasing you, Erin. If you let it go for now, we'll look it up in the encyclopedia when we get home," Brian said. "Okay?"

"Promise?" said Erin.

"Yes, I promise," Brian assured her, relieved when she slipped back down to the back seat. "She doesn't miss a thing," he said, turning back to Grace.

The moment their eyes met Grace realized how foolish she had been. She should have escaped while he was occupied with Erin. She still doubted they were his children, but they certainly were comfortable calling him Daddy. Her stomach gurgled at the same time the food arrived at the window. At that moment Grace decided she might handle herself better if she ate something. A little more time couldn't hurt any, she thought as Brian paid the girl at the window and then turned to the children.

"Erin, come on up here," he said and lifted her from the back seat. "Scoot over a bit so Jack has room," he said before reaching back for the boy. "Don't kick your feet, Jack," he warned.

Grace observed the way he handled the kids. Maybe he was their father after all.

An unexpected image unfolded right before Grace's eyes. All four of them fitted perfectly across the width of the seat. For a moment she allowed herself to pretend she was a part of their lives. Her tender emotions fractured at that moment. She did not belong here. Certainly had no business conjuring up images of things she did not deserve. Even worse than that, he was married.

Grace squashed her dark feelings and prayed she did not fall apart. She watched Brian place a lap tray over the children's legs. Watched as he spread out the paper under the burger and sliced it in two.

"Cut one more time, Daddy," Erin said.

"How many for each of you?" Brian asked.

"Two for Jack, two for me," answered Erin.

Brian handed Grace her burger, then dropped a handful of fries on the paper for the kids. Next he set out a small container of fry sauce for them. Grace had numbly accepted her burger and tuned into their conversation.

"Goop," giggled Erin.

"Frog legs," Jack said as he dunked one fry in the sauce. Before he managed to get the fry into his mouth some of the sauce dripped on his shirt.

"Yuck," Erin said and wrinkled her nose at her brother.

Grace watched Brian use a napkin to wipe the sauce from Jack's shirt. It left a dark smear across the already dirty yellow fabric. Seemingly frozen in place, Grace was still watching them all when Brian began unwrapping his burger. She noticed his strong hands, the same hands that had saved her from falling out of the truck and then prevented her from getting away a short time ago. When his deep blue eyes locked on hers, she quickly looked down. Grace felt her face growing hot and pretended to be totally absorbed with unwrapping her own burger.

Brian recognized her unease and turned his attention back to his meal. He told himself he was concerned for her well-being, not that he was attracted to her. Noticing she was pretty meant he was looking, and he did not intend to look for anyone. No one could ever replace his first love. The mere idea made his stomachache.

*She floated in the air like a feather in the breeze, watching her family with the pretty lady with long dark hair and beautiful blue eyes. With the voice of a tiny speck of dust, Alicia whispered, "She's perfect, my love."*

Brian suddenly jerked up from his burger. He stared out in front of him before abruptly turning on the seat and blurting out, "Did you hear that?"

Grace fought to remain calm when Brian nearly jumped up off the seat. His eyes went wild, looking around as though he had seen a ghost. For the sake of the children, Grace calmly replied, "No."

Still observing his rapid eye movement, Grace reached over and touched his arm. He pulled back from her as if she had burned him. "Are you okay? What's wrong?" she asked.

"Nothing's wrong," Brian hissed. He knew his words were too gruff, but he could not help it. She had been here, right here. He had heard her voice. His Alicia. Overwhelmed, Brian closed his eyes and whispered, "I'm sorry."

Grace did her best to ignore her ill feelings. The man must have a screw loose, she decided as she checked to be sure the children were okay. They seemed oblivious to their father's strange behavior.

Erin picked up a section of the burger and held it up to her brother. "Take a bite, Jack. You gotta be strong and help Daddy build houses."

Grace watched the exchange and smiled when jack bit into the burger with a child sized growl.

"May I have my drink?" Erin asked.

Brian unsteadily handed her the small cup. He concentrated on breathing until Erin started blowing into the straw. Milk bubbled up through the straw hole and dribbled down the sides of the cup. "Hey, don't do that," he scolded. Brian knew an edge of anger had come with his words. He felt ashamed for having Grace witness his loss of control.

Grace frowned and quietly sopped up the spilled milk with her napkin, then gathered up the paper garbage and wordlessly handed it to Brian. Their hands barely touched when Grace felt a mild shock tickling her skin. She dare not look up and meet his eyes. "Thank you for the food," she said softly.

"You're welcome," Brian replied. Anxious to get out of the truck even if for only a moment, he said, "Let's get these two back in their seats." He focused solely on fastening the buckles on Jack's car seat. Before he backed away from Jack, Grace called to him.

"I think you ought to check this," Grace said. "I'm not sure it's secure."

Brian's legs felt numb as he rounded the rear of the truck and saw Grace. He flinched when she took quick steps to get out of his way. Seconds later he closed the truck door. The air suddenly felt too thick to breathe.

Grace stood frozen in place and once again watched Brian try to conceal his wedding band. He seemed to be turning it around and around in nervous circles. She wondered why he did not simply take it off. For a moment she took notice of his scuffed work boots, the heavy denim jeans, the width of his shoulders and his sturdy build. She reached out and steadied herself with her hand on the side of the truck. When he began speaking, Grace held her breath.

Brian looked at his hands, ran his fingers over his ring and struggled to find his voice. "I," he said, swallowing back tears. "I'm married," he said, forcing the words out. "I was married. I lost my wife. She, she died," he whispered. Without another word he turned and walked back around the truck.

Grace was knocked off balance by what Brian said. She leaned up against the truck feeling dumbstruck. She had bashed him for cheating on his wife. Though her thoughts had not been spoken aloud, she had no right to judge him like that. He's all alone and the children have lost their mother.

Grace climbed back up on the high truck seat feeling more confused than ever. He is a widower. The children did not belong to Clay, but to Brian. Her jumbled feelings ricocheted inside her head. She listened to the silence as they drove toward the garage. They passed through the intersection where Clay died. The awful memories made her stomach hurt.

Unaware the truck had stopped, Grace jumped when Brian touched her arm. "I'm sorry, Grace began.

"Gotta pee," Jack called out from the back seat.

"Me too," said Erin.

Brian carried both kids across the asphalt parking lot. In a matter of minutes Grace was standing all alone. Before she managed to gather her wits, Jim Northrup appeared in front of her.

"I hear you had some trouble with that little car of yours," Jim said. "Which tire blew?"

"Back right," sighed Grace. "I don't have a spare. And I have no idea what size they are," she added glumly.

"Don't worry, I know all about that stuff. It's all up here," he said, tapping his head and crossing his eyes.

Grace laughed out loud. It felt good to stop thinking for a minute. "You're crazy, Jim," she laughed.

"It helps," he replied. "Now, you want a round tire, is that right?"

## Chapter 50

"Where's Grace?" Brian asked Jim outside the garage. Erin and Jack chased each other around his legs.

"Hank took her to change the tire on her car. She told me to say thanks. So, thanks," said Jim.

Brian looked out toward the road. Agitated, he reached down and picked up Jack. Erin obviously sensed his tension when she held onto his hand. Brian walked toward his truck with an unexpected feeling of emptiness. He and Grace knew nothing about each other, and he did not understand why it even mattered. "Damn," Brian muttered as he pulled the truck door open.

"That's a bad word," scolded Erin as she climbed up into the truck.

"I guess," Brian said without apology. "Hold still, Jack," he growled impatiently. After both kids were buckled in, Brian looked down the road unable to stop thinking about Grace. Alicia's words came back to him. *"She's perfect, my love."*

Had she really spoken to him or was he going crazy. The balance between madness and peace was tipping too far in the wrong direction. He wondered if there was anything to be gained by pretending today had not happened. Unconsciously, he rubbed his hand over his heart.

Brian turned to his worktable once he had the kids set up on the floor with a large sheet of paper and colored pencils. He propped his sketch pad up against the wall in front of him. He had envisioned the completed houses before he started sketching at the property. Now as he began to work, Brian took the first house apart piece by piece until he reached the bare foundation. His hands almost worked of their own free will, guiding the pencil over the paper.

He noted the dimensions in tiny print on the outer walls. As he added the numbers to each of the rough floor plans, the rooms took shape in his mind. The double garage and wide front porch fit perfectly under the second-story dormer windows. Picture windows in the kitchen and family room welcomed the light during the day and the tranquility of the woods at night. The private living room was situated on the opposite corner, giving it the desired sense of seclusion. A den and laundry room finished out the lower floor. Brian stilled his hands before he got carried away and sketched in furniture. He spread the drawings out over the worktable and studied them closely.

"Make a lizard, Jack," laughed Erin.

Brian glanced down in time to see Erin running her pencil around her other hand on the paper. She began drawing tiny faces on each fingertip before he looked away. He gathered up the drawings for the first house and slid them into a folder. After labeling it he set it aside.

Brian flipped to the next page in his sketch book. The basic structure of the second house was similar to an A-Frame home. Using the same process, he removed the roof and tore the exterior walls down to the foundation. In the next drawings he focused on the high windows in both the living and family rooms, which shared a common wall. Soundproofing the wall worked to make the living room feel cozier. A loft area built over the downstairs bedrooms created a panoramic view from the second floor.

Brian sketched in an island cooktop as the social point of the family room. It was easy to picture a pool table near the windows and overstuffed pillows on a sectional sofa. He looked over his drawings with a critical eye.

Brian's carefully restrained emotions broke free when he unconsciously perceived Clay standing next to him. His friend would tap the sketches with a pencil eraser and ask, why this or why that. Brian blinked away tears, knowing they would never have another brainstorming session. The pencil snapped apart in his hands. Losing Clay and Alicia still seemed unreal. His stomach twisted into knots as he threw the broken pieces against the wall. Gripping his hair in his hands, Brian bit back his anger.

Alicia had been his guiding light. If she had not encouraged him to take the chance and start his own business, he would still be working for someone else. With Clay they had a three-way partnership that clicked smoothly. On the day their first check came in Alicia documented the occasion with her camera. As though she were a pro, she directed them to move this way and that, to get the light just so. In the first photo he and Clay held onto either end of the check. The second one showed Clay kissing Brian's cheek and taking the check away.

Brian recalled what happened next with a sad smile. He had shoved Clay back, but found Alicia slipping in-between them before anything else happened. Clay had stepped up and sandwiched Alicia by grabbing Brian's shoulders with his outstretched arms. Her laughter had them both cracking up. Life had been good back then.

Brian had a mental treasure chest full of memories stored away, but the loneliness hurt too much. Running the business on his own and caring for the children was wearing him down both mentally and physically. He rubbed his face with his hands and exhaled slowly. Putting away the things he had no power to change was easier said than done.

Brian slipped off the stool and knelt down between Erin and Jack. He stretched out on the cold tile and picked up a pencil.

"What are you making?" Erin asked, eager to see what came out of the pencil in his hand.

Jack scooted over to see for himself. "What are you making?" he asked, echoing his sister's question.

Though Brian was pleased Jack was developing his own sense of curiosity, he knew he was in for twice as many questions. "Watch and see," he said.

"Make big buggy eyes," laughed Jack.

Brian drew tiny toes, two black eyes and the tip of the lizard's tongue sticking out of its mouth. He made the tail swirl around, ending up over the lizard's head.

"That's neat, Daddy," Erin said.

Brian continued drawing until Erin tapped his hand. "What?" Brian said without looking up.

"What's whale blubber?" Erin asked curiously.

"Oh yeah, I forgot. Let's go check the animal encyclopedia," Brian replied. He dropped the pencils on his worktable and lifted Jack up by his legs. "Come on, Jack," he said as he draped the little boy over his shoulder.

Erin ran ahead and stopped at the living room doorway. "Turn the light on. Can't see," she exclaimed.

Brian slapped the wall switch and the room lit up. He watched Erin lug the book over to where he sat on the couch with Jack on his lap. "Whales are big and they live in the ocean," Brian began as he flipped through the pages.

"Do they lay eggs?" Erin asked. "When can I read?"

"Soon. Whales are mammals, so they have babies, like dogs and cats or people," Brian explained.

"Uh huh," Erin said, absorbing every word. "They swim in the ocean, right?"

"Right," Brian agreed, then went on. "A long time ago people hunted the whales. They used all the parts of the whale for different things. See the pictures? They used the blubber, the whale's fat, to make oil for lamps. They cooked it in gigantic pots over big fires."

"Do they still hunt them?" Erin asked as she leaned in closer to examine the pictures.

"I don't think so," answered Brian.

"How big are they?" Erin asked next, tapping the black and white picture.

"Well, let's see. That one is as long as my truck," he explained, giving her something to relate to.

Erin looked up at the water stains on the ceiling. "Whales are really big, right?"

"Yes," agreed Brian. He felt Jack slipping down lower on his lap. "Let's get you guys ready for bed. Put the book back, please."

"Can I be a whale when I get bigger?" Erin asked after she pushed the book onto the shelf.

"No, Erin, you get to be a lady when you grow up." Brian lifted Jack up against his chest and stood up. "You want to come up?"

"No, I'll run fast," Erin announced and zoomed down the short hallway.

Half an hour later, Brian settled Jack into his bed and ran his hand over his soft hair. He had almost lost his temper with the boy when he refused to cooperate in the tub. Brian wished he had been able to escape at that point to go out for a long hard run.

"Can I be pretty like the Ladybug Lady?" Erin asked.

Brian sighed and turned to his daughter. "I think you will look like Mommy when you grow up. She was beautiful," he whispered.

"I'm forgetting what Mommy looks like," said Erin.

"We'll look through the photo album tomorrow," Brian told her, tugging the blankets up over her small body.

"Don't cry," begged Erin.

"I'm not," Brian lied. "Please go to sleep."

After only five months Erin was already losing the few memories of her mother. Would she one day have nothing more than photographs to remind her of the woman who gave her life? Alicia's time with him meant everything to Brian. He could not possibly forget her radiant smile, her sunny attitude and her love for him. The chance he might lose some of the details wrenched at his heart. In the dimly lit room, kneeling between the two small beds, Brian prayed silently.

*Julia Robertson*

## Chapter 51

Grace felt like a heel for leaving without thanking Brian, but she needed to escape before she made a bigger fool of herself. She tamped down her negative feelings and focused on the limited view through the tow truck windshield. Now she knew how it felt to be a small child riding in a car. She tried to sit up taller, but still saw more of the truck and the sky than the road.

She glanced over at Hank. The tow truck driver looked like a giant sitting behind the steering wheel. He was easily the biggest man she had ever seen. His glossy black hair curled over his ears. He wore dark gray jeans and huge black work boots. Black T-shirt sleeves fit snug over his heavily muscled arms. By the way his coffee brown eyes twinkled, Grace figured he never stopped smiling. She tapped his shoulder when she spotted her car.

"Alrighty," Hank said as he drove past the car and made a U-turn. "We'll get you back on the road in jig-time."

Grace pushed the heavy door open and carefully climbed down to the ground. "What can I do to help?" she asked as she stepped up next to Hank.

"There ain't much to do," he told her. "I'll check all the tires, then jack it up. You're welcome to sit in the truck if you like."

"No, I'd rather stay here if it's okay."

After inspecting the other tires, Hank shook his head. "I'd say you need to buy yourself a new set of tires. Jim will give you a fair price." Hank squatted down by the rear tire and loosened the lug nuts. "You ever change a tire?"

Grace shook her head. "I've never had a flat before today."

"Want a quick lesson? It's free," said Hank.

"Sounds like a good idea," she replied and stepped closer.

"See here?" Hank said, tapping the lug nuts. "You gotta loosen these up before you jack the car up, else the tire will just spin when you do it. Okay now, with your car you set the jack right here, then ease it on up.

You pump it up, so the tire is up off the ground like this. See?" he said when the tire rose up away from the warm asphalt.

"Is that hard to pump?" Grace asked while she leaned over with her hands on her knees. Hank made it look effortless.

"Here, you try it," he said after lowering the tire back down to the ground.

Grace stepped up and pushed down on the handle. "Hey, this is easier than I thought," she exclaimed.

Hank laughed at her surprised expression. "You betcha. You gotta good jack here, but it don't do no good without a spare."

"You're right about that," laughed Grace. She stepped back and watched him lift off the flat tire and put the new one in its place. He ran the lug nuts down with his fingers.

"Be sure and tighten these down with the lug wrench when you get it back on the ground. Otherwise," Hank said.

"They'll fall off," Grace finished for him.

"Right, you got it," he replied. Hank removed the jack and tightened the lug nuts. "Looks like you're back in business. Jim says for me to bring the old one back with me, but if I was you, I'd buy me some new tires right quick."

"Okay," sighed Grace. She waited while he put the jack and lug wrench back into the trunk. "I appreciate your help. What do I owe you?"

"Settle up with Jim when you come in. He's the boss. I'm just a lowly peon," laughed Hank.

Grace reviewed her day as she drove home. All thoughts of the meeting with the Mills family had vanished from her mind until now. As quickly as Grace began thinking about the newest quilt order, her mind wandered right back to Brian Cooper. Grace knew his name from somewhere else but could not remember where. He and Clay must have been good friends. It was a shock to learn the kids were actually his. After seeing Brian's eyes reflected in those of his son, Grace saw the truth of it.

At home she put the album and tote bag in her work room and looked over the current quilt project. On any other day she would have jumped right back into her work. Her hands were restless, but not for a needle and thread.

Grace stepped into the bathroom and cried out at the reflection in the mirror. A wide-eyed woman with tangled hair and dirt smeared on her face stared back at her. Brian had seen her like this. She recalled practically pulling her hair out with frustration at the side of the road, but how had she managed to smear dirt on her face? She angrily wiped at her cheek. She snatched the washcloth from the towel bar, turned on the hot water and scrubbed her face clean. Grace stripped off her clothes and stepped into the hot shower. The room filled with steam while she struggled to relax her tense muscles.

A few minutes later Grace pulled on a pair of red sweatpants and a light gray T-shirt. She wondered what others saw when they looked at her. Did it matter? Was there any chance someone might actually love her? Was she capable of loving that someone in return? Grace wondered if she had earned the right to be happy.

The same questions had haunted her for years, and Grace feared she knew the answers. Whether it was fate or destiny didn't matter, it dragged her down into the blackness, condemning her to a life in the shadows just beyond hope. She should have gone with her parents. Her fate would have been sealed for eternity.

"Knock it off and get back to reality," she scolded herself. As she began combing out her waist length hair, Grace gave thought to cutting it all off. Roxanne at work had a short boyish haircut and always looked perky. "Perky and cute," Grace groaned.

She grabbed her long hair and held it up on top of her head. For a moment she considered taking her scissors to it. It would take just a few minutes to chop it all off, but then what? Her wet hair fell from her fingers as she frowned at her crazy thoughts.

"You're exhausted," she scolded her reflection. "Stop thinking."

Grace paused to take a serious look at herself. As a teenager she always thought her eyes were too big, but they no longer looked that way. They were rounded and framed by long dark lashes. She suddenly realized they were her mother's eyes. When she leaned in close to the mirror, she saw flecks of gold and green in the dark blue. She assessed her pale skin. Though it was smooth and flawless, it lacked the color some women were lucky enough to have.

Grace frowned at herself again. Was it her personality that kept anyone from getting too close to her? She had a few friends and there had been boyfriends, but nothing serious. Though she was friendly and comfortable around other people, she had to admit she felt empty and lonely. What had Brian Cooper thought of her messy hair and dirty face? She flipped the light off and her reflection vanished.

Every ounce of creative energy drained from Grace while she dragged herself around her empty house. She had no ambition, which made her feel guilty. When the walls began to feel as though they were closing in on her, Grace wandered into the kitchen. She poured a glass of milk and stood by the window staring out into the darkness. The dripping faucet kept up a steady beat, but Grace barely noticed. She kept thinking about Brian Cooper. Kept thinking about the look in his eyes when he told her his wife had died. Moving slowly, Grace lifted the glass to her lips and froze. As if a switch had been flipped on in her head, she realized what she had been trying to remember.

"Cooper," she said and put the half empty glass down on the counter.

Out of habit, Grace had saved the vital statistics section from each newspaper over the past few months. Did she still have that specific section? Seconds later her eyes landed on the only newspaper she had not taken apart. It contained Clay's obituary, which she hadn't written or read. Her hands shook as she opened the folded pages. Upon locating his obituary, the black lettering appeared distorted. She blinked and read through her tears.

"Clayton James Hancock, age 34, died Thursday night. He is survived by his mother, Elizabeth, and his sister, Janine Burns."

He had not been married and did not have children. She scanned down the article and found Brian's name listed among the pallbearers. It must have been awful to walk alongside his friend's body in the casket. She knew death was a natural part of life, but it did not make it any easier to experience.

Grace carefully folded the pages and set them aside. A sense of urgency pushed her to keep searching. Not in June, May or April. Then she came to the stack of papers from March. With great care, she reached out and picked up the folded section. Her heart skipped a beat at the sight of the printed name.

"Alicia," she whispered. "I read about you before. He's all alone and your children still need you. Alicia, it's terrible. What happened to you?" Grace cried for all they had lost.

*Alicia watched and listened to the woman sitting on the floor. Grace Marshall had the qualities to fill the void her death had left behind. Despite the wall she had built around her heart, Grace had spirit, determination and a rare appreciation for life. Brian needed someone who had the strength to help him deal with his losses and rebuild his own spirit. Alicia knew Brian had the power within him to open Grace's heart to love. This home needed to be filled with laughter and love once again. The obstacles standing in the way seemed insurmountable, but Alicia would find a way to convey her messages. The alarmed expression on Grace's face told Alicia she needed to go.*

Grace sat perfectly still with the paper in her hands. The odd feeling of being watched crept into her mind, but she had not heard anything. Breathing hard, Grace set the paper down and stood up from the floor. She knew the back door was locked but did not remember locking the front door. Listening, she stepped up and quickly turned the lock. She rubbed her arms and wondered if someone had been watching her. Her vivid imagination tended to conjure up all sorts of crazy things, but this seemed different. Exhausted, she leaned back against the heavy wooden door. Grace pressed her fingers to her lips feeling a deep sorrow for Brian and his children. Without warning she found herself jerked backward in time and slid helplessly to the cold floor.

With the boat on the trailer behind the car, Grace watched her parents finish packing the trunk. Her pleas for them to stay home went unheeded. She hugged them and cried while they reassured her they would be back in no time, but they never came home again.

Grace rested her forehead against her knees and wept. If she had only tried harder to make them listen. The horrible memories made her stomachache.

*Alicia returned just in time to confirm her earlier observations. Grace had suffered a terrible loss, and though she had not yet come to terms with the tragedy, Alicia saw the possibilities. Alicia also recognized the deep sadness in the woman's eyes. The threads holding her together were barely intact. When Grace looked up with fear in her eyes, Alicia hastened her departure, leaving behind her whispered words.*

Grace watched the lace curtains pull up against the glass, then flutter out and swirl around as if the windows were open. The sight stunned her, but it was nothing compared to the neatly penned words literally floating in the air before her.

"*He needs you. He needs you.*"

*Julia Robertson*

## Chapter 52

Anna smiled when she heard his voice. "Are you still at work?" she asked.

"Yes, I am watching the sunset from my office window. I prefer driving home after dark when it is so hot. I will be glad to bid August goodbye," replied Garrison. "Have you finished packing?"

"I think so," replied Anna. She sat down heavily on the edge of the bed, staring at the brand-new matching suitcases. Not a single scratch marred the sleek surfaces of the powder blue overnight bag and hard sided suitcase with tiny wheels mounted on one end. Even with the well-worn rug beneath them, the sight could have been a photograph out of a stylish magazine. "It's a shame to think of ruining such nice luggage. I ought to use my old ones," she grumbled.

"Anna, you deserve nice things. No more arguments," said Garrison.

Anna actually loved the new luggage, but she found it difficult to accept his generosity. "Paige tells me I'm foolish," she said with a sigh.

"Anna, you are as far from foolish as the moon is from here," Garrison assured her. "I will be by to pick you up at 5 o'clock tomorrow morning."

"I'll be ready," she replied.

Anna's life had been turned upside down. Garrison had taken her out to dinner twice a week and called her nearly every night for the past few months. With his urging, Paige had taken Anna shopping for a new wardrobe. Tomorrow morning they were going on a vacation together. Traveling together but staying in separate hotel rooms as Anna demanded. On that subject she would not budge. She did not deny being nervous, though whether it was about her first airplane ride or spending so much time with Garrison, she was not sure.

During all the years she had been employed by Garrison and his wife, Anna had always been careful to keep her personal feelings in check. Anna never shared any details about the goings on in their household. Only Paige knew the emotional stress she had endured. As close as she was to Paige, Anna never disclosed her longtime attraction to Garrison. Listening to him being verbally assaulted by Contessa often brought Anna to tears. Dwelling on the past only kept the wounds from healing. Anna wanted to think about nothing but the future.

The quiet tapping on the front door early the following morning startled Anna. She saw Paige peeking out from the hallway and hurried over to hug her. "He's here," she said excitedly. "I'll call you tomorrow."

"Have fun," said Paige, rubbing her sleepy eyes.

The tapping came again before Anna reached the door. She pulled it open and turned to get her bags.

"Allow me, Anna. Is this everything?" Garrison asked as he snatched up the two pieces of luggage.

"Yes, I think so," she laughed nervously. Fingers linked together she watched him take the luggage outside. She turned when Paige rushed over and gave her another hug.

"He's crazy about you. Let him take care of you," whispered Paige.

"I never," Anna began, then stopped when Paige shook her head. "Thank you, I'll try." The two women shared one more hug before Anna turned and hurried out onto the porch.

As she approached Garrison Anna decided it had to be a dream, but the chilly morning air told her otherwise. She stopped at the top of the steps when she felt his hands take hold of hers. She felt queasy. Did people their ages fall in love? No words reached her lips while her eyes were held by his.

## Chapter 53

Anxious barely touched how Garrison felt when he parked in front of Paige's house. He sat long enough to gather his wits and calm his nerves before he pushed the door open and stepped out into the cool early morning air. It seemed an eternity before Anna came to the door. When it opened, he felt the long hours of waiting fade away.

"Allow me," he told Anna when she began reaching for her luggage. Only a cad would have allowed such a beautiful lady to carry her own bags. Garrison placed Anna's luggage into the spacious trunk. He fully expected her to produce a few more pieces, but before he returned to the door, she came out holding nothing more than her small handbag. She closed the door behind her as he approached the porch steps.

Garrison was delighted to see her dressed in her new clothes. The pale pink sweater did wonders for her ivory complexion and mocha brown eyes. Her auburn hair, lightly sprinkled with silver, was arranged in a thick braid that reached halfway down her back. For a woman of her age, which he guessed to be in her late 60's, Anna was trim and vibrant back-lit by the porch light. Never in all his years of marriage to Contessa had he known the affection he felt for Anna. She warmed his heart like sunshine on a cold winter's day.

Garrison stopped Anna on the second step up and took her hands in his. Their eyes met and neither of them moved for a few wordless moments.

"Garrison," she whispered.

"I am falling in love with you, Anna," he whispered and kissed her lightly on her cheek. As much as he wanted to remain right where they were, Garrison knew they needed to go in order to catch their flight. He guided her down the last two steps and walked her out to the car.

*Julia Robertson*

Chapter 54

The doorbell rang shortly before noon. Brian ushered the kids to one side and opened the front door. His eyes widened when he saw the woman standing next to Garrison Rivers. He had not expected anyone to be with him. When the mild shock eased, Brian found his voice.

"Welcome. Please come in," he said and stepped back with the kids clinging to him. "They're a little shy around strangers," he explained, compelled to justify their behavior.

"We understand," said the woman. She smiled at the three of them as she stepped inside.

Brian watched the man who was Alicia's father. He stood frozen in the doorway. Brian hesitated a moment before he said, "I have lunch set up on the back patio."

"That sounds wonderful. What can I do to help?" the woman asked.

Brian watched as she glanced back at Garrison. "Everything's ready to go," he said in reply.

"We got teeny pickles," Jack said before he ducked behind his father's hand.

"Daddy," whispered Erin.

Brian knew the kids needed space between them and the two strangers. Truth be told he wanted out of this awkward situation himself. "How about going outside now," Brian suggested. He started toward the kitchen and heard the woman's soft footsteps behind him. At the kitchen doorway, he glanced over his shoulder and saw Garrison closing the front door. Brian could not imagine what Garrison thought of their small, sparsely furnished house. It was nothing like he was accustomed to living in. When Garrison started to walk in his direction, Brian noticed his faltering steps. He turned away at the sound of the woman's voice.

"This is a cute house," she told Brian. "You are renting, aren't you?"

"Yes, we are," Brian replied as he pushed the back door open. The kids raced across the grass toward the swing-set. The woman's voice sounded familiar to him, but he couldn't place her. Out of respect he had not asked her who she was or why she was with Garrison. Brian let it go and asked, "What would you like to drink? We have iced tea, milk, apple juice and water."

"Oh, iced tea sounds wonderful," she replied. "Garrison?" she asked cautiously.

"She looks... she looks like Alicia," Garrison stammered.

"Yes, she does," Brian agreed.

"She is beautiful," said Garrison.

"Like Alicia," Brian said, then waited to see what happened next.

Eyes downcast, Garrison said, "I am sorry." He turned and walked back toward the front door.

Brian forced his tense muscles to relax. He had not known what to expect from Alicia's father. His words had sounded authentic. His apology sounded sincere. Doubt hovered over each of those thoughts. Brian turned toward the woman once the front door closed behind Garrison.

"We've never met in person. I'm Anna," she said, drawing attention away from Garrison's hasty departure.

It took a moment for Brian to digest her words. His eyes widened with genuine surprise. "Anna?"

"Alicia has always been close to my heart," Anna whispered.

Seeing her eyes brimming with tears, Brian blinked hard. "She loved you so much," he sighed.

"Oh my," Anna said, weeping softly.

When Anna held her arms out to him, Brian stepped into her warm embrace. "I'm sorry," he said, unsure where the words had come from.

"I'll get you all wet. I cry big tears," confessed Anna.

"I don't mind," whispered Brian. They both turned to look outside when a squeal broke the silence. The kids were chasing after a red ball.

"You're doing a wonderful job with them," said Anna.

"I'm trying," replied Brian.

"It can't be easy for you. Do they understand she is gone?" Anna asked.

"Erin does, but Jack is too young," replied Brian. "I keep photographs out for them to see. I want them to remember her."

"You're a good father, Brian. I'm happy to be here." Anna wiped her eyes and stepped back a little further. "Coming here has been extremely difficult for Garrison. He's feeling a lot of guilt."

"I'm sure he is. Should we go on with lunch without him?" Brian asked. He had no reason to feel any compassion toward Garrison Rivers.

"Why don't you pour the tea and let me go talk to him. Brian," she said after checking behind her. "You need to know his divorce is final. You also need to know that he and I are seeing each other." She grimaced at Brian's baffled expression. "I know what you're thinking, but he's not the same man. Please give him a chance."

"For you, I will," Brian agreed. "I'll get the kids going on their lunch. Jack still needs an afternoon nap."

Anna patted Brian's arm. "I understand," she laughed. "We'll be right out."

\*\*\*

Anna found Garrison sitting in the rental car with the passenger door wide open. "It's going to be all right," she said as she tugged his hands away from his face.

"I cannot believe I was so damned stupid. Why the hell didn't I step in and save my daughter when it all started?" he pleaded.

Anna watched him sit up and pull a folded handkerchief out of his pocket. His hands trembled while he dried his face. "We cannot change the past, so let's enjoy today and look ahead to tomorrow. I think Alicia knows how you feel now. Do right by Brian and their children and it will help heal the wounds," Anna assured him. "Do right, Garrison."

"Do you think she can forgive me?" he asked.

"Without a doubt," replied Anna. "She's an angel in Heaven. She is everything good."

"Oh, Anna, that little girl," Garrison said, looking up at the house.

"You are not alone," Anna reminded him. She watched him lower his eyes to hers.

"Alicia is not the only angel," he said. "Thank you, Anna."

"You're welcome," replied Anna. "Let's go inside, I'm hungry enough to eat a horse."

"I hope the boy has something more appealing than that. Anna, about what I said earlier today," Garrison said.

"Yes?" she asked.

"I am past falling. I am deeply in love with you," he whispered.

Chapter 55

Brian looked up when Anna and Garrison stepped out onto the patio. Garrison helped Anna with her chair before he sat down next to her. Brian silently wondered if the man had changed. Was such a drastic change even possible?

"Daddy," Erin said, tugging on his arm. "We're hungry."

"Sorry," Brian said as he set the plates down in front of Erin and Jack. Brian's eyes were drawn back to Anna when she began assembling two sandwiches on her plate. He could not help but wonder if Garrison possessed the ability to manage such a simple task. Brian caught himself before he shook his head, mindful of Anna's presence. She seemed so at ease compared to Garrison. Brian was aware of Garrison's eyes darting from Erin to Jack and back again. It took him by surprise when the older man spoke to Erin.

"How old are you, Erin?" Garrison asked.

"I'm five," Erin replied. She held up her hand and wiggled all five fingers.

"I'm this many," said Jack.

Brian patiently moved Jack's thumb and little finger down to his palm. "Pretty soon you'll be able to do it by yourself," Brian said quietly.

"You are three!" exclaimed Anna.

"Daddy says he's gonna be bigger than me. He eats lots," explained Erin.

"They're growing like weeds," said Brian.

"We're not weeds," corrected Erin. "He says we're babies too, but we're not babies."

"Daddies say things like that," said Anna. "It's because he loves you."

"I know," Erin said in a matter-of-fact tone.

Brian wondered what Garrison was thinking about. He must have been concentrating on something unseen when Anna touched his hand.

The man nearly jumped off his chair. "How long are you planning to stay out here?" Brian asked. Regret swamped him the instant the words were out of his mouth.

Garrison sat back while Anna placed his sandwich on the plate in front of him. "Our return flight is in two weeks. I plan on taking Anna to the ocean. She has never seen the Pacific," said Garrison.

"That's a great idea. I can make some suggestions if you don't mind." Brian waited to see how his words settled in Garrison's mind. He knew the man possessed more stubborn than the average mule.

"I am open to any ideas you might have. In truth, I have never been to the Oregon coast myself," Garrison admitted, turning in time to see Anna's eyes grow wide.

"Are you serious?" she asked.

Garrison shrugged. "Yes, I am," he confessed. "I understand we can take dune buggy rides over there. Is that within a reasonable distance?"

"Yes, it is," Brian replied. "They're a blast. We also have a great aquarium, as well as countless viewpoints along the coast highway."

Garrison nodded and said, "Maybe you can mark the map I have out in the car. Thank you, Brian."

Realizing this was their first actual conversation, Brian felt the gentle nudge to keep talking. "While you're here, I'd like to take you to see the houses I'm currently building."

"I'd love that," said Anna.

"How is your business doing?" asked Garrison. "Are you satisfied with the architect who designs the blueprints for you?"

The question should not have surprised Brian. He wanted Alicia to be here with him for this moment. She would proudly explain an architect was beyond their financial means. "No sir, I do everything from the preliminary sketches to the finish work," Brian replied confidently.

"Good, that is good," Garrison replied, nodding his head slowly.

Brian saw doubt in the man's eyes. He probably pictured small box style structures with no fine touches. "I'll be glad to show you my next project. It's all in the rough draft stage, but it is coming right along. I'm designing a two-story home for a couple who bought property outside of town. The acreage is beautiful with a creek and a good number of mature trees. I'd be happy to take you out there if you are interested in seeing it," Brian suggested.

"We can do that," Garrison agreed.

Anna looked from one man to the other. She wiped her fingers on a paper napkin before reaching out for her glass. "Brian, I'd love to have more tea. Would you mind?" she asked.

"I'd be glad to bring it out," Brian replied, thankful for the distraction. He checked the kids before he pushed back from the table and walked toward the back door. No doubt Anna had felt the tension building between him and Garrison. The uncomfortable ordeal was making him feel like he was sitting on a cliff, struggling to keep from falling. "Keep me calm, Alicia," he prayed silently.

After putting the kids down for a nap, Brian walked out to the living room and found Anna and Garrison standing together at the front window. He needed Alicia here to hold his hand and guide his thoughts. When Anna turned from the window, he gestured toward the couch and sat down on the overstuffed chair.

"These are for you to keep," Garrison said as he handed a large manila envelope to Brian. "My lawyer has the original copies. Now you have a record of everything, including paperwork you need to sign and have notarized regarding Alicia's trust fund. I honestly had not remembered her account existed until recently. If any changes are made Nathan will forward copies on to you." Garrison stepped away and sat down next to Anna. He reached up to check the tie he was not wearing, then brushed his hands against his light brown cotton pants. He turned and looked at Anna. She smiled at him before she glanced over at Brian.

Brian held the large envelope on his lap. "So, you were serious about what you said on the phone?" Brian asked.

"Yes, you may read through it now or wait until later. If you have any questions, ask me or contact my lawyer," Garrison explained.

Brian nodded, aware of the weight of the papers in his hands. The slightest movement to his left made him turn, but he saw nothing there. He rubbed his ear and suddenly felt off balance. "I know Alicia is pleased," he said, and instantly wondered where the words had come from. He turned again, but still saw nothing there.

Anna watched Brian and noticed the strange look in his eyes. She glanced at Garrison, then looked back at Brian.

"Perhaps we can look over your sketches," suggested Garrison.

"Good idea," agreed Brian, glad for the chance to leave the room. He set the envelope on a stack of books on his worktable and picked up his sketches. He stood there for a moment longer trying to settle his jumpy nerves. "Alicia," he whispered before he returned to the living room.

Garrison examined the sketches, one after the other. "I am impressed with your work," remarked Garrison.

Brian appreciated what the man said, but recalled a letter Alicia wrote to her parents years ago. He had read the words and told her to throw it away, but she insisted on mailing it. Brian wondered now if Garrison remembered the letter or if he had ever actually read it. Chances were Contessa had destroyed it without telling him. A portion of the letter replayed in Brian's mind.

"If you took the time to see what he can do, you would see what I see. He is bright. He's a good man. He works hard for me, for us."

Brian dragged his thoughts back to the present. "I won't do any more than basic floor designs until the owners choose which one they prefer," Brian explained. "They make the final choices, so I always offer a few options. I won't build anything unless I know it will work out perfectly." It felt strange having Alicia's father study his designs. Garrison seemed genuinely interested with the rough sketches and the potential outcome of the work. Brian finally let down his guard and relaxed.

"How do you get started? When do you see the finished house?" asked Garrison.

"With this project I walked around the property several times. It all comes together for me after a while. I study the layout of the property and visualize the finished house first. Then I take the place apart step-by-step to the framed-in structure and on down to the basic foundation." Brian shrugged since the process was no big deal for him.

"Fascinating," commented Garrison. He looked at his son-in-law with newfound respect.

## Chapter 56

Ponderosa pine trees blocked the sun intermittently along the secluded dirt drive. The car bounced over rocks and ruts in the ground and eventually popped out into the brilliant sunshine again. The picturesque setting appeared before them, dotted with old oak trees against a backdrop of rugged mountains.

"It's beautiful out here," sighed Anna.

Brian parked in the shade, opened his door and gestured toward the downgrade to the left. "The creek runs along the property line over in that direction." He helped the kids out of their car seats while Garrison assisted Anna.

"Hey, this is where Jack found a lizard," Erin said before she was lifted out of the car. The search for the same lizard began as soon as the kids were out of the car.

"They're precious," Anna said as she watched the little ones take off.

"I kind of like them," Brian said. He pocketed the car keys and shifted his sketch book from hand to hand.

"That's easy to see. A happy child reflects a happy home," Anna said with a bright smile. She had not given thought to Garrison being close enough to hear her. "I'm sorry," she whispered, afraid she had hurt his feelings. She reached out and took Garrison's hand in hers. "Let it go, please," she said softly.

Garrison nodded and said, "Yes, you are right."

Anna was grateful when Garrison changed the subject. He had a tendency to sink into mild depression whenever he thought about his past mistakes.

"Where is the house going to be built?" Garrison asked, turning to Brian.

"Over here," replied the younger man. He held up the first sketch as a reference. "I see the house facing this way with the existing trees shading the front porch."

Anna closed her eyes and visualized the wide porch with wind chimes and an assortment of chairs. "It'll be perfect on warm summer mornings to bring breakfast out onto the porch." Anna opened her eyes and found the two men staring at her. "I have a good imagination," she laughed.

Anna listened while Brian and Garrison talked over the setting of the house. Garrison squeezed her hand before he walked away with Brian. Hearing them talking with each other warmed Anna's heart. She turned and slowly made her way across the uneven ground toward the children. She stopped when she was close enough to hear them talking.

"Is this the rock?" Erin asked.

"Yeah," exclaimed Jack as he crouched down close to the ground.

"Was he hiding under it?" Erin asked next.

"Uh huh," replied Jack.

"I'm gonna pick it up," Erin said, tentatively extending her hand to touch the rock. "Be really quiet," Erin warned.

Half listening to the conversation between Erin and Jack, Anna turned to watch Garrison with Brian. Her practical side reminded her to avoid dreams. Dreams had never helped her in the past, but her lifelong fear of being alone in her upper years no longer felt quite so strong. When the men shook hands, Anna allowed herself another tiny fragment of hope. Hope, like dreams, was fragile and easily shattered.

"Why are they doing that?" asked Erin.

"Oh my," gasped Anna, startled to find the little girl standing right next to her. For the sake of the child, she quickly regained her composure. "I think they are trying to make amends."

"Make what?" Erin asked.

"Let me think," Anna replied, pausing to choose her words. "Sometimes when we disagree about something, we find out we're wrong and want to make things right again. Shaking hands is a way of showing that." Anna watched the child process the concept.

"Like when I get mad at Jack, and Daddy says I have to say I'm sorry?" Erin asked.

"That's it, very good," praised Anna. She reached around Erin and gently hugged her.

"Who is that?" Erin asked.

Caught off guard, Anna looked over at Garrison. Before she had a chance to come up with an answer, something else drew the little girl's attention away.

"Hey, look!" squealed Erin. "He found him!"

Jack was laying on the ground with his eyes locked on the eyes of a lizard. Erin scurried over to his side right away. The commotion caught Brian and Garrison's attention as well.

Anna watched Brian walk directly to the kids. Garrison trailed behind Brian and stopped next to her. Anna looked up when his hand slid into hers. Together they watched the scene before them. Brian knelt down and rested his hand on his son's back.

"Let's get closer," Anna said, tugging on Garrison's hand. She encouraged him to kneel down on the rough ground next to her when they were close enough to see the children's faces and hear what they were saying. "Just look at his face," Anna whispered. "He's adorable."

"Yes," agreed Garrison.

"I wonder what he's thinking," she said. Anna loved the way Jack was laying on the ground with his hands fisted under his chin. His chubby cheeks were rosy and his eyes wide with wonder. She glanced up at Garrison and saw the shimmering tears in his eyes. A few minutes later he pushed to his feet. Anna was grateful for his helping hands as she joined him.

Garrison brought his handkerchief out and wiped the dampness from his eyes. As he pushed it back into his pocket he smiled at Anna.

Anna knew she would never forget how she felt at this very moment. Meeting Alicia's family, spending time with Garrison and being in a place she had never so much as imagined seeing, filled her with boundless joy. When Anna saw Brian scoop Jack up from the ground, she smiled. His movements were effortless, as though the boy weighed no more than a feather. She grinned once more when Erin clambered to be picked up in the same manner.

While the laughter of the children touched her, Brian's expression gave her pause. He was still grieving over the loss of Alicia. She wanted to tell him his life would get better, that the pain would ease, but those things were for Brian to discover on his own.

*Julia Robertson*

## Chapter 57

Garrison found the drive out of town quite calming. Compared to where he lived this was wild country. Other than a few small houses and a couple of big barns, there were no other structures to be seen. When they came to a stop, he reluctantly opened the door. There were no sidewalks to step out onto and not a single office building or restaurant in sight.

Garrison might have thought he had landed in an alien land if not for Anna holding his hand. He never allowed himself to dream about participating in the lives of his grandchildren, but here he was watching them running across a dirt field. The bright-eyed little boy, and the girl who would have been Alicia's twin if not for the fact she was Alicia's daughter. So many mistakes, he sighed inwardly. Anna was correct in saying he needed to let the past go and focus on today and the future.

Garrison listened as Brian verbally illustrated the setting. "How do you start a project like this? I mean once you have completed the blueprints, what is the first step?"

Brian checked on the kids before leading the way into the middle of the cleared ground designated for the house. The sun-dried earth beneath their feet crumbled as they walked over it. Brian stopped and flipped to the sketch of the bare foundation.

"We'll drive stakes in to mark the outer corners of the foundation first," Brian began.

Garrison looked over the sketch, doing his best to see what Brian was describing. He knew about building a financial foundation, but taking raw materials and actually creating a physical structure seemed an impossible endeavor to him. "How do you decide how to begin or how much wood you need or how long to cut the pieces?" he asked, feeling no brighter than the clods of dirt under his shoes.

"It isn't so complicated once you've been trained to do the work. I went to college to learn and spent my time away from the classroom doing grunt work to make ends meet," Brian explained.

"Grunt work," Garrison said. "Define that term for me."

"On any construction site, no matter the size, someone needs to take on the task of cleaning up," Brian explained. "Whether it is sweeping up sawdust, washing concrete out of a wheelbarrow or picking up nails and scrap wood, it has to be done. While doing those things you see the hands-on work and eventually take on the simplest of those tasks. Every step is a building block to something bigger."

"Yes, of course, that makes sense," Garrison agreed. He mulled over what he needed to say, scanning the land, the mountains and the many trees within walking distance from where they stood. Garrison considered grunt work might also entail scratching the surface of a problem. It might begin with an offered apology with the hope of building up to something akin to trust. "Brian," Garrison began. "I am sorry for my past mistakes. I sincerely hope you can accept my apology and join me in building the foundation to a new relationship."

Though Brian did not reply, he did offer his hand in peace. Garrison grasped his son-in-law's hand. He saw before him a man who loved his children and had truly loved Alicia.

Garrison wondered if he might have been a good father himself had he made better choices. If he had not fallen for Contessa's lies. If he had known the love he now felt for Anna in his earlier years. He had been incredibly ignorant about what counted most in life. While it was easier to put the entire blame on Contessa, he had to admit equal guilt. Garrison's emotions felt raw.

Erin's delightful squeal drew the men away from each other. No more words were exchanged as they crossed to Anna and the children.

Garrison took note of Anna's bright smile and sun pinked cheeks. When Anna tugged on his hand Garrison followed after her, enjoying the happy sound of her voice. Garrison shifted his attention from the boy to Erin. Her hand rested on her brother's narrow shoulder while their father leaned in close to both of them. Brian projected a calm and confident attitude while describing his building techniques, but he easily switched to his role as a father to his children.

Garrison felt an intense yearning for everything he had never known. He wondered if it was possible to mend a small part of his life through Alicia's children. The impossibility weighed heavily on his mind.

Garrison pushed to his feet and offered Anna his hand. He drew her close and kissed her cheek. When she looked up at him and touched his face with her fingertips, his heart melted. He had never experienced anything like this before.

"They make a nice family, don't they," sighed Anna when Brian started walking toward the creek with the kids.

"Yes, they do," replied Garrison. "Do you think he will allow us to return?"

"From what I've seen so far, yes," Anna replied. "Be mindful of your old ways. Brian is doing everything right despite losing Alicia."

"Yes," agreed Garrison.

"Let's see where they are going," Anna suggested. She began walking with Garrison's hand holding hers. "I'm enjoying this. I've always wanted to go on an adventure, "Anna said.

"Anna," Garrison said, turning her to face him. "If you will have me, you will make me a very happy man."

"What did you just say?" asked Anna.

"Anna, will you marry me?" Garrison asked, lifting her hands and kissing her fingers. "We will have time for adventures. I will take you anywhere you want to go," he promised.

"You can't be serious," scolded Anna. "Don't say things you don't mean," she said, pushing back from him.

"Anna," Garrison sighed. "You have given me a reason for living. Help me through my golden years. Walk alongside me and answer my questions. Share my meals, my idle time, and my bedtime. Please, Anna, marry me," Garrison said, embracing the chance to experience genuine happiness.

Anna looked down at the ground and blinked several times before looking up again. "I can't answer you right now. Please give me time to think," she whispered.

"Take all the time you need. My heart is yours," he replied, gently enfolding her in his arms, marveling at the fact she had not simply turned him down. He tipped her face up and lightly touched his lips to hers. Anna's dark brown eyes sparkled in the sunlight. "You are beautiful," he whispered.

"No," sighed Anna. Though she did not step back, she did look away. "Oh my," Anna gasped.

Garrison held onto Anna and awkwardly eased her down to the ground. Relief came when he found she was still breathing. He held her and brushed her hair back from her face.

"Anna, open your eyes," Garrison said hoarsely. "She passed out," he said when Brian crouched down in front of him.

For Garrison it seemed an eternity before Anna's eyes fluttered open. Brian was right there, and Garrison would be forever grateful for his calm response.

"What happened?" she said with quiet surprise.

"It sounds like you've been out here in the hot sun for too long," Brian said. "Let's get you back to my car."

"Okay," whispered Anna.

Garrison watched Brian help Anna to her feet. By the time Garrison managed to stand up, he knew Anna was in trouble again.

"I'll carry you," Brian said. Over Anna's quiet objections he lifted her with ease and started walking toward his car and the shade under the trees.

Garrison stood there all alone, feeling as worthless as a rock. To his surprise, he found the children standing right in front of him. He had no idea what to do with them. Facing disgruntled and potentially violent employees had not made his legs shake like they were now. Fighting to push through mergers or dealing with major losses in the stock market never created the instant panic he felt taking hold of him. Believing the children were nothing more than smaller versions of adults was impossible. Feeling a terrible tightening in his chest, Garrison cautiously offered his hand to Erin. Erin placed her small hand in his. Garrison had barely registered how tiny her hand felt when Jack scampered around and took hold of his other hand. Assuming he had to lead them, Garrison focused on keeping his steps slow.

"We have to hurry and catch up with Daddy," Erin insisted.

Garrison felt perplexed. What if the little boy could not keep up with them? His concern evaporated when Jack moved ahead and tugged on his other hand.

"Is she okay?" Erin asked.

"I believe so," Garrison replied when he saw Anna. As they drew nearer, he watched the smile spread across her beautiful face.

"Grandpa," said Anna.

Erin peered up at him. "Are you a grandpa?" she asked.

"Maybe," replied Garrison, feeling ill at ease. Of course he knew he had not earned the right to be a grandfather, but had Brian not told the children who he was? He found the idea heartbreaking and looked to Anna for help.

Brian came around from the back of the car and handed a cup of water to Anna. "What did I miss?" he asked, glancing from Anna to Garrison before seeing Erin's wide eyes.

## Chapter 58

"Oh boy," Brian groaned silently. Had they not already had enough turmoil for one day? He ran through the past several minutes, searching for answers, if answers were indeed to be found.

"Alicia," Brian had whispered while he was watching Jack. She would have loved sharing this event, watching their son as he stared at the tiny creature on the rock. Aching for all he had lost, Brian looked up and saw Garrison holding Anna. Jealousy struck without warning. Logic told him it was a natural reaction, but it left Brian feeling off balance.

Alicia had told him about how Contessa had treated Anna. When Alicia had bad dreams late at night, it was Anna who comforted her. It was Anna who read to her and helped Alicia strive toward her independence. Was it conceivable that Anna might help Garrison make better choices for his life?

Still weighed down by feelings of jealousy, Brian became aware of Erin standing next to him. He heard a dozen questions coming from her even before she opened her mouth to speak. He pressed his finger to his lips to silence her.

"Don't go!" shouted Jack.

When Jack scrambled to his feet to give chase, Brian grabbed him from behind. "Let him go. You can look for him next time," Brian said as he draped the squirming boy over his shoulder and patted his behind.

"Me too. Make us rotten potatoes," Erin shrieked with glee.

Brian stood up with both kids over his shoulders. Without a word he turned and walked toward the creek with his children's giggles following after him.

Brian desperately needed some distance between him and Garrison in order to try and settle his conflicting emotions. He would give anything to hold Alicia in his arms again. Though he kept his pace deliberately slow, he wanted to start running and never stop.

They had not gone further than a stone's throw away when Brian stopped walking. Erin was twisting around and grabbing hold of the collar of his shirt. "What's wrong?" he asked.

"Look," said Erin.

Brian turned and saw Garrison hugging Anna again. The sky suddenly turned misty gray, and everything went eerily silent. At that very moment he felt a feather light touch on his lips. A light breeze swept through his hair and he knew. "Alicia," Brian whispered desperately.

She was here, standing right in front of him as real as the first time he had seen her. Alive and here with him. It could not be so. He lost her when she died in his arms. The sadness, the pain, the coffin, he gasped without a sound, unable to catch his breath. How many times had he wished for her to return and here she was, close enough to touch? His Alicia. Brian felt a black hood sliding over him as he fell toward madness.

"Mommy," whispered Erin.

Jerked back to reality, Brian lost his balance, stumbled forward and nearly fell to his knees. Hoping to mask his fear, Brian shifted the kids in his arms. "What did you say?" he asked Erin.

"You saw her," whispered Erin. "She kissed you, Daddy. Mommy kissed you."

Brian was in shock, but he had to keep from sliding further into the darkness. "It's okay," he finally said, though his heart was pounding so loud he barely heard his own words.

Still stunned by what had just happened, Brian saw Garrison struggling to help Anna to the ground. Anna must have seen Alicia too. When he knelt down next to her, he saw the fear in Garrison's eyes. Brian gently squeezed Anna's hand and was pleased when she opened her eyes. She needed to get out of the sun right away, so Brian helped her to her feet. Though she was standing, Brian knew it was too far for her to walk. He lifted her up into his arms and started across the rough ground.

"I feel foolish," Anna complained weakly.

"Consider it my good deed for the day," replied Brian.

When they reached the car, Brian helped Anna sit on the front seat with the door wide open. "Stay put," he told her, earning a smile and a nod.

*Tender Dreams*

Upon returning with water for Anna, the sight of Garrison holding Erin and Jack's hands took Brian by surprise. He looked from Garrison to Anna and back again.

"You both have some explaining to do," Anna said, nodding at Garrison.

Comprehension dawned when Erin stepped up on his boots. He picked her up as he looked into Garrison's eyes. "We'll be back in a minute," Brian said as he hoisted Jack up on his arm. Still rattled after seeing Alicia, Brian needed time to think away from their watchful eyes. He walked out to the shade under a massive oak tree, sat down and held his children close. Jack cuddled against him, something Brian cherished every time he held either of his children. Erin kept looking over toward Anna and Garrison. Brian knew she needed to understand the situation. He kept his explanation simple and her instant comprehension threw him for a loop.

"You mean Mommy had a daddy, like you, like me?" Erin said.

"You are something else, Erin Madison," Brian sighed. Her frown baffled him as he waited for her next thoughts to emerge.

"What about Jack? Can he have a grandpa too?"

"That's how it works, Erin. You have to share him," Brian explained. A few moments of silence passed while a light breeze rustled the leaves overhead and the chatter of birds filled the air.

"He's kind of old," Erin said.

Brian laughed out loud and felt a good measure of his tension melt away. "Yeah, he is kind of old, but that's what grandpas are," replied Brian.

"Do we get to call him Grandpa?" Erin asked next.

"I think he might like that," replied Brian. He kissed her forehead and watched her thoughtful expression. "What are you thinking about?" he asked.

"What about the lady? Is she a grandma?"

Erin fiddled with the buttons on his shirt, then reached over and tickled Jack. Brian felt her concentration fading. "No, but you may call her Anna," he replied. Still holding Jack, Brian stood up and brushed off the seat of his pants.

"Up high," Jack said, climbing up on Brian's arm.

"Hey!" Erin called out as she ran back toward the car. "I get to call you Grandpa!"

From where he stood beneath the old oak tree with Jack on his shoulders, Brian watched Garrison give Erin a hug. He knew the man had never hugged Alicia like that. A light breeze blew warm air against Brian's cheek. "Alicia," he whispered, carefully restraining his earlier fears. He turned toward the warm sensation at the same time Jack leaned down. Jack's slobbery kiss surprised him.

"Jack," Brian laughed as he pulled his son down into his arms. "I love you, little guy."

## Chapter 59

"I don't deserve this," snarled Contessa. She drank the amber liquid straight out of the bottle since she ran out of clean glasses long ago. From the looks of the wine cellar, she was going to run out of booze as well.

Contessa had interviewed countless housekeepers since Anna flew the coop, but none of them suited her needs. "Not a damned one of them," she blurted out.

She slammed the empty bottle down on the coffee table and fell back against the custom-made leather sofa. She grabbed an embroidered pillow and used it to wipe her mouth dry. Then she clenched the pillow against her chest and sobbed. The room swirled around her, creating the sickening image of a tornado right here in her own house.

"My house!" she screamed. "My things!"

Contessa threw the pillow across the room. The empty liquor bottle flew after it, crashing into the glass shelves holding a row of porcelain figurines. Shattered glass and porcelain fragments scattered across the recently installed Spanish tile flooring.

Contessa fell over onto her side and curled up like a baby. Loneliness ate at her until she decided to take a nap. When she woke up, she would look for someone to take his place. As a newly divorced woman she had the right to search. Garrison had no idea she had been cheating on him from the beginning. A smile played across her lips as she lapsed into blessed unconsciousness.

*Julia Robertson*

## Chapter 60

*A thick layer of clouds swept across the moon, blocked out the milky white light and erased every shadow. Her footsteps were left to chance as she ran blindly through the darkness. She heard nothing but her pounding heart and her father's voice urging her on.*

"Run faster, Gracie."

"No, no," she cried, out of breath and scared to death.

Grace broke free from the nightmare, threw back the comforter and frantically hugged her knees to her chest. The sounds and smells had been so real, but she knew she was safe in her own home. Though Grace knew it was nothing more than a terrible nightmare, her father's voice echoed inside her head. Exhausted, Grace buried her face in her hands and sobbed.

*Julia Robertson*

## Chapter 61

"Take a few days off, Grace," urged Roger.

"I don't need to," Grace groaned with her eyes locked on the paperwork before her. Though she knew Roger meant well, Grace wished he would leave her alone.

"As soon as some of the others come back, we're going to lunch," Roger said, turning his back to avoid her nasty looks.

"Shut up," Grace muttered under her breath.

"I heard that," said Roger. "We're still going."

When the lunchtime crowd returned, Grace wanted to crawl under her desk and hide. She pretended to be totally focused on the article before her, though she had not actually read a single word in the past ten minutes.

"Let's go," Roger demanded with his hand on her shoulder. "Don't give me any crap."

Grace forced an exaggerated sigh in hopes he would take the hint and leave without her, but he only squeezed her shoulder tighter. "This is stupid," she muttered.

"I'm driving, so you don't need your purse. Move," Roger said.

Grace shoved her chair back and grabbed her well-worn leather purse out of the bottom drawer. Anything to defy him. While Roger walked toward the lobby door, Grace took her time straightening her soft blue blouse and shaking the wrinkles from her knee-length cocoa brown skirt. She pulled the purse strap over her shoulder and stomped through the office, aware they were attracting too much attention. Once they were outside, Grace slugged Roger.

"Hey, don't do that. I'm delicate," Roger whined, rubbing his arm as if he were severely injured.

"Shut up, Roger. You're such a dufus," Grace responded, forcing a scowl on her face to hide her laughter. She quickened her steps to keep up with his long strides. "Why are we doing this? I have a lot of work to do," Grace continued.

"Just keep telling yourself that," Roger said, clearly enjoying the rare sight of anger in Grace's eyes. "As your immediate supervisor, I know you're a full two weeks ahead."

Grace ignored his remarks. They had a mutual agreement to drop their roles at work the moment they stepped out of the office. "Where are we going?" Grace asked, drumming her fingers on her knees in the passenger side seat.

"It's lunchtime, so what do you think? The zoo?" Roger replied as he pulled out into the light traffic.

"I'm not hungry," Grace sighed.

"Yes, you are," he countered. They both knew she needed to eat and needed to take a break from her busy routine. "Here we go. How many?" Roger asked at the taco stand.

Grace rolled her eyes and left Roger standing at the order window. Feeling rumpled and exhausted, she sat down on the sun warmed bench unable to forget about her troubling nightmares. Each dream revealed a few more details, but not enough to allow her to understand the meaning. If there actually was a meaning to begin with. Grace jumped when Roger dropped the tray on the concrete table.

"This is just the beginning. Hot sauce?" laughed Roger, rubbing his hands together as he eyed the stack of paper wrapped tacos on the tray between them. "Eat up and I'll order more."

"I hope you're hungry, Rog. I'm not eating half of these," groaned Grace. She wanted to kick him for being so darned happy.

"Whatever," he mumbled with his mouth full.

Grace finally gave in and began to eat, grateful for the calm settling between them. With two tacos left among a sea of crumpled papers, Roger looked up at Grace.

"You need to take some time away. You're too tired to do any good at work."

"Roger, you know I never take vacations. I don't have anywhere to go or anyone to visit. I need to work. I have bills to pay," Grace explained.

"You have plenty of vacation time coming. With pay," Roger emphasized. "Take a few days and go somewhere. Do it while you're not fighting a cold or recovering from the flu. Come on, Grace, you know I'm right."

"Those two are yours. I'm stuffed," Grace said in return.

"Grace," he grumbled.

"Roger," she mimicked. The moment Grace remembered that Clay had been sitting right here on this very bench, the fight drained out of her. Carefully hidden scenes from the accident emerged with startling clarity. She stared at nothing while the painful memories replayed in her mind.

"Earth to Grace. Come in, Grace," Roger said. He unwrapped another taco and dribbled hot sauce over it.

"I'm sorry, you're right," Grace said. Being angry with Roger was not doing any good. A vacation probably was a good idea.

Later that day Grace shoved the laundry basket across the floor to the washing machine. Sizing up the first load of clothes, she set the machine on high, pulled the dial out and watched the water pour into the tub. Nothing worked as efficiently as the water pressure in this old house. Thinking about everything that needed to be repaired or replaced made Grace's head ache. After dumping in the detergent, she slowly pushed the laundry down into the warm water.

Grace considered all of the things that needed attention. The carpet, the tile flooring in the bathrooms and the kitchen, the sinks and tub, the old windows, the faded wallpaper and old paint all needed some kind of repair work. Several of the electric outlets had issues and the plumbing had minor leaks. Too many things to pay for while she still had mortgage payments to contend with.

Her parents had taken out a second mortgage on the house to buy the boat and a new car. It added to the balance, but they figured they had plenty of time to pay it off. Following their deaths, Grace inherited the house, but she also inherited the monthly payments. She moved out of her affordable studio apartment in town and back into her childhood home right away. Giving up the house in Chelsea Creek had not been an option. She had taken her first steps in this house. Celebrated family birthdays, anniversaries, her graduation and countless holidays here.

Along with the guilt over losing her parents, the weight of the payments kept Grace locked into her solitary lifestyle. She had to keep her focus on her job, her quilting and keeping her head above water. A house to live in when she grew old did not sound so grand when she sat in the dark knowing she would always be alone. She blinked back her tears and drew her good memories close.

"This house, my home," she sighed. Letting it go would be like losing her parents all over again.

Grace could not count the times she felt like giving up. She felt trapped by the darkness. It loomed over her like a steel cage anchoring her to the ground. Once again she recalled the peace that had shone on Clay's face just before he died. She yearned for the same peace, even while she felt she was betraying the memory of her parents by doing so. Her pathetic thoughts made her pause and shout, "Tell me to stop thinking!"

Half an hour later Grace pulled the wet clothes from the washer and dumped them into the dryer. She wearily emptied the laundry basket into the washer as it filled with water again. She stood there watching the clothes as the machine pulled them down and swished them around and around. Life felt like that for her, constantly being pulled down, running in circles and going nowhere. Her thoughts turned once again to what she might never have. She wanted what her parents had had with each other. She angrily wiped away the blasted tears and shut the lid on the washer.

Grace sat down at her quilting frame, switched on the floor lamp and picked up the needle. The only sounds in the house came from the washer and dryer running down the hall. Her mind began wandering once her fingers picked up the familiar rhythm of the stitches. She had already delivered the sample square to Alexander and Carlena Mills. The intensity of the black and deep blue fabrics together pleased Grace. "Cobalt sky at midnight," she whispered, once again seeing the completed quilt in her mind. How she wished her mother had been with her to experience the thrill of putting the square together.

While she worked on the quilt stretched out before her, Grace freed her imagination. Creating stories about the different fabric scraps helped pass the hours and blur the unwanted images from her bad dreams.

A piece of blue and green plaid triggered the image of a small boy wearing a pair of baggy shorts. His hands and knees were grubby after playing outside in the dirt. Shimmering pink satin had to have been a prom dress for a young daughter. Her date, an awkward boy dressed in an ill-fitting suit, stood next to her in a photograph taken on the front lawn. Two scraps of wildly printed fabrics might have been wide ties sewn for the husband to wear to work. Grace remembered her own father wearing the exact style and grimaced. He always said he loved them, but she knew he had been ribbed by his co-workers. Grace eyed the fabric scraps ranging from flannels for nightgowns and pajamas to seersucker and chambray for blouses and shirts.

Grace scooted her chair to the left and dragged the floor lamp closer. When she started stitching again, her imaginary skylight came to mind. Her hands stilled as she pretended to be gazing up into the night sky. She wordlessly scolded herself for allowing such fanciful thoughts. There were so many more important projects to consider before something as useless as a window for viewing the stars.

Shortly after the dryer buzzed, Grace finished the row of stitches, tied off the thread and snipped it close to the fabric. She slid the needle into a pincushion, set the scissors aside and scooted the chair back. While she folded her clothes, Grace contemplated where to go on her days off. Her parents had loved camping and exploring rather than visiting resorts. She supposed they chose those activities to keep her busy and cut down on expenses.

A drive into the mountains and a cabin in the woods sounded appealing. It brought to mind campfire smoke trailing lazily up through the trees. She envisioned walking along a creek with icy cold water rippling over smooth gray rocks. As much as she yearned for the mountains, Grace also loved the ocean. In her mind, Grace felt the sun warmed sand and heard countless screeching seagulls flying overhead.

Though she loved going to the beach with her parents, she had not been there in years. Grace smiled as she revisited the time she tried to teach her father how to throw a Frisbee at the beach when she was a teenager. He never did master the correct wrist action. Rather than soaring through the air, his attempts always had the Frisbee rolling across the sand. Looking back at that event made Grace giggle. Her father, a man of many talents, simply could not do it.

"You're way too old for this," Teenaged Grace had explained.

"Generation gap," he laughed as he swept her off her feet and carted her back to where her mother was sitting.

Grace slid blouses onto hangers and put them in the closet. She smoothed out a skirt and pinned it to the next hanger. Once everything was put away, Grace returned the basket to the top of the washer and turned off the lights as she walked back to her bedroom. She hoped for a good night's sleep after so many disturbing dreams.

An hour passed before Grace gave up on sleep and went in search of the photographs from the time she had remembered earlier. She sat on her bed, pressed her cheek against her up-drawn knee and ran her fingers over the open album before her.

In one snapshot she and her mother both wore charcoal gray shorts and pink tank tops, with their hair up in ponytails. They smiled at the camera with their arms around each other. The next snapshot showed her parents standing knee deep in the water with Dad's arms around Mom. Grace sighed and closed her eyes. Their life had been a romantic love story.

## Chapter 62

Until the phone rang, Brian had forgotten all about Marlene's call. He left the kids to get dressed on their own and ran to answer it.

"Sorry Marlene, I just took the kids out of the bathtub," Brian explained. He ran his hand through his hair before he realized his hand was still wet.

"You're too busy, Brian," said Marlene. "Our flight comes in late tomorrow afternoon."

"I'm looking forward to having you two here. I made reservations for the weekend." Brian paused and listened to the laughter down the hallway.

"That sounds great," said Marlene. "You go take care of your kids, and we'll see you tomorrow afternoon."

When Brian stopped in the bedroom doorway, he saw Erin already had Jack's pajama shirt pulled on. He waited and watched in silence. The sight of them warmed his heart.

"See, you push the button through the hole like this," Erin explained as she concentrated on the large red button on Jack's pajama shirt.

"Why?" asked Jack.

Brian sighed and closed his eyes. It was the beginning of the "why" period of Jack's life.

"So your tummy doesn't peek out like this," Erin said as she pushed the shirt open, exposing his chubby tummy. To her delight, Jack fell over on the rug when she poked him. "I got you," she squealed. Jack rolled over and hid his face behind his hands.

Brian gathered up the damp towels and took them back to the bathroom. He kneeled and mopped the water off the floor with the same towels. No matter how careful he was, they always managed to get water all over the floor. Some days seemed to drag on endlessly. Having Marlene and Justin here ought to help lift his spirits. He needed the change in routine as well as some grown-up conversation here at home.

A short time later Jack fiddled with the red buttons on his pajama shirt while he listened to the story being read. Pretty soon Jack's eyes began drooping closed.

Erin looked over at her brother. She whispered, "Daddy."

Brian stopped reading and looked down at Erin. "Hmm?"

"Jack never hears the end of the story. He always falls asleep."

"You used to do that when you were little," he said.

"I'm bigger now. I get to go to school," said Erin.

"That's right," he agreed. Brian had been thinking about Erin and school a lot lately. One of the things that bothered him was that the kids always did special things for Mother's Day. What would Erin do? His own mother died long before he met Alicia. She would have loved being a grandmother, laying on the floor and playing games with Erin and Jack. If Anna married Garrison, Brian thought she would gladly fill the role. It seemed appropriate for Erin to make her a card for Mother's Day.

Erin tapped the book. "Finish the story, Daddy. I want to hear the rest."

Later that night Brian stood at the bedroom window with his hands in the back pockets of his jeans. The kids were asleep, and the house felt empty and cold. At times like this the loneliness sucked the life right out of him. Brian watched the twinkling stars and wondered about what Erin had said after Clay died. Were they together? Was Alicia happy? Was he feeling jealous?

What he was thinking was so damned stupid Brian nearly shouted at himself. They were dead and he was alive. No matter how much it hurt, the truth could not be altered.

Brian sighed as he turned around and stared across the empty room. A few steps took him to the side of the bed where he stripped off his shirt and dropped his jeans to the floor. How different his life had been before. The two of them together, raising their children, building their dreams and sharing their love and laughter. Alone, heartsick and broken, Brian lay on his side with Alicia's pillow squeezed tight against his chest.

## Chapter 63

"We're time travelers," Justin said when the idea floated into his conscious thoughts. Flying to the opposite side of the country had been one of his childhood dreams.

"How's that?" asked Marlene. She ran her thumb along the pages of the paperback in her hands while she waited for his reply.

"Well, we left home at 8 o'clock and now it's 8 o'clock at Brian's place. We've been traveling for three hours and we are going back in time," Justin explained as he shifted on the narrow seat, rearranging his long legs with little relief.

"When we head back home, we'll skip ahead," giggled Marlene. Neither of them had been so far from home before today. "What I'm not too thrilled about is the fact we're over 30,000 feet off the ground." She looked out into the nothingness through the tiny window next to her. "I wish we'd made this trip a long time ago," she sighed, reaching out for his hand.

"I know," said Justin. "Let it go."

"I'm sorry," she whispered. Marlene and Alicia had known each other for most of their lives. Their friendship never failed, even when Alicia went away to boarding school. "Did you know Alicia never wanted to have a family of her own?"

"Seriously?" he asked, holding her against him in the cramped space.

"She didn't think she'd be able to love anyone the way she wanted to be loved as a child." Marlene wiped away her tears. The forgotten book slid off her lap and out of sight. "She told me it all changed when she and Brian met each other. Like a lightbulb popped on inside her heart." Marlene took a moment to gather enough calm to speak again. "She said my mother taught her how a real family works."

"She's the best," agreed Justin. He did not say anything about how he had compared his own mother to Marlene's over the years. "Her cookies are the greatest."

"Justin," laughed Marlene. "You have your priorities straight, don't you."

"I sure do," he replied. Justin kissed the top of her head, wishing they were alone rather than crammed inside a sardine can with over 200 strangers. "Does it really bother you that we're seven miles up in the air?"

"Maybe yes, maybe no," she giggled.

"Definitely," chuckled Justin.

## Chapter 64

Brian guessed Erin had checked outside for Marlene and Justin at least a hundred times. When their guests arrived, the kids shouted with delight. Brian watched Marlene squat down and embrace Erin and Jack at the same time.

"You two have grown so much I barely recognized you," exclaimed Marlene.

"How do you keep them in clothes that fit?" Justin wondered out loud.

"It's an ongoing project," Brian replied. What Brian didn't say was that Alicia had stowed away boxes of clothes for their children. Until she became too weak, she scavenged area thrift shops, searched rack after rack of clearance items and sewed with determination, filling box after box with clothing. He had to fill the gaps from time to time, but her stash kept the kids in shorts, shirts and sweatshirts, socks and undies, hats and gloves. Everything was washed, neatly folded and packed into waterproof bags. Brian had not realized then that she had been consumed with the task for months prior to her diagnosis.

Brian struggled to hide his feelings, glad for the confusion surrounding him at the moment. If life only had a replay button to give a person a second chance. Perhaps Alicia's destiny had been to leave for a better place, but it left him hanging by a thread. His dismal thoughts scattered upon hearing Marlene's excited words.

"You're next," Marlene said as she hugged him tight.

"Hey Marlene, you're looking beautiful as ever," he said, holding her for a moment longer before turning to shake hands with Justin. "We're glad to have you guys here."

"We're going to the ocean," said Erin.

"Won't that be fun," Marlene exclaimed, stepping away from Brian and Justin.

"I want to find pretty shells and rocks," Erin said seriously.

"I bet you'll find lots of them," Marlene replied with delight as she crouched down to eye level with the children. "How about you, Jack?"

"Wanna see ottopuss," he said, blue eyes twinkling.

"Octopus, Jack. He can't say it right cuz he's little," explained Erin.

Marlene pressed her fingers to her lips, but the giggles escaped anyway.

"Come see what we did!" exclaimed Erin. She ran inside the house with Jack and Marlene following after her.

"Let's bring your things inside before we start dinner," suggested Brian.

Justin looked after Marlene and glanced back at Brian. "What are they up to?" he inquired.

"Erin's been excited about your visit," Brian answered. "They're probably in the bedroom. Let's go check it out."

Marlene looked up from where she sat on the bedroom floor. "Look what they did for us," she laughed. "I've been introduced to every one of them, I think."

Brian laughed at the sight before him. Erin and Jack arranged their stuffed animals in a semi-circle to welcome their guests. "You look right at home, Marlene," said Brian.

"Cool! It feels like we've stepped into a storybook," chuckled Justin.

Brian and Justin sat out on the patio later that night. "We've been thinking about moving out here. I've been checking into job opportunities and I think I can make it work." Justin looked over his shoulder before he spoke again. "Marlene doesn't know it yet, but I'm going to ask her to marry me."

"That's great, Justin. I'm happy for both of you. She's a super lady."

"She sure is," agreed Justin. He kept turning the glass around and around in his hands. "I'm so nervous my stomach aches." He looked up and saw the grin on Brian's face. "What?"

"You ought to see yourself," laughed Brian. "You're supposed to be nervous. It's a big step, but it's the right one. I mean, you two have lived together for what, two years?"

"Yeah, my mother keeps nagging me about it. I guess I never have followed the rules," Justin sighed. "So, you were nervous before you asked Alicia?"

"Are you kidding?" Brian replied. "I was afraid she'd say no." He unconsciously opened his left hand and looked down at his wedding band. "It was the best decision I have ever made."

"You two made a great looking couple, Brian. I mean, Alicia, well, you know." Justin stopped when the screen door opened behind him. "Talk about beautiful," he said as he stood up and reached out for Marlene's hand. "Come sit with us, honey."

"The kids are sleeping," Marlene said, nestling close to Justin. "You're doing a great job with them. Erin almost reads the words herself and Jack fell asleep," she began.

"Before you finished the book," laughed Brian, carefully hiding away his tormented thoughts.

Marlene leaned back against Justin's shoulder and squeezed his hand. "You're going to need to keep a gun or a baseball bat handy to fight off the boys," she warned Brian. "Erin's going to be a knockout just like Alicia."

"You're right about that," agreed Brian. He changed the subject when his eyes started to burn. This was the time of night he tended to fall apart. "What say we leave early Saturday morning? My crew is all set to do without me," Brian said.

"Sounds wonderful," remarked Marlene.

Brian was vaguely aware of Marlene's reply. His mind suddenly tripped back to their wedding day. He heard his voice stumbling through their vows. Felt his shaking hands sliding the small band onto her finger. Suddenly the final image of her wearing her rings burst to life. Every detail was crisp and clear. He closed his eyes, desperate to erase the terrible sight burned into his mind.

Marlene watched Brian in silence. She turned to see Justin watching him too. She reached up and touched his face.

Justin looked down and mouthed, "I love you."

"Me too," she whispered.

*Julia Robertson*

## Chapter 65

Grace rarely spent time upstairs because of the memories hidden in every corner. So many happy memories, she thought as she flipped on the lights at the top of the stairs. When she reached the second floor she felt a little ashamed of the dust on the furniture, but let it go for now. One of these days she would get it all cleaned up. A familiar aching returned with the unwelcome thought she might one day have to sell this old house. Grace forced the negative thoughts away, knowing it was counterproductive to worry about things beyond her control. She needed to focus on today and the days ahead. Time off and time away had seemed unthinkable until now.

At the end of the hall, she opened the double doors to the walk-in closet. It had been one of Mom's favorite stashing-stuff-away spots. Dad had built floor-to-ceiling shelves inside the six by eight-foot space. Grace reached up and pulled the string for the overhead light. The dusty bulb flickered on and off as it swung on the electric cord snaking down from the ceiling. One more thing that needed to be replaced, she thought while the light created creepy shadows inside the little room. Grace looked up at the two duffel bags on the top shelf. The empty space beside them loomed like a black hole. She looked away, then up again before pushing the larger bag over to occupy that space. The missing items were two suitcases, the ones her parents had taken with them.

"I know I can't change the past," she whispered as she stood on her toes and pulled on the smaller duffel bag. It came down along with a layer of dust. After sneezing several times, Grace turned off the light and made her way back to the stairs.

When it took only a few minutes to load her things into the bag, Grace stepped back and sighed. She held her joined hands under her chin and scanned the room as though she might find something she missed. She sat down on the edge of the bed and wept. Hopelessness threaded its way through her before she gingerly set it aside and turned toward the bathroom.

The sad events from the past few months were eating at her. Maybe her Fairy Godmother would appear and magically pop her into the arms of Prince Charming. Glancing back at the bag, Grace reminded herself that real life had never been easy. A short time later, Grace willed away her worries and fears, as well as the dust and clutter upstairs and prayed for sleep without dreams.

## Chapter 66

Charged with restless anticipation, Grace left the house an hour before sunrise on Saturday morning. She felt exhilarated as she buzzed along the deserted Redwood Highway. The headlights revealed ghostly sentinels standing straight and tall on either side of the two-lane blacktop. As the sky grew brighter over the next few miles, Grace recognized the distinct burnt orange trunks of the Ponderosa Pines. She likened the oval patterned bark to that of a giraffe. The tension she had not been able to ease was now being snipped away. Grace rolled the window down and let the cool air blow through her car. She welcomed the peace and solitude away from her work and her worries, but it did not last for long.

Once she turned north onto the coast highway, her controlled emotions began to fray again. She had not seen the ocean since before she lost her parents. Every memory included the two of them. She pulled off the highway at the first graveled parking area. Despite being alone at this stop, Grace slid down low on the seat and cried into her hands. She heard her father's voice as clearly as if he were sitting right next to her.

"Which way do I need to turn, Gracie?" he asked. He looked over at his four-year-old daughter and laughed heartily. "Turn the map over first. It's easier to read that way."

Today Grace's laughter replaced her deep sorrow. "I can't actually read," little Grace had answered.

"When did you learn that word? Actually? Good one, Gracie, good one," he praised.

Her parents had corrected her mistakes while growing up, but she always knew how much they loved her. "You are the best of both of us," her mother often told her. Grace held their praise close to her heart.

She eased her car up to the guardrail at the edge of the parking area and gazed out across the pewter gray stretching out all the way to the horizon. Except for the rolling waves directly below her, the ocean appeared flat as glass. As a child Grace wanted to go across the water and see what was on the other side. It seemed too far to swim, so she decided to ask a whale for a ride. When her father explained it wasn't possible, she angrily shook her head. Before she had a chance to run off, her father grabbed her and turned her upside down. His deep laughter accompanied her giggles.

When her thoughts strayed toward the explosion on their boat, Grace refocused her attention on today. She drove back out onto the road, eager to continue her adventure.

At her next stop, Grace hiked up the narrow path at Cape Sebastian. She paused at a split log bench and looked out at one of nature's beautiful masterpieces. Through her quilter's eyes she saw the miles long strip of sand connected by ragged stitches to frothy white capped waves, a constantly shifting seam against the endless saltwater. Above the beach, windswept pine trees dotted biscuit-colored ground sparsely covered by faded green dune grasses. Sun bleached driftwood logs appeared to be stitched in place on the dark sand. They made her think of the highlight stitching she added to each of her quilts. Creamy blue sky crowned it all, drawn together by a distinct, yet invisible seam. Grace soaked in the beauty and committed it to memory.

Further up the path the wind-blown trees created an overhead canopy with walls on either side. Someone had meticulously trimmed the tree branches to form the perfect passageway. Grace found herself ducking down unnecessarily to avoid bumping her head. At the other end of the tunnel the narrow path rose up to the highest point on the promontory. Exhilarated after the brisk uphill walk, Grace rested her arms on the wood railing and scanned the surface of the ocean. She caught sight of a ship so far out on the water it appeared no larger than her thumb. She wondered where it had come from and where it was going. It might be a cruise ship filled with passengers. Perhaps a fishing boat or a ship carrying cargo. Maybe a crew following an ancient treasure map. Or pirates with stolen barrels of rum, she thought, imagining her father favoring that scenario.

Grace stood up on her toes and peered down over the wooden railing. To her delight, Grace spotted two harbor seals floating in the shadowed gray water. Their eyes resembled enormous black marbles against their rich brown coats.

"Hey!" she called out. "How's the fishing?" Grace sighed when they disappeared from sight.

She ran her fingers over the silky wood railing and wondered how many other people had enjoyed the view from here. Grace knelt down to see how it might look from the perspective of small children. She imagined bright eyed wonder and countless curious questions. She hoped the harbor seals came to peek up at the same time the boys and girls looked down. What a thrill it would be for them. Children with their parents, exploring together as a family, building memories and sharing their love for each other.

Grace drove into town and stopped at the market for a few groceries before checking into her cabin. She walked out of the store with a single paper bag and nearly collided with a couple deeply engrossed in a verbal battle. She sidestepped them and apologized, but they paid her no mind. At the side of her car Grace was caught unaware by the vicious growls behind her. The unseen dogs were kenneled in the back of a pickup truck and sounded too close for comfort. She glanced back at the market and slid into her car.

Grace checked in, picked up the key and parked in the carport connected to the cabin. She felt right at home the instant she stepped into the cozy space. Four plump pillows were stacked up against the wooden headboard on the queen bed. She walked over to the picture window that framed a view of the ocean. Firewood and kindling were bundled next to the fireplace, ready to use. Grace dropped her small duffel bag on a chair and put her grocery items into the small refrigerator. She drew the lined curtains closed, pushed her shoes off and pulled the covers back on the bed. The luxury of a daytime nap was too tempting to resist. Grace fell asleep as soon as she rested her head on the pillow.

*Julia Robertson*

## Chapter 67

Marlene stepped into the brilliant sunshine and felt it radiate warmth all the way to her bones. Not a single cloud marred the clear blue sky. Her enthusiasm spiked as she clapped her hands and exclaimed, "Let's get this show on the road!"

"Hooray, hooray!" shouted Erin as she danced around the front yard. Jack simply hopped up and down.

"I have some bad news," said Brian. His words instantly caught everyone's attention. "Hey, we're still going," he explained as he turned to Marlene. "The bad news is that you are short."

"What? Is that a crime out here? I can't help being short." She narrowed her eyes and planted her fists on her hips.

Brian pushed his hands into his back pockets and looked over at Justin. "You want to tell her?"

Justin shook his head. "No way, man. I love the woman," he said.

"Brian," growled Marlene, putting on her best intimidating look. "Out with it."

"Justin and I have long legs, so," Brian said, drawing the problem out a little further. "You have to ride between the kids in the back seat."

"Are you serious? That's it? For goodness sake, Brian, that's the best seat in the house," laughed Marlene.

"But we're riding in the car," said Erin.

Marlene wrapped the little girl up in her arms while the men laughed behind her. "We sure are," she whispered, wishing with all her heart Alicia were here.

Shortly before noon Brian pulled off the Redwood Highway and drove toward the entrance to Stout Grove. "We can picnic in here if you guys are ready for lunch." Applause from the back seat conveyed their approval.

Justin bumped his head on the windshield when he leaned forward to look up at the trees. "Will you look at that!" he exclaimed when he saw the first of the redwood trees. "Man, what a place. Marlene, can you see?"

Marlene ducked down and peered out the side windows. "Amazing," she sighed.

As soon as the car stopped moving, Justin pushed the door open and stood up. With his hands on the roof of the car he leaned back and looked up at the trees. He quickly opened the back door, freed Erin and anxiously helped Marlene out.

"Look at this," he whispered, holding her back against his chest. "This has to be a slice of Heaven."

"It's awesome," sighed Marlene. Surely only whispering was permitted in such a majestic place. Marlene could not believe what she was seeing.

"I read about these trees, but I never imagined coming here," said Justin. "This area is part of what's left of the old growth forests. They say these trees are on the average 500 years old. Some reach to over 350 feet tall with a diameter of 16 feet and more."

"Incredible. They don't look real, even up close. I want to touch one of them," Marlene said.

"Yeah, let's do it," agreed Justin.

"Wait a minute. Look," Marlene told Justin.

Justin stilled and together they watched Alicia's family. Marlene brushed her hand across her cheek and sighed.

"Can we climb up to the top?" Erin asked, looking up at the first branches.

"No, they're too big to climb," said Brian. He squatted down and lost his balance when Jack tumbled back against him. "Hey," he chuckled, sitting with Jack sprawled across his lap. The boy's eyes remained locked on the tops of the trees.

Erin climbed up on Brian's back. "How did they get so big?" she asked, stretching up as tall as she could.

"Big, big, big," said Jack.

Marlene walked hand-in-hand with Justin toward one of the nearby trees. With her back against the oversized tree, Marlene looked straight up the trunk and watched it sway. "It's like a tall building the way it's moving up there."

"Imagine the noise one of them makes when it falls," said Justin.

"Too sad," whispered Marlene.

"The bark is almost soft," Justin said. He ran his fingers over the deeply furrowed gray-brown bark. "It looks like it's been shredded by gigantic claws," commented Justin.

"It's shaggy," marveled Marlene as she pressed her hands against the tree's uneven bark. She took Justin's hand as they walked back toward the car.

"This path leads down to the river," said Brian. "We can picnic down there."

"I'll get the cooler," said Justin.

"And the blanket," added Marlene. "Do you want me to take one of the kids?"

"No, I've got them, thanks." Brian started down the path, stopping when Jack stumbled on an exposed root. Before long he was carrying both kids.

"Did we come here before?" asked Erin.

Brian let her think for a moment longer. He imagined the tiny snippets from the past flashing through her mind.

"With Mommy?" Erin asked.

"Yes, we've been here before. When Jack was a baby," Brian said. "You and Mommy took off your shoes and walked in the shallow water. In the warm sunshine," he sighed. Brian came to a stop on the path.

"Don't be sad," said Erin.

"Hug me," said Brian. Both of his children reached around his neck and squeezed tight.

A short distance up the path, Justin stepped over a fallen log and set the cooler down. When he turned around, he saw that Marlene already knew he was up to no good.

"If you wish to cross this log, you must first pay the toll," Justin said sternly.

"And what might the toll be?" asked Marlene.

"A dozen kisses," he ordered.

"A dozen kisses. May I take out a payment plan?" she inquired.

"Let me think," Justin sighed, tapping his index finger against his chin. "Maybe, but only if you make a down payment immediately. One kiss, with the balance to be paid at my will."

"They sound like pretty harsh terms. I suppose I have no other choice," said Marlene.

"No other choice," agreed Justin. "Pay up."

Marlene leaned forward and kissed him. Without another word, she was lifted over the log and placed down on the soft ground, but he did not release her. "What?" she asked but knew.

"One additional kiss, not to be counted among the eleven you owe, for lifting you over the log."

"You're tough," she said and complied.

Upon reaching the end of the path, Brian stopped and put the kids down on the ground. Before he let them go, he warned, "Stay out of the water. Keep your shoes dry."

"Look for lizards," Erin told Jack.

"This place is magnificent," Marlene sighed as she stepped up next to Brian. She flung out the dark green and brown plaid blanket and knelt on one corner. "What comes after this?"

"There's a special grove of trees not far from here. We can walk the path and wear the kids out. And if you think these trees are big, just you wait," said Brian.

Obviously anxious to find out what Brian meant, Justin flipped open the cooler and asked, "How fast can we eat?"

After lunch, Brian drove further into the grove and parked in the designated parking area. From there they started walking down the steep paved path. The ground on either side of the path was lush and green, littered with wood rose and sword ferns.

"It feels like we're walking into a cave," Marlene remarked. She glanced over her shoulder as they reached the end of the paved path and stepped onto the reddish-brown dirt. "Hey, is there another way out of here or do we have to walk back up that steep hill?"

"Well," laughed Brian.

"Okay, I won't think about it," groaned Marlene. "What's that?" she asked. "It looks like fluffy green carpeting."

"It's called Redwood Sorrel," Brian replied. He stopped to show the plants to Erin and Jack. "It blooms in spring with dainty violet three-petaled flowers."

"Can we pick some?" Erin asked.

"No, we can look and touch, but we can't take anything with us."

The wandering path eventually led them to where it dipped down underneath a fallen tree. Justin passed under the gigantic remains of the tree ahead of the others. Very little sunlight came down through the overhead canopy, but when Marlene followed him, a single sunbeam

*Tender Dreams*

touched her golden red hair and made it sparkle. Justin reached out for her hand.

"I never imagined seeing anything like this," Marlene said with delight. She watched Brian duck under the tree with his kids in front of him. His smile wasn't enough to hide his lingering sorrow. In contrast, Erin and Jack's happiness shined in their eyes. Jack's red T-shirt was smudged with dirt. Erin seemed to notice every single plant and rock. "Thank you for bringing us here, Brian."

"Alicia always said this place is a gift that has to be shared," Brian told them. He lifted Jack up so he could pat his hands on the rough bark of the downed tree.

"Look!" squealed Erin.

Brian watched Marlene crouch down close to his daughter. Jack scampered over to join them. Marlene reached out and touched the reddish colored snail on the path, the object of their attention.

"He's hiding," Erin said after seeing the snail's head slip into the shell.

A loud creaking noise momentarily caught everyone's attention. Brian stepped around Marlene and the kids. He took his camera out and snapped a photo while they were still studying the snail.

"What was that?" asked Justin, alarmed even while no one else seemed bothered by the noise. When Marlene tugged on his hand in her haste to keep up with Erin and Jack, Justin obediently followed along. He continued staring up at the trees.

"The branches rub together sometimes," explained Brian.

"Hey, let's get a shot of the two of you by that one," Brian suggested, gesturing toward one of the largest trees in the grove.

"Man, it would take at least a dozen people to reach around this one," Justin guessed. "Probably more." He held Marlene's hand and reached as far as he could along the trunk of the tree.

"We must look like ants from the top," exclaimed Marlene.

Brian snapped the photo before resting his hand on Erin's head. She clung to his leg as she rubbed her eyes.

"I'm sleepy," Erin said softly.

"I bet you are. It's time to hit the road," Brian told Justin and Marlene. "These two are beat."

"Okay, Jack, come on up," said Justin. He offered the boy his hands and laughed when Jack jumped up as though he could bounce up into his arms. "Hey Marlene, we ought to get one or two of these for ourselves, don't you think?"

A few steps ahead of the others, Marlene turned around and smiled at Justin. "Only one or two?" she asked. She giggled when Justin's eyes widened and his mouth fell open. She barely contained her laughter and held up two fingers in his direction. Her heart yearned to see a baby of their own nestled in his strong arms.

"Man, he's already out," Justin remarked when Jack nodded off.

Brian smiled at Justin before turning his attention to his daughter. "Take a snooze," he said as he guided her head down to his shoulder. Before they were halfway up the steep hill to the parking area, Erin was sound asleep.

"Let me take a shot of the four of you," Marlene said as she plucked the camera out of Brian's pocket. She ran a few yards ahead of them, then turned and snapped the shot. She captured the two great looking men and the sleeping children with the giant redwood trees all around them. "It feels like we're in a living post card," sighed Marlene.

Back at the parking area, Justin settled Jack into his car seat. "This is like putting down a big bag of warm mashed potatoes," he remarked as he fastened the buckles.

"That's great," laughed Brian. "I'll have to remember that one."

## Chapter 68

Brian, Justin and Marlene rode in silence on the drive out onto the coast highway. They passed through Brookings and continued north until they reached Gold Beach, their destination for the night. By the time Brian picked up the keys for their cabin, the kids had fully recharged. Marlene grew antsy in the back seat, looking out one side of the car and then the other. "Tell me that's not ours," she exclaimed as they drove toward a big two-story house.

"That's not ours," replied Brian. "That one is."

"It's beautiful," she exclaimed. She studied the smaller two-story cabin with its weathered gray walls and lovely front porch.

The five of them spilled out of the car without delay. As much as they wanted to hit the beach, Brian ordered a potty stop first. He unlocked the cabin's front door and pushed it open.

"This is incredible," remarked Marlene as she explored the downstairs rooms. She stopped to look out the big window facing the ocean and sighed. Marlene had always tried to see every day as an adventure. Today was no different with so many new things to discover. She could not hold her excitement inside any longer. "Let's go to the beach!" Marlene exclaimed. When she spun around, she ran into Justin.

Justin stumbled backwards, surprised with her sudden movement. "Slow down, honey. Let's wait for Brian. We have lots of time."

"I'm sorry. It's so nice here and I feel like I'm going to pop," she said, unable to stand still or think straight.

"Shut up and kiss me," said Justin. To his delight, Marlene complied.

After finding hats for the kids and the elusive tube of sunscreen, the five of them started along the narrow path to the beach. Marlene giggled and declared, "We must look like ducks following one after the other."

Justin laughed at Marlene's humorous description. "I feel like we've stepped into another universe. Nothing back home looks anything like this."

The hard packed ground eventually gave way to soft sand. Brian picked up Jack while Justin reached out for Erin. They climbed up the steep dune with Marlene trailing behind. Brian turned in time to witness her reaction to seeing the ocean for the first time. They had seen glimpses of it on the drive north, but it was nothing compared to the panoramic view before them.

"Oh my!" gasped Marlene at the top of the dune. The roar of the ocean registered mere seconds before her visual senses were impacted. The peeks at the ocean from the car hadn't felt anything like this. She pressed her hands to her cheeks and took it all in. She absorbed the miles and miles of dark sand, rolling waves and water that went on and on forever. Experiencing the Pacific Ocean for the first time had her heart dancing. Marlene pulled her shoes off and grasped them in one hand. Unable to restrain herself for another second she grinned at the men, slid down the dune and ran toward the water.

"You okay here?" Justin asked with a glance back at Brian. He wasted no time in following after Marlene.

Marlene had visited the ocean on the East Coast, but this place sparked her passion in a new and unexpected way. Could a person share a kindred spirit with a body of water? She closed her eyes and absorbed the awesome sounds enveloping her with joy. She stood in the frigid water and let it pull the sand out from under her feet. She raised her hands and shouted her happiness to Heaven above.

"You're loving this, aren't you," Justin said as he stepped up behind her.

"I've always wanted to come out here. I wish," she said softly. "I wish Alicia was here with us."

"I know," Justin agreed.

Marlene sighed and leaned back against him.

Justin wrapped his arms around her and held her snug against him. Accompanied by the thunderous roar of the ocean, Justin kissed her cheek. "I planned to do this differently, but," he said as he turned her in his arms and framed her face with his hands. "Marlene, will you marry me?"

"Oh yes, yes," whispered Marlene. "I thought you'd never ask." She pressed her cheek against his chest and cried with joy.

"You're the best," he said. Justin lifted her feet off the sand and walked away from the water. "My feet are numb," he groaned while her laughter vibrated against his chest.

The persistent dark clouds weighed heavily on Brian while he watched Justin start across the sand toward Marlene. He squeezed his eyes closed and wished for things that could not be. "Stop it," he scolded himself.

"Can we take our shoes off?" asked Erin.

Brian heard the echo of Alicia's voice in their daughter's request. "Sure, let's sit down over there," he suggested, pointing to a large chunk of driftwood. He tucked their socks inside their shoes and set them together against the wood.

"Don't go near the water without me. The ocean is pretty, but it is dangerous for little kids. Understand?" Brian asked.

"Yes," replied Erin. She wiggled her toes into the soft sand. "It's warm."

Jack watched his big sister, then pushed his hands down into the sand. He laughed when his hands disappeared. "Hands all gone," he chuckled.

"Is there sand under the ocean too?" asked Erin.

"Yes," Brian replied.

"Does it float?" Erin asked next.

"It sinks," Brian replied. "Let's walk down toward the water. Hold my hands."

If Alicia were here, she would take them down to the water's edge and get their feet wet right away. Keeping them a safe distance from the waves, Brian walked Erin and Jack down to the cooler damp sand. He glanced over and saw Marlene running her fingers through the water swirling around her. If Alicia were here the two of them would be knee deep in the water by now. Brian pulled in a deep breath and turned away with his children.

Erin kept peeking over her shoulder while he held her hand tight. "Daddy, look," she said, tugging hard to make him stop.

Brian looked back, but when Justin lifted Marlene off the sand he had to look away. He knew exactly what that kind of love felt like. Knew exactly how much it hurt to lose it. Brian desperately wanted Alicia back in his life.

Brian was grateful when he spotted the rocks scattered across the wet sand. "Let's look for agates."

"What's that?" asked Erin.

"Come over here," Brian said as he guided the kids over to the rocks and crouched down. He picked up several rocks before he found one.

"Look," he said. "This one is an agate. It looks a little like butterscotch candy. Hold it up to the sky. See how the light almost comes through it?"

"It's pretty like gold," exclaimed Erin.

Intrigued, Jack found a pitted rock and picked it up. "Like this one," he said and held it up to the sky.

"You can't see through that one, Jack. It's not agate," said Erin. "But I like it too."

"Me too. Lotsa pokey holes," said Jack.

Brian gazed out across the water. Though he knew it was foolish, he wished for Alicia to come home. The need seemed to increase with every wave rolling in toward shore. He sighed and turned back in time to see Jack wiping the sand off a rock with his T-shirt. Then the boy pushed the rock down into the sand.

"Jack's hiding rocks," said Erin. "Here, hide this one too," she giggled.

## Chapter 69

She gracefully swept her wings through the air, skimmed above the treetops, caught the warm updraft and let the currents carry her out over the meadow below. Instinct guided her toward the fast- flowing river. Her dark eyes scanned the land below, took in every detail and monitored every movement. Drifting lower and lower, she flared her wings and extended her long feathered legs just before she touched the ground. A smooth, soundless, beautiful landing on the bank of the river. Standing in place, she trembled, invigorated by the freedom of the flight.

Grace blinked and felt somewhat deflated when she realized where she was and who she was. Not the elegant hawk soaring on the winds, but just Grace. She rolled from the soft bed and touched the floor with her bare feet. She stretched her hands up over her head, drew in a deep breath and came to find herself fully rested for the first time in countless months.

Grace checked the clock on the nightstand, surprised to see she had slept away the afternoon. She pushed the curtains open before getting her lunch out of the refrigerator. Sitting on the bedspread, she had a makeshift picnic with a turkey sandwich and shrimp pasta salad from the grocery store's deli counter. She reached out for the television remote, then stopped her hand with a sigh. The reason for coming here was to leave anything related to stress behind. After she'd eaten some of the salad, she snapped the lid on and pulled the plastic wrap around the second half of the sandwich. "Tomorrow's lunch," Grace said out loud as she tucked the food back into the mini refrigerator.

A quick glance at the clock told her she had plenty of time to walk down to the beach. She would be back long before sunset. Grace pulled on her tennis shoes, laced them up and went outside. She snatched her windbreaker out of her car and walked around the cabin to where the beach access was posted.

Grace followed the meandering path leading to the ocean. The hard-packed ground had been worn smooth by countless footsteps. Patches of flat olive-green grass interspersed with long narrow blue-gray strands sprouted out among the curling branches of the low growing ground cover on either side of the path. Grace crouched down to examine the overcrowded vegetation, remembering her mother's warning from when she was a little girl.

"The grass might be sharp, Gracie. Best not touch it," warned Marianna.

"Sharp," whispered Grace, cautiously fingering the tiny barbs on the wider blades. A rustling sound drew her attention away from the grass. The pale green ground cover resembled oversized mounds of moss and created the perfect hiding places for any variety of small creatures.

Still crouched down, Grace listened to the sweet song of an unseen bird. It probably had a nest in one of the scruffy pine trees. Every single tree tipped toward the cabins behind her. They appeared to be running away from the wind blowing up from the ocean.

Grace hadn't expected the overwhelming feelings that came once she reached the top of the dune. The sound of crashing waves and the steady roar of the ocean focused her attention on the vast body of water. Grace became no larger than a speck of dust by comparison. Her life's priorities suddenly realigned themselves. The dark dread of possibly losing the only house she had ever called home melted away. Along with it went the mounting bills, concern about her aging car, stress related to her job and her worries about what might come next. Even her wishes to attain peace through death lost clarity. Life mattered and people mattered she knew, even as feelings of loneliness threatened to creep back into her conscious thoughts. This weekend was for renewing her spirit. "One small step at a time," she reminded herself.

Grace tugged off her shoes, knotted the laces together and draped them over her shoulder. She cut a straight line across the sun warmed sand toward the incoming tide. No one heard her squeal when the first wave splashed around her legs, swirling high enough to wet her rolled up pant legs. The outgoing water pulled the sand out from under her feet. For a moment she was a child again, holding onto her father's hands. Childhood delight and heartfelt grief collided as she turned and began walking north, mindful of the incoming tide.

Grace stopped to pick up a broken sand dollar. If she came down here early in the morning and found one of these intact, she would sketch the intricate design to use on a future project. The combination of colors had to be a creamy ecru like the shell itself, mixed together with pale antique pink and brushed nickel gray. Scattered pieces of the imagined quilt fell into place as she continued on.

Grace noticed a few clouds thickening overhead and contemplated the possibility of rain for tomorrow. Spending the day sitting near a crackling fire, reading a book and listening to the rain appealed to her. She continued walking north, staying on the damp sand and breathing in the sea air. Caught up by the ocean's awesome power, she turned once again to face the waves. How likely was it that someone just as enchanted with the sea was standing out there looking in her direction thinking the same thoughts? One day she might travel across the ocean and see for herself what it looked like. Though her mind rejected the idea, her heart said anything was possible.

Mesmerized by the brilliant strip of magenta hued sunlight far out across the water, Grace stood frozen on the sand. She squinted when the light began fading away. "Just a little longer, please," she whispered as darkness pushed the sun down into the ocean. She sighed, feeling both happy to have witnessed such a beautiful sunset, and sad to have taken it in all alone. She remembered her parents sharing moments just like this. Grace stood alone, deeply troubled by her empty feelings.

"No," she whispered softly. "Today is a gift and I thank you for it."

Grace knew she ought to go back to her cabin, but the desire to cling to the peaceful feelings overwhelmed logic. She allowed herself a few more minutes to take it all in. The magnificent sunset, the peaceful night and the rhythmic rolling waves.

*Julia Robertson*

*Tender Dreams*

## Chapter 70

Brian took the kids upstairs for a bath after dinner. He plunked Jack down in the tub next to his sister. Erin's expression told him a question was coming.

"How did sand get in here?" Erin asked. "Hey, it doesn't float!" she exclaimed. "Look, Jack, sand."

Jack tried to pick the tiny bits of sand off the bottom of the tub, but his fingers kept coming up empty. Brian eased back on his heels and marveled at how their minds worked. They bounced from one thing to another, deep in thought one moment and off to something else the next. Brian had come dangerously close to the breaking point on several occasions since losing Alicia, but the threads that kept him from shattering were sitting before him. Then again, he knew as much as the children needed him, he needed something they could not possibly give him. His heart felt broken beyond repair. He shelved his despair and focused on the task at hand.

Jack's mouth opened wide with a huge yawn. "You guys had a good day," he said as he wrapped his son in a towel. He plopped Jack down on one of the beds. The boy was too sleepy to climb down and get into trouble. Back in the bathroom he wrapped a towel around Erin and dried her off.

"I'm sleeping," Erin said.

"I see that, honey," Brian said as she stood before him with her eyes closed. It was a wonder she hadn't collapsed on the floor. He cradled her in his arms and carried her into the bedroom. "You're my baby girl."

"Not a baby," she whispered with her eyes closed.

Brian dressed both sleeping kids in pajamas before covering them with blankets. Though he needed to sleep himself, he decided to get outside and seek refuge down at the beach.

"Hey, would you guys mind if I go for a walk?" Brian asked at the front door. Marlene's smile gave him the answer he was seeking. "I won't be long," he said as he pulled his windbreaker on and reached for the doorknob.

"Take your time," Marlene said. "We'll keep an eye on the kids."

Brian needed the solitude. Being here was dredging up more memories than he could handle. "Thanks," Brian said as he stepped out onto the porch and quietly shut the door behind him. He hoped a long walk might relieve the headache he had had all day.

While he enjoyed showing Marlene and Justin some of the places Alicia had loved, every turn reminded him of how much he had lost. Even now in the early evening, the flowers planted all around the property seemed to be shouting at him. Alicia spent time on one of their visits taking photographs of every flower in bloom. She created an album of her best shots, complete with hand printed labels identifying each photo. Everything from vivid red foxglove to yellow lupine with their long-fingered leaves and hedges of dancing ballerina-like fuchsias filled every page. She planned to use the photos to create her own note cards. Yet another dream lost forever.

Brian retraced their earlier walk to the ocean. Alicia had always loved to walk in the water. She would trail ahead of him, drawn toward the water, confident of her every step. Once they reached the beach, they would hold hands and walk side-by-side. Soon she would stop to slip off her shoes. Her words came back as though she were standing right next to him.

"The water's too cold," he usually argued.

"Aw Brian, how often do we get to do this? I'll go by myself if you don't want to join me," she said in return.

"You're nuts," he sighed, already giving in to her wishes. Today Brian stared out at the water, aching to hold her hands again. The unwanted image of them placed together in the coffin flashed through his mind.

Dragging his misery along with him, he began walking close to the water's edge heading south. The spongy wet sand pulled at his shoes with every heavy step.

Brian paused a short time later and turned to face the ocean. He watched the sun sink down into the water, leaving behind a slice of rosy golden light along the horizon. It felt like someone had pulled a window shade down to bring an end to the day. If tomorrow was as nice as today, he would take Erin and Jack out to search for shells and rocks. They might get to explore a few tidepools as well.

A crisp image of Alicia kneeling with Erin appeared before him and lingered for several seconds before it crumbled and fell away. Brian's weariness allowed the scene from Clay's funeral to return. He felt the weight of the coffin in his right hand.

Brian's concentration kept faltering. Everything that happened over the past year kept tumbling through his mind. Though he knew both Alicia and Clay were gone, he still found it impossible to accept.

Brian looked up in time to see the last sliver of light before it vanished. With the horizon virtually invisible, Brian felt the weight of darkness take him back to the day with Anna and Garrison at the prospective building site. He had nearly lost it. His world had transformed into charred ashes with all of his senses temporarily paralyzed. He had to stave off the terrifying feelings he had felt that day. Erin's words alone had saved him from plunging into a bottomless pit.

*Julia Robertson*

*Tender Dreams*

## Chapter 71

Larry Baker stormed out of the lousy motel room. He was fed up with his girlfriend. Reina bitched constantly. He just plain wanted her to shut up. Whether they argued in private or in public, it was all the same to her. Today's fight at the supermarket had pushed him past his limits. She did not know it yet, but he was going to dump her.

Larry heard her following him, but he kept his eyes on his dogs as they crossed the road toward the beach. The dogs needed to get out and run as much as he needed to escape. Reina complained about the sand getting into her shoes, the shows she was missing and how she needed to go back and put on her new nail polish. He did not bother arguing with her. He wished she would just go back to the room and let him be.

The wind had picked up considerably since they came down here earlier today. He started over the steep dune toward the beach without looking back. Larry let Tank and Butch pull him down the sandy dune. They were powerful dogs and he loved them. As strong as they were, Larry still had more power. He simply snapped his fingers to make them listen. If Reina worked that way, he would have it made.

Larry reached the bottom of the dune and the two dogs instantly sat down. He unclipped their leashes and grinned as they eagerly awaited his next command. He pointed his finger at the dogs before he turned and walked away. They did not budge. "Not an inch, not a silly millimeter," he chuckled to himself. He had seen other dogs wiggle until their butts were off the ground and they took off running, but Butch and Tank stayed right there. They did not so much as blink. They were so intense it was amazing. Totally awesome dogs, totally under his control.

*Julia Robertson*

## Chapter 72

Brian walked along close to the water contemplating the years past and the memories he held dear. Some days he felt like he was carrying the weight of the world on his shoulders. The kids needed so much from him. He stopped and focused on the invisible horizon.

"I'm going to start looking at houses, Alicia. I need to have a little more room for the kids." He spoke as if she were standing right next to him. He did not question why he felt so close to her out here. "I read your letter to Erin. She asked me to keep it for her, to keep it always. She's so bright. And Jack, he doesn't miss a thing. He's a tough little guy, but he has such deep feelings. He gets this look on his face when he knows Erin is sad. It's something to see."

Alicia was not here, could not possibly be here, but the tenuous connection he felt in this place kept him staring out at the dark water. He linked his hands behind his head and closed his eyes.

"Help me see what to do, Alicia," Brian said. "Please help me. I feel like I'm losing my mind. If I can't keep myself together, what's going to happen to our kids?" Overwhelmed with the reality of his words, Brian fell to his knees in the wet sand and bowed his head.

*Her whispered words drifted across the surface of the water and rose toward Heaven. "I cannot do this alone," she prayed. "Please light the way for him." Alicia lay a kiss on the palm of her hand and gently blew it away.*

Brian's eyes burned when he felt the feather light touch. "Alicia," he cried, "please come back to me."

*"No," she whispered in the wind. "She needs your help. She needs you right now."*

"I don't understand," he cried out. "Don't leave me!"

Brian raised his hands up to the night sky. Her voice, her words, they had to be real. Resigned, he said, "Show me what to do."

He pushed his hands into his pockets when the air suddenly grew colder. He reluctantly turned away from the water and wondered if he had actually heard anything. Perhaps it had only taken place inside his weary mind. If Alicia had spoken to him, who was she talking about? Who needed his help?

Brian started walking back up the beach feeling confused, exhausted and completely lost. When he came across a piece of driftwood, he reached down and picked it up. The wood's finish felt smooth and almost silky. He decided to show it to the kids even though Erin would come up with countless questions.

## Chapter 73

Grace looked out across the dark water thinking about the night her parents died. The explosion had literally blown their boat apart. Recovering their bodies had not been possible. Her parents had loved and respected the ocean, so she found comfort in knowing they would have chosen to have their ashes scattered upon the waters of the Pacific.

Grace abruptly looked away from the water. A shiver of unease tickled the back of her neck. Without delay, she started walking back toward the path to the cabins. It was foolish to be out here after sunset.

Feeling disoriented, Grace studied the lights above the beach. What made her think she could find her way back in the dark? She remembered thinking a giant lumberjack had stacked the big pile of logs near the path to the cabins. She moved closer to the grassy dunes, afraid of what she could not see. Grace squinted, trying to bring things into focus. All she had to do was spot those logs.

Bright as lightning on a dark night, the nightmare came to life. Her body went rigid when a familiar voice whispered in her ear.

*"We've always told you not to run, Gracie, but this time you must. Get away as fast as you can right now, Gracie, right now!"*

"Oh no," she gasped. "This can't be happening," She felt his strong hands pushing her. "Daddy," she whispered as she turned and ran.

The wind shifted and drew the clouds together like curtains in front of the moon. Grace wanted to wake up in her bed, but she knew it was not going to happen this time. Her thumping heart echoed inside her head. She barely heard her feet pounding the sand. Already out of breath, she knew she was not going to be able to keep up the pace for much longer. A quick glance over her shoulder made her cry out. She scrambled up the soft sand dune and into the brush and long bladed grass above the beach.

*Julia Robertson*

## Chapter 74

Larry counted to one hundred before he turned around. He whistled for Butch and Tank at the same time he realized they were not sitting where he left them. After all her bitching about the dogs not listening to her, Reina managed to call them away. If she thought for a moment he would let her stick around, she had another thing coming. He ran back, thankful there was enough moonlight to study the sand to see which way the dogs had gone. Not over the dunes again to where Reina was probably still waiting for him, but down the beach in the opposite direction. Larry was consumed by the damp heat broiling his body. He swiped at his eyes with the sleeve of his shirt. Everyone warned him about this particular breed of bulldog, but he never believed any of it. They would never freak out and harm anyone. They were loyal to him. They listened to him. "They wouldn't," he cried as he ran, following their tracks.

Larry clambered up the dune where he guessed the dogs had gone, slipping several times before he reached the upper edge. He stood up, wiped his eyes again and scanned the land. What if they had gone after someone? Their jaws were like steel traps. He had to find them before anything bad happened. What if they managed to get out onto the highway? When visions of his dogs ripped to bloody pieces flashed through his mind, Larry took off running.

*Julia Robertson*

## Chapter 75

Out of breath and scared to death, Grace could not afford to look behind her. "God help me please," she prayed as she ran. The dune grass was cutting her skin just like in her dreams. "No," she cried when she heard heavy breathing behind her.

Grace wished she had gone back to her cabin earlier. Wished she had stayed home and dealt with the nightmares in her own house, on her own time. Even through the terror, Grace worried someone else might possibly be in danger. "Help me!" she gasped. "Please help me!"

What seemed to be level ground during the daytime turned into a series of small hills and valleys covered by brush and long grass. Grace did not have time to study each step. She raced helplessly, trying to ignore the pain while her pursuers grew ever closer. Her foot caught on some unseen object and she tripped, gasping for air, frantically trying to keep her balance. Her chance for escape vanished when she stumbled down into the deeper darkness of the next shallow valley. One of the dogs literally tore her jacket off while the other one grabbed her leg. Desperate to get away, she clawed at anything near her fingertips.

"Help me, find me, please find me," she prayed. Hopelessness overwhelmed her when one of them grabbed her right hand. She prayed for God to take her life and save her from the pain.

Grace did not question why the dogs suddenly released her, but she knew she had to hide before they came back. Without the benefit of light, she pushed her way in under a thick clump of brush and hoped it was enough to conceal her. Grace held her injured hand up against her chest in the confined space, unable to stop trembling. She bit back the need to cry and felt the tears pouring from her eyes. "Find me, please find me," Grace pleaded silently.

Grace made herself as small as possible in her hiding place. She could no longer hear the dogs, but she knew it did not mean they were gone. She had to remain motionless and absolutely quiet. "Please find me," she wept silently.

Grace inadvertently moved her fingers and felt the pain radiate all the way up to her shoulder. She bit her lip to hold back the scream waiting to burst from her lungs and tasted blood. Would she be able to crawl out of here in the morning? Surely the dogs would not hang around out here all night long. She closed her eyes, too afraid to fall asleep and once again prayed.

## Chapter 76

Larry stumbled to a stop and whistled for his dogs. A huge driftwood log nearby provided a good lookout point. Awkwardly balanced on top of it, he spotted the dogs and yanked their leashes out of his back pocket. He jumped down to the ground and fell on his ass. His dogs were safe. They had not hurt anyone. They had not been flattened by a truck. Waves of relief rolled over him while they ran toward him.

Larry clipped the leash on Butch, then reached out for Tank. Before he was able to wrap his fingers around his collar, the dog bolted. Butch tried to follow, but Larry corrected him with a sharp jerk on the leash. "Shit," he spit out as he wrapped Butch's leash around his hand and ran after Tank. He spotted someone moving in the dark a short distance away. "Watch out for that dog!" he shouted, doubling his pace.

Larry held his breath knowing Tank was not going to stop. "Holy shit," he groaned. "Don't hit him, please don't hit him!"

Sick to his stomach, he kept running with Butch straining on the leash. "Tank, come here!" shouted Larry. "Please don't kill him!"

*Julia Robertson*

*Tender Dreams*

Chapter 77

Brian continued walking back toward the cabin, deliberately keeping his pace slow. Once inside he would have to mask his dark feelings again. Marlene and Justin were playing cards when he left and he had no desire to join them.

"If Alicia," he said out loud. "No, stop it," he ordered himself. He switched the chunk of wood from one hand to the other, trying to dispel the growing tension.

*Alicia blew the words in his direction. The sounds swirled around him like sparkling dust. "She needs your help."*

Brian spun around on the sand, the wood now a weapon in his hands. "Who's there!" he called out. Was he losing control or actually hearing Alicia speaking to him? Once again Brian feared his sanity was shredding apart. What if the urgent plea to help someone in trouble was real and he ignored it. It was not in his nature to do such a thing. "Who needs my help?" he asked, feeling the urgent need to move.

Brian charged up the dune, away from the ocean's constant roar. At the highest point he stopped and listened carefully. "Which way am I supposed to go?" Brian asked, searching, but seeing little in the dark. Turning, he carefully scanned the beach, then looked back again. A moonbeam spilled down from the sky, illuminating someone running in the brush. It vanished two seconds later.

Stunned, Brian froze. "What the hell was that?" he gasped and started across the uneven ground.

Brian halted abruptly when he heard the desperate plea for help. He turned slowly, studying the area and listening intently. "Show me the way," he said softly. Before he took another step, Brian heard the warning and saw the dog charging toward him. Gripping the wood with both hands, he braced himself for the attack. No way was it going to keep him from helping someone in trouble.

Brian slammed the dog with the driftwood and hoped it was enough. He watched it hit the ground, then slowly get back up on its feet. He stood ready for a second blow and heard someone yelling again. He watched the dog as a man with another dog came into view.

Spitting mad, he shouted, "Why the hell do you have animals like this? What the hell's wrong with you?"

"I'm sorry," Larry apologized as he clipped the leash on Tank's collar and pulled him away. "They have never done anything like this before. Really, they are good dogs. He didn't hurt you, did he?" he asked, holding his breath as he waited for an answer.

"Did you see anyone else out here?" Brian asked urgently.

"Say what?" Larry replied, anxiously jumping from one foot to the other.

"What's your name?" asked Brian. The guy was nervous about something, but Brian did not have the time to figure it out. "Come on, you do have a name, don't you?"

"Ah, James, yeah," Larry Baker said, nodding at his choice.

"James what?" demanded Brian. No doubt the guy was not telling him the truth.

"James Cook," Larry replied with a grin. "Listen, I'm sorry about this. I'll get these guys back to their kennels right away. No harm done, right?" he said as he backed away with the dogs in tow. Tank wobbled on his feet, still stunned from the blow.

Despite the dim light, Brian was able to get a pretty good look at the man and the dogs. He would report the incident to the local authorities later. He turned away from them and gave his full attention to finding the woman in trouble.

When the desperate plea came again, Brian realized the words had not been something he heard, but something that emerged from inside his head. It was almost too much to take. "But she needs me," he cried out, his body quaking. "This is real, she is real, I'm not crazy," he said with growing rage. He had to find her before he lost it, before it was too late for both of them. Gruffly wiping away his tears, Brian turned in a slow circle. "Show me where she is," he whispered.

## Chapter 78

Brian mentally retraced his search. Once he felt sure he had not gone too far, he let his senses guide him further. He stopped a few minutes later, cupped his hands around his mouth and called out, "Where are you? I'm here to help you!"

"I'm here," she cried silently.

Brian ran toward the voice. He charged up over the next rise and down the other side before he came to a stop on the uneven ground. He stilled once again, hands braced on his knees, listening intently. "Where are you?"

"Down here," she replied without a sound.

Brian stumbled backwards when he heard her. He searched the dark shadows, startled when moonlight suddenly revealed her bare foot. "Are you hurt?" he asked, though he felt he already knew the answer.

"Yes, yes," she sobbed.

Brian carefully tugged back the tangled brush and saw her. "What happened?" he said, hiding his shock. Brian assessed her injuries as best he could in the dim light. He debated whether to go for help or take her back to the cabin. "I can carry you, but it's going to hurt," he cautiously explained.

"Please don't leave me here. The dogs," she cried.

"They're gone," he assured her, guiding her up to sit. Brian pulled his windbreaker around her, carefully positioned her injured hand and carried her toward the cabin. Despite all the movement, she had not made so much as a whimper.

She clung to him with her fingers in his shirt. "How did you find me?" she asked in a hoarse whisper.

"I heard you calling for help," replied Brian.

"But I didn't," she whispered. "Never said it out loud," she mumbled before she went limp in his arms.

Feeling lightheaded, Brian came to a stop. "But I," he began, looking back toward the ocean in wonder.

*Julia Robertson*

## Chapter 79

At the sound of thumping on the front door, Justin crossed the room with Marlene on his heels. Illuminated by the front porch light, they saw Brian through the glass panel in the door. Justin pulled the door open and stepped back.

"What happened?" Marlene blurted out.

Justin nudged her back a few steps to give Brian room to come inside.

"She needs an ambulance," Brian said without delay.

"I'm on it," Justin said, already heading for the phone at the main office.

"I'll get a blanket and towels," Marlene said as she scurried off to the bedroom.

Brian was not surprised to see Erin coming down the carpeted stairs. No doubt she heard him banging on the door. She stopped on the bottom step, rubbing her sleepy eyes. Brian knew Erin would not be able to go back to sleep without some answers. While he waited for Marlene to return, he sat down on the edge of the sofa and beckoned her over.

"What are you doing?" asked Erin. She stood up on tiptoes to look at the lady he was holding. "Who is," she began, then froze.

Brian saw her stunned expression. "Erin, honey, go sit on the chair until Marlene comes back," he said.

Marlene rushed into the room and dropped her armful of things on the sofa next to Brian. "Sit over here while we take care of her," she told the little girl.

Brian watched Erin. "Go on now," he told her.

Marlene reached out for Erin when she did not move. "Come sit down, sweetie."

"Daddy," Erin whispered softly. "She's the Ladybug Lady."

"No," Brian said, though he had not yet seen her face.

"What happened?" Erin asked.

"No," Brian repeated as he turned toward the light from the kitchen. "Marlene, the lights, please, turn them on," he said haltingly.

Marlene reacted immediately, switching on the lamp at the end of the sofa. "Do you know her?" she asked, picking up the blanket when he stood up. She swiftly opened it out and put the pillow down. "Brian?"

"I'm not sure. Maybe," he murmured as he eased her down onto the sofa and knelt on the floor. "Grace," he said, touching her cheek. "Grace, can you hear me?"

Erin pulled free of Marlene's hands and moved back to see the lady again. "Why is she so sad?" she asked. Erin grabbed her father's hand with tears streaming down her cheeks. "Is God going to take her away?"

Brian felt himself fighting for calm. Was life going to deal them yet another horrible experience? He reached around his daughter and pulled her in close. "I hope not, baby."

Erin bit her lower lip and reached out to touch the lady's face.

"Gentle," warned Brian, somehow knowing she needed to be a part of what was happening.

Marlene interrupted at that point. "Here," she told Brian, passing him a towel. "Her hand," she urged, pulling Erin out of the way.

"Yes," Brian said and focused on what needed doing. Until help arrived, he had to slow the bleeding. For Grace's sake he kept a firm hold on his growing panic.

"Brian, they're here," Marlene said a few minutes later. "Erin, come with me, we need to give them room to work."

Erin nodded and took Marlene's hand. "Will they make her all better?" she asked.

"Yes," Marlene said as they moved quickly over to the stairs. "Let's go check on Jack."

"Grace, you're going to the hospital now. Can you hear me?" Brian asked as he gently brushed her hair back from her face. He quickly stood up and stepped back when the paramedics arrived. He gave them a brief run-down of what he thought had happened to Grace. He shoved his hands into his pockets and watched helplessly.

Brian did not really know Grace, but he knew fear when he saw it. Different from the fear Alicia had experienced, but certainly no less frightening. The need to step in and be sure she was okay kept him on edge. Every sound, every movement had him starting to step closer.

"Brian," Justin said at the open doorway.

Brian turned and stepped out onto the porch. He glanced back when he heard Grace's muffled whimpering. "What?" he asked Justin.

"You need to talk to the Sheriff. They need to know what happened," Justin said, tugging on Brian's arm. "You can't do anything else for the victim right now, come on."

"But," Brian argued.

"No," Justin said sternly. "It will do more good if you can be sure whatever happened to her doesn't happen to someone else."

Brian knew Justin was right. He followed him across to where the deputy was waiting. Brian gave a detailed description of the man on the beach, the two dogs and the events he personally witnessed. He excused himself when the paramedics rolled the gurney out onto the front porch of the house. On the way to meet them he told Justin, "I want to go along to be sure she's okay."

"Not a problem," Justin replied. "We'll take care of your kids."

"Thanks," said Brian. He talked with the paramedic at the back of the ambulance for a minute before going back to the house to talk with Erin. He could not leave her without an explanation.

"Daddy!" Erin cried.

Brian caught his daughter when she ran out onto the porch in her pajamas. "Listen, honey," he said, holding her tight. "I'm going to go to the hospital."

"I'm scared," Erin wept.

"I know, I know," he said, kissing her soft cheek. "You go back to bed and get more sleep. I'll talk to you in the morning, okay?"

"Tell them to make her all better, please," Erin said.

"I love you," Brian whispered. He stood up and carried Erin back inside to where Marlene and Justin were waiting. "Are you sure you're okay here?"

"Yes," Marlene said as she took Erin from Brian. "You do what needs doing. We'll talk when you get back."

"It might not be until morning," Brian said, turning to watch the ambulance pull out onto the road.

"Don't worry about anything here. Now go!" Marlene urged, pushing Brian out the door.

*Julia Robertson*

## Chapter 80

"Are you warm enough?" the nurse asked as she arranged the blankets and turned to set up a drinking cup and straw on the nightstand. "If you need anything the call button is attached to the railing."

"Thank you," Grace replied.

"You sleep for now," the nurse told her. "The light meds are going to make you drowsy, so take advantage of it and rest."

"Yes, I am sleepy," Grace replied. She actually felt like her mind and body were disconnected from each other. Everything appeared blurry, probably due to the mild concussion the doctor had tried explaining to her earlier.

"Are you up to having a visitor?" the nurse asked when she reappeared beside the bed.

"Visitor?" asked Grace. Nobody but Roger knew she was here, she thought with bewilderment. "Okay," she finally whispered.

"I'll tell him he can't stay for too long," the nurse assured her.

Grace lay in the quiet, her mind swirling with fractured bits and pieces of whatever had happened to her.

"Hello Grace," said the male voice accompanied by soft footsteps.

From where she lay, Grace could not see who it was. Her back was to the door and the night darkened window was out of focus.

"How do you feel by now?" he asked as he came around to the side of the bed.

Grace watched as the hazy image of a man appeared and crouched down in front of her. He had dark hair, but his features were blurred. Not Roger, but who else would be here looking for her? Confused and frustrated with her inability to clear his image, she asked, "Who are you?"

"I wondered if you would have any memory of what happened tonight. You had a rough time of it," he said. "May I sit down for a few minutes?"

"Sure," Grace said, struggling to recognize his voice and finding it impossible to do so. The figure turned and seemed to be moving a chair in closer. "I don't know who," she began.

"Grace, I'm Brian Cooper," he said. "Do you remember me?"

"Brian?" she said, her speech slurring slightly.

"Yes, we picked you up when you had a flat tire, remember?" he asked.

"Brian," she repeated, reaching into her memory and picking out a fractured image. "Yes, maybe," she said then.

"They must have given you some powerful meds. I'll let you sleep," he said.

"Maybe," mumbled Grace. She remembered now. That day in the hot sun, the ordeal with her car and leaving without saying thank you to him. Even while she felt her mind sliding toward sleep, she felt the heat of shame climbing up her neck. "My car, thank you," she said. Her eyelids grew heavier. Despite her best efforts, Grace glided into the quiet dark, taking with her the knowledge that he was right here in the room with her. The how and why mattered not.

Brian watched without making a sound as she relaxed into sleep. After all she had been through, healing had to be her first priority. Brian eased back on the low-slung seat and folded his arms over his chest. He decided to close his eyes for just a few minutes to recharge.

Neither of them saw the night nurse come in, nod approvingly and walk away singing, "Young love..."

## Chapter 81

Brian rose from the chair and walked to the window. It was too dark outside to see anything beyond the lighted parking lot one story below. The past two years had been full of turmoil and grief for Brian and his children. He and Alicia had too few years together. The good years overflowed with joy. They had given their all into building a family and channeling everything positive and happy into every part of their adventure. When the tragedy of Alicia's illness began tearing their world apart, Brian was at a complete loss. He did everything he could to help Alicia deal with the medical appointments. He took care of the children so she could rest. He gradually accepted the changes Alicia assured him would make it easier to cope with life later on. As he had thought so many times before, Brian had no doubt he would have married Alicia even if he had known the end was so near. People often said a person battled cancer with courage, but Brian knew Alicia was fighting for her family, to build their strengths and their hope for the future knowing she would not be a part of it. She told him often that she was not afraid of dying, but afraid of leaving him all alone to raise their children. Brian's life had turned completely upside down. Not a single day passed without aching for Alicia's company and encouraging words.

The events of the past few hours had swept Brian further into unknown territory. Had Alicia really been out there on the beach? Had he actually heard her voice? Dare he deny it after her words guided him to the place where Grace had been hiding?

Brian rubbed his face with his hands fearing his mental well-being might be fractured beyond repair. He was conscious, a fact he verified by touching the chilled glass before him. Did someone who was insane feel things like hot and cold, fear and happiness? His jumbled thoughts churned inside his head as he closed his eyes and tried to make sense of it all.

Brian turned far enough to confirm Grace was in the bed behind him. She had been injured and he was here with her. Actually here and not the result of an insane nightmare.

More questions rose as the minutes ticked by. Did he have any business being here? Was he intruding on her privacy? Had she come to the coast with someone or by herself? Would she be angry when she emerged from her drug aided sleep?

He eyed the door, contemplated leaving and returned to the chair. For now, he would stay put. He felt some level of obligation to her. She needed to understand his role. He needed to offer his help. He needed to keep his distance. Helping someone with a flat tire did not earn them the right to expect anything more than a mere word of thanks.

Once again overwhelmed with unease, Brian folded his arms over his chest and closed his eyes. Grace needed time to heal. He planned to stay long enough to see if she needed his help. After that he needed to leave her alone. He knew his place, and it was with his children.

## Chapter 82

*There was no escape as their jaws locked on her leg, gripped her arm and dragged her out of her hiding place. The pain was excruciating. Hopelessly doomed, Grace whimpered, unable to free herself, unable to cry out for help. She shook violently while her flesh was being ravaged.*

"Help me," she screamed without a sound.

"Grace, wake up, you're safe," he said calmly.

Heart pounding in her ears, the terror continued. She felt hot and freezing cold at the same time.

"Grace, can you hear me?" he asked.

"Help," whispered Grace. "Please help me."

"There's nothing to be afraid of now, you're safe," he said.

"The, the dogs," she wept.

"They're gone, Grace. They're not here, you're safe. Believe me, everything's okay," he told her calmly.

Warm fingers lightly brushed her face. Grace was unsure whether to pull away or sigh with the unfamiliar touch. She found herself wishing for more, wishing to open her eyes and find herself somewhere beautiful, living a life so far from her own she would not recognize her own image in a mirror.

"Grace," said the person behind the voice.

Befuddled came to mind once she had the presence of mind to think clearly. "Clearly befuddled," Grace thought to herself. "Where am I?" she managed to say out loud.

"That's a good starting point," he replied. "You're in the hospital."

"Oh," Grace sighed with disappointment.

"I bet you are confused," said the man. "You had a rough time last night."

Grace gradually opened her eyes and found she was looking at a faceless silhouette. The harsh sunlight from the window behind him made her squint, but even then his features were lost to her. When his hand slid in under hers, Grace wondered if she was still sleeping and he was only a part of her dreams.

"Grace, I need to leave for a few minutes," said the man, easing her hand free and touching her face one more time before leaving the room.

"Good morning, Miss Marshall. How are you feeling this morning?" asked a woman's soft-spoken voice.

Grace blinked, surprised when a light flickered on overhead. The bright light revealed a middle- aged woman dressed in white scrubs. "Tired," Grace replied. "and sore."

"That is to be expected. You'll feel better once you are able to sit up and eat a little something. Let's check your vitals before we do anything else. The doctor will be in to see you eventually," she said as she slipped the blood pressure cuff around her patient's arm.

"Thanks," Grace said, closing her eyes and wishing for more sleep. The dream felt so real, but was it anywhere close to what actually happened to her? Would she ever know the whole story? She had been down at the beach all alone and had not seen any other people. Had she done something to provoke the attack? The attack, she knew, something or someone was chasing after her. Tears seeped from her eyes as the memories burst to life. She drew her legs up and felt the pain charge through her body. "No," she whispered. "No," she mumbled as she drifted into restless sleep.

## Chapter 83

"She's sleeping," the nurse said as she stepped out into the hallway. "She will probably do so throughout the morning." The woman patted his arm and walked toward the nursing station down the hall.

While Grace slept, Brian decided to make the phone call. He left a message at the desk for Justin and Marlene and the clerk said they would deliver it right away. He had to remind himself the children were in capable hands. Upon returning to the room, he listened at the doorway and then entered quietly.

Grace's eyes were closed. While he watched her sleep, Brian wondered if he had any right to be here. He considered leaving, but leaving her alone seemed more wrong than staying. Getting some answers to a few questions would serve to ease his concern, but she had to be awake in order to accomplish that. He pulled in a deep breath and let it out slowly as he settled back on the chair to wait.

Brian closed his eyes from time to time but did not allow himself to fall asleep. When he noticed Grace's fingers moving, he sat forward on the chair. He braced his elbows on his knees and waited. Her eyelids fluttered open, closed and then opened again. It was so like watching Erin or Jack when they woke from a nap. It seemed to him it was the brain awakening bit by bit, activating one particular function at a time until awareness sharpened and the brain became fully alert. And so Grace awoke, her eyes open, her lips parted and the fingers on her left hand curled into a fist.

"Good morning," Brian said softly. He waited as she processed his brief greeting.

Grace blinked, watching cautiously. Her fingers opened, reached up and touched her lips.

"Are you thirsty?" he asked. She blinked in reply, though he doubted she fully grasped the question. "You're still asleep, aren't you."

"Some," she replied, clumsily brushing her fingers against her face.

Brian noticed several strands of her hair laying tangled across her cheek. Images of Alicia in bed flashed through his mind as he tentatively reached out and brushed the loose strands back in place.

Grace's hand returned to where it had been before. She blinked again, licked her lips and drew in a relatively deep breath.

Brian wanted to pepper her with questions, but kept quiet and let her float along. The meds were most likely to blame for her drowsiness. Only time would release her from the aftereffects. For now he eased back on the chair and continued waiting. He felt a sense of belonging that both pleased and angered him. He was not ready to feel anything resembling desire. He told himself to be concerned for her well-being and absolutely nothing more. Once again, he wanted to blurt out his questions and get back to his children. He looked up at the doorway, contemplated a quick escape and remained sitting.

An hour passed before Grace awoke again. This time she came fully awake, eyes open and a frown darkening her expression.

"Hello, Grace," Brian said, sitting up on the chair, careful to keep some distance between them.

Grace watched the man. "Brian?" she murmured.

Brian saw the effort it took to manage the single spoken word. "Yes, how do you feel by now?"

"Not sure," she replied.

"That's okay," Brian replied. "It's going to take some time for you to feel better. There's no rush, you are here to heal."

"Heal?" she said, sounding confused.

"Are you thirsty?" Brian asked, deciding she needed to be more alert before he offered any further explanation. "I'll help you."

Grace accepted the straw and sipped gingerly. "Thank you," she said.

"You're welcome," Brian told her as he set the cup aside. "Let me know when you want more." He waited and wondered what she was thinking, how much she remembered and what might happen next.

"Good morning," Dr. Orland said as he entered the room.

"I should go," Brian said and rose from the chair.

"Are you family?" the doctor asked, reaching out to shake hands. "It is good Grace has someone here with her today. She is going to need some help for the next few days. I understand she is not from our area."

Brian looked from the doctor to Grace and back again. "She's not quite all with us yet. I really ought to go," he said.

"I prefer she is not alone at this time, young man. Please sit and let's talk," Dr. Orland explained. "Grace, would you like to sit up some?" he asked.

"Yes," replied Grace. She looked at Brian with apprehension.

Reading her expression as a silent plea for him to stay nearby, Brian stepped back far enough to give the doctor room to work. He stood still and observed while the doctor spoke quietly with Grace. He watched as he checked her eyes, examined her hand and repositioned the Velcro brace. Brian stepped aside even further when a nurse entered the room. They folded the blanket back and removed tape from Grace's leg, applied something he guessed was an antibiotic or antiseptic, and put fresh bandages in place.

The nurse left the room and the doctor waved Brian closer. "Grace is doing fine, but we would like for her to stay with us for another night. She suffered a minor concussion, and we would like to be sure her leg is healing properly before she is released to return home," Dr. Orland explained. "Once she goes home, she will need to see her personal physician. We recommend she has someone helping her for at least a week. I am counting on you to help her out. Yes, good man, thank you."

"I," Brian replied, dumbfounded after being put in charge of Grace's care.

"I will see you later today, Grace. Rest and take advantage of our excellent nursing staff. Let them know what you need," Dr. Orland said before he picked up the chart and exited the room without another word.

Brian had not moved an inch. He glanced over at the open door and shoved his hands down into his pockets. A week of care, he thought to himself. Why didn't he tell the doctor he was not responsible for her? He looked down at the floor, then up at Grace. She made him think of a wounded bird with her sad eyes and broken body. "Grace," he said softly. Then he saw the tears.

Grace nervously pulled up on the upper edge of her hospital gown. Tears streamed down her face. "You don't have to help me," she sobbed. "Just go, please, just go."

Brian thought he knew what she was feeling. After all she had suffered down at the beach and here, with what the doctor had said and his own presence during her unexpected crisis, she was certainly overwhelmed. He moved over to the side of her bed, crouched down and did his best to help her calm down. She looked utterly lost.

"Grace, I'm sorry. "Hey, you're going to be fine, really, you will be just fine."

"Go away," whispered Grace.

"Did anyone come over here with you? To the ocean I mean," he asked, doing his best to analyze the situation.

"No," she sobbed.

"Is there someone I can call to come help you?" he asked next. "Family, your husband, someone?"

"No," she repeated. "There's no one."

"Surely your parents," Brian began.

"There's no one," she said again. "I have no one at all."

"Damn," whispered Brian. He had not meant for her to hear him. She turned away from him as far as she could manage, but her injuries did not allow her to move freely. Brian stood up and sat on the edge of her bed, offering her comfort with caution. "I'm under doctor's orders to help you. I cannot disobey him, Grace. You saw him, he's bigger than me," he explained and was rewarded with a tiny smile through her tears.

Brian gently squeezed her uninjured hand. "Listen, you relax and let me think about how we can handle this."

"You don't need to," said Grace. "I can take care of myself."

"You planning on hobbling home when they kick you out of here?" Brian asked, trying to inject some humor into the mix. "How about we get you something to eat and then we can figure out what to do for you."

"Okay, but you aren't responsible for me. I've been alone for a long time, I mean," she cried, having lost control once again. "Just go away and let me do this alone."

"And have me arrested for disobeying direct orders?" Brian replied. "I can't do that. Let's find something for you to eat before we say anything more."

## Chapter 84

Grace operated in a fog, overwhelmed with everything that was happening to her. It felt more like she was floating than sitting on the bed. Felt more like someone else was occupying her body. When the food arrived, it looked incredibly inedible.

"They said you are on liquids only for today," Brian explained. "It doesn't look very appetizing."

Grace looked up from the tray feeling like a fool. Here she was, once again in an awkward situation with the man she had once created in her mind. She had been too far from the car to have seen any of his detailed features, but his eyes, his hair, his build, were all on target. Foolish, she knew, but incredibly accurate.

Grace tried to distance herself from her thoughts and gave her full attention to her meal. She suddenly realized she was very hungry. The bowl, the cup, the other two containers all had lids on them. Plastic lids that required two hands to open them. She had a spoon, a fork, a knife, salt & pepper, a napkin and a small packet with a wet wipe inside it. "Impossible," she whispered under her breath.

"Allow me the pleasure of helping you," Brian said, stepping up close to the tray of food. "What do you want first? Jell-O, broth, coffee or apple juice?"

"The broth sounds best right now," Grace replied. "I'm sorry, but my hand," she tried to explain.

"Don't apologize for being unable to do things, Grace. None of this is your fault," Brian said as he pried the lid off of the cup of broth. "This feels warm, but not hot. Do you want the spoon, or can you manage picking it up to drink it?"

Grace slid her left hand in around the small cup and lifted it carefully. She took a sip of the chicken flavored broth and melted with relief. "It's good," she said right away and sipped more of the liquid.

Brian sat down and watched as Grace slowly consumed the broth. She slipped the napkin free and dabbed at her mouth once she was finished.

"I need to thank you for helping me with my car, but even more so I must apologize for leaving without saying so," Grace confessed. "There's no excuse for being rude, I'm sorry."

Brian nodded and stood to help her open something else on her tray. "We were both worn out, so let's let it go," he said. "Here, I'll open the juice and the Jell-O. Dessert is served."

"Who has dessert after breakfast?" asked Grace. She felt slightly breathless while Brian pulled back the foil lid on the juice. Her eyes followed his every movement. He switched the Jell-O with the empty broth cup and opened the plastic wrapped spoon. Remembered images flashed before her eyes. Cutting the burger on the paper wrapper.

"How are your children?" she asked without thinking. His hands stilled as he set the spoon into the Jell-O. "That's none of my business, I'm sorry."

"Grace," Brian said, pushing his hands into his pockets.

"I should not have asked, really, I'm sorry," Grace quickly apologized. Her appetite vanished and she started to push the tray away.

"Grace, don't," Brian said.

"Maybe you ought to go," Grace said softly. Her heart hurt and she wanted to cry.

"No, I am delighted you asked about them," Brian remarked. "You caught me by surprise. They're doing great."

Grace did her best to calm her rattled nerves. "They're beautiful," she managed to say, carefully avoiding his eyes.

"Yes, they are," laughed Brian.

## Chapter 85

Brian brought the tray in closer to Grace once peace settled between them. He felt they had just stepped over a huge hurdle. "Erin watches for your car whenever we're out on the road. In fact," he said once she reached for the spoon. "In fact, she's the one who recognized you last night."

"Recognized me?" Grace asked, clearly perplexed.

"Last night," Brian said. "You can't remember?"

Grace set the spoon down and turned to him. "I must have missed something. I definitely remember the dogs, but were you out on the beach with Erin?"

"Wow, we have a lot to talk about. Why don't you finish eating first. I'm going to go to the cafeteria and see if they have something I can bring back here, if you don't mind my eating in front of you."

"Of course, I hadn't even thought about you being hungry too," Grace apologized.

"I won't be gone for long," Brian said. He left the room, left Grace behind and immediately felt deflated. He contemplated leaving the hospital and returning to the kids. They could pack up and be on the road for home in an hour's time. "Coward!" he sputtered as he strode toward the small cafeteria.

The dining area was bigger than he had expected. Following after an older couple, Brian picked up a tray and viewed the offerings behind the glass partition. He chose a turkey sandwich on whole wheat bread and filled a paper cup with iced tea. After pressing the lid in place and picking up a straw and napkin, Brian approached the cashier. "Can you tell me if taking food up to a patient's room is permitted?" he asked, pulling his wallet out to pay for his meal.

"Of course," replied the cashier, a woman in her late 60's.

Brian smiled at her happy expression and took back the change. "This is a very nice dining room."

"Yes, it is," remarked the woman. "We try to make the families feel welcome and accommodate their needs."

"I appreciate your efforts," Brian said as he picked up the sandwich and drink.

Arriving back in Grace's room, Brian met her eyes. Despite her injuries Grace was a beautiful woman. He wondered what she looked like without dirt on her face or bruises marring her skin. She still had the dark shadows he had seen before. Her past showed there, something he supposed he bore himself. She had seen it, having witnessed his unease while he turned his ring restlessly when they sat together at the Drive In. The ring remained on his finger. Brian was still married to Alicia. He was, wasn't he? He forced away the irritation as he made his way around her bed and eased down on the chair.

"Real food," Grace sighed dramatically from her place on the bed.

Brian laughed. "I'd share, but your stomach might object and then we'd have some explaining to do."

"I can wait," Grace replied. "It's an opportunity to shed a few pounds," she added.

Brian looked up and raised his eyebrows. "Seriously?" he asked, and instantly felt ashamed. "Forget I said that. Your statement was private. I'm sorry."

Grace laughed and said, "I was kidding. I tend to eat less than I should."

"You look good to me," Brian said cautiously. After he finished eating, he would pose a few questions and try to make some plans for the next two days. While he ate, Grace eased back against the pillow, tugging on the blanket and pulling it close around her shoulders. Her eyes were closed, and Brian thought his chance to ask her anything may have melted away.

Brian mentally sifted through the coming days. Justin and Marlene's flight home was on Wednesday. The original plan was to drive home on Monday. He had to go back to work on Tuesday morning. They also had last minute preparations for the start of school next week. Erin was excited about starting kindergarten. As always, Brian felt his eyes burning with the knowledge Alicia would not be there for Erin's big day. He acknowledged they had a lot more time ahead when they would mourn her loss. He used the paper napkin to wipe away his tears, doing his best to make it look like he simply had something in his eyes. Since Grace was dozing it seemed a foolish thing to be concerned about, but when he looked up, he found her watching him. He had been caught once again.

*Tender Dreams*

Chapter 86

Grace was well aware of the noises out in the busy corridor. Carts constantly rattled past her doorway, people chattered endlessly, and the phones rang out quite regularly. Grace blocked it all out and kept sneaking peeks at the man sitting close enough to touch. Knowing she had no real idea what he was thinking did not keep her from speculating. Surely he was still hurting from the loss of his wife. She guessed it must take a long time to find some semblance of peace after such a tragedy. Her own grief never seemed to reach a peaceful point. The lingering "what ifs" constantly haunted her. Depression chased after her every step. It would have been easy to swallow pill after pill in an effort to numb the pain in her heart, but so far she had resisted. Rather than medicate she found places to hide and avoid facing the truth. She retreated into her work, let her quilting absorb the remaining waking hours available outside work and diligently turned down every opportunity to date or socialize with anyone. When she grew fatigued, she crawled in under her favorite comforter and slept. Dodging any chance to open her heart blocked the possibility of losing someone who mattered again. The wall she had constructed around herself protected her from harm and sheltered her from having to face reality.

Grace studied her hands. For the first time since she had been able to think clearly, she realized she would not be able to quilt with her right hand in the brace. She checked her fingertips with her left hand, feeling each for numbness. While three of her fingers felt warm to the touch, her thumb and index finger felt swollen and chilled. Had the doctor explained what was wrong with them? She pondered removing the brace to look for herself, but stilled her hand when the chance it was something serious shot through her mind. What if she could no longer thread a needle or work neat rows of stitches.

She raised her injured hand to her chest and shut her eyes against the fear bubbling up in her throat. She had to either type or write for her job and needed to use a needle for her quilting. She was doomed without either of those skills.

Feeling lost and broken, her troubles multiplied by leaps and bounds. If she fell behind on the mortgage, she would lose her home. "No," she gasped.

Brian crumpled the sandwich wrapper and threw it into the wastebasket. He set his drink on the floor and stepped over to the bed. "Grace," he said, crouching once again to be in her line of sight. "Hey, what's wrong?"

Grace had forgotten Brian was here. She felt embarrassed and foolish when she opened her eyes and looked at him. There he was again, watching her and turning her insides upside down. "I'm sorry," she said humbly.

"Aw Grace, you know you're safe here, don't you?" he asked.

"Yes, but," she mumbled, looking down at her hands.

"What is it?" Brian asked.

"I'm afraid," she managed to say then.

"Of course you are," Brian replied. "What happened to you must have been terrifying. You need to put it all behind you now. You're going to be fine once you heal."

"My hand," Grace cried out.

Brian watched as she touched her thumb and index finger over and over. He took the chance and reached up for her hands. "Did you understand what the doctor told you?" he asked.

"I don't remember. I wasn't able to grasp it all. I mean, I was, oh," she confessed.

"Worrying won't help. When the doctor comes back later you can ask him. I can be here if you want so you won't miss anything he tells you," Brian assured her.

"But you need to take care of your kids," Grace objected. "They need you more than I do."

"My friends are taking care of my kids for now, so don't worry. I can stay until the doctor returns," Brian reassured her.

"I can't feel my thumb, can't feel my," she wept, gently cradling her injured hand.

"I'm sure they will get better with time," Brian replied, wishing he could take away the pain.

Grace turned and slid down lower on the bed. "I want to go home," she cried.

"Is someone there to help you once you get home?" Brian asked.

"No," she whispered. Grace pulled up every ounce of strength she had left and fired back, "I can take care of myself."

"I'm sure you can, but the doctor doesn't want you to be alone for a week or so," Brian reminded her.

"I don't have anyone. Please, I want to go to sleep now," she wept.

"Okay, you do that. I'm going for a walk, but I will come back later," Brian said as he lowered the bed down until she looked comfortable. He tugged the blanket over her and backed away from the bed. After he picked up the drink cup, he walked out of the room.

Grace felt sick to her stomach. What kind of future did she have if she could no longer work? Grace slipped into the memories of the night of the storm, back to the rain-slicked road and the moment Clay left this world. She had seen the peace come over him and felt the radiant warmth as his spirit rose toward Heaven. Grace prayed her time was near. She yearned for eternal peace and forgiveness for all the mistakes in this life.

*Julia Robertson*

## Chapter 87

As the hours slipped by, Brian made a mental list of the things he needed to discuss with Grace. He thought he ought to contact her employer and let them know where she was and basically what had happened. And where was she staying? She had to go home, but how would they get her there? His initial solution was to have Justin or Marlene drive one of the cars since he guessed Grace had driven over here. They would get her home, possibly tomorrow, at which point she had to make arrangements for her care. It seemed like a reasonable plan to him, but would Grace agree?

He walked the perimeter of the hospital's parking area. The wind was picking up and it felt like rain was coming. He needed to drive back to the cabins tonight. It was not fair to leave Justin and Marlene stranded with the kids for too much longer.

With the tentative plan in mind, Brian started back toward the hospital entrance. As he reached the doorway to Grace's room the doctor appeared beside him.

"Good to see you, young man," said Dr. Orland. "I'm just about ready to depart for the evening. Let's see how your lady is doing by now."

"My lady," Brian murmured under his breath. He shook off his unease and followed the doctor into the room.

Still hesitant to intrude on her privacy, Brian kept his distance. Then he recalled telling Grace he would help by listening in case she missed something important. He stepped closer and stood at the foot of her bed while the doctor spoke.

Dr. Orland removed the brace, described her injuries and the treatment while watching Grace's eyes to be sure she understood his explanation. He gently positioned the brace and fastened the Velcro straps. "The wounds need time to heal," he explained. "I recommend physical therapy once the wounds are healed. Keep in mind the nerve damage will likely take longer to heal. In due time you will regain the sense of touch, though to what degree I can only guess."

Brian recognized the panic in Grace's eyes. He moved without thinking and stood to one side of the doctor. Tears had escaped Grace's eyes. He stepped over and pulled several tissues out of the box and tucked them into Grace's left hand.

"Let your young man take care of you, Grace. You need to be careful moving about until the stitches along your ankle heal. You may put weight on your foot, but sparingly. Again, healing takes time. Your biggest concern is for your hand. Your concussion is coming along just fine. The blurred vision will clear after a few days and you may take pain meds to help with any discomfort. Are you able to comprehend all of what I've told you?"

"I think so," replied Grace.

"Any questions?" he asked, in no rush to leave his patient.

"Yes," Grace said, her voice wobbling with fear. "I am a seamstress. I hand sew quilts. Not as a hobby, but to make ends meet," she explained. "My hand, I'm afraid," she said, swiping at her eyes with the tissue.

"You must give it time to heal, Grace. I cannot predict the end result. Only time will reveal that for you. I will check back with you tomorrow before you are released. You two have a good night," he said as he rose and left the room.

Brian felt ill at ease. No wonder Grace had been emotional when she discovered the numbness in her hand. She was a quilter, he thought as he pulled the chair close to the bed and sat down.

"Grace, are you okay?" he asked.

Grace sat frozen on the bed. "No," she whispered. She stared at her hands. Tears streamed from her eyes.

"Grace," Brian said as he sat down on the edge of the bed and gently gathered her into his arms.

## Chapter 88

Brian wished he had grabbed his jacket the night before, but there was no help for that now as he ran across the hospital's dark parking lot to his car. The rain was coming down so hard it soaked through his shirt in a matter of seconds. By the time he dropped down on the front seat he was soaking wet head to toe. He turned the key and started the engine. While it warmed up, he wiped the water from his face with his wet hands, doing no more than assuring him the rain succeeded in hitting every inch of him. Brian backed out of the parking space and drove toward the coast highway. Strong winds buffeted the car and blew the rain sideways. Typical weather for coastal areas, he thought as he focused on the road while the windshield wipers continued moving back and forth at a steady clip.

Brian and Grace had worked out a plan to get her and her car back to town, but not until the day after tomorrow. Grace had insisted she needed to go to work tomorrow, but there was no way she would be able to handle driving, let alone going to work and using a keyboard. She could answer phones but taking notes with her hand in the brace was not likely to produce legible messages. Brian had contacted her immediate supervisor and explained the situation to him. Roger had been very understanding and told Brian Grace had plenty of sick time coming and health insurance to help cover her bills for the next month. Roger asked him to convey the message to Grace so she could stop worrying about everything but her recovery.

Brian shared the details of the call with Grace that afternoon in her hospital room. Though she stubbornly objected, Grace was now resigned to putting work aside, taking time off to heal and regain her strength.

Brian had no idea how she was going to arrange for help at home, but that was her problem and not his. No matter how many times he told himself that, Brian still felt dismayed. He had his business to run and had to take care of his kids. As far as Grace's personal life was concerned, he vowed to keep his distance. So why did it bother him so much, he wondered as the miles of roadway stretched out in front of him. The windshield wipers swished, the tires splashed water up from the road, the wind buffeted the car and his inner turmoil continued.

When he finally parked the car, Brian noticed the lights were on upstairs. Maybe the kids were still awake. He pushed the door open and ran for the front door.

"Brian," called out Marlene. She threw him a towel from the top of the stairway. "I thought I heard a car pull up outside. We're taking a bath up here. Justin's down there somewhere."

"Thanks," Brian said as he toweled off his hair and dragged the towel over his arms. He pushed off his shoes and peeled off his soggy socks.

"Hey, Brian," Justin said, coming out of the kitchen. "Man, look at you."

"Yeah, it's sprinkling out there," Brian laughed.

"Looks like," laughed Justin. "I'll stoke the fire. You ought to get some dry clothes and hit the shower down here. Marlene is probably ready to get the kids out of the tub by now."

"Good idea," Brian replied, taking the steps two at a time. Moving fast, he ducked into the bedroom, gathered up sweats and dry socks and rushed down the stairs to the shower. He nearly melted under the hot spray. In his mind he saw Grace again, cradling her injured hand and crying. She had unknowingly burrowed into his heart and he had no idea how to deal with it. Brian froze when he realized he was thinking about Grace, not Alicia. Standing naked in the shower and thinking about Grace. His hand shifted to the lever and turned the water cold.

"Daddy, Daddy!" shouted Erin and Jack when he came out of the bathroom. He squatted down and hugged the kids tight against him. Tears burned his eyes as he walked into the living room with his children in his arms.

"They missed you," Marlene exclaimed.

"I missed them too," Brian replied as he sat down on the oversized sofa and kissed his kids. "Did you two grow while I was gone?"

"Daddy, we can't grow that fast," exclaimed Erin.

Jack rubbed his hand against Brian's beard roughened cheek. "Gotta shave," he chuckled.

"What have you been up to?" he asked.

*Tender Dreams*

"We played on the beach and made a sandcastle," said Erin. "And Jack found a starfish."

"Big star," Jack said seriously, bobbing his head up and down.

"Is that right?" asked Brian.

"And we walked to town," Erin added. "And we had ice cream."

"Nilla scream," Jack said.

"I bet you had some on your nose," Brian said to his son, kissing him again.

"And in his hair," groaned Erin.

"We've had fun," Marlene said as she sat down across from them on the oversized chair.

Justin moved in, scooped Marlene up and sat down with her on his lap. "It was a good test for us. We're planning on having kids sometime in the near future."

"A dozen," giggled Marlene.

"Two," sighed Justin. He cuddled Marlene close.

Quietness descended upon the room as the kids relaxed and yawned sleepily. Marlene curled up on Justin's lap and Brian closed his eyes. He had not realized how tired he was, or how much he missed his kids. Their small bodies were warm from their bath, and dressed in their pajamas, they were all ready for bed. He was in no hurry to take them upstairs. Right now, Brian needed the comfort they gave him just by being in his arms. Alicia's children, he sighed. Her blood ran in their veins, her beauty shone on their faces. How he missed his first love. An hour later Brian opened his eyes when Justin spoke to him.

"Let me take one of them for you," Justin suggested. At Brian's nod he lifted Jack up and ascended the stairs.

Brian shifted Erin and followed Justin. His mind was foggy with sleep as he trudged up the stairs.

"Good night," Justin said when he passed by Brian.

"Thanks," Brian said. He nestled Erin in her bed and kissed her cheek.

"Daddy," whispered Erin.

"Yes baby," he said, kneeling on the floor and stroking her soft hair.

"Is the Ladybug Lady all better?" she asked with her eyes closed.

"She's much better," he replied. "Go to sleep now. I love you."

"Love you," Erin said as she drifted into sleep.

As he had done so many times in the past, Brian remained kneeling on the floor between his children. He prayed for guidance, prayed for strength and ached for the answers to so many unanswered questions.

Brian let his guard down and felt tears running down his face. From the moment Alicia heard the doctor's devastating diagnosis, she began removing herself from their lives. She knew it had to be that way in order to build them up to the point where they could stand independently from her. Brian had not been able to so much as consider doing that.

"I think I understand what you did, but I can't let you go. Not now, maybe not ever. I still love you. You are still in my heart. How can I ever let you go?"

## Chapter 89

"I think we can guess her size close enough to make her comfortable," Marlene said as they walked into the coastal town's only variety store. "Let's go with sweats. Something warm, something loose," she said as she led the way into the sportswear area.

Brian followed along behind Marlene. He watched with fascination as she deftly sorted through several racks of clothing. In a matter of minutes, she held up a pair of charcoal gray sweatpants, a zip up sweatshirt in light pink and gray and two pairs of gray socks with pink heels and toes. Delight shone on her face. "Very nice," Brian agreed, taking the clothing from her.

Marlene stood frowning for a moment before she signaled for him to follow. Brian looked down, then went after her. By the time he caught up with her she had chosen a dark green button up pajama top and a matching pair of loose-fitting bottoms.

"She can wear these and feel at ease around all of us strangers. I think that does it," she proclaimed, handing the pajamas to Brian.

"So, are we ready to go?" he asked.

"Yes, we're out of here," she laughed.

Their next stop took them to the small grocery store where they purchased enough food for the next two days. Marlene chose sandwich fixings for the trip back to Brian's home. Brian admired her efficient planning and was happy to push the cart and nod at her choices.

"We're all set," Marlene said after they carried the groceries inside. "Now you can go and bring Grace back here. We'll take the kids down to the beach for a bit. By the time you get back I'll have them down for a nap. It'll be quiet for Grace so she can rest. The ride is going to wear her out."

Brian said goodbye to the children and walked out to his car. He brought along the sweat suit and socks for Grace to wear out of the hospital. Grace had given them permission to get into her cabin and bring some of her own clothing, but no one wanted to rifle through her belongings. Since she could not yet be alone, they set things up so

Grace could stay in the downstairs bedroom and turn in the keys for her rental cabin.

After yesterday's heavy rain, the clouds had cleared, and a dome of blue sky spread out overhead. Brian felt the warm sunshine through the windows whenever he reached a spot where the sun cut through the trees along the road. He used his alone time to sort out the events of the past few days. Being out on the beach that night must have been preordained, if such a thing even existed. Alicia had spoken to him. She had somehow directed him to find Grace. Brian felt certain the dogs would have gone after Grace again if he had not been there. Her hiding place put her out of sight, but dogs didn't need visual contact to tell them someone was nearby.

Brian ran his fingers through his hair and groaned. If he let his imagination overwhelm common sense, he might think he was supposed to find Grace, fall in love and make her his own. How dare he even think such crazy thoughts? No one had the right to intrude on anyone's personal life, take command and direct their every movement. That was what he was doing, wasn't he? "Shit," Brian swore, once again dragging his fingers through his hair.

Grace needed help, a fact verified by her doctor, but the help was limited to watching out for her to be sure she had food and a place to stay. As he told himself before, she had to find someone else to care for her in her own home. Merely contemplating doing it himself was foolish and inconsiderate. He had no business letting his feelings control his actions.

"Damn it," he swore. "I'm bringing her back to the cabin so we can all cooperate, get Grace and her car back to town and then go our separate ways. End of story."

Brian pulled into a parking space, grabbed the bag of clothes with too much force and slammed the car door too hard. Feeling anything but calm, Brian waited as the automatic doors yawned open. His aggravation spiked as he entered too quickly and bumped his shoulder on the still opening door. He cursed under his breath, rubbed his shoulder with more force than necessary and stormed toward the elevator. He knew he had to settle down before entering Grace's room. He paced the upstairs corridor until he regained control. Being here was nothing more than doing a good deed for someone in need. Brian let out a long-held breath and tapped lightly on the partially open door.

## Chapter 90

Grace could not stop fidgeting. She was anxious to go home, but she knew it was out of the question. She had agreed to stay in Brian's cabin, sharing the space but also having a room to herself. Staying with virtual strangers, though she had to remember she had met Brian and his children before. Even as she remembered Brian's odd behavior and short temper at the Drive In, she had to admit she had been a frazzled mess herself. Worry kept her brow furrowed and her shoulders tense. How had her short vacation turned into a mini drama?

Grace hated being the center of attention. She preferred living her life in the shadows, moving from one task to another unnoticed. Her only goals were to keep up with the bills, keep her childhood home and keep her hands busy.

Gloom descended over her when images of the accident that claimed Clay's life flashed before her eyes. She debated the pros and cons of telling Brian she was the one who was with Clay that night. Grace immediately pushed the idea away. There was already too much going on right now. It was probably best to let it go, get through the next two days and hope she could manage on her own once she was inside the walls of her home. She yearned to be in the shelter of the house she loved. Her sanctuary, her fortress, where she and the mute walls alone knew of the love that once thrived there.

Grace quickly brushed at the forming tears when someone knocked on the door. She knew there was no need to answer since anyone and everyone simply pushed the door open and entered unbidden. When she saw him her heart skipped a beat. Brian came in looking like a warrior returning from a battlefield. She knew better than to judge him even though his expression seemed to mirror her own dark mood. It took great effort to sit up straight and greet him with a smile.

"I'm happy to see you," Grace said cheerfully. Inside she felt anything but cheerful.

"Good afternoon," Brian said as he rounded the bed and sat down on the chair. "How are you feeling?" he asked.

Grace sighed and replied, "Shall I sugar coat it and say I feel great?" Her words apparently registered in the same manner with Brian. His eyebrows rose up before he quickly looked down at his shoes.

"So we both had a bad night?" he asked sheepishly. "I'm sorry, let's start over." He ran his fingers through his hair and looked up. "Are you ready to check out of here?" he asked.

"I think so," Grace replied. "Someone is supposed to come in with paperwork for me to sign. I'm not sure how long it will take."

"It might take all day," Brian said as he sat back on the chair. "Have they brought you anything to eat? I can go down to the cafeteria and sneak something back up here for you."

"I did have breakfast," she laughed. "Eggs, toast and juice. I guess I've been cleared to eat something more substantial than liquids."

"That's good," Brian said. "Want me to smuggle in a pepperoni pizza?"

Grace laugh without restraint. Brian's eyes lit up with his suggestion. As to whether or not he was serious, she could not be sure, but laughing felt good. "I'm not a fan of pepperoni," she confessed.

"Sausage?" Brian asked hopefully.

Grace shook her head. She hid her eyes behind her hand when his mouth turned down in a frown. He looked so much like his son when the little boy talked about her flat tire. Once she regained her ability to speak, Grace said, "Pizzas can be made half and half."

"That's true enough," Brian said, once again running his fingers through his hair.

Grace wondered what he was actually thinking. He seemed on edge and doing his best to hide it from her. Feeling anxious, she rubbed her numb fingers, wishing they would heal faster. The doctor had been in earlier and reminded her that there was no set length of time regarding healing nerve damage. Fear that some of the numbness might be permanent frightened Grace the most.

Brian sat up on the chair and handed the bag to Grace. "I brought you some clothes for the ride back. Maybe someone can help you get dressed. That is if you need help. Take a look and see what you think of Marlene's choices," he suggested.

Grace was puzzled by his smug expression. The same glint was in his eyes that had been there when he read the food items to his children at the Drive In. She timidly opened the bag and slid her good hand inside.

"What's this?" she asked, holding up a pair of socks. "These aren't mine," she exclaimed. "I love the pink toes, but they're not mine."

Brian did not look away. He sat forward on the chair with a grin on his face. "They are now," he replied. "Look in the bag again."

Grace frowned, but secretly delighted in seeing how happy he looked. She slowly slid her hand inside again, this time pulling out a pair of gray sweatpants. "Wow, these are soft," she exclaimed as she ran the fabric against her cheek. "Brian, these things are nice, but they are not mine. I don't understand."

"One more thing, Grace," Brian replied, nodding toward the bag and ignoring her last remark.

Grace sighed and pulled out a beautiful pink and gray sweatshirt. The wide tooth plastic zipper was pink, and the fabric was as soft as the other items. "Did you buy these for me?" she asked.

"You deserved something nice," Brian said.

"Give me the receipt so I can pay you back right away," she demanded.

"Nope," he replied, folding his arms over his chest.

"Brian, I will pay you back for these things and for your time and the gas it has taken for you to drive back and forth. I'm not a charity case."

"No one suggested you were," Brian said, pushing forward on the chair. "Can't you accept a gift from people who care?"

"But," sputtered Grace. "No one, no one, I've never, I can't," she wept, holding her hand over her eyes and turning away.

Brian was saved from trying to figure out what to say or do when a woman dressed in a dark skirt and pink sweater came into the room with a stack of paperwork. "Grace, here," he said, pressing a few tissues into her hand. "I'll wait in the hallway." He awkwardly squeezed her hand and walked away.

Grace sniffled, wiped her eyes dry and did her best to put on a brave face.

"I bet you are ready to get home to your own bed," said the thoughtful clerk. "I'm here to explain a few things before you go."

*Julia Robertson*

## Chapter 91

Brian walked down the hallway, giving Grace time to deal with the process of checking out of the hospital. He certainly had not intended to upset her with the new clothes. Looking back, perhaps they should have retrieved something from her cabin, but they all felt she needed a distraction after her life had been turned upside down. She was obviously upset with the injury to her right hand. When he tried to put himself in her place, he thought he understood her distress. Then again, Brian thought, he really did not know Grace. For all he knew she might be a stalker. Maybe her ex was hounding her, trying to make amends. She might have several children and had simply escaped for the weekend. Maybe she was a runner, trying to find refuge from whatever was chasing after her.

"Shit," Brian muttered, bracing his hands on a low windowsill in the waiting area.

Brian needed to stop thinking. He had to get back on track, focus on helping Grace get back to her home and then walk away. Grace did not owe him any further explanations. It was a simple case of someone facing trouble and another lending a helping hand.

Brian wandered back down the hallway to the doorway to Grace's room. He heard voices, turned and walked away again. He hoped someone was helping Grace get dressed. Brian realized then that he had not brought any shoes for Grace. He turned in time to see two nurses come out of Grace's room.

"She's all yours," one of the nurses called to him.

He raised his hand in acknowledgement and pondered her words. "All mine," he said, taken aback by his reaction.

Brian took a moment to gather his wits before walking into Grace's room.

"It sounds like you're all set," he said, doing his best to appear cool and collected. He was far from calm when his eyes found Grace. Wearing the new sweatsuit, complete with the crazy socks, she looked radiant perched on the bed. Brian bit his tongue when he realized what he was thinking. His fingers curled so tight into his palms it hurt.

Brian watched her for a moment longer before crossing to the bed. She was working her fingers through her hair, making him regret not bringing her a brush.

Grace looked up and said, "I guess I have to wait for someone with a wheelchair before I can leave."

"Hospital policy, right?" Brian said as he sat down on the opposite side of her bed. "You look nice in your new duds," he remarked. Where those words had come from was a mystery to Brian.

"They're comfortable," replied Grace. She touched her toes and smiled up at him. "I could get used to these."

"Marlene enjoyed the shopping spree," Brian said.

"I'm looking forward to meeting her," Grace admitted. She went back to threading her fingers through her long chestnut-brown hair.

Brian was grateful when the hospital volunteer arrived with the wheelchair. "Your limo," Brian said, standing up from the bed. "Can you manage moving to the chair?"

"Yes, I'm fine," Grace said as she shifted on the bed and moved awkwardly to the wheelchair. She picked up the paperwork and two containers of medications and held them on her lap. She met Brian's eyes as the chair was turned around.

"I'll go ahead and get my car. I had to park across the lot, so it'll take me a few minutes."

"You go ahead, young man, we will be along directly," the volunteer chirped.

Brian rushed outside and hightailed it out to his car. He saw Grace being wheeled out at the same time he pulled up. Worried she might try standing, he rushed around to stop her.

"I can do it by myself," Grace argued.

"You're not supposed to be on your feet unless you have to. At this time, you don't have to. With your permission I'll transfer you to the car," Brian said, once again hoping he had not overstepped the line.

"I can't let you do that," argued Grace.

"He looks like a strong young man," the volunteer said, leaning over her passenger's shoulder. "Your husband is very handsome." She patted Grace's hand and smiled up at Brian.

Neither of them corrected the woman. Brian took the meds and paperwork from Grace, put them in the car and turned back to her. "May I?" he asked.

"This is embarrassing," whispered Grace.

Brian had plenty of experience caring for Alicia. He knew exactly how to lift her without hurting her. He eased Grace down on the seat in his car, pulled the belt down and fastened it for her. "Now that wasn't so bad, was it?" he asked.

Time froze when his eyes locked on hers. Overcome by the unsettling urge to kiss her, Brian quickly pulled back and shut the door. He had to grit his teeth as he sat down behind the wheel.

"Thank you," Grace said, cradling her injured hand on her lap.

Brian nodded in reply. The drive was quiet as the tires rolled across the road, covering mile after mile. Brian kept sneaking glances at Grace, wary of her comfort. She was holding her injured hand, and he felt certain she was worrying about its healing. Curious, he asked, "Do you sew a lot?"

Grace nodded before replying, "Yes."

"What do you like to create?" He asked.

"Well," she sighed. "I can sew anything, but for the most part I quilt."

"You mean comforters?" Brian asked, doing his best to keep the conversation going. He noticed when Grace shifted on the seat. "Are you okay?"

"I'm fine, thanks," she replied.

Brian knew she was hurting. Once again, he reminded himself to back off and let her deal with her troubles.

"I create one-of-a-kind quilts," Grace said. "Most of my work is done for clients who are giving them as gifts. You know, wedding gifts, baby showers and the like."

"That must take a lot of time," Brian remarked, checking the rearview mirror and accelerating for the upcoming hill.

"Since I do it all by hand, yes," she explained. "In fact, it takes so much time I have trouble when it comes time to deliver the finished quilts."

"I understand that feeling," Brian said.

"What kind of work do you do?" Grace asked. "I remember Erin saying you build houses."

Brian was surprised. "I build, but I also design," he said.

Grace turned on the seat far enough to watch him. "When I start a project, I see the finished piece first," she began.

"I do the same thing," he replied, waving his hand in front of him as he spoke. "I have the completed house in my mind, then I take it down to the bare bones."

"Exactly," Grace said, smiling brightly. "I take my time going backwards in my mind until I can see every piece fitting together, stitches and all."

"Like disassembling a jigsaw puzzle," Brian added.

"That's it," agreed Grace. "People don't understand my method unless they do the same thing, which is rare."

"Interesting," Brian said, touching the brake pedal as they started down the hill. The quiet descended once again and Grace turned toward the passenger side window. "I don't know what I'm going to do. My work, my hand," she said. "I have to go to work as soon as I get home. I can't not work."

Brian saw a large parking area coming up on the right side of the road. He slowed the car and eased off onto the gravel covered surface. The tires crunched loudly until he came to a stop. The quiet was sudden and almost deafening. Brian wondered if his read of her conflict was correct. He plunged ahead, hoping to ease her tension.

"If you don't mind, I'd like to say something," he began. He watched Grace lift her good hand in resignation. It was the same gesture she had used in his truck that day at the Drive In.

"There are times when we encounter obstacles in life that seem insurmountable. We can't let ourselves be destroyed by the unknown, but we do need to keep our heads above water. It's something like the tides," he said, gesturing toward the ocean. "The tide comes in and goes out, over and over in an endless cycle that continues no matter whether the sun is shining down on it or a storm has roared in on top of it. It just keeps going and going. Our lives are similar to that unbroken cycle."

Brian paused again, listening to the noise from the ocean as the waves rolled up over the sandy beach below. "We know little about each other, but I feel we know enough for me to share this," he said, running his fingers through his hair and reaching for the proper words. He needed the correct words to convey his message without wasting time.

"I lost my wife earlier this year, as I told you before. I've been consumed with her death and afraid of the future without her to help raise our children. Inadequate barely touches how I've felt. Until the other night on the beach I doubted I had the strength to go on for much longer. Too many things have happened that had me thinking I was going insane. I was walking on the beach that night and I swear I heard my wife speaking to me," he said, pausing to look over at Grace. "I know it sounds crazy. Hell, I wouldn't believe it if it hadn't happened to me. When you called out for help I realized she really had been there with me," he said, stopping for breath.

"I never said anything out loud," whispered Grace. "I was afraid the dogs would hear me. I prayed for help, but," she said, watching Brian.

"Are you sure? I mean," he said, pausing once again. "You told me after I found you, but I thought, I figured you were in shock."

"Not a sound," Grace replied. "I was too scared."

Brian stared out across the gray expanse of water. "Then it's stranger than I imagined."

"I don't understand it either," Grace said, rubbing her numb fingers.

Brian nodded as his thoughts came together. "I think we were brought together for some unknown reason. I mean your flat tire that day on the road, then here on the beach," Brian said, turning to face Grace.

Grace bit her lip and nodded before she said, "And Clay."

"Clay?" Brian said with surprise.

Grace stared down at her hands. "Yes," she whispered. "I'm the one who called you. I didn't mention my name since it didn't seem important at the time. I was there," she said, then looked up.

Brian's mind whirled. He blinked several times before he said, "You were with him. That means everything to me. Clay wasn't alone," he said. Brian reached out for Grace's hand. "Thank you for being there, for trying to help him."

Grace stared at him without saying a word. She nodded as a tear slipped down her cheek. "I'm really tired," she whispered.

Brian wiped away her tear with his thumb. "I bet you are," he said. "Sit tight." He rushed around the car and opened the passenger side door. "Is that more comfortable?" he asked after he lowered the back of the seat down.

"You have beautiful eyes," whispered Grace.

*Julia Robertson*

## Chapter 92

*Little Grace held the paper angel in both hands. Glitter and glue stuck to her fingers, her cheeks and her elbows. "Gonna fall," she cried out.*

*"I've got you, Gracie. Put your angel on top of the tree," said Daddy.*

*"You can do it, sweetie, just a little further," encouraged her mother. She lifted the camera to her eye, clicked the button and captured the moment.*

*"We did it," whispered Gracie. She curled her fingers around the collar of her father's shirt, still unsteady on his shoulders.*

"Grace, can you hear me?" he asked, prying her fingers loose from the front of his shirt.

Grace opened her eyes, confused and exhausted. She heard the voices, but they were not those of her parents. She worked to clear her mind and focus. Finally the face closest to her stopped swimming and she recognized Brian Cooper. Frightened by his nearness, Grace shrunk away and cradled her injured hand against her chest.

"Grace, I just brought you in from my car. You're in our cabin. There's nothing to be afraid of here," Brian assured her.

Grace watched uneasily. Her eyes left Brian and darted over to another figure standing several feet away. She saw a friendly smile framed with pretty red hair.

"Grace, meet my good friend Marlene. Marlene, this is Grace. She's worn out from the ride back from the hospital," Brian explained.

"Hello, Grace, I'm pleased to meet you," Marlene said as she moved in closer. "Why don't you take a nap. If you need anything just let me know."

Grace watched her touch Brian's shoulder, then turn and leave the room. Grace glanced back at Brian. Feeling more frightened, she kept looking around the unfamiliar room. "I can't stay here," she said.

Brian moved off the bed and crouched down at eye level with her. "Listen, Grace, you're perfectly safe here. No one will harm you. Let's see how you feel tomorrow and then we can decide when to head back to town," he suggested. "I think you ought to take your meds. What do you think?"

"Yes, maybe," Grace agreed hesitantly. "I am tired."

"Marlene brought a glass of water in for you," Brian said. "May I help you with the meds?"

"Please," said Grace. After she took her medication and handed the glass back to him, Grace said, "I'm sorry."

"For what?" Brian asked, capping the pill bottles and turning back to her.

"I really do appreciate everything you're doing for me. It's just that I'm used to doing things on my own, you know what I mean?"

"No need to apologize," Brian replied. "Sleep for as long as you need. Marlene will come check on you later on. She's a nice lady. You'll like her," he said, rising to his feet. "Are you comfortable?"

"Yes," Grace replied as the fatigue drew her toward sleep. She heard the light switch click and the room went dark. The peace and quiet enveloped her like a cloud in the soft bed.

Chapter 93

Marlene stood at the sliding glass door in the kitchen watching Erin and Jack playing with Justin on the deck outside. She thought of Justin with Jack in the redwoods. He looked so at ease holding the sleeping little boy. Was there a child or two in their future? Would they make good parents? What chance was there they might lose each other to bitter squabbles, or even to one of them dying like Alicia? She bit her lip, wincing at the pain brought on by the mere idea. "Until death do us part," she whispered for her ears only.

Quiet footsteps behind her told her she was no longer alone. When she turned, she saw Brian standing close by with his hands buried deep inside his pockets. "Life is never fair, is it," she sighed.

"No," replied Brian. He turned toward Marlene. "Take it one day at a time and remember there's no promise of another tomorrow."

Marlene nodded in agreement, unable to speak for the moment. She wept when Brian wrapped his sturdy arms around her. "Life sucks," she sighed.

"It sure as hell does," Brian replied.

Marlene stayed there in Brian's arms for a long time thinking of her own life, Alicia being gone, how lonely Brian was all the time and the woman in the far bedroom. In a storybook life the handsome young man with his broken heart would sweep the damsel in distress off her feet and ride off on a big white stallion. If only, she thought, patting Brian's chest as she stepped back from him. "Go join them, they missed you so much," she ordered as she reached for the sliding glass door handle.

"Daddy!" shouted the children.

Marlene listened as their small feet thundered across the wooden deck toward Brian. Filling the role as both father and mother, Brian swept them up in his arms. They clung to him with all their might.

"Magical," whispered Marlene. She wiped tears from her face and turned back to the kitchen to begin dinner preparations.

"What are we grilling tonight?" Justin asked, sliding his arms around her and pulling her back against his warm body.

"We're actually making sandwiches so we don't have a big mess to clean up. Turkey and salami, cheeses, stuff like that," she said, resting her head back against Justin.

"Sounds great," whispered Justin. "Let's walk the beach alone later tonight," he suggested.

"I'd love that," she replied. "I never want to leave this place."

"I know what you mean," he replied, kissing her neck until she turned in his arms. "I love you."

"I'm the luckiest girl," she said, sliding her hands around his strong body and resting her cheek against his chest.

"We fit just right," Justin said as he brushed his cheek over her soft hair.

"Yes, we do," giggled Marlene.

While Brian played with his kids outside, Marlene went in to check on Grace. She found her in a scrambled mess of blankets and clothing, weeping softly. Marlene shut the door and crossed to the bed.

"Grace?" she said, reaching out and touching the young woman's shoulder. "Let me help you," she said, tugging back the blankets and urging Grace to sit up.

"I'm sorry," Grace apologized.

Marlene worked slowly, gently pulling the tangled sweatshirt around and down Grace's left arm. "Hang on until I can get the cuff over your brace," she said, aching for Grace and her confused state of mind. "There we go, that's much better," she said, laying the sweatshirt over a chair and returning to the bed. "Are you hurting a lot?" she asked. Grace shook her head in reply, but Marlene doubted it was true. "If you can stay ahead of the pain you'll be much better off, Grace."

"Can't," mumbled Grace. "Need to go home."

"Tomorrow," Marlene replied. "We'll pack up everything tonight and get an early start in the morning."

"Umm, yes, okay, guess so," mumbled Grace.

Marlene helped Grace lay down again, then gently pulled the blankets over her. "You sleep for now. Don't worry about anything."

"Sleep," whispered Grace as she drifted away.

Marlene watched her for a minute before leaving the room. "Grace is so lost," she whispered.

## Chapter 94

Brian tapped lightly on the bedroom door before pushing it open. He waited and listened before stepping into the room. "How's our patient doing?" he asked.

Grace blinked at the light coming in through the doorway. "I'm fine," she whispered.

"Getting hungry?" Brian asked.

"Yes," Grace replied as she pulled the blanket up across her lap. "Please tell me where the bathroom is," she said, pushing her hair back from her face.

Brian looked back to the doorway, trying to work out how to get her to the bathroom with the least amount of trouble. He winced when Grace slid her feet to the floor and tried to stand up. He barely caught her as she tipped forward. "Grace," he said. "That was close."

"I can't," she whimpered.

"I see that," he replied, easing her back down on the mattress. "Let me carry you to the bathroom," he suggested.

"But," Grace whispered, swiping at her tears.

"Marlene can help you, but you need to get there first."

"Brian, is she awake?" Marlene asked from the doorway.

"Yes, she needs the bathroom. Can you help her once she's there?" Brian watched Grace, read the dismay on her face and knew the situation was tearing her up. "Let's not think too hard about this. I moved you from the car without any trouble. Let's go," he said, moving swiftly, but gently.

"I feel foolish," Grace said, hiding her eyes behind her hand.

"I feel like I'm in a storybook with Prince Charming rescuing the damsel in distress," Marlene said.

Brian had to grin at Marlene's choice of words, but then narrowed his eyes at her. He thought he heard a muffled giggle from Grace, but he could not be sure. He eased Grace down so she was standing at the vanity. "Are you okay?" he asked Grace. Before she had a chance to answer, Marlene tugged on his arm.

"Brian, go away. I'll yell when we're ready for you. Shoo," Marlene added, waving him out of the room.

When he backed away, Brian accidentally bumped up against the door. Something inside him twisted into knots as he shifted, stepped into the hallway and closed the door behind him. Marlene's laughter seeped through the door. Despite the feelings sparking inside his mind, Brian knew better than to open his heart to anyone or anything. He already had too much going on in his life. An invisible force seemed to be pushing him toward Grace, but she was a stranger to him. Sure, he had helped her, but he knew virtually nothing about Grace. "Alicia," he whispered when it struck him. Who else could it be? She had been at the Drive In, had spoken to him at the beach and guided him to find Grace. Was something so extraordinary actually possible?

"Daddy!" Erin called out, running up and grabbing his legs.

"Whoa," said Brian, caught off guard by her boisterous behavior. "What's going on?" he asked, reaching down and picking her up.

"When can we see her?" Erin asked, bouncing excitedly in her father's arms.

"Soon," replied Brian. "When the time comes you must behave. No jumping around or squealing. Can you do that?"

Erin nodded, calming down and growing serious. "Is she all better now?"

"Almost, but she's still very uncomfortable," Brian explained. He took her hand and traced his thumb across the soft skin on her palm. "Her hand is hurt right here," he explained, showing Erin the path of the stitches on Grace's hand. "And she hurt her ankle, so she can't walk for a few more days."

"Is she still sad?" Erin asked next.

"A little bit," replied Brian. "You go play with Jack for now and I'll ask Grace if you two can come visit her in her room."

Erin nodded and scampered off after he put her down. Brian was glad to see Erin content with his explanation. He did not want to get into describing the dogs attacking Grace. Erin was smart, but too young to fully comprehend the depth of the violence. He hoped when it came time to tell her about such awful things he would know what to say. When Marlene called to him, he put aside his worries about the future.

"At your service, ladies," Brian announced as the door swung open. He saw Grace flush with embarrassment. When he lifted her up, he said, "This is no big deal, Grace. I don't mind helping you."

Chapter 95

Grace did her best to relax in Brian's arms. The past few days left her feeling like she was living inside someone else's body. Nothing resembled her real life. Grace had never allowed herself to imagine life as anything beyond working to earn money in order to keep her childhood home. Her anxiety always increased when it came time to pay her bills. If she couldn't work there would be no money coming in.

An unexpected sense of gloom darkened Grace's mood even further. Once again she felt Clay letting go. She yearned for the chance to free herself from her troubles and find the peace she had seen surround him during his final moments. It would have been better if the dogs had ended her misery out on the beach. If she had not run from them, she thought with regret. Guilt and regret had walked beside Grace every day since the deaths of her parents. She desperately wanted to correct her mistakes and bring them back. Denying herself any level of happiness was the most appropriate way Grace had found to punish herself. She had failed every attempt to cope with the constant turmoil.

Grace tried to focus on where she was at this very moment. She wanted to ask Brian to keep holding her. His warmth radiated through her, bringing to life an array of tangled emotions both fragile and frightening. Grace let herself feel safe, comforted and pleasantly content, even though she knew she had no right to think of such things.

She was meant to live alone, work her fingers to the bone and step cautiously toward the days ahead. Grace had never been reckless and did not intend to change the pattern she had created for herself. Life was a one-way journey with a preordained destination. She compared it to a brook running through a meadow, twisting and turning until it eventually spilled out into the place fate alone directed.

Grace suddenly realized she was challenging fate by being here. These strangers knew nothing about her. At the same time she had no real knowledge of who they were. For all she knew, they had orchestrated the attack on the beach. The dogs might belong to them. Brian finding her might have been planned. She wanted to cry and wanted desperately to leave this place. Her heart knocked erratically as she fought to conceal her rising panic.

Brian eased Grace down on the bed. Marlene stepped in and handed Grace a washcloth.

"Here you go, honey. I'll get your brush," she said after placing a hand towel on Grace's lap.

The warm cloth felt good in Grace's hand. She forgot about the others while she ran the damp cloth over her face, holding it there until it grew cold. She reluctantly lowered it and picked up the towel. It was then that she looked up and saw Brian. "Oh," she said, hiding her face behind the towel for a few seconds before peeking out to see if he was still there.

"Erin asked when she can come see you," Brian said as he walked toward the framed photograph on the far wall.

Grace realized he was trying to give her some privacy. "I would scare them looking like this," she said.

"I don't think so," replied Brian. "Please give it some thought. I'll go now."

Grace wanted to call him back, but remained silent when Marlene came into the room. The emptiness she felt as Brian disappeared from view took Grace by surprise. How dare she feel anything at all. She bit back the need to break down and cry.

Marlene smiled and sat down on the bed. "May I help you brush out your hair?" she asked.

"Ummm, I guess," Grace said. "My mother used to do it for me, but that was a long time ago."

Marlene began brushing the ends of Grace's waist length hair. "It's gorgeous. Gosh, my own hair is so thin," she sighed, brushing small sections with great care.

"Your hair is beautiful," Grace said softly. "I've given thought to chopping mine short."

"Seriously?" Marlene exclaimed. "You mean short short?"

"Maybe," sighed Grace. "I probably won't do it, but it would be less fuss getting ready for work in the morning."

"And you'd spend even more time getting it cut every few weeks," Marlene remarked.

"I suppose," said Grace. "Where are you from?"

"My East Coast shows, doesn't it," laughed Marlene. "Justin and I are from Massachusetts. Alicia and I grew up together."

Grace was not sure what to say in return. She was thankful she was turned away from Marlene's direct gaze. How did you console someone who had suffered a terrible loss? She had no idea even after losing her parents. She concluded there were no words and remained silent.

"Alicia was one of those people who brought sunshine to everyone around her," Marlene said. "She put everyone at ease without even trying."

Again, Grace remained quiet. She picked at the loose threads on the towel as Marlene drew the brush through her tangled hair.

"Brian misses her so much. He thinks he's hiding his emotions, but it's right there in his eyes. Might as well be written all over his handsome face," Marlene said, lowering her voice to keep her words between the two of them.

"I know," Grace replied, taken aback when she realized she had spoken the words aloud. It was none of her business. She pressed her lips together, determined to avoid being drawn in further.

"I'm sorry. My thoughts spill out of my mouth from time to time," confessed Marlene. "Change of subject," she said next. "I understand you're from the same town where Brian lives. Have you known each other for long?"

"No," Grace replied, then decided to revise her reply. "We do live in the same area. We met just once before."

"Yes, I guess Brian did say something like that. Do you think you are up for the drive home tomorrow?" asked Marlene.

"I hope so," sighed Grace. "I can't believe how weak I feel. I was fine before all of this happened."

"It's a normal reaction following a traumatic event, Grace. Don't give it any thought," Marlene said, drawing the brush down the full length of Grace's hair. "Thank you for allowing me the pleasure of brushing your hair. I hope we have a little girl one day," she sighed.

Grace glanced over her shoulder. She watched Marlene while she slipped into a future that only she could see. "She'll be beautiful just like you," Grace sighed, hoping afterwards that any sign of envy had not been in her tone.

"She'll have freckles and red hair, no doubt," laughed Marlene.

"Maybe. And cute as a bug," laughed Grace. She unconsciously drew her fingers through her hair.

"Do you have a boyfriend?" Marlene asked, flipping the brush over and over in her hands.

"No," Grace replied, turning away from the woman.

"Not married?" Marlene asked next.

"Never," sighed Grace.

"That's good," replied Marlene. "Hey, I'd better go see what everyone else is doing. The kids will be ready for dinner soon."

Grace sat alone after Marlene left the room. She felt somewhat like an alien from another planet. Here in body, absent in spirit. She drew in a deep breath and fingered the brace on her right hand. How was she going to sew with her hand so confined? She considered pulling the brace off and taking a chance with the healing, but then felt guilty for even thinking about doing so. She carefully pulled the elasticized band of the sleeve down over the brace. There was no hiding it from sight. Even under the sleeve it showed since it was many times bulkier than her own wrist. She had avoided looking in a mirror, wondering now how bad her face looked. She fingered her bruised lips and felt the raised bump on her forehead. She did not have any memory of hitting the ground, but she had obviously landed hard. Once again she wished the dogs had taken her life. Where would she be by now if they had, she wondered as tears burned her eyes. Her body tingled at the remembered feelings with Clay. She yearned for that kind of peace, longed to be held by her parents and wished to slip away from this life into whatever waited for her on the other side.

## Chapter 96

Brian avoided seeing Grace for the rest of the afternoon. He let Marlene know he was taking the kids for a walk and headed down to the beach. It might very well be the last chance to do so. He pulled the small baseball cap over Jack's head and set him down on the sun-warmed sand. Erin's beach hat was tied under her chin. The ruffled edges fluttered in the breeze. Alicia had made the hat for Erin. It was pink with yellow and white daisies decorating the rounded top.

Brian pushed his hands into his pockets and followed after the kids. They knew better than to wander down to the water, but he kept an eye on them nonetheless. The area was strewn with countless distractions. Driftwood logs, fractured crab and oyster shells, rocks and the crashing waves were all attention grabbers for both kids. Jack's attention was instantly captured by a group of squawking seagulls. He ran as fast as his chubby legs could carry him in a hopeless attempt to reach the birds. As soon as he drew near them, the birds jumped up from the sand and flew up and over Jack's head. Erin was busy with a stick, drawing pictures in the damp sand. Every now and then she drew an arrow pointing in the direction she and Jack were going. Brian found himself stepping around the drawings, knowing Erin would be searching for them on the return trip to the cabin.

A strong gust of wind sent the open edges of Brian's jacket up from his body. He fastened the zipper and pulled the jacket down. He wanted to hear Alicia again, but he heard nothing beyond the laughter from the kids and the gulls overhead. Had he truly heard Alicia? The slight disconnect from reality kept nagging at him. If Grace had not spoken aloud, how had he known she needed help? If he had heard her, then he could not explain any of it.

Brian watched Erin draw circles around Jack while the boy stood still on the sand. Jack leaned over and pressed his hands into the sand. Erin adjusted her steps and made a bigger circle around her brother. When Jack sat down on the sand, she adjusted once again, patting her brother on his head as she moved, never missing a step. Brian wished life were that easy. Wished the worries and losses he had suffered had not left him feeling hollowed out inside. He had not been able to adjust, to compensate for all that had happened.

Brian pushed his hands into his pockets and looked out toward the horizon. "I know you're gone, but I can't do this all alone," he said. He felt his insides twist into knots that might never loosen again. "I miss you all the time!"

Brian turned to check on the kids. At the same time, Erin squealed at something on the sand. Jack squatted down to examine it more closely. Brian came up behind Jack and lifted him up onto his shoulders.

"Why is that fish laying there?" asked Erin.

"It died," Brian answered. He knew the simple answer would not be sufficient.

"Why?" asked Jack as he tried to lean down closer to the fish.

Brian kept Jack on his shoulders and squatted down next to Erin. "It's confusing, but everything dies. It's sad that the fish is dead, but its body will feed other creatures now. It'll wash back out into the ocean when the tide comes up." He watched Erin while she stared at the fish.

"Somebody is sad today," she said softly. "Can we bury him?"

"That's a good idea, honey," Brian replied. He knew if they left it behind, she would never let the subject drop. He knew she was thinking about her mother.

They found a wide flat piece of driftwood to serve as a shovel and dug a hole deep enough to conceal the fish. Brian reminded the kids not to touch the fish since they had no place to wash their hands until they returned to the cabin. He made the hole large enough, but also small enough so it would be easy to fill in. With gentle movements he lifted the fish with the driftwood and slipped it into the hole. Jack handed him several pretty rocks and Erin brought over three pieces of driftwood no bigger than the fish itself.

"I think he'll like having these things buried with him. You two have nice ideas," Brian said as he thoughtfully placed the rocks and driftwood around the fish.

"He can be happy now," said Erin.

"Now we'll fill the hole in with sand to protect him forever," Brian said. "Go ahead and push the sand into the hole."

Jack dropped to his knees and began pushing the sun-warmed sand over the edge of the hole. Erin joined in, watching the sand spill down. Brian helped, but watched his children at the same time.

"Who makes the sand?" Erin asked. She pinched a few grains between her fingers.

"I'm not sure," replied Brian. "It seems to me it's made of tiny fragments of the shells and driftwood."

"And dead fish," said Erin. "I bet his body will turn into sand one day."

"You are probably right about that," Brian said, astounded she had figured that out on her own.

"Do people turn into sand too?" she asked, rubbing the sand on the palm of her hand.

"That's something we can research one day," Brian said. Her next question made him wince, but he hid it as best he could manage.

"Did Mommy turn into sand?" she asked.

"I don't know," Brian whispered. Erin climbed onto his lap and was joined by Jack a moment later. Brian let the tears come as he held his children.

"I believe our spirit lives inside our bodies, Erin. When you die your spirit leaves and goes to Heaven," he explained, afraid his attempt was far beyond clumsy.

"Okay," whispered Erin. "Mommy's spirit didn't stay in the box."

"That's right," Brian replied.

"Heaven is a nice place, isn't it," Erin said next.

"Yes, it's beautiful," Brian whispered.

*Julia Robertson*

## Chapter 97

"Brian, come give me a hand in here," Marlene called from the bedroom.

"What do you need?" he asked as he stopped just inside the doorway.

"Please help me get Grace to the bathroom. She's feeling a little lightheaded, but we both think she's exhausted and nothing more."

"Okay," he agreed and crossed to the bed. Grace did not look up as he lifted her from the bed and started across the room.

Marlene walked ahead of them and waited inside the small room. "Stay close," she asked Brian once Grace was standing next to the vanity.

"I'll be right outside the door," he replied.

"Are you sure you're okay, Grace?" Marlene asked.

"Maybe," replied Grace. "I'm not sure."

Marlene brushed Grace's hair back over her shoulder. "You're not running a fever, but it's been a while since you had anything to eat. I'll make something for you and then we can see if you feel any better."

Out in the hallway, Brian waited, leaning up against the wall. He could not erase the event with the dead fish on the beach. He had hoped by now Erin might be able to get past seeing Alicia in the coffin. It was stupid to think that since he had had no luck doing it himself. As if with a branding iron, the images were seared into his mind. He ran his fingers through his hair and wished he could fix the past and make everything right again. Turmoil seemed to be a constant part of his life and he hated it.

"Brian," Marlene called out.

He came into the room and saw Grace sitting on the closed toilet lid. She looked like a discarded ragdoll, so small and so bruised. "Ready to go?" he asked. She did not answer, so he took it upon himself to carry out the task. Once again, the image of a discarded ragdoll came to mind. He turned and walked back to the bedroom, wishing for a moment he could sit down in a big overstuffed chair and hold her forever. The mere idea astounded Brian. He had no interest in sharing his life with anyone but Alicia. He did not intend to put himself in the position of losing someone again. His heart could not take it. It would tear him to shreds if he lost someone again. There was already enough to do with raising the children and keeping them safe. He had to keep a distance between himself and this obviously lonely woman. She certainly needed someone, but that someone was not him.

Brian set Grace down on the bed with great care, then stepped back before he turned and left the room. He was not aware of the tears in Grace's eyes. Nor did he see her slide down to the pillow, close her eyes and weep silently.

Grace wanted to die. She wanted to slip away and escape the heartache and headache. She wanted peace and silence forever, no matter if it was Heaven or Hell. She ached for it, yearned for it and wept for it.

Grace jumped when someone touched her shoulder. She pried her eyes open and found Marlene crouched down close to her.

"You need to eat something, Grace," Marlene urged. "Sit up now, come on."

Grace wanted to say no so she could fall into sleep and stop thinking. The sudden appearance of the child at Marlene's side jolted Grace back to reality.

"Is she all better?" asked the child.

"Erin, she doesn't feel good," Marlene said. "Maybe you should," she began, then stopped.

Erin placed her hand on Grace's cheek. "Don't die," she whispered. "Please, don't die."

Grace felt heartsick as she struggled to sit up. The little girl's soft brown eyes spoke to her in a way Grace had not known since childhood. How often had her own mother reprimanded her, and sometimes praised her by only the look in her eyes. "I'm fine," she lied.

Marlene arranged pillows behind Grace, brushed her hair back from her face and tugged the blankets up over her lap. "Comfortable?" she asked.

"Yes, thank you," Grace replied.

"I'll be right back," Marlene announced before she rushed out of the room.

Erin moved in closer. She touched the brace and asked, "Does it hurt?"

"Yes," replied Grace. She knew the truth was always better than a lie. And it did hurt. She did not want to take more pain pills since they made her feel dizzy. She preferred dealing with the pain, or so she thought now that she was sitting up and the child was right there in front of her.

"We found a dead fish," Erin said. "We buried him on the beach."

"That's sad," said Grace. Erin had very expressive eyes.

"Can you go to the beach?" Erin asked.

"Not for a while," replied Grace. "My ankle is injured, and I can't walk for a few more days."

"Daddy can carry you to the beach," Erin said, furrowing her brow in concentration.

"Not this time," Grace said with a smile. "It's too far."

"Daddy's strong," said Erin. "He can't pick up our car, but he can pick up really big things. Big like you."

Grace had to laugh. "Then he is truly very strong," she agreed. "How old are you?" Grace asked in hopes of sidetracking the child.

"I'm five," Erin answered with obvious delight. "I get to go to kindergarten."

"Kindergarten will be fun," said Grace. "Do you know the alphabet letters?"

"Most of them," said Erin. "I can write my name. And I can write Jack's name."

"That's very good," remarked Grace.

"We're going home tomorrow," Erin said. "Are you coming with us?"

"Yes, I am," replied Grace.

"Will you come to our house?" the child asked next.

"No, I'm going to my own house," replied Grace. She wondered how much the little girl understood. She was inquisitive and thoughtful, but how much she comprehended was a mystery.

Marlene came into the room followed by Jack. He appeared to be hiding behind Marlene, peeking around her legs with his bright blue eyes open wide. Grace pulled her own eyes away from the boy as Marlene set a bowl and a glass on the nightstand.

"Here's a towel so you have a place for your soup bowl," Marlene said, placing the folded white towel over her lap. "I hope you like chicken soup with stars. It's the only soup we had left. Sorry it's not homemade," she apologized. "I have sandwiches ready in the kitchen for you two monsters."

"Can we make a picnic in here on the floor?" Erin asked.

Grace looked from Erin to Marlene and back to the child again.

"I don't know, Erin. We shouldn't bother Grace with your noise," Marlene explained.

Grace's heart raced with a sense of intrigue. "It's fine with me," she told Marlene. Her answer obviously pleased the child.

"Grace, are you sure?" asked Marlene.

"Yes," Grace said. "Why not."

"Find your beach blanket, Erin. Jack can help you spread it out on the floor," Marlene instructed. She laughed when the children ran out of the room with their giggles filling the quiet spaces. "They're easily excited."

"They're delightful," sighed Grace.

In a matter of minutes the children were sitting on the blanket. Marlene set them up with paper plates. She placed sandwich halves on each plate, added some carrot sticks and pickles, then handed each of the kids a napkin.

Grace smiled while she watched them start to eat. Erin's ponytail swung around as she talked about the ocean and the sand. Jack bounced up and down as though he were sitting on a spring. When Brian appeared in the doorway, Grace's heart fluttered. Had she overstepped her boundaries? Should she apologize for allowing his children in the room? She could not be sure if he was pleased or disturbed by the sight.

"I wanted ants to come to our picnic," Erin said, waving a carrot stick in the air. "Ants need to eat too."

"That's true," agreed Grace. "But they must stay outside."

"We agree on that," Brian said, walking further into the room and kneeling down next to his children. He picked up a napkin and wiped a glob of jam from Jack's cheek. "He tends to absorb most of his food," he explained when he looked up.

Grace was rendered speechless when his gaze met hers. She felt the same fluttering in her heart as she had that day in his truck. She tried to turn her attention to the soup on her lap. Her movements were clumsy due to the brace. Using her left hand was not typical for her. She brought the spoon up, but caught Brian's eyes on her again. She hoped she did not miss her mouth and end up wearing the soup.

Marlene came into the room with a plate stacked high with sandwiches. Justin trailed behind her, waiting by the door for a moment.

"Grace, have you met Justin?" asked Marlene.

Grace shook her head. "Nice to meet you," she said softly.

"Feeling better?" Asked Justin.

"Somewhat," replied Grace.

"Our vacation is almost over," Marlene said.

Justin pulled a chair over and sat down, then gestured for Marlene to sit on his lap. Grace watched the scene play out before her eyes. Marlene first offered Brian a paper plate and sandwich, then slid the platter with the remaining sandwiches onto a nearby dresser. She picked up two sandwiches and giggled as she sat down on Justin's lap. Grace wondered how it might feel to be a real part of this gathering. To belong, she considered for a moment. It was a foolish thought. She turned her attention to her soup and tried to keep her tears at bay. She had not been a real part of a family unit since before her parents died. She felt an icy cold lump growing in her chest. She wondered if anyone would notice if she slid down under the blankets. When Erin giggled, Grace looked up. Jack was bouncing up and down on the floor again. Brian reached over and stopped Jack's movements with his hand on the little boy's head. Grace noticed how Brian responded as naturally as one might scratch an itch.

"Silly Jack," giggled Erin.

"What time should we aim for in the morning?" Marlene asked, looking from Brian to Grace.

"It usually takes three hours to drive back, but I think we need to plan on more stops than we made coming over," Brian said.

"I agree," said Marlene. "I'll pack sandwiches for everyone."

"That's what I was thinking," Justin added. "We can order pizza or stop and pick up something on the way into town rather than going out for dinner."

"By the time we get there the kids will be ready to play outside. We can eat out on the back patio and let them run wild," Brian said. He ate the last of his sandwich before reaching for the glass on the dresser behind him.

"Can we get a puppy?" Erin asked.

Everyone looked at Erin. Marlene giggled and covered her mouth with her hand.

"Maybe sometime," said Brian. "Not right now."

"Do seals wear jackets?" Erin asked next. She ran her finger along the edge of her sandwich, then licked the peanut butter and jam off her finger.

Laughing, Marlene nearly fell off Justin's lap. Justin grabbed her and held on tight.

"I think they should wear jackets. The ocean is cold," Erin said.

"Erin, they're warm enough with their thick coats. People need jackets if it's cold, but not seals."

"I guess," Erin sighed.

Brian hoped that was the end of her questions. He looked up and saw that the conversation was entertaining Grace. Her unease had faded some and her eyes held the hint of a sparkle. "Let's be on the road by 10 o'clock. How does that sound to everyone?"

"I'm fine with that," Justin agreed. "Marlene has no choice. Where I go, she follows."

"So now you're my boss?" Marlene said, jabbing him with her elbow.

Brian glanced over to see Grace's reaction and was pleasantly surprised to see her smiling this time. "If we pack up everything we can tonight it'll make tomorrow morning easier," he said, thinking through the possibilities. "Grace, do you know how much gas is in your car?"

"Maybe half a tank," she replied, furrowing her brow.

"Okay, we'll check on that tonight. We'll stop in Brookings and fill up both cars just to be sure."

"You lead the way, Brian," Justin suggested. "We can all take turns driving."

"I want to drive," said Erin.

Brian tipped forward when she climbed up on his back. "You're always driving us nuts," laughed Brian.

"Me too," chuckled Jack as he joined his sister.

Marlene picked up the paper plates and handed them to Justin. "Let's get packed up, make sandwiches and check on the cars. Maybe we can take a walk on the beach before bedtime."

Amid the cheers from the kids, Brian looked over at Grace again. She looked drained. He was concerned about her health and worried the drive might be too much for her. After the kids ran out of the room behind Justin and Marlene, Brian remained sitting on the floor. He waited a beat, then gathered up the blanket. He stood there feeling awkward and out of place.

"Your time over here wasn't what you had planned," he said, stepping over and sitting on the foot of her bed. Grace looked like a little pixie sitting up against the stacked pillows.

"No, nothing like I had planned," she agreed.

"You'll have to come back once you're healed," Brian suggested.

"I don't know," she replied. "I never take vacations. This one was foolish. I should have stayed at home and worked. None of this would have happened if I had stayed home."

"Everyone needs a break from routine," Brian said. "Most people feel it recharges their brain cells and makes them more productive at work."

"Mine did not work out that way," sighed Grace. "And then I ruined your vacation as well."

Brian saw her happiness vanish as she pondered her situation. He reminded himself to keep his distance and let her figure things out on her own. She was broken and bruised and far beyond exhausted. "You've hit a rut in the road, that's all. Give yourself time."

"Daddy, we have to pack our stuff," Erin shouted as she ran into the room. "If we pack fast, we can go play on the beach."

Brian reluctantly nodded. "Don't beat yourself up over this, Grace. None of it was your fault."

*Julia Robertson*

## Chapter 98

Grace lay awake on the bed, wishing she could remain secluded from the rest of the world forever. She knew any movement she made was going to trigger the pain. Eyes closed, she focused on her breathing, slow and steady, calm and quiet. Her mind began to float toward sleep, but it did not last for more than a minute. Quiet footsteps drawing nearer told her she would not have her way.

"Grace," said Marlene. "It's time to wake up. We'll be ready to go within the hour. Let me help you get dressed."

"Thank you," sighed Grace. She slowly pushed herself up to sit on the side of the bed. Her leg throbbed, but she refused to take more pain meds. She wanted to be alert as possible for the drive home even though she dreaded the hours in the car.

"It's beautiful outside again this morning," said Marlene. "It's a little foggy right now, but it's supposed to burn off before long."

"That's good," Grace said as she followed along with what needed doing. She wished she could shower, but it was out of the question until she could stand on both feet for more than two minutes at a time.

"Have you anyone to stay with you at home?" Marlene asked as she carefully brushed Grace's hair.

"I'm not sure," said Grace. She fingered the brace on her right hand, disturbed once again that her finger and thumb remained numb. "I'll be fine on my own."

"I'd like to offer to stay with you at least for tonight. I mean, you should be okay putting some weight on your foot tomorrow, according to the doctor. We can set up an appointment with your doctor as soon as we get back to town."

"You'd do that for me?" Grace asked, astounded by the offer. "But it's your vacation, you don't need to waste time helping me."

"Grace," Marlene said, her voice tender and thoughtful. "Every now and then we all need some help. It's nothing to be ashamed of.

Besides, if I didn't want to help you, I wouldn't have offered. We're friends now and that is that."

"Friends," whispered Grace. The word was as foreign as walking on the moon for Grace. She was friends with Roger and Maggie, but having friends who would take care of her like this, well, she had to be dreaming.

"Grace, I'm going to get Brian to help you to the bathroom again. I understand you don't want that, but for now that's the way it goes."

"But," retorted Grace, still reeling from Marlene's offer. She put her feet on the floor and eased off the bed far enough to put some weight on her injured foot. The pain was still there, but not nearly as bad as it had been. A sense of hope floated into her mind as she bit her lip and lifted her foot up from the floor.

"Taxi," Brian said as he entered the room. "Ready to go?"

Embarrassed, Grace nodded. With all that had happened, all the times she wished to escape life, she found herself wishing once again for his warmth to remain this close forever. The mere idea had Grace blushing immediately. She prayed Brian did not notice. She kept her face averted when he set her feet down on the floor. "Thank you," she said, pretending she needed to wipe her eyes.

"You're welcome," Brian said on his way out of the room.

Grace forced her crazy thoughts away as she and Marlene managed her needs. Upon returning to the bedroom, she had to fight off the urge to hang onto Brian. She did not understand what she was feeling, but she knew it was something she did not deserve. The burden he carried from day to day was already more than he ought to have to bear.

Once Brian left the room Grace worked the buttons free on her pajama top. Marlene helped her pull the sweatshirt sleeve up over her brace.

"I have breakfast ready for you. Do you want coffee this morning?" Marlene asked.

## Chapter 99

Once Brian eased Grace down onto the front seat of her car, he pulled down on the seat belt. He was surprised when she took it from him and fastened it herself, fumbling for a moment with her left hand. He felt a knot forming in his stomach as he stepped back and closed the door. Hands shaking, he pushed his fingers through his hair.

"It's time to hit the road," Justin announced.

"We'll stop for gas in Brookings," Brian said, doing his best to hide his emotional turmoil. Grace had not even looked at him. Why did that bother him?

"Got it," called out Justin before he sat behind the wheel in Grace's car.

Brian glanced over his shoulder before pulling out onto the coast highway. His stomach was still churning. While the kids were occupied and content, he let his mind wander. After a lousy night of tossing and turning he felt unusually irritable.

Brian barely noticed the scenery as they moved along the two-lane road. More often than necessary he checked the rearview mirror to be sure Grace's car was still there. His eyes landed on Grace sitting in the front passenger seat every time he looked. He wondered what she was thinking. Even more so, he wondered what she was feeling.

Brian sighed, tried to draw his attention elsewhere, but kept returning to Grace. How had she managed to totally disrupt his grief? Mourning over losing Alicia had dominated his life. It started shortly after her diagnosis and grew more powerful as her time with him came closer to the end. He clung to it like a lifeline even when he found himself thinking it was not good for him nor his children. Letting go of his grief felt like a sin, like he was breaking his vows to Alicia.

"Until death do us part," he whispered, the words barely making it past his lips. At the time he and Alicia had spoken those words he had not imagined them ever coming to reality. Neither of them had considered it happening until they were old and ready to leave this world together.

Brian hated himself for his misguided thoughts. Accepting the way life had turned out was imperative, but damned if he could manage to do so. Alicia dwelled in his heart forever. How could it be any other way, he thought.

Brian thumped the steering wheel, angry with himself and the direction his mind kept taking him. "What am I supposed to do?" he cried silently.

Brian cursed himself for falling into the dark hole. It was a familiar place, but a place he had no right to go. His kids needed him to keep it together.

When the town came into view, Brian signaled and pulled into a gas station. Justin pulled up on the opposite side of the pump and stood up, stretching his arms up over his head. Brian watched with amusement as Justin removed the gas cap. He had not yet grown used to the idea that Oregon had attendants at every gas station. Pumping your own gas was not permitted. He saw Justin's smile grow as a young girl in black jeans and a blue and gray flannel shirt stepped up and snatched the pump from his hand. She was shaking her head as Justin apparently apologized. The same girl appeared at his window a moment later and Brian asked her to fill it up.

"Wish we had such attention back home," Justin said as he stepped up next to Brian. "Imagine how many jobs it would create."

"Yes, I agree," said Brian. "Some folks see it as a waste of good money, but we like it this way. The benefit of more jobs is icing on the cake."

"You bet," Justin agreed.

"You ought to stop staring," Brian suggested. "Umm, Marlene's taking notice."

"Oh yeah, thanks," Justin said, immediately turning to look down the road.

"Unless we need a stop beforehand, let's stop in Cave Junction and find a place to eat our lunch. It's early, but it will give everyone a break from sitting."

"I'm all for that," agreed Justin.

"How's Grace doing?" Brian asked next. He tried to avoid looking in her direction, but had caught sight of her twice while Justin was moving about next to him.

"She's awfully quiet, but I think she's okay," replied Justin.

Back on the road, Brian focused on the blacktop and listened to the kids talking behind him. They had their pocket games out and he was glad for the handy entertainment. He thought he knew a spot where the kids would have room to run around and burn off some energy before getting back into their car seats after lunch.

Brian envisioned a time in the future when the kids would be old enough to go for hikes up in the woods. He imagined camping trips and rafting on the river. Right now they were too young and grew weary too quickly for big adventures. Alicia had often talked about taking the kids to museums, state and national parks, fishing trips and simple daytime outings to trigger their imaginations.

Brian suddenly realized if she had been out on the beach, if she had spoken to him and warned him about Grace, if she had been there at the Drive In, perhaps she was watching them all the time. Had she seen him when his anger got out of control? Was she disappointed with him? Had she wept whenever he found himself losing hope?

Why was he thinking about things like this? Nothing would change what he felt, nor would he ever forget about Alicia. Loving her was all he had ever needed in his life. He mentally kicked himself and put aside his troubling thoughts.

Brian spotted the pull-off and signaled early enough to let Justin know he was going to stop. He stepped out of the car and stretched his back before unbuckling the kids. "You guys ready to get out for a little while?"

"Daddy," Erin said. "We should have brought a sea lion home with us."

"Erin, that's silly," he said as he set her down. "Let's wait for Marlene to get out first." Before he had a chance to get the kids to the restroom Marlene offered to take them.

"You okay here for a minute?" Justin asked, following Marlene without waiting for an answer.

Brian was left standing alone outside Grace's window. Feeling awkward once again, he tried to sound at ease as he leaned down and said, "Grace, why don't you stand out here for a few minutes. You might be too stiff to get out if you wait until we're home," he said cautiously.

Grace sighed as she shifted on the seat. She was already stiff and uncomfortable, but she refused to complain. "Okay," she agreed. Brian opened her door when she tried unsuccessfully to unlatch her seat belt.

"Allow me," Brian said, leaning inside and releasing the belt.

Grace trembled at his closeness. What was wrong with her? She held her breath and waited for him to move out of the way. She felt dizzy even before she turned on the seat. "I want to try standing on my own," she insisted, fearing her reaction if he touched her again. Her efforts proved futile when she failed to find the power to lift herself up.

"Here," said Brian. "Let me help you. Are you sure you can balance?"

Grace wanted to cry. She did not want any help. She wanted to go home and crawl into bed and stay there forever. "Yes," she finally replied.

What happened next caught them both by surprise. Two black & white dogs came running toward them barking furiously. Grace cried out with fear and Brian instinctively wrapped her in his arms. He turned his back to the dogs, completely blocking her from the potential danger. The dogs scrambled under the car and one of them came out with a red ball clamped between his teeth. They raced away as quickly as they had appeared. Someone shouted an apology from across the parking lot.

Grace was shaking like mad in Brian's arms. The nightmare flashed before her eyes. The terror felt real even while she tried to convince herself they were not the same dogs. They could not possibly be the same dogs. She clutched the front of Brian's shirt in her left hand and struggled to quiet her weeping.

"There, you're safe with me, Grace," Brian said. "I won't let anything harm you, I promise."

Grace finally settled down, warm in Brian's embrace and comforted by his calm words. Her head fit snug against his shoulder, tucked in under his chin. She shuddered with awareness when she realized she was in his arms, not in a dream.

"I've got you, Grace, don't be afraid," he whispered.

Grace had to ignore her impulse to cling to Brian. She had to be independent. Relying on someone else, counting on that person to be there for both comfort and support was a gift of such magnitude it overwhelmed her senses. She did not deserve such a gift, not after what she had done, or not done for her parents. The burden of blame weighed her down like an anchor. Relying on someone else meant, in turn, that person would rely on her and she could not bear to put anyone in that position. She would surely fail them, and the end results would destroy what was left of her damaged spirit.

The next period of time passed in a blur for Grace. By the time she let herself focus again they were on the road with Marlene at the wheel. Grace unconsciously rubbed her injured hand. Her eyes felt raw. She could only guess she had been crying again.

"Hey, you okay?" asked Marlene. She reached over and touched Grace's left hand. "Grace?"

"Yes," Grace replied, though she felt anything but fine.

"If you need to talk," Marlene said, stopping when Grace shook her head. "Okay, just sit back and relax as much as you can. I guess we may have another hour and a half left to go."

Grace noticed Justin in Brian's car, then automatically glanced into the back seat.

"We're playing musical chairs," said Marlene. "I think the kids are getting a little restless in their car seats."

"It can't be easy being restrained like that," commented Grace.

"You are right, and you know first-hand how it feels," said Marlene.

"I guess," replied Grace. She watched out the passenger side window, barely noticing the trees along the side of the road. Her life had taken a drastic detour, one she wished she had avoided. If she had simply stayed at home, she thought with a frown.

"What's wrong?" Marlene asked. "You look sad."

"Nothing," lied Grace. "Everything," she amended. She pulled tissues out of her pocket and wiped away the tears she could not control.

"Hey, you're going to be fine," Marlene assured her. "Your life will be back to normal in no time."

Grace stared at her hand and wondered if it would ever be normal again. Marlene's idea of normal had to be the complete opposite of what Grace lived day-to-day. Grace dreamed about things that other people must wish for, but allowing herself any sense of happiness was out of the question. She had to work, keep up with the bills and remain within her self-imposed boundary lines. Even though she had no idea how to interpret the feelings she experienced when Brian was too near, she refused to explore them. She had no right, absolutely no right at all.

Brian needed a good person with inner strength, the ability to show him how valuable he was and how to reach his full potential. Grace was not that person. Her heart plummeted when the remembered words flashed before her eyes. *He needs you. He needs you.*

## Chapter 100

The following weeks passed without any significant changes for Grace. She was able to walk, but her pace continued to be slow and unsteady. She went back to work, but accomplishing her daily tasks proved frustrating. When the stitches were removed from her hand Grace faced more disappointment. Physical therapy had started, but the numbness remained. The nerve damage in her hand needed time to heal and nothing she did would alter the final outcome. It would either get better or it would not.

Coming home from work one afternoon, Roger turned his car into Grace's driveway. "Are you okay?" he asked.

"Just fine," groaned Grace.

"Call me on Sunday night and let me know if you need a ride," he urged.

Grace nodded in reply. Her throat felt tight with her frustration as she fumbled with the door.

Not for the first time Roger said, "There's nothing wrong with asking for help, Grace."

"I know," sighed Grace. She pushed the door open and eased her feet out onto the gravel driveway. "I really do appreciate your help. I'll be okay."

"Don't forget to call," Roger said just before the door slammed closed.

Tears burned her eyes the moment Roger drove away. She bit her lip as she fumbled with the keys and walked into her cold and lonely house. Every time she came home she saw the unfinished quilt project staring at her. She had to call and explain her situation to Carlena Mills. Finding the words was not as daunting as knowing she was going to cry while she explained the need for the delay. She dared not put a finish date on the project now. She might never finish it. That awful prospect weighed on Grace's mind as she walked down the hallway to her bedroom.

Out of habit Grace always made her bed every morning. At least she had until her trip to the coast. Tonight her comforter and sheets were a tangled heap on one corner of the mattress and one pillow was on the floor. She hobbled over, leaned down and tossed the pillow on top of the messy bed. Grace dropped her keys on the nightstand before she sat down on the bed. She pushed off her shoes and unzipped her lightweight jacket. It ended up on the floor on top of her shoes. With awkward movements she shed her blouse and her slacks, not caring where they ended up.

Grace turned and crawled in under the mound created by the rumpled sheets and comforter. With some pulling on the comforter and twisting around she eventually found a position that was comfortable enough. She tugged a pillow under her head and closed her eyes.

As she had done every day since returning to work, Grace drifted into restless sleep. She had no desire to do anything except sleep. Going to work forced her to leave the house. The bills waiting to be paid were the only reason to go to work. Unsettling dreams haunted her sleep. She often awakened crying, so confused she did not know where she was.

When morning came Grace turned away from the sunlit window and held her hand to her chest. She wanted the darkness to stay forever. The entire day passed without leaving her bed. The house was silent, her mind numb and her heart ached for release from her life. Grace constantly prayed to be freed from life and taken into whatever existed beyond her time on earth. She knew in her heart her prayers would never be answered.

Grace ignored the housework, skipped eating anything all weekend and dealt with headaches every waking moment. Life simply did not matter. It was not long before she cancelled her physical therapy appointments and stopped thinking about regaining the use of her hand. By her calculations she had lost about 90 percent of her worth. Everything that had gone wrong was the result of taking time off to spoil herself. She did not deserve anything better than grief and hopelessness. Life simply was not worth the trouble.

## Chapter 101

"I can't work with this," Shane Kelly complained in his booming voice as he held the papers out in front of him. "You must have let your kids draw up this one."

Brian was furious. The electrician was pushing him past his limits. "If you don't want the work, I'll hire someone who does. You're not the only electrician in the valley," he shouted, taking the papers out of the man's hand.

Shane stepped back. "I sure as hell want the work. Cool down and get back with me. You need to check out what you have there before you kick my ass off this job," he said, standing his ground while the other workers gathered around them. "Call me when you get yourself straightened out." He turned and walked away.

"Damn it," growled Brian. He became aware of his crew watching the heated exchange with Shane, but had not been able to get control of his anger before the man took off. He frowned at the crumpled plans in his hand. "Show's over," he told his crew. "Get back to work."

Grumbling, the men did as they were told. Bill walked up to Brian, waiting until the others were out of earshot before he spoke. "Hey, what's going on?" he asked cautiously.

"What the hell does that mean?" barked Brian. He knew he was wrong, saw Bill wince at his words, but could not take them back.

Bill raised his hands and took a few steps away. "There's talk of walking off this job site, Brian. You're going to be in trouble if you don't make some changes right away."

"There's nothing wrong," Brian said, clamping his mouth shut and pushing his fingers through his hair. He turned away from Bill and held his breath. "Leave me be, just leave me be."

"I can't guarantee anyone will be here on Monday, Boss," bill explained. "I can't do the work without the others."

"I can't, I won't," Brian said with both hands in his hair as the forgotten papers fluttered to the ground. "I can't think. It's just, I can't."

"Go home, Boss. Let me get things in order here. I'll take care of what needs doing for today," Bill said. "Let's start fresh on Monday."

Brian nodded, unable to get himself under control. He wanted to smash something, anything, just pound out his anger on something.

Brian watched Bill lumber across the uneven ground to where his crew stood waiting. How had things gotten so messed up, he wondered. He reached down for the ruined blueprints and turned toward his truck. Maybe Bill was right. Maybe he needed to leave and let Bill shut down for the night. As he walked away, he felt like he was dragging the weight of the world behind him.

Brian did not look back as he pulled out onto the road. Consumed by guilt and exhaustion, he was not aware of anyone in the crosswalk near the school.

"Hey, watch where you're going!" someone shouted. "Get off the road and sober up!"

Brian noticed then that the man had two children walking with him. They were about Erin and Jack's ages. He had almost hit them. Brian pulled to the side of the road and slumped down in the seat. Tears welled up in his eyes. "I almost hit them," he cried.

By the time Brian pulled himself back from the pit he had fallen into, the sun had set and his head was throbbing. Bill had made it crystal clear with his statement. He was going to lose his business if he did not make some changes. His personal tragedies and inability to cope had contaminated everything in his life. He had built a career for himself, one that gave him great satisfaction and pride. With Alicia they had created a beautiful family that warmed his heart and gave him a purpose for living. With Clay he had a good friend and partner at work and in his private life. With those things he felt fulfilled and worthy. All of that had been destroyed, leaving him feeling shredded beyond repair and lonely beyond belief. Not a day passed without thinking about Alicia and what might have been. He rarely reached the end of a workday without looking over his shoulder for Clay. How often had he started to ask him a question, or for his opinion only to realize he was no longer there to put in his two cents worth.

Brian sighed as he straightened up on the seat of his truck and turned the key in the ignition. Everything he had worked for was gone except for his children. Why weren't they enough for him to keep going? As though a cold wind were blowing through him, Brian felt empty and abandoned. He felt lost in the fog without a clue as to which way to go next.

Brian stopped at a pay phone and called the house. He asked Kathleen if she could stay for another hour. He did not understand why she was so patient with him when she agreed and told him to take all the time he needed. Brian heard Erin's laughter just before the call was disconnected. Guilt tripped through his heart as he put the phone back in its place. He stood alone on the side of the road for several minutes before he finally pulled himself away and walked back to his truck.

Brian had been a mess since returning from the coast trip with Marlene & Justin. He had not been able to shake off the events on the beach and could not stop thinking about Grace. From the few conversations they had shared he knew she was dealing with her own set of challenges. She certainly did not need to add his grief and anger to her own. The lingering images of her despair following the doctor's blunt statement kept haunting him. There was nothing he could do for her. Hell, he thought, he could not deal with his own personal problems, let alone those of another broken person.

On a day-to-day basis Brian lost his temper more often than not. Whether it was with his crew on the job or at home with his children, he often found himself feeling outraged. Shouting and throwing things when he lost his temper had become commonplace occurrences. Guilt followed each outburst, and he no longer had control when irritating situations arose. He refused to acknowledge the need to make any changes before it was too late.

Upon returning home each night after work he seemed to stir up something to churn the waters with Kathleen. Small as she was, she stood her ground, getting right in his face, but Brian refused to budge. The children were his, not hers, the house his responsibility, not hers. Even while he often put the kids to bed and let them cry themselves to sleep, it had not cut deep enough to open his eyes. Despair followed his every step. Shame filled his fractured heart.

Brian drove across town and parked in front of an old two-story house. He saw the light on in the living room window. Several minutes passed while he pondered the wisdom of following through with his plan. Brian gathered his courage and walked up to the front door, knocking several times before stepping back with his hands in his pockets. The door swung open and a shadowed figure appeared. A moment passed before anything was said.

"You gonna stand out there all night?" the man asked gruffly.

Brian stepped inside, turned and shut the door. Unsure of how to begin, he decided a simple apology might suffice. "I'm sorry," he said.

"Shut up and sit down," barked Shane Kelly.

"Right," sighed Brian. He made his way around the man in the recliner and sat down on the edge of the couch. There was nowhere else to sit in the dimly lit room.

"What's eating at you?" Shane asked.

There was no beating around the bush when it came to Shane Kelly. Brian kept his eyes averted from the man and said, "I'm about to lose my business. My crew has had it with me."

"Obvious to anyone who ain't blind," Shane remarked. "And what do you plan to do about it?"

"I don't know," said Brian. He sat with his hands pressed between his knees, eyes downcast, lost in thought.

"You looking for suggestions or pity?" Shane asked in his straightforward manner.

"Pity?" Brian asked.

"You know what I mean. Feeling sorry for yourself," Shane replied.

"Damn," groaned Brian. He stood up intending to leave. He already felt rattled.

"Park your ass!" barked Shane. "There's no shame in sharing your feelings, Cooper."

"But," Brian argued.

"Shut up," groaned Shane. "Stay put, I'll get us a beer."

"I don't want," Brian began, but the man was out of sight before he had time to finish.

Shane came back into the room with his bare feet scuffing across the old wood plank floor. "Here, drink," he ordered, pushing the can into his hands.

Brian had to laugh. He held a root beer, not beer. "Shit," he laughed as he popped the lid open.

"Yup, I do like my beer," laughed Shane. "Living on the wild side gets me through the day."

Brian sat back on the lumpy old couch. "Life sucks," he finally admitted.

"That it does, that it does," Shane said with a sigh. "You can either roll with the tide or let it wipe you out. Ain't no other choices."

Shane's comment surprised Brian. It was so close to what he had told Grace. It was much easier to dish out advice than to face it personally. He stared at the can clamped between his hands. He flicked the pull tab, swallowed hard and looked over at Shane.

"How do you get from day to day?" he asked with his voice so soft it was barely audible. "I mean, how can I ignore everything I've lost?" He did not expect an answer. He knew better than to think there was an easy solution.

"The way I see it is," Shane began. He sipped the soda and stared at the blank wall. "You set a goal for yourself. Don't lose sight of it. It's gonna look unattainable at times but keep aiming for it. Never give up, just do not give up on yourself. No matter what you think, you're never as alone as you feel. I'm not so sure about God, but something's there, just there," said the older man. "You can't touch it, can't smell it, but it's as real as you or me. Behave, work hard, do what's right and it will still be there when your time comes. You can count on it just like you can count on the sun rising every morning."

Brian took in every word. Something stirred in his chest. "Never actually alone," Brian said, nodding as he let the concept sink in.

"Some folks are meant to share their lives," Shane said with the can audibly crumpling in his tightening fist.

"Share their lives," Brian whispered. He glanced over at Shane and wondered how the older man had seen what his heart was actually feeling. It really didn't matter how, he thought, staring down at the floor once again. Brian hated living alone. He hated having to take care of everything without someone actually standing beside him.

Brian slowly sat up on the lumpy couch. "I think you're right."

"Most times," Shane snorted. "Like your drawings. They're crap."

"Maybe," Brian admitted with regret. "I haven't been able to focus lately."

"No kidding," laughed Shane. "Try running."

"What's that?" Brian said, pushing his fingers through his hair.

"Running," said Shane. "You know, putting your feet on the ground and making them move fast."

"Shit," groaned Brian. "I don't have the time."

"Make the time," Shane barked. "You're messing everything up lately, so make the time and you'll feel the difference. Clears the mind, realigns your priorities."

Brian nodded again and said, "You're a wise old man."

"Yup, that's me, a wise-ass," grunted Shane.

"Damn, that's not what I said," Brian laughed.

"Whatever," Shane grumbled, waving his hand in the air to dismiss the remark.

"I need to go home. Kathleen's probably wondering where I am by now," Brian said as he stood up. "Thanks for the drink. And thanks for the advice," he said, reaching out to shake Shane's hand. "I appreciate you listening to my troubles."

"Don't sell yourself short, Cooper. You're a good man. You're gonna get through this rough period and come out smelling like a rose."

"I hope you're right," Brian said.

With failure biting at his heels, he had to move fast or chance losing even more than he already had. The conversation with Shane gave Brian a temporary reprieve from his troubles. He told himself he was fine, that the troubles of late were manageable. Shane had planted the seed that should soon grow into something resembling normal. His past mistakes were fixable, Brian thought as he drove toward home.

When he turned onto the road leading to the rental house, the all too familiar dread suddenly rose up in his chest. His heart started beating erratically and his shoulders tightened. It was happening again. There was no way to stop it. By the time he came to a jolting stop in the driveway his stomach was in knots.

"Please have the kids in bed and sleeping," he whispered. "Please."

Brian did not want to be alone, but even more so he did not want to deal with the kids tonight. Another confrontation with Kathleen had to be avoided at all costs. He rubbed his neck in a vain attempt to ease the tension. He fought to keep his hands from fisting as he pushed the truck door open and stepped down. "Calm," he ordered himself. "Stay calm and be nice."

Brian listened as the doorknob turned in his hand. He heard nothing as he stepped inside. Quiet footsteps approached as he turned around. The thrumming of his blood through his veins sounded like a freight train in his ears. His shoulders dropped with relief at the sight of

Kathleen standing alone and watching him warily. "Sorry I'm so late," he apologized without delay.

"No need for that," whispered Kathleen. "I'll be on my way. If you need me tomorrow just call. I have no plans for the weekend, none at all." She patted Brian's arm before making her silent escape, pulling the door shut behind her.

Brian doubled over with relief, hands braced on his knees, eyes squeezed closed. He had not had supper, but he was not going to chance waking the kids. He pushed off his boots and padded silently down the short hallway into his bedroom. He skipped brushing his teeth and stripped down to his underwear before crawling into bed. Kathleen was a saint for making up his scrambled bed for him. He pushed away the troubles of the day and tumbled headlong into restless sleep.

*Julia Robertson*

## Chapter 102

*Gloomy darkness leached all the colors from the scene playing out around him. His hands were held behind his back as blood ran from his mouth and dripped down on the filthy ground at his feet.*

*"Keep your eyes open!" a faceless figure shouted. "Look at what you've done!"*

*Without warning someone kicked the back of his knees. He fell to the ground and gasped for air.*

*"You did this!" the same voice shouted.*

*Erin and Jack were a few feet away, frantically trying to get free. "Please, don't," cried Brian. "They didn't do anything wrong. It was me, not them."*

*"You had your chance. You ruined them. Now you will suffer the consequences," the angry voice shouted.*

*Someone grabbed his hair and wrenched his head back. Brian cried out when he was kicked repeatedly. He wanted to lay down and die but his body was held upright, still on his knees, unable to fight back or draw in a breath. When the latest attack stopped, he saw them separate the children. Erin screamed in protest until a large hand clamped over her mouth. Jack was tossed from one man to another as though he were a football. His small body was limp, dressed only in his pajama top.*

*"Stop!" shouted Brian, though he knew his words had not been heard. "Please, please stop," he begged as the terror continued. He tried to look away, but his captors wrenched his head back again.*

*"Keep looking, you sorry bastard," said the gruff voice. "This is all your doing."*

*"Please," he pleaded, tears converging with the trails of blood running down his face. "Please stop."*

*The children were suddenly taken away. The night went black as his body fell into the gutter. He was vaguely aware of the water running underneath him. His head had cracked hard against the concrete curb. One arm was twisted up behind him and the other lay out across the filthy blacktop. His fingers were out there, but he could not move them, nor could he see them. Guilt penetrated his heart when he realized he was going to die here in the gutter, knowing it was a better place to be than wherever his children had been taken. He should have taken better care of them. He ruined their lives. They were suffering because of his stupidity and selfishness.*

"*No,*" *he wept as the night swallowed him whole.*

"Daddy," whispered Erin. "Wake up, wake up."

Groggy and disoriented, Brian opened his eyes. They felt gritty as he fought to bring her image into focus. It had all been a dream, nothing more than a terrifying dream. Erin was here, it was morning and she was safe. "I'm awake," he mumbled.

"We're hungry," Erin said.

"Okay, I'm getting up now." Brian forced his legs over the side of his bed. He barely touched the floor when he shuddered with fear. Where had the nightmare come from and how was he going to safeguard his children. The room appeared to tilt sideways as he made his way toward the hallway.

## Chapter 103

Grace scraped up every bit of courage she could muster and stepped into her work room. She did her best to ignore the dust collecting on her fabrics and sewing supplies. Feeling sick to her stomach with fear, she dragged the old wooden chair up to her worktable and studied the sections already sewn together. She ran her left index finger over her expertly sewn stitches. Grace was a perfectionist when it came to her sewing skills. She knew exactly where the threaded needle needed to go, penetrating the fabric and drawing the length of thread in behind it. When the barely audible sound of the thread following the needle came to mind, a smile lifted the corners of her mouth.

"I can do this," she whispered, envisioning the first stitches she would make. She tugged the needle from the pincushion, held it up in the fingers of her left hand and slowly lifted her right hand up to the same level. Grace agonized over what might happen when she grasped it with her right hand.

"Guide my fingers," she whispered. Her mother's spirit was always with her when she worked on her projects. She was always there to answer her questions or nod at the next step she chose to take. Today Grace felt utterly alone. Tears welled up in her eyes as her left hand gingerly passed the needle to her right hand. She saw the needle come between her thumb and index finger, but she could not feel it there. Determined, she willed her fingers to hold onto it, but as soon as her left hand released the needle her right hand failed.

Grace instantly broke down. Salty tears dripped down onto the surface of her marred worktable. Grace stumbled backwards as she awkwardly stood up from the chair. She caught her balance and clumsily turned toward the hallway. Moving without thought, she made her way to her haven from the world and crawled in under the comforter.

Misery clung to Grace like a second skin. She needed her parents to come back, to comfort her and encourage her to make the best of her life. The mounting bills swirled around her like a tornado as Grace drew further into herself. Loneliness and despair were sucking the life out of her. She squeezed her eyes closed tight and buried her face against the pillow.

## Chapter 104

As the minutes ticked by at a painfully slow pace, Brian gave thought to what Shane had suggested the night before. He wondered if running had any chance of ending up as anything but another waste of time. How could he manage, he wondered hopelessly? He was tethered to life by work and his children. Brian froze as he stepped into the kitchen. He had to be losing his mind.

"Tethered," he groaned. What happened to the way he had felt with Alicia? Where had the feelings of gladness gone for having the kids and knowing a part of her would be with him always? What the hell was wrong with him?

Brian turned and looked around the house. It was small, sparsely furnished and littered with the memories of his family. His children were his family. Even without Alicia they were a family. Fractured, but functioning as a whole. Well, they would be if he pulled his head out of his ass and found a way to make things work again.

"I can do this," he murmured, once again looking around the kitchen. "This place doesn't belong to us," he whispered. "What if we bought a new house, made it our home and built new memories and set new goals?" he wondered out loud.

Jack came running toward the kitchen. Erin chased after him, shouting at him to stop. Brian reached down and lifted Jack up from the floor.

"He has my toothbrush!" Erin shrieked.

"No," ordered Brian. He held his temper and spoke in a quiet tone. "Stop shouting right this minute. We are not going to shout anymore."

"But I'm mad!" Erin screamed, her face reddening with anger.

"I messed us up for too long," Brian said, crouching down and grabbing hold of his daughter. "I'm sorry for being angry all the time, Erin. I need to start over and make us all happy again."

"Happy?" asked Erin. "Why?"

Brian saw an expression on her face he had not seen in months. He looked into her beautiful brown eyes. "Because we're a family," he said. "I love you two with all my heart."

Erin reached over and took her toothbrush away from Jack. "You have your own toothbrush," she said calmly.

Jack slumped down low on Brian's shoulder. "He needs a nap, Erin. Let me get him in bed and we can talk, okay?"

Erin still looked puzzled. She followed after her father and brother but stopped at the doorway to their shared bedroom. Brian settled Jack down and covered him up.

"Close your eyes, little man," he said, kissed the boy's soft cheek and walked to the doorway. He picked up Erin, put her toothbrush in the bathroom and walked out to the kitchen. Brian shifted his young daughter in his arms until he had her cradled against him. "I used to walk around holding you like this when you were little," he said, brushing her tangled hair back from her face.

"When Mommy was sick," Erin said.

"You remember," Brian sighed. He wished the darker times had been forgotten by now.

"Mommy was sad all the time," Erin whispered. "I didn't want her to go away. I still need her."

"So do I," Brian replied. "I'm sorry I've been so angry."

"Me too," Erin said. She smiled, but her eyes were still sad. "Kathleen said we need to be happy too. She doesn't want us to cry."

"She's right," agreed Brian. "I lost my way. Sometimes the days are too busy and I don't have time to relax and have fun with you and Jack. We need to change that."

"How?" Erin asked as she relaxed and let her head rest on her father's shoulder.

"I'm not sure," Brian confessed. "We might need to ask for help. How about we start with you telling me what you've been doing in school."

For the remainder of the day Brian focused on his children. They played out in the back yard and he chased them, tickling each of them, enjoying their laughter. When he found himself laying on his back on the grass, Brian wondered how he had let himself fall into a black hole. Jack climbed on top of him and Erin was there in a flash.

"You two," he laughed as he wrapped his arms around both of them and held on tight.

After dinner Brian bathed the kids and left them to play in their room. He went out to his truck and picked up the crumpled papers Shane had thrust at him the day before. At his drawing table he carefully flattened them with his hands. Now that he cleared his mind and accepted the fact he had to repair his life, he found the drawings looked terrible.

"Sloppy," he groaned. He spent the next hour working up new drawings. Though he knew the work needed more details, he was satisfied with what he had accomplished so far. For a moment he considered calling Shane but decided to check on the kids instead. They needed to go to bed soon, he thought as he turned off the lights and walked to their room.

Brian found their room empty. There were a few toys scattered across the floor, but the kids were gone. The nightmare flashed before his eyes. Momentary panic had his heart beating like crazy. In a rush he turned back and checked the bathroom. It was empty too. Out of breath, he stumbled into his bedroom and found them both asleep on his bed. Relief washed over him as he slumped back against the door jamb and waited for his heart to calm. "Just a bad dream," he whispered.

*Julia Robertson*

## Chapter 105

Over the next few months life became a steady routine of work and sleep for Grace. Her ankle injury had healed to the point she was walking with only a slight limp. Her hand was a totally different story. Her doctor had reprimanded her for stopping the physical therapy, but she denied she needed it and disregarded his repeated attempts to convince her to resume therapy. Although the swelling had nearly disappeared and the jagged scars had healed properly, she saw no sense in wasting time sitting with a physical therapist. Her fingers would either heal or they would not. As far as she was concerned it no longer mattered. Her spirit was crushed, and she saw no point in trying.

Grace's health insurance had provided her with additional income to allow her to work part-time and still meet her most urgent bills. She knew the length of time they would pay was limited, but she simply did not care. Maybe it was better to consider moving into a small apartment and selling the old house and its contents. All she needed was her bed and a small kitchen. She had no friends, went nowhere and had no interest in changing her life. She had become accustomed to sleeping whenever she was not at work. Working part-time suited her just fine since it gave her more time to sleep. She was floating along like a leaf on the wind without a care as to where she landed at the end.

One afternoon as she drove through town toward home, she saw him. She was so caught up in the sight that she nearly hit another car. Certain Brian had not noticed her, Grace drove directly to her house, slammed her car door and ran inside. She locked the door, threw her purse on the floor and raced to her bed. Tears streamed down her face as she kicked off her shoes, threw her clothes on the floor and frantically wrapped herself in the sheets and comforter.

Grace cried herself to sleep after praying once again for God to take her life, to spare her the pain and sadness, to bring peace to her fractured heart.

*Drawn unwittingly into the dream, bits of golden light sprinkled down all-around Grace. She rose up from the bed and reached out when a hand appeared before her. Balancing awkwardly, she reached out and knew instinctively that she had but one chance to grasp it and be saved from further punishment for her mistakes. She saw her hand draw closer, witnessed her fingers touching the hand, but could not feel anything. It was like trying to pinch falling water. Trembling with horror, Grace witnessed the hand disappear into the white fog hovering all around her.*

The cold mist settled down around her and forced her back under the comforter where she curled into herself, shivering with fear.

Lightning burst through the night dark sky, lighting Grace's bedroom in stark white light. She came awake at the same time the thunder exploded and rattled the windows. Grace wiped her face with the corner of the sheet and tried to calm her panic. She must have been asleep for hours and the dream still held her in its grip. She struggled to sit up and pushed her hair back from her face. If she had to interpret the dream, she had no idea where to begin. She did not move until the next lightning bolt lit the room and she was able to find her way to the side of the bed without falling. Once she found the lamp on the nightstand, Grace clicked it on, but nothing happened.

"Oh no, no power," she sighed. Fumbling for the side of the bed, Grace made her way to the small bathroom. It was a good thing electricity was not required to flush a toilet, she thought ruefully. Of all the things to think about while she sat in the utterly dark room.

## Chapter 106

Heading out for work that morning, Brian felt he was getting his life back on track. His patience level with the kids had risen to what he considered normal and his relationship with Kathleen had grown into that of friendship again. She caught him slipping from time to time, but he did his best to listen to her advice with an open mind rather than taking it as criticism. Kathleen had loved Alicia like a daughter and Brian had nearly forgotten that fact. She was closer to being a grandmother to their children than their babysitter. For a woman who never raised any children of her own, Kathleen possessed a nurturing instinct that surpassed average by leaps and bounds. He tried to remember to thank her every day for what she did for the kids, and for all she did for him.

Several months had gone by since the ocean trip and Brian had found a moderate level of peace in his heart. Shane's lecture about some people needing to share their lives replayed every now and then, but Brian was learning to let life progress at its own pace without trying to direct it. If it was meant to happen, he would have to consider the pros and cons and decide if taking the chance was worthwhile. Then again, he thought to himself, he might have to accept wandering through life all alone.

Brian frowned at the vision of himself as an old man sitting all alone in a dark room with no one to talk to but the walls. A deep sense of sorrow rippled through him as he recalled the conversations he had with Alicia, sharing their dreams for their future. He had to put those dreams away. Better yet he ought to throw them away since they had no chance to evolve into reality.

"Pretending won't get me anywhere," he groaned as he drove along the road. Detour signs ahead caught his attention. He checked his watch and knew he was going to be late meeting with his crew. Brian had no doubt Bill would have assigned tasks to everyone by the time he arrived. Bill was a good foreman and took pride in his work.

Brian appreciated Bill and made a mental note to thank him again for being there to cover for him when his life fell out of balance. If not for the frank warning from Bill, he might have lost his business months ago. Bill had stepped into Clay's shoes without a hitch. Brian counted him as a good friend.

While following the detour signs leading back to the main road, Brian saw it. It should not have surprised him to see the car since she lived in the area, but he had not seen it since returning from the ocean.

"The Ladybug Lady," he whispered, feeling a little foolish for using Erin's nickname for her. "Grace," he said, pulling his attention back to the heavy traffic around him.

All the way to the job site Brian thought about Grace. The strange feelings he had felt while near her at the ocean came back, filtering through his heart and bringing a smile to his lips. What was it about her that touched him so? Her eyes held a deep sadness Brian had not understood and had no right to question. The way he saw it now, he had overstepped every boundary of privacy during the time she was hospitalized and recovering at the cabin. He wanted to delve further into the time with Grace, but doing so while driving felt too distracting to be safe.

Brian quickly shelved his thoughts upon arriving at the job site. His work crew was gathered around Bill. What was going on, he wondered to himself as he pushed the truck door open and jumped down to the rocky ground.

Bill raised his hand when he spotted Brian. When all the men turned toward him, Brian stopped short. Were they planning to walk off the job despite the changes he had made? He thought he had repaired all of his past mistakes and had not expected any more backlash. For a moment he considered running for his truck, but remained rooted to the ground. Fear and anger collided as he waited. Waited for what, he thought miserably. Brian felt the hope that had been growing begin to fade away.

"Hey, Boss," Bill said, leaving the crew behind him.

Brian braced himself for the bad news. It was coming, he knew it was coming. He locked his knees to keep from falling as Bill's sturdy hand clamped over his shoulder.

It was then that Brian became aware of the odor in the air. He turned toward Bill and saw the proof of it. A plume of cigar smoke rose from Bill's mouth and sucked the oxygen out of the air. Brian turned and coughed while Bill laughed and patted his back.

"Can you guess what we're celebrating?" he said before clamping the thick cigar between his teeth.

Brian turned, wiping his eyes with relief. By then the entire crew had surrounded the two of them. Danny, the tallest of the men, stepped up and handed Brian a cigar.

"Gina and I have a healthy baby boy," Danny announced. "I wanted to bring him with me this morning, but Gina put a stop to that right off."

Brian took the cigar but refrained from lighting it. Instead, he stuck it in his shirt pocket and shook Danny's hand. "Congratulations," he said. "How's Gina doing?"

"She's a trooper," laughed Danny. "She's got guts. And she wants another kid as soon as possible. If it were me giving birth to a big baby, well, he'd be an only child."

Laughter erupted from the others. Everyone slapped Danny on the back and one by one they began heading toward the house-in-progress.

"There's no reason for you to stay around today," said Brian.

"Naw, I'm staying. Gina said I should keep busy while she's in the hospital. That way she can sleep when she can and not have me bugging her."

"That's probably a good idea," Brian agreed. "Let me know what kind of time off you need and we'll accommodate you and Gina."

"Thanks," Danny said, taking one last draw on the cigar before he broke off the end and smashed it into the dirt. "Man, these things stink."

Brian watched Danny follow after the other men and wondered why he had doubted his crew. He pulled the cigar out of his pocket and rolled it between his fingers. He and Alicia gave out bubble gum cigars after the births of their children. He still had one for each of them tucked away in the back of his dresser drawer. There was a pink one for Erin and a robin's egg blue for Jack. Memories crowded into his mind until Bill broke the silence.

"You okay, Boss?" Bill asked.

"Yeah," replied Brian. "Yeah, I'm okay, thanks."

Later that night Brian stared up at the water-stained ceiling in his bedroom. The events at the job site earlier in the day had stirred up the ashes of his marriage. He was a lucky man to hold the memories of a woman who loved him more than life itself. How many people muddled through life without a clue as to how that kind of love felt. Never knowing the touch of a woman's soft hands or the feelings that came when they made love. Brian knew the miracle of birth and the wonder of a tiny hand wrapped around his finger. He knew all about the pure joy that came while watching his wife with his children. Even while the joy was overshadowed for so long by the tragedy of losing her, he had to work past the sadness and hold tight to the love they had shared.

"I can't completely let you go," he whispered in the dark. "I think I'm beginning to understand I need to move on and build a new life. I'm not sure I can handle the changes that will arise if I find someone new to share my life with, but I will do my best when the time comes. If that time comes," he amended. "Love is a precious gift, something rare and beautiful that makes your spirit breathe and grow. I don't have all the answers I need, so please stay close enough for me to depend on. You were there at the ocean, so I know you're here with me now. I will always love you," he whispered.

Brian turned on the bed and pulled Alicia's pillow against his chest. Not a body, nothing warm, but a fragile reminder of holding his first love.

*Not so much as a whisper of breath moved as she touched her fingers to her lips and sent her kisses to him. If she had the power to mend his heart and give him the gift of love, she would do it. Her spirit rose and slipped away into the night.*

## Chapter 107

The new year arrived without any further complications for Brian and his children. The construction business was keeping him busy and Erin was enjoying school. Jack quickly adapted to Erin's absence and Kathleen managed them all.

Brian passed by the newspaper office in Jameson on his way back to the job site. He found himself thinking once again about Grace. Dare he contact her, he wondered as he tapped the steering wheel while he waited for the light to change. There were people crossing the busy street and something clicked in Brian's head. Today the people were bundled in heavy jackets and warm boots, but he was not thinking about cold weather. Not a snowy day like today. It had been cool and cloudy though, he decided, still watching the passersby. He sifted through the past months, reaching back toward last summer. It was right after Clay died.

Brian drove on but glanced back at the corner. The kid at the crosswalk, he realized. The woman he had nearly collided with, he thought. The woman who had smiled at the boy. She was Grace. He remembered in vivid detail her waist length chestnut brown hair and her expression of sorrow that mirrored his own mood on that terrible day.

"Hell," groaned Brian. Of course she had been gloomy after witnessing the accident and being unable to save Clay. How many ways was Grace tied to him, he thought. How many times had Alicia played a role in bringing them together? It was mysterious, but was she drawing them toward each other for a reason?

"Alicia, is Grace, could she and I, I mean, is it meant to be?" he asked out loud, hoping others around him did not see him talking to himself. He pushed his fingers through his hair and sighed. "Yeah, I know, take it easy, one step at a time."

*Alicia watched, brushed her fingers ever so lightly against his cheek and then slipped away without a sound.*

Brian felt her presence. He pressed his hand to his cheek. She was with him, he felt certain she was still with him.

## Chapter 108

Grace sat in her car outside the house until she began to shiver. Getting groceries had taken every ounce of energy she had left after working all day. Discouraged barely touched how she felt as she pushed the car door open and stepped out onto the frozen ground. It was then she heard the light pattering of tiny hailstones hitting the car.

"Perfect," Grace groned as she ducked inside the back of the car and lifted out the paper bag. She turned her face up to the sky and whispered, "What next?"

After leaving the bag in the kitchen and returning to lock the front door, Grace noticed her dirty footprints on the hallway floor. Feeling foolish, she pushed off her boots and left them near the door. She trudged toward her bedroom, retrieved her slippers, picked up a hanger from the closet and walked into the bathroom. She slid her wet jacket over the hanger and hooked it over the shower curtain rod. The slow dripping sounds told her she would have another mess to clean up if she did not position a towel on the floor to catch the runoff.

"I can't do this," she wept. Grace walked into the kitchen and placed everything from the bag onto the counter. Moving as though she were mired in mud, Grace put the cold items into the refrigerator, tried to fold the paper bag and gave up when she started crying.

Grace let the paper bag fall on the floor and dragged herself back to her bedroom. Her doctor would probably diagnose her with depression and put her on some sort of medication, but Grace craved sleep more than escape via drugs. Fumbling clumsily, she worked the buttons free on her blouse. She pushed off her jeans and kicked them out of the way. Her car keys tumbled out onto the hardwood floor, but she did not care. She didn't care about anything. Loneliness and regret drew her toward sleep. Nothing mattered as much as getting into bed and sleeping away the day.

The bills, her job and fixing meals were no longer important. She moved through her days at work like a robot. She spoke to no one unless required to do so. Grace acted as close to what she hoped others considered normal as she made her way through each day. Here at home, where she was hidden behind closed windows and locked doors, she felt nothing. If the walls collapsed and the roof fell down on top of her, Grace could not have cared less.

When the phone rang later that night, Grace ignored it. She had not thought to pull the plug on it. She would do it later. Just like the dirty dishes piling up in the sink and the overflowing laundry hamper, none of it mattered anymore.

Grace was giving up on everything. If she weren't so weak, she might have attempted suicide. As it was, she had no idea how to do it if she actually found the courage. When the phone finally stopped ringing, Grace stared at the wall. The past year had taken her apart bit by bit. She knew the worst had been witnessing the terrible accident during the storm. She could still feel Clay in her arms, still hear his raspy voice in the final moments leading up to his death. She had never recovered from that experience. Nor had she recovered after the deaths of her parents. Guilt came first, regrets flowed close behind and wishing for her own death came right on its heels.

Grace watched her fingers tracing over the patterns on her pillowcase. Tiny white daisies with sunny yellow centers, a mass of flowers surrounded by green leaves and long stems. They should have made her smile, but she felt nothing but sadness. She pulled her right hand up next to her left hand. Her index finger and thumb still felt numb. They hurt when it was cold, like it was today. The pain was a deep aching that refused to ease even when they should have felt warm.

While she stared at nothing, unwanted images flickered through her mind. She squeezed her eyes closed, but they lingered still, vivid with color and details. First came Jack's silly expression when he asked for frog legs at The Drive In. Next came Erin in the cabin asking her if her hand hurt. There was something in the little girl's beautiful brown eyes that touched Grace's heart. If those images were not enough to rattle her, the next one made her heart skip a beat. Brian's features came to life before her with his thick brown hair and his penetrating blue eyes. She thought of his gentle manner when helping her, his quick temper when Erin spilled her milk and his fierce reaction when the dogs in the parking lot came running toward them. The same tingling she had felt too many times flashed inside her now as she lay under the comforter, warm and comfortable, but desperately lost and alone.

Grace saw the words floating before her eyes, the same words that had remained as clear as the first time she had seen them.

*"He needs you. He needs you."*

They remained frightening, yet oddly compelling. Had they really been put there by Brian's late wife? Were things like that actually possible? Or, to Grace's dismay, were they merely the product of the imagination of a broken woman. She bit her lip and closed her eyes while her tears soaked into her daisy covered pillowcase.

Grace did not deserve to be happy. Her life was an emotional disaster, a tangled mess Grace knew was sucking her into a bottomless pit. Where she had felt the peace Clay's spirit radiated as it rose from his body, she knew her own spirit was destined for eternal torment.

*Julia Robertson*

## Chapter 109

Brian put the phone down and rubbed his hands over his face. He had been thinking about making the call for the past few weeks. Marlene's earlier call had pushed him far enough that he had actually dialed her number and let it ring a dozen times before hanging up. Had he dialed the wrong number? He felt certain he had gotten it right. It was probably best it had not worked out. His life was busy enough with work and his children. "Busy enough and lonely as hell," he muttered as he started down the hallway to his bedroom.

It was time to read a couple of books to the kids. It had become their nightly ritual since the earliest signs of Alicia's illness. "Alicia, what am I supposed to do," he whispered as he sorted through a stack of books on the floor.

"Want Go Dog book," Jack shouted as he ran into the room. He climbed up on his father's back and latched his arms around his neck.

"Jack, slow down," sighed Brian.

"He's all nutsy," Erin announced as she came into the room carrying her stuffed rabbit.

"Great," Brian said as he stood up with Jack still hanging onto his neck. "Two books and off to bed with both of you. Down you go," he said as he flipped Jack over onto the mattress. Brian sat up against the headboard and opened the first book.

"Dogs can't really drive cars," Erin said. "Can they?"

"No, dogs don't drive cars," Brian assured her. "These books are pretend. They are stories people made up just for fun."

"Books are pretend?" Erin asked, puzzling over the matter.

Brian watched her, still fascinated by her thought process. "There are all kinds of books. Some are stories that are made up, some are stories about things that have really happened. The encyclopedias are all facts, things that actually happened."

"Cartoons are pretend, right?" she asked.

"Right," agreed Brian. "Now let's enjoy this one before Jack nods off."

Brian read the book, turning pages as he moved along. Erin was enthralled with the story as usual, but Jack nodded off long before the male dog was content with his lady counterpart's choice. The book was complete nonsense with dogs of all colors.

"Is one book enough for you?" he asked Erin.

"Okay, if you carry me to bed. I'm sleepy," she sighed, cuddling her bunny closer.

"Jack first," he said, setting the book aside and scooping Jack off the bed. The boy felt exactly as Justin had described him in the Redwoods. Exactly like a bag of warm mashed potatoes, Brian mused as he settled Jack down on his little bed and covered him up. He returned to his room and picked up Erin. She turned her face in against his chest with the bunny squashed between them. Erin did not have one favorite stuffed animal she liked more than the others. She loved them all. Brian could not help but wonder if she planned on growing up with all of them. He might encourage her to take them with her when she was ready to leave home. Among others, she had bunnies, bears, a turtle, a frog, a pumpkin and two elephants.

Brian settled Erin into bed much as he had done with Jack, kissing her as he covered her up with her blankets. He had years of this routine ahead of him. He stood for a moment watching his children sleep. There was a magical feeling flowing around them in sleep and he wondered if Alicia had something to do with it. It would not surprise him in the least. Then again, maybe all children looked the same when their brains shut down for the night. He had no idea about any children other than his own.

"They miss you," he whispered to Alicia. "So do I," he said as he crossed the hallway back into his own bedroom and his empty bed. He pushed his hands into his back pockets and wished to know what was in store for them for the future. Just a glimpse would be helpful, he thought, knowing information like that was unattainable.

Brian spent most of the night staring up at the dark ceiling. He kept jumping from the plans for the upcoming house project to Grace and back again. The more he tried to focus on work, the more he wanted to bring back the images of Grace. Guilt intruded when he realized Alicia had not been on his mind since he put the kids to bed. Exactly how much time was he supposed to spend thinking about her?

And missing her, he added as the guilt weighed him down like an anchor. He felt the ring on his finger growing warmer the longer he pondered the problem. Brian sat up abruptly and dropped his feet down on the cold floor.

"So, I guess you know I tried calling Grace tonight," he said, confessing to his first love as though he had committed a sin. "I'm not sure if I'm required to feel guilty, but I do. I mean I can't figure out how I'd feel if our roles were reversed and I was the one who died. How would I feel if you were thinking about replacing me?" he said, feeling his anger gaining strength. "It makes me sick to tell you the truth. Having someone else touching you," he cried out now. "Alicia," he gasped, grasping the edge of the bed. "Damn," he sighed as he fell back on the bed and grabbed Alicia's pillow. "You'll always be a part of me. I cannot make that part of my life disappear. You were here, you're in my heart, I want you back."

*Julia Robertson*

## Chapter 110

Roger picked up the phone and greeted the caller. "Hold on, I'll check," he said and turned toward Grace. He tapped out a message on his computer and sent it to her. "Brian Cooper calling for you," it read.

Grace reacted immediately, her face growing hot as she pounded keys, fumbling to get the correct ones. "Please, tell him I'm not here," she wrote.

Roger nodded and conveyed the message, shaking his head as he turned back to Grace. He looked around the office to be sure no one was too close. "It would do you good to talk with someone," he urged Grace, not for the first time.

Grace said nothing and hoped he would drop the subject. Though Brian had been on her mind for months, she simply could not deal with anything in her life beyond work. Work had become almost unbearable. Keeping a brave front in the face of debilitating depression was growing more and more difficult.

"Let's go out for lunch," Roger said after coming to stand next to Grace at her desk.

"I can't," sighed Grace.

"You need to eat," Roger said.

"I have too much to do here," she replied, her eyes burning with the lie. "Thanks anyway."

"Aw, Grace," Roger said.

Grace listened to his footsteps as he left the office. Her shoulders slumped with both relief and regret. Her troubles were not only hurting her, but hurting Roger too. He had been trying for weeks to get her to come over and join them for dinner. She begged off every time he brought it up. She knew she was losing weight and knew it was going to kill her if she did not do something soon. Her hands trembled while she drew herself back into her work.

As had become her habit of late, Grace walked into her empty house and dropped her purse on the floor, kicked off her shoes and tossed her jacket over a chair in the kitchen. Her neat and orderly home had become a shameful mess. Grace did not care. Her work room had not changed since the day she tried to work a few stitches in her current quilt project. The needle was still somewhere on the floor underneath the quilt frame.

Grace reached the kitchen counter and stared out into the back yard. Spring was coming soon. Dried leaves were scattered all over the grass. She had not raked at all last fall, partially due to her hand, but more so because of her lack of desire to take it on. The yard looked all brown. She supposed the grass was growing new soft green shoots beneath the dried out leaves. No one saw any of it except for Grace, and she no longer cared.

Grace shoved herself away from the counter and nearly fell down. When her body could not catch up with the motion, she found herself on her knees on the floor. The room tipped and swirled while she remained on the floor with her eyes closed tight.

Several minutes passed before she managed to get to her feet, using the refrigerator to keep her balance. She pulled the door open and rummaged around for some cheese. She grabbed it and slammed the door as she turned to the sink to find a relatively clean knife. The thick slab of cheese seemed to dare Grace to eat it. She lifted it and took the smallest bite, held it in her mouth and waited for calm to return. She felt as though her mental being had become separated from her body. The creepy sensation remained while she took a second bite, then a third. The bites were no larger than a mouse might manage, she thought with a groan. She took a bigger bite and began to feel the creepy sensation easing off. Several minutes ticked by before Grace felt back together.

"How does that happen?" she asked no one. Frowning, she looked down at the sink. Both sides were overflowing with dirty dishes, glasses and silverware. She considered washing everything, thought again and walked away still holding the slice of cheese.

Grace stepped into the bathroom and looked into the mirror. The woman looking back at her was a stranger. Seeing the shadowed eyes, blotchy skin and tangled hair, Grace's heart began beating hard. The tempo increased when she realized her old self was gone. She looked half dead. No wonder Roger was trying so hard to help her. What was the point? She had nothing to be happy about, nothing at all.

Grace dropped the cheese and fumbled with the light switch before stumbling into her bedroom. She nearly tripped over the pile of clothing on the floor, caught herself and sat down hard on the side of the mattress. Prayers were getting her nowhere and she wanted so badly to walk out of this life. Heart aching, Grace tipped over onto the bed and buried her face in her pillow.

*Julia Robertson*

## Chapter 111

"Why do dogs have four legs?" Erin asked.

Brian looked up from his drawing table where he had his ledger opened out before him, calculating his crew's paychecks. Alicia had taken care of the many details of the business before the bad days arrived. Though Brian had dealt with them for over two years, he still found them incredibly tedious. He kept the rows as neat as possible and worked hard to make every entry legible. When it came to drawing blueprints or creating sketches, every detail was perfectly clear. Some mysterious mental block kept him from feeling the same gratification when working the ledgers.

Brian put the pencil down and looked at Erin. "I have no idea why dogs have four legs," he replied.

Erin stepped up on his boots and pressed her small hands against his knees. "I want four legs," she said seriously.

"That's an interesting request, but I'm afraid I can't fulfill it," he replied, raising up the toes of his boots one at a time. Erin's giggles started instantly.

"Cars have four tires, cats have four legs, the mowlawner has four wheels," she sang out.

"And Erin has two legs, two feet, two hands and two ears," Brian added.

"I guess," sighed Erin as she pressed her pointy little elbows into his knees, rested her chin on her fists and looked up at her father.

"Next question?" Brian asked. It was always easy to see when she had more questions ready to pop out of her mouth.

"Can you do magic?" she giggled.

"What would you ask me to do?" Brian asked even though he already knew the answer.

"I want you to turn Jack into a puppy," she said, bouncing up and down.

"And I'll turn you into a frog," he told her as he lifted her up onto his lap. "What makes you so silly? Are you full of silly worms?"

"No worms in me," squealed Erin.

Brian suddenly realized he had not seen Jack since Erin started with her questions. He held onto Erin while he closed his ledger book and moved it into the file drawer. He quickly locked the drawer, pocketed the key and stood up from his chair.

Brian learned the hard way to put away any and all of his paperwork. Adept at climbing shortly after he had learned to walk, Jack climbed up and decorated one of his ledger books when it was left open on the drawing table. He found it the next day with crayon marks all over the pages. It was creative, but also destructive. Now he never left any important paperwork out unless he was sitting right there.

Brian carried Erin over his shoulder and went in search of Jack. The first signs of trouble came as soon as he turned down the short hallway. A line of toilet paper trailed out of the bathroom, across the hall and into the bedroom. Brian slid Erin down on the floor and told her to stay put.

"Don't move," he told Erin as his shoulders tensed. "Stay calm," he ordered himself. He remembered putting a new roll on the holder no more than an hour ago. Jack had dragged it out of the bathroom, into the bedroom, across both beds and into the closet. The white panels ended up in a pile inside the closet, but there was no sign of Jack. Brian sighed, muttering as he crossed to the bathroom. The room, which was positioned in the center of the small house, had no windows and was always dark unless you flipped on the overhead light.

A month ago Brian would have exploded at his kids for disrupting his day. He might have spanked Erin for interrupting his work, might have lashed out at Jack for wasting the toilet paper even before he knew what else he had done. Today he relaxed his shoulders before he took another step. He kept his anger in check and let out his breath to ease his rapid heartbeat.

Brian slapped the lightswitch and saw Jack. He was sitting on the toilet seat with his bare feet in the water. Bobbing around his feet were the rubber ducks and plastic fish usually reserved for time in the bathtub.

"What are you doing?" Brian asked, grabbing a towel before he lifted Jack up off the toilet seat. He let the water drip from Jack's feet before he wrapped the towel securely around his small body.

"Ducks wanna swim," Jack said.

Brian hid his laughter. Jack had made a picture of innocent cuteness, but allowing him to do it again was out of the question.

"Ducks don't like yucky toilet water," Erin groaned at the doorway.

"Happy ducks," Jack assured her with his head bobbing up and down, wearing a big smile.

"Good grief," sighed Brian. By then his socks had absorbed some of the water on the floor. He needed to get back to the ledger book and write out paychecks, but it appeared his plans were going to have to wait.

Brian sat Jack down on the floor and ordered him to stay put. He hoped the boy listened better than his sister. He rolled up the toilet paper first, then turned on the hot water in the tub.

After scrubbing the bathtub toys and giving the kids a bath, Brian mopped the bathroom floor. He gathered up the damp towels and carried them out to the kitchen. It made sense to get them washed right away. Once the machine was filling with water, Brian headed back to get the kids dressed. They were sitting on their bedroom floor playing with stuffed animals. Brian folded his arms and leaned against the door jamb. Did anyone make straightjackets for children? Brian shook off the idea, knowing it bordered on cruelty and opened the small chest of drawers.

"Put these on," he said as he dropped Erin's pajamas down on her lap. "Come on, Jack, let's get you dressed too. It's almost dinnertime."

"Do we have any dog food?" Erin asked.

"No," replied Brian. "Do you want to eat some?"

"I want to feed it to Jack and make him a dog."

"He's a boy, Erin, not a dog," Brian said firmly. "When you two are older we might think about getting a dog."

"Can we name him Woof?" Erin asked excitedly.

*Julia Robertson*

*Tender Dreams*

Chapter 112

Two weeks had passed since Brian called the newspaper office. During that time Marlene called him several times, urging him to contact Grace. Besides wanting to find out how Grace was doing, she wanted him to take Grace out to dinner or to the park with the kids. Brian might have been irritated by her relentless suggestions, but he was actually encouraged and appreciated her enthusiasm. He was lonely and he liked Grace. He did not want to use the unfortunate situation at the ocean as the only reason to contact her. He wanted it to be because he liked her, not that he felt pity for her. After finally taking the first step he felt slightly bruised by her not taking the time to return his call.

"She's shy," Marlene told him. "She feels you deserve someone stronger than her."

"Damn it, Marlene, she's more than I deserve. How can I tell her without making me sound desperate?"

"You both need someone special, Brian. I can still see the fear in her eyes, and the same dark loneliness in yours. If you don't try, you'll never know."

Brian saw Grace's red car parked at the newspaper office on his way to the job site that morning. He considered going in right then, but thought it might be too much too soon for Grace. Putting her on the spot at her place of employment was wrong. Before he reached the job site, he stopped at a pay phone outside a gas station.

"Valley Post," said the male voice. "This is Roger, how may I help you?"

Brian wondered if Roger was the receptionist since he had answered the phone both times he called. "Good morning, Roger, this is Brian Cooper. Is Grace in today?" He knew the answer and waited for the man's reply.

"Is there any chance we could meet at lunchtime today?" Roger asked.

Brian noticed Roger's voice sounded muffled. "She's there, isn't she?"

"Yes, but," Roger began.

"Tell me what time and where," Brian replied.

Brian kept an eye on the time throughout the morning. He already let Bill know he had an appointment he could not miss. He focused on the work at hand and the upcoming start on the house for which he recently completed the blueprints. It was the house he had made the preliminary sketches for on the same day he and Grace met for the first time. He was anxious to get that project underway. There was something about building from the ground up that gave Brian an extreme sense of gratification. Of course the renovation job they had taken on gave him immense satisfaction as well.

They were currently pulling out old carpet and linoleum tiles, wallpaper, ceramic bathroom tiles and the cupboards in the kitchen. The place needed new wiring and new plumbing throughout. They were painstakingly removing old wood trim and molding, salvaging every piece possible. The stairways had been found in incredibly good condition and the slate rock entryway was as solid as the day it had been installed. With new windows and layers of insulation they would make the house tight as a drum.

Brian thought of the times when he simply dreamed of running a crew of good workers who were skilled as well as willing to learn new techniques. Long hours of studying and working hands-on had taught him to understand the work environment from every perspective. Except for dealing with Alicia's illness and the aftermath of her passing, Brian felt confident and in control. The low periods of his life had shown him life from yet another perspective. He hoped and prayed for peace in the future. Adversity might build character, but Brian knew even the strongest person could crumble under too much pressure. He had been brought to his knees countless times over the past two years.

Brian never shirked his responsibilities and took on any job he was offered. He was glad for the work and grateful he had advanced to being well known in the community for his skills and integrity.

"Hey, Boss," Bill called out.

Brian lowered the hammer in his hand and looked back at his foreman. A quick glance at his watch told him he had no time to waste.

He stepped down from the ladder and walked over to Bill. "I should be back within the hour," Brian said.

"We can get along just fine without you," Bill said with a grin.

"I appreciate your honesty," laughed Brian.

Brian approached the small café and pulled the door open. He let the two women coming up at the same time enter ahead of him. A quick glance at the other customers revealed only two men sitting alone at two different tables. When the man with light brown hair dressed in a sweater vest over a long-sleeve gray shirt raised his hand, Brian walked over to him. Brian guessed it was his own clothing that gave him away. The other men in the café had to be office workers. Brian wore well-worn work boots, heavy denim jeans and a lined denim jacket over a black T-shirt.

"I'm Brian Cooper," he said in greeting.

"Roger Phelps," the man said as he offered his hand. "Thanks for coming."

Brian shrugged off his jacket and draped it over the back of the heavy wooden chair. He sat down across from the man.

"I haven't ordered yet," Roger said. "I'll wave the waitress over when you're ready."

"That's fine," agreed Brian. He quickly scanned the menu and made his choice. Once their orders were placed, Brian settled back in the chair.

Roger appeared ill at ease. He shuffled his feet, drummed the table with his fingers and sipped his coffee. Still he said nothing. Brian realized he had to get the conversation rolling. "How is Grace doing?"

"She's getting by, but," Roger replied. He looked down at his hands, offering no further explanation.

Brian wasn't sure what Roger meant by that statement. Was Grace still dealing with her injuries? It struck him then that Roger might be trying to ask him for help. How long might it take before Roger said anything more, he wondered, then decided he'd push once again. Brian did not have all day to sit here.

"Listen, I'll be heading back to work as soon as we're finished here. I don't have a lot of free time on my hands," he said. Brian saw he had Roger's attention when the guy's mouth dropped open and his eyes went wide. "Just say what's on your mind."

"My apologies," Roger said quickly. "I guess I'm concerned Grace might be angry when she finds out I've talked with you, but she needs help." He sat up straighter on the chair and stared across the table. "She's falling apart. It all started after the accident during the big storm last summer. She never fully recovered after that experience. She moved from day to day without any sparkle at all. It's like a part of her died inside."

Brian nodded, but said nothing. He thought it best for Roger to get everything out without any interruptions.

"Then I suggested she take a few days, head out of town and do something out of the ordinary to clear her mind. I mean, it works for me."

"Sure," agreed Brian.

"Well, as you well know that turned into a disaster that no one could have predicted. She is still walking with a limp. And her hand, well," he said, running his fingers over the exact areas where Grace's hand was injured.

"Do you mean she still hasn't been able to sew?" Brian asked, taken completely by surprise by the news. "I figured that was all behind her by now."

"Yeah, it might have been. She cancelled the physical therapy after just a few sessions. She wanted to work and not waste time with what appeared not to be working, but she did not give it enough time to help. I tried," he said, stopping when their food was placed on the table.

"Thank you," Brian told the waitress.

Roger picked up a French fry and bit into it. "Wow, these are hot," he warned, setting the remaining half of the fry back on the plate. "She won't like that I'm telling you this either, but she's not eating, she's losing weight and she looks terrible."

Brian lost his appetite with the last remarks. "How can I help?" he asked without delay.

Roger sighed audibly. "I was hoping you'd offer," he said, letting out a long-held breath. "You're into construction, right?"

Brian looked up and replied, "Yes."

"I have an idea," Roger said with a grin.

Brian listened as Roger explained his plan. He nodded and at the same time concentrated on the food before him until Roger seemed to run out of steam. "You don't think she'll see through your plan?"

"If we're careful, no, I don't think so," Roger explained. "Under normal circumstances Grace is bright, but lately, well, it's like she's only half there."

"Damn," sighed Brian. "Here, take this," he said, pulling a business card out of his wallet. "Get things lined up and then call me. I'll do anything I can to help get Grace back on her feet."

"The old Grace, the one before the accident last year was quiet, but nothing like she is now. I'm hoping we can bring her back to life."

Brian checked the time and sighed. "Hey, I hate to end this, but I have to get back to work. If I'm not at home, please leave a message with Kathleen. She takes care of my kids during the day and she will be happy to help us with this endeavor. What do I owe on that?" he asked, pointing at the bill under Roger's hand.

"My treat," said Roger as he pushed his chair back. "I have a good feeling about this. It's going to work."

The two men shook hands before Brian left the café and headed back to the work. He had to put the baffling situation aside before he reached the building site. Distractions created accidents on a job site. Brian knew that all too well. Before turning onto the long driveway, Brian recalled Grace's fearful expression the day she learned her hand might take a very long time to heal. It had broken his heart at that time, and it did so again just thinking about it. "You're not alone, Grace, you are not alone."

*Julia Robertson*

*Tender Dreams*

## Chapter 113

Exhausted, Grace decided to take two sick days and delay facing her co-workers until the following week. Roger had been badgering Grace so much she felt near the point of breaking down if she didn't get away from him. She knew in her heart he meant well, but Grace had run out of excuses for saying no to dinner invitations, no to lunch out and no to going back to the physical therapist. Grace hated seeing his defeated expression with every no, but she simply could not face anything other than going to work so she could earn her paycheck. A paycheck that left her short on money every single pay period. Another good reason for taking two sick days was that her car was almost out of gas again. She did not like asking anyone for a ride to work since she lived in Chelsea Creek, ten miles outside Jameson and the newspaper office.

Grace put the phone down after making the call to work. She knew she had only a few more sick days with pay coming this year, but she had to stay home. Her wallet held a few dollar bills. A handful of coins were loose in her purse. She had nothing else left until payday at the end of next week. If she put the last of her money into the gas tank, she might be able to hold out until her check arrived.

When she went to the front door to be sure it was locked, she caught sight of her quilt project. Dust was building up on everything. She unconsciously held her right hand up against her chest.

"I'll never," she wept, turning and rushing down the hallway to her bedroom. Her bedroom, her haven from the world and all of her troubles.

Birds were singing outside the window. A neighbor's dog was barking. Someone was running a lawn mower at the property behind hers. Life went on as usual everywhere but inside Grace's home. Grace was mired in quicksand, sinking ever so slowly toward an unseen destination. Trembling with fear, she sought refuge under the bulky weight of her sheets and comforter.

*Julia Robertson*

## Chapter 114

"Roger, I need help," Grace said.

Startled by the tone in Grace's voice, Roger almost dropped the phone. A myriad of terrifying scenarios raced through his mind. An accident, an injury or maybe someone breaking into her house, he feared. "Are you okay, Grace?" he inquired, ready to rush out to Grace's house right away.

"There's water all over my floors. Something broke and I don't know what to do. Do you know a reliable plumber?" she asked desperately.

Roger saw it was already nearly 6 o'clock. He doubted a plumber would make a call this late without charging extra, especially on a Friday night. "Take it easy, Grace. Let me make some calls. I'll get back to you in a jif," he said and quickly disconnected the call. Cradling the phone between his ear and his shoulder, Roger rifled through the debris cluttering his desk. "Be there, be there," he chanted as he dialed the number, then crossed his fingers for good luck.

*Julia Robertson*

## Chapter 115

Grace wandered through the house wearing her rumpled sweatpants and a hooded sweatshirt. Having abandoned her slippers for a worn-out pair of socks, she paced the wet floor feeling anxious and hopeless.

"Not the sinks, not the bathtub and not any of the toilets," she told herself as she waited for the repairman's arrival. Roger had called back right away, but that was an hour ago. While she waited, she used towels to build a dam along the floor in the dining room. It seemed to her the house must be tilted slightly toward the back yard since the water had not flowed as far as the entryway.

For a short time, Grace's imagination had her checking to be sure someone had not pushed a hose in through a cracked window and turned it on. Why would anyone consider doing something so dreadful, she wondered, scolding herself for her crazy thoughts. Her stomach ached with worry and frustration. Grace let herself imagine she was walking along the beach. The floor was the sand, and the water was flowing in from the ocean. Even Grace's vivid imagination could not maintain the fictional depiction without an ocean breeze or the sound of seagulls squawking overhead. Not the ocean, she admitted regretfully.

Grace forced herself to face her current reality and began fretting over the rugs in the dining room, the old linoleum tiles on the kitchen floor and the wooden chair and table legs sitting in water. Tears seeped from her eyes, seemingly nudging her toward her bedroom and the refuge under her comforter. She wanted to believe sleeping would erase whatever disaster had occurred. Nothing was farther from the truth.

A terrifying image flashed before her. The plumber's hand jotting down dollar amounts on his notepad, calculating the figures out loud until her stomach lurched. Grace braced herself against the bathroom door jamb and sucked in air. She didn't have enough money to fill her gas tank, let alone pay the service call for the plumber. She felt the sudden need to call Roger and have him cancel the plumber. She could mop up the water and keep mopping until she figured out what to do.

When she recalled the water meter out by the road, Grace wondered if she could turn it off herself. She had no clue what it looked like, but it had to resemble a faucet handle. Why hadn't she paid more attention when her parents were still with her, she groaned as she began searching for her shoes. Searching for a flashlight was imperative since it was already dark outside.

Grace whirled around when the doorbell rang. "I'm coming," she said as she hurried to open the front door. She saw the toolbox and the dark denim shirt with an emblem on it. Despite his being backlit by the front porch light, Grace noticed the baseball cap pulled down low on his head. She quickly averted her gaze in hopes he did not see how dreadful she looked. As she turned away she thought he touched his fingers to the bill on the cap, making her imagine a cowboy using two fingers to touch his well-worn cowboy hat. She would not have been too surprised if he said, "Howdy."

"Please come in. Be careful on the slippery floor. I have no idea where it's coming from. There's no water in any of the sinks or the bathtub."

Frantic, Grace headed to the kitchen. She heard the front door close and the heavy footsteps following after her.

"Roger told me you're a good plumber," she said, scrambling to make conversation. She had not cleaned the house in months and felt embarrassed and ashamed for the way it looked. The dirty dishes in the sink were piled high. It was all too obvious they had been there for a long time.

Grace stopped at the doorway to the kitchen, nervously twisting the dish towel in her hands. "There's a small bathroom next to the laundry room, and I thought the toilet was overflowing, but it's not."

Grace wished she could run and hide. She had been crying all afternoon, leaving her eyes puffy and red.

"May I have a look around?" the repairman asked.

"Of course," Grace answered timidly. She did not dare make eye contact with the man, but she was aware he was walking toward the laundry room by the sound of his wet footsteps.

"Is this the water heater closet?" the man asked, tapping the narrow floor-to-ceiling doors across from the laundry room.

Grace looked toward his voice and was suddenly overcome with embarrassment again.

"Yes, it is. I never gave that any thought," she groaned. She had to look away. She had to settle her jumpy nerves. Grace had no notion when the doors to that closet had been opened last. She had forgotten how they used to creak until the plumber pulled them open. The sound made her turn and look back. He was half hidden behind the open doors.

Grace bit her lip waiting for the outcome of the inspection. "Be something simple," she whispered. "Something inexpensive, please."

What came next had Grace letting out a strangled whimper. She pressed the twisted dish towel against her eyes and turned away.

*Julia Robertson*

## Chapter 116

Before he rang the doorbell, the repairman positioned the ball cap down so low it nearly covered his eyes. He momentarily thought he had pulled into the wrong driveway as soon as the door swung open. Address numbers on houses in this area of Chelsea Creek were few and far between. The road had no streetlights, and few people used their front porch lights at night. His words of apology for bothering her slid down his throat as soon as he heard her voice. She spoke to him without looking up. Her tone reflected the exhaustion written all over her face. When she immediately turned and walked away, he noticed her steps were out of balance. He moved inside and closed the door before following her toward the back of the house. As he entered the kitchen, he realized she was wearing socks. Wet socks, he thought silently.

While she had her back to him, he touched the water on the floor. Although it was not warm, it was not as cold as water running from the tap. That was his first clue. There was no dishwasher in the kitchen.

"Have you run the washing machine today?" he asked.

"No, not for a few days now," she replied, twisting the dish towel and shifting her weight from one foot to the other.

Nervous, he easily deduced. He put the toolbox up on the counter to keep it dry. The repairman checked with Grace before he looked under the sink, then went to inspect the washer. Before stepping into the laundry room, he noticed the louvered panels on the two narrow doors in the short hallway. He recognized her dismay when she confirmed it was the water heater closet. Even before he tugged the doors open, he felt the heat radiating from the oversized heater.

Crouched before the ancient water heater, the repairman wondered if the old relic ought to be donated to the Smithsonian. Talk about things that were made to last. Apprehension stilled his hand as he reached out for the valve. He wondered if it had ever been turned off and if it was going to break off in his hand, but it turned easily despite the initial squeak of protest. Once the valve was shut off the dripping ceased immediately.

"Okay, you're going to need a new water heater," he said, still leaning into the closet space. "Chances are this one was put in when the house was first built." He rose from the floor and left the doors standing open. The water on the floor needed to be mopped up, but other than that there was nothing to be done here. "I can install a new water heater for you tomorrow morning if that works for you."

"No," Grace said softly.

"What's that?" asked the repairman.

"No new water heater," she said, eyes glued to the kitchen floor.

He turned from the open closet doors and stared at her. "It can't be repaired. Besides being ancient I can't get parts for it. It needs to be replaced," he explained carefully.

Without another word Grace turned and walked away.

The repairman looked back at the old water heater, shook his head and closed the double doors. He heaved a sigh, retrieved his toolbox and followed after her. She was standing by the front door, head down and shoulders slumped.

"Thank you for coming," Grace said.

"I can bring a new one tomorrow before noon. It won't take long to install." He watched her shake her head. The statement that Grace was "getting by," struck him then.

"I can't," she began.

"There's no need to worry about paying right away. Next week works, or next month. I'm sure we can work something out," he said, speaking cautiously. She looked like she was done in.

Grace swiped the back of her hand over her eyes. "No, thank you," she mumbled. She tugged on the door and let it swing open.

"Grace," he said.

She looked up then, her swollen eyes filled to overflowing. "I can't do this," she wept. She drew in a ragged breath and met his eyes. For a moment time stood still.

"Grace, let me," he said, reaching out to touch her shoulder.

Grace flinched and blinked hard. "Brian?" she gasped.

"Let me explain," he said, setting his toolbox down with a thump. "Grace."

"How did you," she gasped, stepping back and bumping into the wall.

"Careful," he cautioned.

"Why are you, how, who told," she said, babbling with confusion.

"I'm here to help," he explained. For the first time, Brian got a good look at Grace. She was too thin, he thought, remembering Roger telling him she had lost weight. She was ghost-white and had dark smudges beneath her reddened eyes. "What happened to you?" he asked, instantly regretting his choice of words.

"Nothing," she replied, swiping at her eyes again. "Why are you here?" she said.

Brian heard the trembling in her voice. "You needed help," he said, gesturing toward the kitchen and the water on the floor.

"I thought," she cried. "I thought, you, you're a builder, not, not a plumber."

"Can we talk?" Brian asked. "Please, Grace, can we sit down and talk?"

"No, I can't, it doesn't, we, you, please," she wept uncontrollably.

It was obvious she was weak and very upset. He looked around and saw a heavy wooden chair in what appeared to be her work room. "Let's sit down," he suggested.

"I can't," she said. "Go away, please, just go."

Instead of doing as she asked, Brian stepped into the work room and scanned the space. Another chair was in the far corner, piled with fabrics. He crossed the room, set the stack on the nearby table and carried the chair over to the first chair he'd seen.

"Come sit down," he said, pushing the front door closed and taking Grace by her arm. "Don't argue with me, Grace," he said, watching her as she took measured steps toward the two chairs. "Sit down," he told her, leaving no room for her to object. Without a word he crouched down and pulled off her wet socks. "

You shouldn't be walking around in these. Where can I find dry ones?"

"No, please stop, I can't," she said, pushing at his shoulders.

"I'll be right back," he said and walked away from her, down the hallway opposite the entryway. Brian passed a bathroom and stopped at the first bedroom. He felt certain it was her bedroom. He saw the messy room, but focused his attention on finding the socks. In the second drawer he opened he found them. The drawer was a jumbled mess, but he found two socks that appeared to match and pushed the drawer closed. Something told him the room had not always been like this.

Without saying a word, he knelt once more and pulled the socks over her cold feet. "You're not doing so good, are you," he said in a matter-of-fact tone. He did not expect, nor did he get a reply. "Looks to me like you're stuck in a rut. How about allowing me to offer a helping hand."

## Chapter 117

Grace could not stop trembling. Brian was here, right here in front of her. Though the circumstances were altogether different, it took her back to the hospital room after the dogs attacked her at the ocean. At that time, she blamed the medications and her injuries for the confusion she had felt. Today her extreme exhaustion was clouding her thoughts.

How had this happened? Why was he here? Who told him she needed help? How had she not recognized him when she opened the door to let him inside?

Brian was close enough to touch. When his warm hands held her cold foot she sighed. She had been so cold for a long, long time. It suddenly became clear at that point. She was dreaming, floating in the fog of sleep and caressed by her childish desire to be loved. Her eyelids drifted closed.

After a time, her hands, moving on a path her brain had no control over, found their way into his hair. In her mind she saw the ball cap fall backwards off his head, forgotten as it hit the floor behind him. Silky soft strands warmed her cold fingers as she found pleasure in its plush softness. Her body ached for something so alien to her she had no way to imagine it. She wanted a tub filled with hot water and scented with lavender and mint. She conjured images of a half dozen candles in stained glass holders lining the edges of the tub. Two glasses-long-stemmed and filled with wine stood waiting on a wood framed tile table on sturdy cast iron legs. Grace breathed in deeply, filling her lungs with the soothing scents and the steam rising from the water. Relaxed both physically and mentally, she eased back against the side of the oversized tub.

*Julia Robertson*

## Chapter 118

Experience had taught Brian how to massage a woman's foot to warm it and caress it with pressure from his hands. As soon as Grace began to relax, he knew he had not lost his touch. When her ankle became pliable, he increased the pressure, running his thumb down the length of her small foot. Her toes curled under like those of a baby.

He refrained from saying anything when Grace closed her eyes. She was slipping into a place beyond consciousness, making him wish he had taken her into her bedroom. She needed to sleep. He wondered how long it had been since she slept through the night. Lack of sleep took a toll under normal circumstances, and Grace had experienced too many stressful sitfuations during the past year. Not stressful, he amended, but terrifying.

Had he been asked for his opinion he would have said Grace was on the verge of a mental breakdown. He had no training in such matters, only his personal experiences from which to draw from. It was more like a reflection of his own up-close and personal life-altering tragedies. Sometimes experience gave a person more insight than countless hours spent in a lecture hall.

Brian turned and shifted close enough to lift Grace's other foot and give it the same treatment. The relaxed foot remained resting on his thigh, close enough to hold if she indicated the need.

Early on in Alicia's illness, she benefitted from massage therapy. He learned from the therapists who came to the house every other day. The therapist generously taught him what to do, what not to do and how to watch for signs that she'd had enough or if she needed something more. By the way Grace was reacting he thought he was doing a darned good job. If she began slipping off the chair, he'd carry her back into her bedroom.

Brian deliberated his options now that he had worked over her other foot. Kathleen didn't mind staying with the kids, but she deserved to go home before it got too late. He checked his watch, then said, "Grace, we need to talk before I leave." Nothing happened. She sat against the back of the hard chair with her eyes closed and her features completely relaxed. "Grace?" he said. What happened next took Brian by surprise.

Grace's hands reached out and pushed off his baseball cap. He froze, wondering if she was awake or in a deep sleep. If he woke her would she lash out and scream? If she woke up suddenly would she recognize him? Or, he wondered next, was she willingly suggesting more intimate actions?

Brian's unease spiked when her fingers delved into his hair. If he did anything wrong, she had the right to take legal action against him. The mere thought of being imprisoned sent a chill down his spine. He hadn't smelled liquor on her or seen any in the kitchen, but some people were well versed in concealing such habits. Had her parents been alcoholics? Children often followed such a pattern, even without intending to do so.

Her fingers moved slowly, almost seductively through his hair. Brian found the intimacy disturbingly arousing and quickly reached up and took hold of her hands. He had to stop her before something more happened. He had responsibilities and could not afford to destroy what he had with his children and his business. There were too many ways to lose it all. The recent nightmares had portrayed a disaster he had no intention of having come true.

"Grace," he said sternly, raising his voice loud enough to wake the dead. "Grace, wake up," he said one step louder.

## Chapter 119

Startled out of sleep, Grace shot up on the chair. Her hands were held captive in Brian's much larger hands. "What happened?" she blurted out. "What are you doing? Let me go!"

"Grace, I think you were dreaming," Brian explained as he set her hands on her lap and eased her feet down onto the floor. "You must be exhausted."

"Sleeping? I fell asleep?" she asked as comprehension dawned. "I was dreaming," she sighed. "I'm sorry, I didn't mean to fall asleep. I'm sorry."

Brian smiled at her. "Don't worry about it, Grace. You need to go to bed. I'm going to mop up the water in the kitchen and dining room. I don't want you to risk falling down while you're here alone." He moved back from Grace and stood up.

"No, don't do that," Grace argued.

"Listen, I'm bringing a new water heater over tomorrow morning. I don't want any arguments from you. Go to bed and let me take care of the floor," Brian told her before he picked up his hat and turned toward the hallway.

"I can't let you do that," Grace said desperately. "I can't afford to pay for it, or to pay you for your time. Please go home," she pleaded. To her dismay Brian waved off her words and walked away.

"I'm not listening," he called out.

Grace sat down and stared at her feet. They felt marvelous. She remembered his warm hands on her feet and smiled.

Grace rose from the chair, walked to the entryway and looked around the corner. "No," she whispered when she saw Brian on his knees, sopping up the water and wringing the towels out into a bucket. She still didn't understand how he had come to be here. Had Roger called him? It did not make any sense. When Brian finished mopping up the water where she had dammed it with towels earlier, she stepped up on the entryway floor.

"I thought you were a contractor, a builder," she said, braced with her hand on the wall.

"I am, but I can do most things that need doing. Some plumbing problems are within my limits. If it had been more complicated, I would have called the plumber I use on my job sites. It works that way," Brian replied, shrugging his shoulders.

"But why you?" Grace asked, inching closer to where he knelt on the floor. "How do you know Roger?"

"Well, I called the newspaper office from the hospital at the coast. I dealt with Roger at that time. And then," he said as he sopped up more water. He wrung out the towel until it stopped dripping. He looked up and said, "I called the office several more times after we came home. You never called back."

"I didn't, I couldn't," Grace said, her voice quavering with the words.

"Yes, well, I met with Roger just a few days ago. We decided, rather, he decided to keep an eye out for an opportunity for me to come here and help you."

"So why did you come here?" Grace asked, feeling anger rising as her shoulders tightened.

"Initially it was to allow me to ask you out on a date. Roger seemed to think the plan was airtight," he said, stopping when her expression turned to that of anger. "Look, Grace, I only wanted to ask you out to dinner, that's all."

"You're here to ask me for a date?" she said.

"Yes, that's right," Brian said. "No, wait," he said next, dropping his head back and staring up at the ceiling. After a few beats, Brian sighed, sopped up more water and wrung out the towel with more force than necessary.

"If that's what you planned on doing, why are you kneeling on my floor like that?" Grace blurted out, pointing her finger at him.

"Excuse me, Grace, but you needed help. I'm not the kind of guy to see someone in trouble and walk away because it's inconvenient. I am here to help, yes. And even more so to ask you out."

"Good grief," retorted Grace.

Brian loved her honest response. He shook out the towel and moved the bucket. Without another word he dragged the towel over the next standing puddle of water. He did not look up until it was time to wring it out again. She was still watching him, so he smiled at her.

Grace wore a dark green sweatshirt that was too big for her small body, and oversized gray sweatpants that completely hid her legs. Her chestnut brown hair was extremely messy. He guessed she hadn't brushed it after sleeping. How often had Alicia been up during the night with one of the kids, leaving her hair looking exactly like that?

"I'm too tired to care about my hair," Alicia liked to tell him when he made a face at the tangled mess hanging down around her shoulders.

Brian wiped his sleeve over his eyes, blotting the tears that always came whenever he pictured Alicia during that happy time of life. He turned away from Grace and focused on the job at hand. He set aside his tender feelings and sighed. There was no way to bring her back or get a second chance to fulfill their dreams. Today, right now was what mattered most. He could not change his past, but he had a future waiting out there for him. Whether it was a future of life alone or a life shared was not known yet, but he had to look ahead. Looking back and wishing for things he could not change had taken up enough of his life.

After mopping up more water, Brian stopped and looked back at Grace. Disappointment struck when he found she was no longer standing there. A little voice told him to go find her, but another told him to stay put and finish the job. He worked diligently until the floors were dry and the towels deposited in the washing machine. When he turned off the overhead lights in the kitchen and dining room, Brian found the house was dark. The only sound he heard was the ticking of a wall clock somewhere nearby.

Brian stood by the entrance to the hallway for several minutes before turning toward his toolbox. After a moment of thought he drew out his wallet, extracted a business card and went back into the kitchen. Once there he stood the card up on the windowsill above the sink.

He locked the front door, pulled it closed and walked to his truck. As he stepped up into the cab he looked back at the house. There was no light glowing behind any of the windows. He yearned to know what Grace was feeling. Did she think he was crazy for coming today? Was she intrigued or dismayed with his wanting to take her out on a date?

While he sat in the dark, he looked back toward the house again. He wondered what it felt like for Grace living here all alone.

Brian thought about his own life. Lonely, yes, but never actually alone. He recalled how he felt when Clay took the kids to the park the day he cleaned out Alicia's things. He remembered the wrenching pain he had felt when he imagined them never coming home again. That particular fear was so intense it made him feel sick to his stomach. He unconsciously closed his eyes while he relived some of those feelings. When he caught sight of the car coming into the driveway that afternoon with Clay behind the wheel and the children asleep in the back seat, Brian sighed silently with relief. He was thankful Clay was too tired to notice his weakness.

"Clay," whispered Brian. "If you were here, I'd call you and tell you about Grace. I miss you working beside me, talking with me and pushing me past the anger and guilt I felt for so long."

Brian sighed, let the memories from the past float away and backed out onto the road. He drove at the posted speed limit back toward his small rental house. Back to his children and the life they had together. Grace was behind him, alone in her big house. She looked so lost and worn out. He wondered how bad it was for her financially. Her quilting was a big part of her income and he knew her hand was not healed sufficiently for her to start sewing again. Hearing the bad news about her hand from Roger allowed him to avoid bringing up the subject tonight.

Brian pondered his own financial situation. While he usually had enough to meet his expenses, he also knew how it felt to be down to the last few dollars in the bank. What money they had managed to save had gone into the business and then into the doctor bills for Alicia.

Garrison signed Alicia's trust fund over to him not too many months ago. The older man made it clear it was money to be used, not money to be socked away for the children. Garrison had funds lined up for Erin and Jack's college educations if they chose to attend college. Brian still had issues with Garrison, but he also had learned there was a good side to the cold-hearted father of his beloved wife.

"Get off that subject," Brian demanded as he turned onto the narrow road leading to the little rental house. The front porch light was on, a beacon in the dark welcoming him home.

"My home, my family," he said. "She's all alone. Please watch over her," he whispered before pushing the truck door open.

"They're down for the night," Kathleen told him the moment he stepped inside.

"Thank you," Brian replied. He pushed off his boots and set them aside before walking over to Kathleen. She was pulling on her pink sweater and fastening up the row of tiny buttons. She always dressed elegantly, even on the days she cooked or baked for him. "You're an angel, you know that?" he said, giving her a hug.

"I have my moments," Kathleen laughed softly. "If you need help tomorrow, let me know. I have no plans for this weekend. Maybe for the next weekend, but not this one."

"Have you got a hot date lined up?" Brian teased.

"Actually," Kathleen whispered. "I've met someone."

"Keeping secrets from me?" he asked with a grin.

"I'll let you know more when I feel the need to share," she said firmly. "Right now I'm going home. You call me in the morning."

"I'll do that," Brian assured her. "I might be installing a new water heater for Grace tomorrow."

"Grace," sighed Kathleen. "I love her name. I'd like to meet her one day. I have a good feeling about the two of you."

*Julia Robertson*

## Chapter 120

Grace burrowed in under the comforter. Clearing her mind took every ounce of concentration she possessed. She willed Brian out of her mind. Roughly shoved aside the worries over the cost of a new water heater as well as the cost of removing and replacing it. Her stomach lurched, but she ignored the need to eat.

Did Brian say he wanted to take her out on a date? It must have been part of the dream that sparked to life when she fell asleep on the chair with him rubbing her feet. Her toes curled under as she remembered the luxurious feelings he evoked with his hands. If he were here right now and massaging her bare feet, she thought she'd melt into sleep in a blink.

"Shame on me," Grace scolded. "I have no business thinking about Brian like that. Even if he does want to take me out, I can't go. My life is such a mess. I can't put that burden on anyone, especially someone so good." Grace finally drifted into a restless dream-filled sleep.

*The fog billowed up around her, obscuring her vision and blocking out the path beneath her. Her bare feet were hidden from sight in the thick mist. Grace raised her hands and wiggled her fingers, desperate to make her eyes see them. When she pressed her hands to her eyes and the scene before her remained the same, Grace gasped with alarm. Scared out of her wits, Grace fell to her knees. She looked to the sky that was not there and prayed silently, "I'm so lost, please help me find my way."*

At the sudden ringing noise Grace automatically reached out for the phone. Still mired in the frightening dream she mumbled, "Hello?"

"Grace, this is Brian Cooper. I can be there by 10 o'clock if that works for you," the caller said.

"Ten?" Grace said as she pulled herself up on the bed and found the sun shining through the blinds on the window.

"Did I wake you?" Brian asked. "I'm sorry, call me back when you're ready for me to come over."

"How," Grace began before she realized she was not dreaming, that the fog was gone, that her hand was raised up before her eyes and she could see it. "Give me an hour," she finally said, then glanced at the clock. "Oh," she sighed. "I had no idea what time it was."

"Grace, are you okay?" Brian asked.

"Uh huh," she replied dumbly. "I'm fine, 10 o'clock is fine. I'll be ready." Grace could not believe it was already close to 9 o'clock in the morning. She dragged her feet over the edge of the bed and stood up slowly, waited for the spinning room to slow down, then walked toward the bathroom.

A mad search through the drawer in the bathroom vanity produced her toothbrush. Grace scrubbed her teeth clean and wondered when she had brushed them last. She peeled off her clothes, left it all in a heap on the bare floor and stepped into the steaming shower. The nearly empty shampoo bottle produced enough liquid to shampoo her hair. The bottle fell down on the floor outside the tub when she set it down again. Grace followed her normal shower routine, ending up with combing out her long hair and squeezing it out with her towel. A quick walk to her bedroom had Grace searching for clean clothes to wear. Dressed and scuffing along in her slippers, Grace started for the kitchen. She considered leaving the mess on the floor in the bathroom, reconsidered, gathered up dirty clothes and the wet towels and made her way out to the laundry room.

At first the sight of several wet towels in the washer puzzled Grace, but then she remembered all the water on the floor. A moment of thought had her dumping the clothes into the hamper, the towels into the washer and pouring in some detergent. The washer started filling as she walked into the kitchen. The repairman was coming in half an hour. Brian was coming in half an hour, she corrected. Grace gathered her wits and assessed the sink filled with dirty dishes. A dishwasher would have been handy at this point, but Grace was the only dish washer in the house. She had no one to blame but herself.

With hopes there was enough hot water left, Grace began filling the sink, squirted in some dish soap and stacked the dirty plates and bowls, gathered up the silverware, set the glasses along the back of the counter and picked up the wash rag. She scrubbed, rinsed and dried until the sink was empty and the cupboards full. "Why did I wait so long to do this?" she groaned.

Grace scuffed back to her bedroom and stared at the scrambled mess of sheets and the rumpled comforter. It was too late to think she could wash it all and re-make the bed, so she hastily straightened it out, fluffed the pillows and tugged the comforter into place. She picked up all the clothing from the floor and the chair and hurried out to dump it all into the hamper. The lid snapped closed at the same time the doorbell rang.

*Julia Robertson*

## Chapter 121

"Good morning," Brian said when the door swung open. He was pleasantly surprised with the sight before him. Grace was dressed in clean jeans, a button-up denim long sleeved shirt and slippers. Though she still looked exhausted and slightly haunted, her hair was brushed, and her eyes were definitely brighter than they were yesterday.

"Come in," Grace said. She looked around Brian, then back up at him. "Where is it?" she asked.

"In the back of my truck. I'll remove the old one first."

"Okay, but we need to discuss payment first. I can't give you anything today except a post-dated check, but," she said, stopping when he raised his hand.

"Let's not ruin a good start to the day, Grace. We will talk about the bill later. Right now I want to get the old relic out of the closet. I brought along some wood to build a platform for the new one."

"Oh," Grace said, frowning with worry as she linked her fingers before her.

"The wood is all scrap, so there's no cost involved but a handful of nails," Brian said cheerfully. Toolbox in hand, he walked to the kitchen and over to the double doors. "This looks good," he said as he crouched down to inspect the floor.

"How do you know what to do first?" Grace asked.

Brian sat back on his heels and looked up at Grace. Curiosity shone on her face. He wanted to wipe away the dark smudges beneath her eyes. He wanted to bring a smile to her face. "I'll disconnect the power and then drain the water."

"Drain it?" asked Grace. She leaned down and peered inside the closet. "How do you do that?"

"We have two choices on that matter. We can either drain it out all over the floor," he said, earning himself a stern frown from Grace. He laughed and added, "Or hook up a garden hose to it. I brought along a length of hose." He twisted around to confirm there was an outside door in the laundry room. "I'd like to drain it out into the yard if you don't have any objection."

Grace looked into the laundry room. "Sure," she said. "I haven't had that door open in years. I hope it still works."

"We're going to find out shortly," Brian replied. He watched Grace turn back toward him. When she rested up and regained some color and a few pounds she was going to shine like a new penny. Her long hair intrigued him. He fisted his hands to keep from reaching out to touch it. The slight curl at the ends had the look of a child, but he knew better. He had carried her in his arms. Although he had been careful to not feel her body, he had been very aware of it.

Brian suddenly realized he was staring at Grace. He turned his attention back to the water heater, regained his composure and stood up. "I'm going to get the hose and get this started."

Brian welcomed the cold air outside as he walked to his truck. He should have grabbed the hose and returned to the house, but lingered a few minutes longer to get himself cooled off. Grace was wary of everyone and everything. If he pushed her she would probably push back. If it was going to work out in the manner he hoped for he would have to give her time, let her set the pace and give her a chance to make a decision.

Brian long ago made a vow to treat women with genuine care. He knew what a controller did to a woman's spirit and how difficult it was to repair the damage. A controller isolated his prey, battered her self-esteem and then molded her into what he wanted, that is a servant and slave.

Brian fisted his hand and thumped the cold tailgate. He looked up through the trees and said, "Never, I'll never do anything to hurt her." Brian sucked in a deep breath and pulled the coiled hose up over his shoulder. He picked up the stack of boards and headed back toward the house.

Brian worked methodically, focused on the job and averted his eyes from Grace whenever she came back into the kitchen. He opened the laundry room door to the back yard and discovered a vast collection of spider webs. Some resembled rotted basketball nets, while others were silky white artistic masterpieces. "Holy smoke," he sighed as he set the garden hose down on the floor near the water heater. "Grace, do you have an old broom and some bug spray handy?" he asked.

Grace stepped into the kitchen. "There's a broom out on the back porch. What did you find?" she asked.

"Is there another way to get out there?" Brian said, wincing at the idea of opening the screen door. He was surprised when Grace appeared next to him.

"Disgusting," groaned Grace as she quickly backed out into the hallway. "I apologize, please, let me clean it up. You don't have to take care of that."

"Tell me how to get out there first," Brian said as he swiftly pushed the door closed. He secretly hated spiders, but he never shirked his responsibilities at home and had no intention of doing any less for Grace. "I'll take care of it. Bug spray?"

"Up over the washer, I think," Grace replied as she moved toward the overhead cupboard.

Brian moved in the same direction and inadvertently knocked Grace up against the door jamb. When she yelped, he instantly reached out and took hold of her upper arms. "Sorry, my fault, you okay?" he asked.

Grace rubbed the back of her head, nodding in reply.

"Let me see," he said as he turned her far enough to see the back of her head. There was no blood, but he noticed her hands were shaking. "Hey, you need to sit down," he urged, guiding her toward the small table by the kitchen window. "Have you had anything to eat today?" he asked, leaning down to look into her eyes. She said nothing, clearly avoiding eye contact with him.

"Grace, have you had anything to eat?" He demanded. He tipped her face up with his hand underneath her chin. "What's going on?"

"Nothing, I'm not hungry," Grace finally answered, biting her lip as she tried to turn away from him.

"Damn it," Brian snarled before he turned and opened the refrigerator. "I'll fix," he said, but froze when he found the refrigerator nearly empty. "Why don't you have any food in here?" he asked, closing the door slowly as he turned to her again. Once again Roger's words raced through his mind. "Grace is getting by," Roger told him.

Brian searched for the best solution to the problem. Grace very obviously needed help. He set aside the water heater repair and focused solely on Grace. She was crying, but she was not making any sound at all.

At that point he decided it was time to take charge. Brian stepped closer, crouched down and took hold of her hands. "Grace," he whispered. "I'm going to bring the new water heater inside, then I'll go get some groceries. You probably don't feel up to going with me, do you," he said, offering her the option of coming along. When she tried to pull her hands free, he gripped them tighter. "Okay, you stay here. I won't be long."

Without thinking, Brian kissed Grace's damp cheek. "It's going to be okay. Everything's going to be okay," he assured her.

As soon as Brian closed the front door, Alicia silently slipped into the room. Grace sat at the kitchen table. Embarrassment and hopelessness shone on her face. She rested her head on her arms and cried herself to sleep. *Had she the ability to feel emotions Alicia would have been crying too. Brian and Grace were following the right path. She lingered until he returned, then left the room without so much as a whisper. She knew neither of them felt the temporary presence of her spirit.*

## Chapter 122

Brian made quick work of loading several bags of groceries into his truck before heading back to Grace's house. Once there he took two bags inside. He stopped short when he found Grace asleep right where he had left her.

"Oh boy," he sighed. What if he had not been here? What if she had spent the entire weekend as weak as she was without food or help? His heart ached for her. He put the bags on the counter, turned and rushed back out to his truck. Once he shut the front door and returned to the kitchen, he began emptying the bags into her refrigerator.

Brian searched the cupboards for a skillet and a roasting dish. Working rapidly, he switched on the oven, set the skillet on the stove and turned the burner on. He cracked two eggs into a bowl, whisked them with a fork and dropped a dab of butter into the warm skillet. By the time the eggs began setting up he had cheese grated and deli ham sliced into strips. While the omelet cooked, he cut an onion into quarters and set a whole fryer into the sink. He turned the omelet, took down a plate and poured a glass of orange juice.

"Grace, wake up, I have something for you to eat," he said, jostling her gently yet firmly. "Wake up and eat."

"Not hungry," mumbled Grace.

"It isn't nice to turn down food when I've worked so hard to prepare it for you," Brian said. "Come on, eat it while it's hot."

Grace raised her head and rubbed the sleep from her eyes. "What did you do?"

"The grocery fairy came to the door," Brian said, tapping the plate with the fork until she finally focused on the food in front of her. "Eat," he said firmly. He turned and left her alone, crossed to the counter and opened the plastic bag. He rinsed the chicken and set it in the roasting dish. Once the onions were placed in the chicken and he sprinkled it with salt and pepper, Brian searched for hot mitts, found a mismatched pair and deftly slid the dish into the very hot oven.

The next search started at that point. "Where's your timer?" he asked, turning to Grace when he ran out of places to look.

"Timer?" Grace said.

"You know," replied Brian. "A timer. It ticks down the time when you're cooking. You must have one."

"Up there," Grace finally said, pointing to the refrigerator.

Brian looked until he saw the round timer magnetically mounted on the side of the large appliance. "Clever," he said as he turned the dial to 60, then backed it off to a little less than 30 minutes. "Okay, aluminum foil?" he asked, even though he had run across it during the earlier search.

Grace pointed in the direction of the set of drawers on the left side of the sink. "I think I have some," she added.

"Got it," Brian said. He snuck glances at Grace to be sure she was eating before he went into the laundry room, found the bug spray and gave the spiders and their webs a generous dose. If it did nothing more than slow the spiders down the work of clearing them off the screen door might be easier. He shut the inside door and returned to the sink. Grace was still taking bird-sized bites, but at least she was eating. "Good," he whispered as he dropped the eggshells into the trash basket, then washed his hands. He was thankful the old water heater still had some hot water left in it.

"How's your omelet?" he asked as he walked over to the table and sat down across from Grace. She looked lost, but he tried to pretend everything was normal, that she was simply eating breakfast like any other day. "More juice?" he inquired.

"No, but thank you," Grace said. "I wish you hadn't," she began, but stopped short.

"I'd like to think we're friends, Grace," Brian said, quickly interrupting her thoughts. "I mean after what happened at the ocean and what you did for Clay, well, that adds up to friendship to me."

"I guess," sighed Grace. She absentmindedly pushed the remnants of the omelet around the plate with her fork.

"Okay, good," Brian said. "I need to get back to work on the water heater. I was thinking," he said, pausing until she finally looked up. "You ought to consider donating that old relic to the Smithsonian."

Grace could not stop the smile. A giggle escaped before she clamped her hand over her mouth and shook her head.

*Tender Dreams*

"There has to be a collector out there who would pay big bucks for it. I mean it's pretty nearly ancient."

Grace's fork clattered to the plate when she covered her eyes with both hands. Brian stepped closer, kissed the top of her head as he might have done for Erin, then got back to work.

Grace remained hidden behind her hands even as his footsteps told her he was not standing next to her any longer. She lowered her hands as slowly as she dared when her face finally cooled down. Her heart was still beating too fast.

Grace felt glued to the chair as she watched Brian run the hose out into the back yard. A short time later he backed out of the closet with the hand truck, tipped it back and rolled the old water heater through the kitchen and out of sight through the open front door. Feeling useless as an old shoelace, she watched him wheel the new water heater into the kitchen. He stopped short of the closet doors, turned and picked up his toolbox. When he moved back inside the closet, she wondered what he was doing. The narrow door was just wide enough to block everything but his legs and boots.

Every now and then he backed out far enough for her to see up to the top of his jeans. Dare Grace admire the view? She felt her face growing hot and frantically tried to cool down by waving her napkin at her face. Falling prey to her growing curiosity, Grace walked over to see what he was doing.

Brian held a row of nails between his lips. One of his hands held a hammer, the other the sections of wood. She watched as he tapped the next nail into place as though he were sliding a needle into a pin cushion. She realized then that he was building the stand for the water heater to rest on. She noted the precise corners when he rested back on his heels.

"That looks great," she commented.

"It'll work," Brian said, nodding as he turned to face her.

Grace felt it then, that queer tumbling of her insides as his eyes locked on hers. Those penetrating blue eyes, the same eyes that had infiltrated her heart at the Drive In. She almost looked away, but kept her eyes open and on him. He looked good kneeling there on the floor. She saw it all, his broad shoulders, well-muscled arms, skilled hands and his very handsome face. Her heart fluttered, making her step back against the cupboards.

"Be careful," Brian warned.

Grace nodded, raised her hand and ran her fingers over the bruise on the back of her head.

"Does it hurt much?" Brian asked.

Grace looked up, surprised to find him standing in front of her. Her mouth went dry. "Not bad," she replied.

"You smacked the door jamb pretty hard. It'll be sore for a while. Can I get you some Tylenol or Aleve?" he asked.

"No, but thanks," Grace replied. She avoided taking any medications unless absolutely necessary. A bump on the head was nothing these days.

"I'm sorry for what happened," Brian apologized. He reached out for her, but then the timer rang and he turned toward the oven. "I need to, I'd better," he said, stumbling over his words. He turned back to her and ran his thumb down her cheek. "There's something between us, Grace. Something special," he said. "Damn, I need to take care of the chicken or it'll burn."

"Chicken?" Grace said, dumbfounded by his words, his intensity and the touch of his hand.

Brian stepped away from her, grabbed the hot mitts and lifted the roasting dish out of the oven. He set it on the stovetop and turned the temperature down to 350 degrees. He grabbed the box of foil, pulled out two lengths and spread them over the roasting dish. With quick deft movements, he crimped the edges of the foil over the dish and double-checked his work before sliding the dish back into the oven.

Grace watched him work without moving. Her mother had cooked and baked with ease, but her father had never made anything but peanut butter and jam sandwiches. "I'm impressed," she admitted, surprised the words had come out in logical order. She had not meant to say it aloud.

"I had a good teacher. And it was a matter of survival," Brian said as he put the hot mitts on the counter. He set the timer for an hour and put it back on the side of the refrigerator. "I can work a French braid and change diapers too," he said with his hands spread wide.

"Super Dad," giggled Grace. She hid her smile behind her hand.

"I have my moments," Brian admitted. "It hasn't been all fun and games."

Grace's smile faded into a frown. "I'm sorry," she sighed, looking down at the floor to break the spell.

"Life isn't fair for a lot of folks," Brian said.

"You're right," agreed Grace. She wondered what was happening here in her kitchen. Brian stood only a few steps away from her. He watched her while she watched him.

Grace's imagination formed an array of images that mentally drew Brian closer to her. The colors so vivid, the details so real Grace felt tears in her eyes.

A shadowed figure peeked out from behind Brian's knees. Twinkling blue eyes and a cap of light brown hair adorned the little boy's face. He darted back, hidden completely out of sight. Grace blinked and looked again. This time she saw Brian balancing an infant against his shoulder. A girl, Grace thought as she stared with disbelief. Brian's sturdy hand patted gently, soothing the infant as though she were made from porcelain.

Grace so wanted to see the baby's face, to study her features and learn the identity of her mother. She unknowingly took a step closer to Brian, but discovered the infant was no longer there. She realized neither of the children had been there in the first place.

Grace's heart sank.

At that very moment Grace realized she had to get help. Perhaps she needed to admit herself to a mental facility. Lack of sleep, skipping too many meals, fretting over the past and her nonexistent life had all congealed into a state of mental instability beyond words. She had no idea what to do first. No clue who to call for help or how one went about admitting oneself to a center for the mentally insane. For that was what she must be by now.

"I need," she began, staring down at the old linoleum floor. "Damaged, broken, lost, hopeless," she mumbled under her breath.

"No," Brian said as he reached out and took hold of Grace's hands. He slowly pulled her in against him, gently wrapped his arms around her fragile body and tucked her head under his chin. He felt her trembling and so, held her tighter.

"Hush," Brian said when she started crying. "I've been where you are, Grace. I understand what you are going through. Not long ago I came so close to the edge of sanity I thought I would never find my way back again," he explained. "Let me help you find your way. You are not alone," he said soothingly. "I'm here, I'm here."

*Julia Robertson*

## Chapter 123

Brian looked back on that day as the beginning and the end. Both an ending to his life with Alicia and the beginning of his life without her. What came next was still out there waiting to be discovered. He hoped the future included time with Grace, but he had to let things develop slowly.

Brian and Grace started going out on dates and spending time together over meals out. They walked along the river and talked about the past, the future and his children. He kept their conversations light, listened as she described her visits to a counselor, nodding with her as she noted her progress. Brian knew Grace had to love herself before she had the room in her heart to love him. He held her hands, kissed her tenderly, loved her immensely and restrained from pushing her for anything more. She needed time and he most certainly had that to give her.

"Grace," Brian said one night while visiting on the phone. "Would you like to join us for a walk in the woods?"

"Us? You mean with your kids?" Grace asked.

"Yes, exactly," Brian said. Until now he had not included the children because of her need to regain control of her life. Brian noted her progress and felt she was ready to take the next step. She was working full-time now and gaining back some of the weight she had lost. She smiled more than she frowned and openly strived toward presenting her positive side. He knew just by looking at her she was growing more content with her life. His internal radar told him he had a lot to do with her current happiness.

Early the following morning, Brian walked up to the door and knocked lightly. He grinned at Grace when she stepped out into the morning sunshine. "Don't you look dandy," he exclaimed.

Grace wore tan hiking boots, well-fitted blue jeans and a bright red T-shirt. She carried a small tote bag and a dark gray hooded sweatshirt. The sun lit up the gold strands in her chestnut brown hair.

Brian looked down when the gold highlights reminded him of Alicia. Always his first love, though he knew he must put her one step away in order to make life with Grace a possibility. He reached for her hand and felt his insides ripple as she stepped up close to him.

"You're beautiful," Brian said before opening the truck door for her. He hitched his chin toward the back seat. "They're excited about having you join us," Brian said. Then wishing to boost her self-esteem, he leaned down and kissed her lips. Grace grew rosy with his intimate gesture, but did not pull away or object. "Ready for an adventure?" he asked.

Grace nodded, then looked up into the cab of the truck. "Let's go," she said enthusiastically.

"That's my girl," Brian said, keeping an eye on her as she stepped up onto the high seat.

Brian's words made Grace want to dance with delight. Such feelings were so foreign to her she was not sure how to process them. Grace did not sleep much the night before. Her mind kept trying to imagine the next day, their very first outing with the four of them together. She felt certain Brian had come up with the idea in order to test the waters with his children in the mix.

Grace felt she and Brian were making positive strides with their relationship. She had begun sharing more about her past and the tragedy of losing her parents. She knew there was more to learn about Brian, but she was not sure he was ready to open his heart to her. Her counselor had suggested she give him time. Suggested he might be allowing her room to heal before he opened up to her. Grace agreed and hoped the counselor was correct.

Today was a definite break-through. She didn't think Brian was being overprotective. His children were precious to him. She felt sure he would never put them in a situation that would harm them in any way.

Grace had stared at herself in the mirror that morning. Was the woman looking back at her strong enough to take on the future? What if Brian wanted to join his life with hers? Would he be disappointed to know she knew nothing about raising children? If he knew would he turn around and walk away without looking back? How did a person know if he or she was strong enough to cope with another person's excess baggage? Grace herself had a trunk-load of troubles. Doubt crept in when she considered what it might look like to Brian. Was she asking too much of him? She had not yet allowed herself to imagine a life with him beyond their brief visits. Grace could not afford to set herself up for another mental disaster. She had to force the negative thoughts out of her mind and focus on life one day at a time as her counselor had taught her. Then again, what if, she sighed silently.

As the truck rolled out onto the road, Grace pondered the last few minutes. Seeing Brian at her door had made her heart skip a beat. She had momentarily considered running back inside her house to hide. The old Grace yearned for the sanctuary of her bed, ached for the weight of her bulky comforter and the darkness in her bedroom closed off from the rest of the world. The new Grace, even while she felt the panic rising, held her head up and locked her gaze on Brian's beautiful eyes. When He had taken her hands in his, his warmth radiated up her arms like an electric shock. Before she stepped up into the truck, he kissed her. Grace's mind had lost track of everything at that very moment. It felt as though they were standing alone on top of the world.

Grace carefully returned to the present and focused on the road ahead. She stole glances at Brian from time to time, still feeling like she was living in a dream. She peeked at the kids too, but they were engrossed in a game, passing a pad of paper back and forth between them.

The next few hours passed too quickly. She delighted in the antics of Erin and Jack as they followed the well-worn path through the trees. Jack stopped each time he spotted a bug. He investigated every little sound from the underbrush. Erin inquired about the bird songs and touched each flower in bloom along the trail. Grace's eyes opened wider with each new discovery. She had no doubt she learned more about the woods than she ever realized existed. Brian had unlimited patience with all the questions his children came up with. He promised to get out their encyclopedia to search for more answers when they got home later today. Grace's legs grew weary after a time, but she never complained and pushed herself to keep up with the three of them.

"Let's take a break," Brian announced, obviously noticing her fatigue.

"I'm fine," she assured him.

"Maybe I'm the one who needs a break," Brian said, yawning expansively. "Stay close," he reminded his kids as he sat on the edge of a flat-topped rock.

Grace gladly joined him and kept a fair distance between them. She did not want to give the kids the wrong impression. She had no sooner sat down when Brian stood up and moved closer. He brushed loose strands of her hair back from her face. She turned to look up at him and saw the twinkle in his eyes.

"Thank you for inviting me," she said.

"I'm glad you agreed to come with us. The sunshine is good for you," Brian said as he brushed the back of his fingers over her cheek. "You're glowing."

Grace blinked away her threatening tears, looked from Brian to his children, glanced into the trees in the distance and back at Brian. She bit her lip and remained quiet even while her mind whirled with her jumbled emotions. Here she was surrounded by the beauty of nature, sharing the day with a man she had strong feelings for. Hearing him so easily put his thoughts into words, while she herself was unable to explain what she was feeling. She drew in a deep breath, turned her face up to the sky and felt a sense of peace she had never known before. With the sun shining warm on her face, her heart sang with tender dreams. The joy she felt made her want to dance. her eyes filled with tears.

"Hey," Brian said, reaching out and turning her face toward his. "What's wrong? You're crying."

Grace shook her head. "No, no," she sighed as heat rose up her neck. "It's been a perfect day."

"What are you thinking that's making you cry?" he asked, slipping his hand around hers.

"It's lovely out here. Simply beautiful," she said, her voice barely audible. "It's just, it's only," Grace babbled, unsure how to explain her inner turmoil.

"Spill," Brian said. "Share your feelings. Share your thoughts."

"It's just, it's me," she whispered. The all too familiar trembling began in her fingers and quickly spread throughout her entire body. "I'm not, I can't, it's just me, it's me," she said, dealing with an array of complex emotions she had never felt before.

"Okay, there we go," Brian said as he held her close, rested her cheek against his chest and kissed the top of her head.

"I'm not, I'm not good enough for you," Grace confessed.

"And who says you aren't," Brian asked while he held her healing hand in his.

"Me, me," wept Grace. "You deserve more."

"Aw, Grace, I'm just a regular guy who's falling in love," Brian said. He gently kissed the palm of her hand.

"You can't," wept Grace as doubt stripped away all the progress she had made over the past few months.

"Grace, look at me," Brian said as he turned her face up toward his. "I'm crazy about you. There's no doubt in my mind how I feel."

Grace saw his eyes turn darker than the night sky. Was he angry with her? Fear ignited her unease and she wished she could hide under the rock. He held her so tight she knew she could not have crawled away if she tried. "I've never been in love. I don't know anything about it," she confessed.

"We'll find our way together," Brian said, hugging Grace against him.

Grace felt the trembling slowly abating. She felt safe and secure in his arms. His strength seemed to be sinking into her. Should she take a chance with him? Dare she let herself love? She finally let her arms encircle his body. Grace wished to stay like this forever, wrapped in his arms and warmed by his love.

While the wind whistled through the treetops and the children's laughter floated on the air, Grace whispered, "Please don't let go."

*Julia Robertson*

## Chapter 124

Grace felt their lives coming together like one of her quilt projects. Bits and pieces of time were being trimmed, pressed and pieced together. The intricate stitching created a design that was uniquely theirs. She found herself amazed with how the pieces from their lives, cut from mismatched templates fit together so beautifully. As the years of loneliness slowly faded away, her happiness grew brighter.

Grace walked into her empty house feeling exhausted after a long day at work. Startled by the ringing phone, she dropped her purse on the floor and grabbed the receiver. "Hello," she said.

"Are you home?" asked Brian.

"No, I'm shopping," she answered in a matter-of-fact tone.

"All right, are you up for some company?" he asked.

"Of course," laughed Grace. "Where are you?" she asked when she heard the traffic noise over the phone.

"At a phone booth not too far from your house," Brian replied.

Intrigued, she quickly changed into an old pair of jeans and pulled her comfy clover green sweatshirt down over her head. She pushed her tired feet into her faded yellow slippers and scuffed out of the bedroom. By the time she reached the end of the hallway Grace heard his truck outside. To her delight she found two bright smiling faces when she opened the door.

"Hi, we have a surprise," Erin announced as she and Jack scampered inside.

"It's secret," said Jack.

"Is that right?" remarked Grace. "Did you two come here all by yourselves?"

"No," giggled Erin. "Daddy's outside. We have to stay in here until he comes in."

"It's secret," Jack repeated.

"Coming through," Brian called out with the three-foot-long cardboard box balanced on his shoulder.

"What did you do?" Grace asked, stepping back against the wall with the kids. There was no way to know what was in the box or how heavy it was by the way he moved.

"We found something for you." He set the box down and opened his pocketknife.

"Can we have the box?" asked Erin.

"Sure," replied Brian. He dumped the contents out onto the work room floor, checked the flaps for staples and put the empty box down near the front door. "How do you like it so far?" Brian asked, scanning the pile of unassembled parts before looking up at Grace.

"Looks promising," she laughed. "Need a screwdriver?"

"Nope," he said, pulling a screwdriver and wrench out of his back pocket. "Want to help?"

"Sure, but I'm getting a pillow," she said, gesturing to the hard floor. By the time she returned with her pillow, Brian had already sorted through all the pieces, lined them up and had the seat partially assembled.

"How'd your day go?" Brian asked, tapping the screwdriver against his knee.

"Pretty good," replied Grace, sitting down on the pillow with her legs folded in front of her. "I made it through the day without having to come home early."

"You look like a princess perched on a tufted stool," Brian said as he set the tools aside. He cleared a path through the parts and crawled over to her on his hands and knees. "You're so pretty," he said, touching his lips to hers. "I love you."

One look from Brian made Grace tingle with delight. She still found it next to impossible to believe someone like him wanted her. Grace had told him about her parents, about the guilt she lived with and her inability to let the past go. Brian assured her they could mend her damaged spirit, just like she was healing from the injuries to her hand. With his love and a good deal of time, she was learning to believe him.

"I love you too," she whispered, running her fingers through his silky soft hair. It was warm, just like him. "Oh my," she whispered breathlessly.

"I can't get enough of you, Miss Marshall." Brian kept his hands on the floor, but kept his eyes locked on hers and kissed her again. "I'd better get this thing put together."

Grace bit her lower lip as she touched his face, then reluctantly let her hands drop down on her lap. "Yeah, I guess," she sighed, admiring how the dark blue polo-style shirt fitted over his broad chest.

A short time later Grace sat down on her new softly padded roll-around chair. It had a lever to adjust the height and swiveled as well.

"It's perfect. I love it. Thank you," she said, looking up at Brian with delight. "I could sew all day with this." She spun the chair around to face the unfinished quilt and felt the familiar sensation tickling her fingers. She studied her hands and wondered. The brace was gone, but her hand had not completely healed yet. She worried about the loss of feeling that ran from the base of her thumb to halfway up her thumb and forefinger. Worried she might never be able to accurately guide a needle again, Grace hid her scars beneath her left hand.

Brian swiveled the chair around and squatted down in front of her. He gently took both of her hands in his. "Soon," he murmured. "Soon everything will be good again. You will see. Give yourself a little more time." He raised her hands and kissed her palms. "They're beautiful."

Grace had not known true love until she met Brian. His kind words sent shivers racing down her arms to their joined hands. "Life changes," her mother had told her time and time again. How often had she sat in this very room wishing for those changes to come? Foolishly wishing on shooting stars. Wishing for someone as special as Brian to come along and sweep her off her feet. Grace looked up at the commotion drawing nearer.

Erin squealed and ran into the room. "There's a monster! I can't find Jack!" shouted Erin.

Brian turned to his daughter. "What did you do with your little brother?"

"Come on, Daddy," she pleaded, tugging on his hand. "Help me find him."

Grace held her warm hands against her cheeks and watched them go. It touched her heart when he went along with the game. She stood up and moved closer.

Erin stopped near the box, shaking her head and holding her hands up in the air. "He was here, but now he isn't," she said, looking everywhere but at the box on the floor.

"Let me think," Brian contemplated. "Did you throw him outside?" Erin shook her head. "Let's see, where might a small boy go?" Brian asked, walking around the box and nudging it with his shoe. "Maybe I'll get this out of here and we can search the house top to bottom. Every inch of it," he said as he slowly lifted the end of the box.

Grace watched Erin's hands fly up and cover her mouth. Her pretty brown eyes grew wide when a soft thud came from inside the box. Grace giggled at Brian when he acted surprised with the sound.

"What's in this box?" Brian asked after setting it down again. "I'm going to have to see." He knelt down and peered inside. "What's this?" Brian exclaimed as he pulled out one shoe clad foot. He tugged the red shoe off, dropped it over his shoulder and ran his fingers up the bottom of the small foot.

Erin squealed as she reached out to touch, but pulled her hand back as if it were on fire. "Is that Jack's foot? Where's the rest of him?"

"I'm not sure. I'm afraid I will have to tickle this." Brian pulled off the sock, tossed it aside and ran his fingers over Jack's bare foot.

Grace held her hand over her mouth to muffle her giggles as Jack's deep laughter rose from within the box. Erin dropped to the floor and wiggled inside with her brother. Grace watched Brian. Marveled at the delight shining in his eyes. She shook her head when he gestured for her to join them.

"Please," whispered Brian.

Grace shyly walked toward him, her footsteps silent on the hardwood floor. She did not protest when he tugged her closer. Did not object when he drew her down onto his lap. The moment he kissed her, she felt herself melting into him.

"You are sure, aren't you," she whispered.

"Completely. Let's get married right now, today, tonight," he insisted. He ran his fingers into her soft hair. "Please be mine. Be with us. Be a part of us. Please marry me."

His words took her breath away while a thousand thoughts raced through her mind. Saying yes meant committing their lives to one another. Raising his children together. No longer utterly alone. Becoming a real part of a family. Grace's heart filled with joy. Why was she questioning the chance of a lifetime? She looked up into his eyes with a single word dancing upon her lips. Grace whispered, "Yes."

Brian kissed her, held her close and kissed her again. "I love you," he whispered.

Erin watched from the opening of the box. She tugged on Jack and slid out on the floor. "What about us?" she asked quietly.

Brian reached out and pulled Erin in close.

"Me too," said Jack. Grace shifted over to allow the kids room. "May I give a hug too?" she asked. Erin nodded and Grace's eyes filled with joyous tears. She reached around Erin as Jack squeezed in against Brian to complete their big hug.

"Do we get to keep her?" Erin asked.

Brian kissed Grace again. "Yes, we get to keep her."

*The scene playing out before her was a dream come true for Alicia. Everything had fallen into place. Her first prayer after her diagnosis had not been for herself, but for Brian. He had too much goodness in his heart to spend his life all alone. Alicia savored the sound of their laughter and their happy expressions. When Erin's eyes found hers, Alicia lingered for a moment longer. Alicia touched her fingertips to her lips and sent kisses swirling around her family in a dazzling display of jeweled lights. "Be happy. I love you always," Alicia whispered before her spirit vanished from sight.*

Jack scrambled down from Brian's lap and tried to capture the elusive bits of light. Erin watched in wide-eyed wonder.

"Alicia," Brian whispered breathlessly.

Grace turned to look up at him and found he was ghost-white. Erin had not moved an inch and looked as shocked as her father. Jack was still trying to pick up the diamond-like bits of light on the floor.

Grace was not sure what to do first. She reached up and touched Brian's face. "You okay?" she asked.

"Did you?" he began, unable to finish the question.

"Yes, I saw her," said Grace.

"Mommy," Erin cried out.

Grace carefully pulled Erin up against her, hoping her own calm might transfer to the little girl. "I think she was saying goodbye," Grace finally managed to tell them.

"Maybe," Brian said, clearing his throat and doing his best to hide his unease.

Grace lifted Erin and sat down on the floor with her. "Get Jack," she told Brian.

Brian obeyed, moving slowly as he reached down and lifted his son into his arms. Jack chuckled when Brian cuddled him like a baby.

Grace noticed the bits of light were gone, and the slight breeze she felt when Alicia disappeared had stilled.

"She sent us kisses," whispered Erin.

"She loves you," Grace assured the child.

It was a long time before Brian took his children home. Grace wandered around her empty house and wondered about the mysteries of life. Perhaps they were not supposed to figure it all out, but to trust enough to let things work out with time. When the phone rang, she jumped, then ran for the bedroom phone.

"Hi," said Brian. "Doing okay over there?"

"Yes, I'm fine. How about you?" she asked.

"She's gone," he said softly. "I can feel it inside me, but I can't explain it."

"No need to explain, Brian. I was here, I saw her too," she replied, sitting down on the side of her bed.

"I think she was waiting for me to find you," Brian said. "I mean, to find out we are meant to be with each other. Does that make any sense at all? I feel a little insane at the moment."

"It makes perfect sense," she sighed. Grace flopped back on the bed. "She's been watching over you and the children. She wanted you to be happy, like she said."

"If I had heard this story from someone else, I would have told them to go jump off a cliff," Brian admitted.

Grace laughed. "Yeah, it's enough to make a person question everything," she said. "You're going to have to help Erin understand."

"Yeah, once I get it all straight in my own head, and with your help," Brian added.

"I'll help as much as I can," Grace told him.

Silence spread out for several minutes before Brian spoke again. "Grace," he whispered.

"I'm here," she replied.

"What do you think about a late summer wedding?"

Grace sighed with delight. "I love it," she exclaimed. "On the anniversary of you finding me on the beach?"

"That's appropriate, isn't it," he agreed.

"A new beginning," Grace said softly.

"I wish I could crawl into bed with you right now," Brian sighed. "I'll wait, you know I'll wait, but it won't be easy," he sighed dramatically.

"Brian," giggled Grace.

*Tender Dreams*

Chapter 125

Nestled in among the tall pine trees, the little church looked like something out of a fairytale. Late afternoon sunshine streamed through the tree branches and lit up the narrow stained glass windows. The simplicity and elegance made it the perfect setting for the gathering within.

Brian stood near the first row of pews, watching as Grace stepped into view from the entryway doors. Her floor-length antique lace dress suited her to perfection. To his delight, her cascade of chestnut brown hair flowed freely down to her waist. His heart sang when her eyes met his.

Grace's quiet footsteps were accented by the occasional creak of the old oak floor. Brian waited patiently, savoring every moment of their special day. As Grace took the final step to stand facing Brian, the air warmed noticeably between them. It swirled around their legs, ruffled the many rows of handmade lace adorning her dress and lifted the ends of her hair. Grace clutched a bouquet of snow-white daisies and velvety lavender rose buds as they joined hands and together turned toward the minister. A moment later, Grace passed her bouquet to Erin. While Erin, the Bridesmaid, and Jack, Brian's Best Man, looked on, Brian and Grace exchanged vows.

"For a time our lives ran along two parallel paths," Brian began.

"Two separate lives overshadowed by sorrow and grief," Grace said.

"When our paths crossed a spark was ignited," Brian said.

"And we found love that was meant to be," whispered Grace.

"I promise to love you and cherish you, protect you and walk beside you," Brian told Grace.

"For all the years of our lives, I will take your hand in mine and share your laughter and your tears," Grace sighed emotionally.

Brian squatted down and helped Jack retrieve the rings from his front pocket. He brushed his hand over his son's blonde hair before he stood and faced Grace again. The love in her eyes took his breath away.

"With this ring," they recited together.

Erin never took her eyes away from Grace and her father. Jack held onto his father's pant leg and rubbed his sleepy eyes. The minister nodded and pronounced them husband and wife.

Brian kissed his new bride. "I love you," he whispered.

Marlene leaned against Justin while they watched the newlyweds. Standing next to them, Roger and Maggie held on to each other. Kathleen wept with tissues held in her trembling fingers. Garrison glanced over at Anna. He pulled a clean handkerchief out of his pocket and pressed it into her hand. Anna laughed with everyone else when Brian swept Grace up into his arms. Beaming, Brian carried Grace through the church and into the bright sunshine outside. Following behind them, Erin carried the bouquet and held Jack's hand. "We got married," she told her little brother.

While summer's heat lingered, the scattering of golden leaves on the bare ground told of the approach of autumn.

"When Grace pressed her face against his chest and cried, Brian was bewildered. "Are you sad?"

"No, no, I'm happy," she wept. "Did we, are we?"

"We sure did, Mrs. Cooper. You're all mine," declared Brian.

"And you're mine," Grace sighed, brushing away her tears.

"What about us?" asked Erin.

"They're not just my kids, Grace, they're our kids," Brian said and kissed her again.

"Our kids," whispered Grace.

Still holding Grace, Brian squatted down. "What do you two think?"

"Can we call you Mommy now?" asked Erin.

Grace's eyes glistened with tears. "Yes, please," she whispered, reaching out to hold their hands.

Marlene and Justin, Roger, Maggie and Kathleen watched the newlyweds. Anna and Garrison stepped out and stood behind the others.

"They're precious," sighed Kathleen.

"How about a few photos before we leave. Stand here in front of the church," Roger instructed as he readied his camera and walked out toward the road. "How about the newlyweds first," he suggested.

He took several shots, including one before Brian put Grace down. Grace's eyes sparkled with happiness. She looked elegant in her antique lace dress standing close to Brian. His dark brown suit, cream colored shirt and deep purple tie were a perfect match. They were so beautiful they might have stepped out of a fashion magazine promoting antique wedding gowns and late summer country weddings.

"Kiss the girl," called out Justin.

Marlene jabbed him with her elbow. "They look incredibly happy," she sighed.

Brian held Grace close for several more shots. When Grace reached up and straightened his tie, Brian laughed with delight. Roger's camera clicked again.

Everything about today was perfect. Brian turned toward Roger and requested, "Hey, now with our kids."

"I like that," said Roger. "Hold the bouquet up a little higher, Erin. Good, that's very nice." He snapped off several more photos.

Erin wore a knee-length dress a shade darker than the flowers in the bouquet in her hands. Her sturdy ankle-high boots added a touch of the Old West to the shot. Jack looked up at his father before Erin tugged on his hand. His slightly rumpled brown pants fit snug around his waist. Like his father, Jack wore a dark brown jacket over a cream-colored shirt. Rather than try to fit him with a tie like Brian's, Grace had pinned a small rosebud to his narrow lapel. Grace had neatly braided Erin's hair at the little girl's earlier request. A tidy deep purple ribbon adorned the end.

"Okay, Garrison, take Anna up there next," called out Roger.

"You two look beautiful," said Anna. "We're so happy to be a part of this, thank you." When Garrison stood beside her, she looked up at the camera.

"You know, it would be fun to have one of all of us here. I'll set it up," Roger said as he moved to the closest car parked on the dirt road. "Everybody go up to the newlyweds. On either side," he instructed as he set the camera on the car's rooftop. He took careful aim, checked the group and set the timer. "Here I come," he called out as he ran toward them.

He had barely stepped in next to Maggie when the camera clicked. "One more," he shouted as he made a mad dash back to the parked car. "Everybody ready?" he called out. He set the timer and raced back again.

"He's funny," said Jack.

"Say cheese," Erin instructed.

The camera clicked and forever captured the small gathering in front of the old church. At the same time, a single brilliant sunbeam shone through the trees and lit up Brian and Grace in each other's arms.

"Hey everybody, let's do one more," suggested Roger.

"Does he have issues?" asked Justin.

Maggie smiled. "No, he's just that way. He loves to do this kind of stuff. Humor him a minute more and I'll take the camera away."

Brian didn't mind at all. The kids were happy, and Grace was his, all his. He closed out the others and turned to her. He did not notice Roger running back. Nor did he hear the click of the camera as it captured him kissing Grace.

Chapter 126

Grace moved a few of her belongings into Brian's rental house following their wedding. They wanted to give the children a chance to adjust to her being with them before they took the next step. Their options were moving into Grace's family home or selling it and building or buying another house. Brian put the final decision in her hands. Grace knew her own heart but hated putting so much on Brian.

My workload is light for the next two months," Brian explained. "Let's make a list of what needs to be done, the time needed to complete the work and the total cost involved. After that, if you think we should build, then that's what we'll do."

Grace leaned against him feeling an inner turmoil that made her head ache. "I'm not sure what to do," she confessed as she rubbed her temples with both hands.

"Your house has plenty of room, but we don't have to stay there permanently," Brian said. "I can build anything you like."

"Anything?" Grace said, needing to escape her unsettled emotions. "An elevator, a walk-in refrigerator, an indoor pool and two hot tubs?" she began. Her words evoked no response. She leaned back and looked up into his eyes. "A barn with eight stalls, a tennis court and private landing strip?"

When he still did not react, Grace tapped his head with her small fist. "Anybody home?"

"If that's what it takes to make you happy," said Brian.

Grace quickly pushed away from him and turned her back. "Material things don't make a person happy," she sighed, folding her arms over her chest.

Brian slid his arms around her waist and pulled her back against him. "I have everything that makes me happy right here," he said, kissing her neck and squeezing her tighter.

"Brian," she said, drawing in a deep breath. "I want us to live in my house, but it needs too much work."

"Nothing is too much. The house is sound. It has a sturdy foundation and a good roof," he explained.

"But things are falling apart. The flooring, the plumbing," she began.

"It's all repairable," Brian told her, kissing her with loud smacking noises.

"Daddy's eating Mommy!" shrieked Erin. "Help me, Jack, help me!"

Grace listened to the kids running toward them. "They love me more," she giggled.

Brian kept kissing Grace while Erin pulled on his arm. Kept kissing her when Jack latched onto his belt at the back of his jeans.

"Tickle him," laughed Grace.

Erin squealed. Jack started climbing up his leg.

"If you two are still here when I count to three," growled Brian. With that said, the kids disappeared in a flash.

"Let's hide," shouted Erin.

Brian turned Grace around in his arms. "Let's make your house our home," he said, tipping her face up to his.

"I'd love that," sighed Grace. "I've always been afraid I'd lose it one day," she whispered as she pressed her face into his chest.

"We won't let that happen, honey. We'd better go find those kids," he said after a minute.

"I'm with you," Grace giggled, following after him.

"Where do you think they're hiding?" Brian asked Grace.

"I have no idea. They could be anywhere. Do you think they might be in there?" she asked, holding back her laughter knowing the kids heard every word.

"In the closet?" Brian asked. "Maybe," he said as he swept the door open with a flourish.

Erin held her hands over her mouth. Jack tumbled out onto the floor. Erin hid her eyes behind her hands.

"Good grief, we found one of them," Grace laughed, delighted with Erin's giggles. She picked up Jack and kissed his little boy face.

Brian lifted Erin out upside down. "Something happened to this one. I think it's broken."

"I'm starting supper," Grace said as she left the room with Jack in her arms.

"We're going to go out and check the mailbox," laughed Brian.

Grace turned in time to see Brian pull Erin up and over his shoulder. Erin's giggles accompanied them out the door before Grace turned back toward the kitchen. She set Jack up with his coloring book and crayons at the kitchen table. She was standing at the sink when Brian came into the room with Erin still draped over his shoulder. Grace loved how Brian interacted with his children. "Our children," she thought, biting her lower lip.

Erin scrunched up her face while she examined the lettering on an envelope. "I need to go to school more. I can't read this. All the letters are hooked together."

"You're learning, Erin. It takes time," Brian said, taking the envelope and sliding Erin down onto an empty chair.

Grace walked up to Brian when his expression darkened. "You okay?" she asked, drying her hands on a dish towel.

"It's from Garrison," Brian said.

"Brian," Grace sighed as he handed her the unopened envelope. She knew he still held ill feelings toward the man who was Alicia's father. "Let it go," she urged, opening the elegantly addressed envelope. "It's an announcement, a wedding announcement."

Grace waited while Brian walked toward the back door. His hands were balled into fists at his sides. She knew he was holding back from saying anything negative in front of the children. Grace waited a moment longer before saying, "Grandpa married Anna."

"We got a grandma!" Erin said excitedly.

Brian walked back to Grace and hugged her tight. "I'm sorry," he apologized. "Some things are impossible to forget. I hope he takes good care of her."

Grace turned with Brian when Erin spoke up with her usual excited tone. She always had something to share after a day at school. Grace rested her head against Brian's arm while they waited.

"Sherri at school, her mommy is big like this," Erin said, holding her arms out in front of her. "She said her baby is grown almost all the way and gets to be born soon. Do we get to have a baby too?"

Caught by surprise, Grace blurted out, "Let's get supper on the table." Heat rose up her neck and she knew her face was turning beet red. She rushed over to the sink and busied her trembling hands.

Brian watched Grace but answered Erin. "We'll have to wait and see. You two go wash your hands. Scoot," he told them. Once the kids were out of sight, Brian approached Grace. "Honey, are you okay?"

She pressed the damp towel to her face and nodded. She couldn't say anything yet. Not this soon.

Brian gently turned her to face him and lowered her hands. Her eyes glistened with tears and he knew. "Are you?" he asked, his voice barely a whisper.

Grace searched for the proper words. Unable to meet his eyes, she pressed her forehead against his chest and whispered, "Maybe."

"I love you," Brian said, rocking her gently in his arms. "I guess we'd better get busy with the house."

Grace sighed with relief. She had been agonizing over how to handle this for days and he made it so easy. She felt safe and warm cuddled against him. "I've always wanted a skylight in my work room."

"We can do that," he laughed.

## Chapter 127

Over the next few weeks, Brian and Grace spent time poking into every nook and cranny of her house. "I can see what it will look like, but I can't see how to get there," Grace said. Her expression reflected her frustration.

"I'll show you," Brian said. "First we'll bring the plumbing and electric up to code."

"Okay, that makes sense," Grace said. "New outlets and switches too?"

"Yes, several of them are coming apart. All new wiring throughout. Let's check this out," Brian said, flipping open his pocketknife and cutting into the corner of the worn-out olive-green carpeting in the living room. He yanked it back far enough to expose the flooring beneath it. "This is real oak," he said, smiling up at Grace. "You said you want the old floors refinished?"

"Can we do that?" she asked, squatting down next to Brian and looking at the flooring.

"With a little elbow grease," Brian replied, snapping his knife closed. "I have the entire project in my head. Let's go make a list of supplies and I'll get my crew lined up to start on this tomorrow."

"Tomorrow?" Grace said. "Seriously?"

"Unless you've changed your mind," he replied, watching her eyes dance with delight.

"No, my parents would love what we're going to do here. We're breathing new life back into their home. The kids, their laughter, it's precisely what it needs," Grace said.

Brian loved her sentimental attachment to her childhood home. "Putting a skylight in your work room is a great idea. How about putting one in our bedroom too?" he asked, delighted with her happy response. He loved how she appreciated the little things in life. He picked her up and danced her across the worn-out carpet.

An hour later, Brian heard the light tapping on the front door and mentally added a doorbell to the list. "Hello, Kathleen. What a nice surprise," he said as they shared a hug. He sensed something was amiss, but her expression did not give him any deetails. "Grace is upstairs contemplating the possibilities for the master bathroom."

"I'll go up and join her, but I have to give you something first," Kathleen said, producing an envelope from her shoulder bag. She placed it in his hand and patted his arm. "She wanted me to give it to you once you found your way. It seems to me you have."

"What's this?" Brian asked, taken aback at the sight of Alicia's handwriting. "Um, thank you."

Brian watched Kathleen as she met the kids in the hallway and escorted them up the stairway. His stomach ached while he fingered the flap and slid it open as he walked out into the back yard. Brian sank down on the edge of the patio and squeezed his eyes closed. "Alicia," he whispered.

Thick gray clouds drifted down from the early evening sky and showered the ground with tiny raindrops. The rain became heavier, rhythmically drumming the shingles and splattering the patio chairs. Brian was oblivious to it all while he read the letter again and again. He barely heard the quiet footsteps behind him.

"Brian," whispered Grace. She knelt down beside him in the rain, glancing up when a mourning dove cooed from its place on the corner of the roof.

Brian swallowed hard, unable to respond.

"Come inside, honey," urged Grace. "Kathleen took the kids back to the rental." She slid her arm around his neck and pressed her lips to his damp face.

"She did it," Brian whispered. "She wanted to be buried back there so I wouldn't, couldn't, go to her grave. She, she," he wept.

"She loves you," Grace whispered, glancing at the handwritten letter. "Brian, it's getting wet."

The rain began to smear the inked words on the pale-yellow stationery. Grace reached out to steady Brian's hand and gasped. They both stared at the single line left untouched by the rain.

*Healing your heart Begins with loving Grace.*

"Brian," whispered Grace as she looked up into the darkening sky.

"How did she," he began, aware it was beyond comprehension. Shaking, Brian clung to Grace.

"Tears from Heaven," whispered Grace.

The dove cooed twice more before it fluttered by and disappeared against the dark gray clouds.

*Julia Robertson*

## EPILOGUE

Three years later

Grace ran the needle through the layers of cotton and batting while she reflected on the changes in her life since she and Brian committed their lives to each other. Raising their children gave her life purpose and loving Brian filled her heart with endless joy.

She recalled her near frantic call to Brian at the work site two years earlier. Nothing had prepared her for the quick delivery of their son. They had made it to the hospital with only minutes to spare. Samuel Marshall Cooper was born with his eyes wide open and a smile on his face.

When the soft sounds reached her ears, Grace quickly slid the needle into a pincushion and rolled the chair back from the quilting frame. "Hi there, sweetie," she whispered as she scooped up the tiny bundle from the infant seat on the floor.

She sighed and kissed the baby's soft cheeks. From behind her she heard the small footsteps and quiet giggles. She turned and found them watching her. "Come see," she encouraged them all.

Brian came in with the children and knelt down next to her. Nine-year-old Erin's soft brown eyes were wide while she guided little Sam in closer to the baby. Jack, now seven years old, came up beside Erin and reached out to touch his baby sister's hand. Sam wiggled free from Erin and climbed up on his father's lap. Brian caught him around his waist before he lost his balance.

The center of attention was a baby girl with wispy blonde hair. Her tiny hand wrapped around Jack's much larger finger.

"She has teeny fingers," remarked Jack. "Were mine this small when I was a baby?" he asked.

Grace watched Brian nod in reply. Their marriage still felt like a beautiful dream. She cherished the nights when she woke up and watched him sleeping next to her. Her life with him was a fairytale come true.

"Can we call her Beth?" asked Erin. "Elizabeth is a pretty name, but it's long, you know."

"That's a wonderful idea. What do you think, Beth?" Grace said, brushing her fingers over the baby's feather soft hair.

"She said yes," said Sam.

Brian kissed his youngest son's cheek. "I think you're right, Sam. Beth is a beautiful name."

"Beth stinks," said Sam, covering his nose with his hands.

"Babies do that," said Erin.

"Phew," sighed Jack.

"Anyone want to clean up our little stinker?" asked Grace. She carefully lifted the baby and stood up from the chair.

"Not me, not me," said Sam. He rolled onto his back making gagging noises.

"I'm helping," said Erin.

"Gross," said Jack. "I'm glad I don't wear diapers."

"Me too," agreed Brian. He reached out and grabbed Jack before the boy ran off. "Let's go get the charcoal started. We're grilling hot dogs tonight."

"I want mustard!" shouted Jack.

"Me too," echoed Sam.

Grace listened to the conversation as she slowly made her way down the hallway. A moment later she heard the boys running toward the back yard. "Elizabeth Marianna Cooper is a long name," Grace said as she and Erin walked into the bedroom. She settled the baby down on a blanket on the bed. "What do you think?"

"It's a pretty name. I like it," replied Erin. She brought over a diaper and rubber pants. "Does she need something clean to wear?"

"Yes, I'm afraid so. Please pick out a sleeper for her. It's a bit cool in the house, don't you think?" asked Grace, pleased with how Erin was handling her role as the big sister to three siblings.

"I agree," replied Erin. "Her toes and fingers get cold easy. This one is cute," she said, picking up a red sleeper with snaps up the front.

"What color do you think her eyes will be?" asked Grace.

"Probably blue like everyone but me," replied Erin.

"You're lucky to have such beautiful brown eyes," said Grace.

"Yeah, but it's funny not being like everyone else in the family."

"Always think of them as your mother's gift to you. When Daddy looks at you, he sees her and it warms his heart," Grace explained.

"Do you think he misses her anymore?" asked Erin.

"Yes, he does," replied Grace. She thought of the nights when he awoke in tears. She knew how lucky she was when he shared his feelings about Alicia, but there were times when he had to go for a run in order to work through his dark moods. Alicia would always be his first love. Now that Grace had experienced the beautiful sensation for herself by loving Brian, she understood how he felt. Losing something so precious left scars. Scars that Erin had to deal with herself.

"But he has you now. How can he still miss her?" Erin asked.

Grace slid the sleeper sleeves over Beth's tiny arms and snapped up the front. She lifted the baby and sat down on the bed. "Erin, you will understand better as you get older. You can never run out of room for loving or missing those close to you. It's a natural and wonderful feeling. Missing her means you still love her," Grace said. She caressed her baby's soft cheeks.

"That's good because I do," Erin said quietly. "Sometimes it hurts and I cry, but I try to hide it." Erin stepped closer and held her baby sister's tiny hand.

"Don't hide it, honey. Share your feelings with us. That's what families do," said Grace. "I wish my parents were still here. I wish they could have spent time with you and the boys."

"And Beth," said Erin.

"And Beth," agreed Grace as she ran her hand down the length of Erin's silky blonde hair.

"I miss Clay too. He called me Lady Erin, like I was a real princess," Erin said.

"I barely knew him, but I wish he was here too," agreed Grace.

"I was thinking," said Erin. "If Mommy were still alive, you wouldn't be here with us. You'd be all alone and sad."

"Life is a mystery, Erin. We can't spend too much time analyzing the why's and how's. We must accept the gift of life and never take love for granted. I'm lucky to be loved by all of you," said Grace.

Erin looked from her baby sister to the woman holding her. "Thank you," she said. "I'm glad I have my mother's eyes. Does that make me unique?" she asked, using the new word for the first time.

"It certainly does," agreed Grace. "Let's go see what the boys are doing. Would you like to hold Beth while I help with supper?"

"Yes, please," Erin said excitedly.

Side-by-side, they walked out to the kitchen where Erin sat down on a cushioned chair. Grace nestled the baby on Erin's lap, glad for the bond they shared. She looked up when Brian stepped up beside her.

"I love you, Mrs. Cooper," Brian said as he gathered her into a hug.

Grace wanted him to carry her to bed and hold her for the next 24 hours. They both needed that much sleep. Grace turned in his arms and rested her cheek against his chest. His strength flowed into her as she reached around him and held on tight. Together they watched Erin holding the baby on her lap. Two precious gifts created with love. The boys suddenly came crashing into the house from the back yard. Life bounced from sweet serenity to utter chaos in the blink of an eye. Brian lifted Grace up and slowly danced her around the floor.

*From a sacred place beyond the stars, those gone before them watched over the home filled with laughter and love.*

Made in the USA
Las Vegas, NV
09 May 2021